Connie's Wars

Connie's Wars

A Novel

G. N. Bell

Library of Congress Control Number:		2016907492
ISBN:	Hardcover	978-1-5144-9895-8
	Softcover	978-1-5144-9894-1
	eBook	978-1-5144-9893-4

Print information available on the last page.

Rev. date: 05/06/2016

To order additional copies of this book, contact:
Xlibris
800-056-3182
www.Xlibrispublishing.co.uk
Orders@Xlibrispublishing.co.uk
726686

PREFACE

History tells us time and time again, that when the Governments of the world and their leaders create for themselves insurmountable differences and disagreements, The result of these disputes undoubtedly lead these countries into war with each other, in many cases bordering counties on both sides are also dragged willingly or even unwillingly into the dispute. Thus ensuring that a large number of the young men living in these duelling nations are forced to rush to the defence of their country. Once entered into the conflict these young men would be subjected to the most terrifying and horrendous conditions imaginable. Pain, suffering and death would inevitably follow, all of this would be endured in the name of their countries government. In many cases these terrifying conflicts would last for many years, so when the day finally arrived that this man-made catastrophe had finally grinded to its brutal conclusion. One thing would always remain the same, win or lose. That one constant would be that when the brave young fighting men returned home they did so with a lot less than when they had taken their first steps to defend their country. Sadly, in too many cases millions of these brave young gladiators never returned home at all.

The response of those fore-mentioned Governments to the appalling high price which the young men under their keep were made to pay was, to erect august cenotaphs and monuments in their remembrance. Rightly so one would say, but surely this was the least their leaders could do for them by way of gratitude for the immense personal sacrifice that these brave young men had made willingly in the cause of their countries. What of the families the mothers, the wives, the brothers, the sisters, the small children left fatherless. What of those that had lost husbands, sons and brothers and other family members? What was to become of them in this brave new world? Much had been written over the years on the subject of war, and the young men that fought so fearlessly in them again, rightly so but what of the other casualties of these horrifying conflicts. What of the ones that were left behind? Their stories are never glamorized in quite the same way as that of the young fighting men, but in their own way they were every inch the warrior too because you can be assured without any doubt, that they all suffered just as much as the young men who found themselves overseas fighting. Not only did they suffer pain and immense sorrow they did so without a word of complaint, they showed great strength, great courage and great heroism, to equal the highest decorated soldier. So I ask you, the next time you stand by one of the many cenotaphs in this or any other country please give a thought for all those mothers, wives, children and sweethearts who sent their sons, husbands, fathers and lovers on that perilous journey. Knowing that they did so not just for themselves, but for the ones that would come after them, you and me.

This is the story of one of them... told for all of them.

CHAPTER 1

Someone once said, "I don't like Mondays." I never really understood the thinking behind that statement and have often wondered what was so different about Mondays. Until today that is, because this particular Monday has the potential to be one of the worst Mondays of my entire life. Allow me to introduce myself and explain. My name is Bill Clark, aged twenty-two and I share a large wooden desk with my good friend Thomas Westwood in the press-room of the Belfast Telegraph. If I were to describe myself to you I would prefer to do so as others see me. It is often said that I am a chubby, cheeky faced young man who carries a joker's smile fixed firmly upon his face. It has also been said that the full head of thick black hair that I have been blessed with always looks as though it is in need of cutting or grooming or even both, but I tell you this, until today I have always been content and comfortable about myself.

As for my good friend Thomas Westwood, well he is the other side of the coin. He is also twenty-two years old and of slender in build with a thin almost gaunt expression etched on his face. His hair is brown and wispy in appearance and, although he would never admit it, the onset of baldness is getting nearer by the day for young Thomas. Thomas is inclined to be a little more serious about life than myself and on many occasions he fails to see the funnier side of things. Now you might be wondering why this Monday is proving to be such a pain in the neck for the both of us. I will tell you why. A few weeks ago we were given an assignment by our big boss, Mr Austin Packingham, features editor, and at twelve-thirty today both Thomas and I have been cordially invited to have lunch with him. The purpose of this lunch is for Thomas and myself to inform Mr Packingham of our progress with this assignment. Well, as we have made little progress in this matter, you will understand our reasons for us not liking this Monday morning.

Mr Austin Packingham is a tall sour faced individual with a mop of thick bright red hair that continues to grow down the side of his face in the form of thick sideburns. Now, as if this isn't silly looking enough, Mr Packingham then allows this ginger growth to keep on going until it eventually joins up with a splendid military styled moustache. As if this expanse of facial hair wasn't enough to make him stand out in a crowd and make his appearance look even more ridiculous, Mr Packingham had decided to plunk a pair of rimless spectacles on the end of his nose.

Mr Austin Packingham had been a newspaper man for the best part of forty years and always demanded work of the highest standard from his reporters, be they old hands or novices like Thomas and myself and that's the rub. You see, this was the first time that Thomas and myself had been granted the opportunity to work on a story totally by ourselves, so we are both understandably more than a little apprehensive about our lunch with Mr Packingham. When this offer came our way we were both more than willing to grasp this wonderful opportunity with both hands, knowing full well that if we came up with a good story it would go a long way in raising our stature on the press-room floor. We were both well aware of the fact that this assignment was not going to be an easy one to pull off as the only instructions that Mr Austin Packingham had given us was that he wanted a human interest story, something that would grip both sides of the political divide that existed here in N. Ireland. A story that would hold its place in the forthcoming Millennium Edition of the newspaper.

Up to this point both myself and Thomas had explored a host of different avenues to find our story, all without any luck it has to be said. We had spent hour upon hour discussing several topics and ideas in our search for a story worthy of inclusion in the newspaper's Millennium Edition. Sadly as yet we had come up with nothing that could be considered as mind-blowing or even anything quirky. Nothing that remotely fitted the criteria that Mr Packingham had handed down to us. You see both of us wanted this story to be something really special, something that would capture the attention and imagination of all readers throughout N. Ireland. Unfortunately for Thomas and myself this was a Monday we could have really done without. We just hoped that Mr Packingham was in a good mood this Monday lunch time.

As I looked across our large wooden desk I could see that Thomas was in deep quiet thought. His eyes were shut tight and his face ever so slightly crumpled as he sat rattling his black fountain pen pensively against his teeth. Is he onto something, has he discovered the story we need I wondered. Getting up from my chair on my side of the desk, I picked up my cup of morning coffee and walked around the desk to where Thomas's was sitting. I then conveniently place my back-side on the edge of the desk, my body facing inwards towards Thomas. I couldn't help but notice that Thomas's polystyrene cup of coffee remained untouched, as did mine at this point. Foolishly I took a sip of this strange brownish brew that passed for coffee in the press-room and the instant my tongue came into contact with this lukewarm, brownish liquid I remembered just how unpleasant this brew actually was. With this polluted swill still washing around inside my mouth, I placed my polystyrene cup down on the desk beside Thomas's.

"Tell me Thomas," I said. "Why the hell do we drink this shit day after day?"

Thomas glanced down at his cup of untouched coffee, which was resting harmlessly by his telephone. Slowly he raised his eyes in my direction and said,

"It's this shit or nothing mate. That's why we drink it."

Thomas gave a playful smile because deep down he knew that it wasn't so much the coffee, dreadful as it may be, that was making me so grumpy. It was the lack of progress being made in our quest for a good story for Mr Austin Packingham's Millennium Edition.

The total lack of progress in their hunt for a story was beginning to get to the two boys, making them somewhat irritable, as they were well aware that their futures depended on them making this a success.

"Come on Thomas," said Bill. "The millennium story. Have you got any ideas at all?"

Thomas declined to answer. Bill then he picked up the desk calendar and held it out in front of his friend Thomas.

"Look Thomas," he continued, "It's the 12th. of August and we've been working on this for three weeks now and as yet we haven't come up with anything useful."

Thomas began to rattle his black fountain pen against his teeth once again, then he said, "What if we find a story that began a hundred years ago Bill? A story that will grip the people of Belfast and excite them. That would do it wouldn't it Bill?"

Thomas's eyes now became fixed on his friend's face as he waited in anticipation for Bill's response.

"Yes it would Thomas, but what?" replied Bill.

"Maybe there might be something hiding amongst the old stories in the vaults. The ones that never made it into the paper." said Thomas.

"You know Bill you just might have something there." replied Bill.

Both men jumped to their feet and headed for the newspaper's vaults, deep in the bowels of the building. The two boys did have one slice of luck that Monday, when one of the newspaper's runners delivered to them a message from Mr Packingham saying that he regretted to inform them that he would have to cancel their lunch meeting due to other important business.

Over the next few weeks the two young men ploughed through a plethora of old stories that were stored in the newspaper's vaults. Evening after evening both Thomas and Bill worked tirelessly, staying behind in the press-room, on occasions until gone midnight. Unfortunately for our two young scribes, this was proving to be a fruitless task, as no matter how hard they searched, they found nothing. Thomas was sat alone at his desk on what seemed to be yet another fruitless Friday morning in late September. He was quietly reading yet another of the archive stories that he and Bill had found in the vaults of the newspaper offices. Suddenly out of the blue, old Peter came lumbering past on his way to the dreaded office coffee machine, his trade mark cigarette burning slowly from the corner of his mouth. When old Peter reached Thomas's desk, he suddenly stopped and tapped Thomas on the shoulder and then asked politely,

"Have you found anything of interest yet young man?"

Thomas looked up at old Peter, somewhat surprised by his interest.

"No, nothing yet, Peter but thanks for asking." said Thomas as he quickly turned his attention back to the old manuscripts he had been reading giving old Peter no more attention. Again old Peter tapped Thomas on the shoulder and said,

"Try looking up Colin Woodard's last story. The one he was working on when he tragically died of a heart attack in 1996. I know he would want to see it get published. It was always very special to him but when he died it somehow got pushed to one side and forgotten about. I think it just might be what you're looking for, young man. Also you would be doing Colin a big favour because he always wanted this story to see the light of day. It was that important to him. Trust me, just look it up son, just look it up. I really think that it's what you are looking for."

Old Peter's voice was low and he croaked as he spoke. His speech was interrupted every few seconds by a muffled cough to clear his throat. Most of the younger reporters compared him to Methuselah.

Thomas looked at old Peter somewhat bemused because old Peter was the last person on earth he had expected the offer of help from and it had taken him a little by surprise. So, by the time Thomas had composed himself enough to thank old Peter, it was too late and the old hack was already on his way, shuffling slowly across the press-room, his cigarette ash dropping on the floor as he continued towards the dreaded coffee machine. Old Peter had worked at the newspaper for over sixty years and he was now in his late eighties. He was a small, frail, wrinkly old man, somewhat bent in stature. His appearance was at best dishevelled, his teeth were a kind of brown in colour and it always appeared that he hadn't shaved properly as he would always have facial hair growing out from under his shirt collar. Nowadays, old Peter only worked two days a week for the newspaper, even then he never seemed to be actually doing anything of any use. It was more a case of him just turning up on the allotted days so he could be seen around the place. At least that was the impression most of the junior reporters had of him and for that reason they found him a bit of a joke and never gave him too much attention. In fact, in Thomas's two years at the newspaper this was the first time he had ever spoken to the old man, but for some reason Mr A. Packingham held this old hack in high regard and would not hear a bad word said about him on the press-room floor. As Thomas watched the old man shuffling across the press-room, he thought to himself, why have I never spoken to that old guy before today? I see him two days every week and I have never even said as much as good morning to him. Thomas whispered under his breath, somewhat belatedly,

"Thanks Peter. I will look it up right now."

It took Thomas over two hours to find Colin Woodard's old manuscript but find it he did. Thomas returned to his desk and immediately began to read through the pile of old dog-eared papers marked 'Colin's story on Connie Gallagher'. Thomas spent the next two hours reading Colin's story, so engrossed in it was he that he hadn't noticed that his friend Bill had returned to the press-room from yet another wild goose chase.

Bill's face was like thunder as he roared angrily,

"What a total waste of my time and effort that was!"

Thomas made no attempt to respond to Bill's outburst. Needless to say, the lack of interest being shown by Thomas at his return only angered Bill even more.

"I do hope that pile of old tatty papers that you are reading, Thomas are very interesting because you seem to not have noticed that I have returned empty handed yet again." snipped Bill.

Again Thomas did not replay instantly to his friend but instead raised his hand as if to say, wait for one minute.

"Thomas!" snapped Bill loudly.

As he was now becoming even more irritated by Thomas's non response, Bill was just about to shout his friend's name once again when Thomas raised his head from the manuscript, smiled broadly at Bill and said,

"Found it Bill. Bloody well found our story!"

"What is it, Thomas? What have you found?" asked Bill, his anger now gone.

"I think I have found our story, Bill and it's all thanks to old Peter."

Bill laughed out loud for several seconds then he scowled scornfully at his old friend saying,

"Have you taken leave of your senses Thomas or did you pop out to The Morning Star for a few drinks? Whichever it is, please tell me that you're not serious!"

"No Bill listen to me, it's good. It's really, really good Bill, trust me." beamed an excited Thomas.

"Can't be if old Peter has anything to do with it, Thomas." sneered Bill.

"Just sit down and listen for a minute Bill." said Thomas.

Bill dragged a chair from the desk next to the one Thomas was sitting at and sat down.

"Go on then Thomas, I'm all ears. Convince me if you can." said Bill mockingly.

Thomas quickly turned the pages of the old manuscript back to the beginning, then with one quick sharp glance at Bill he said,

"Okay Bill, pin back your lugholes and listen."

"Ready." grinned Bill,

"Ready." said Thomas.

Thomas began to read Colin Woodard's old story about a woman from East Belfast called Connie Gallagher.

CHAPTER 2

"I first met Connie in the July of 1995, a frail elderly lady I recall. As I looked at this lady for the first time I couldn't help but notice that her face, although pleasant on the eye, seemed to be carrying more than its fair share of the ills of life. As I was to discover later, more than a few of life's tragedies had without a doubt been brutally tossed in her direction. One thing about this lady's appearance that has remained embedded deep inside my memory from the very first moment I set eyes on Connie. I noticed it straight away. From that first day onwards, every time I met Connie, this strange oddity remained constant. I can see it even now as I sit here in this smoke filled pressroom, typing her tragic yet courageous story for all to read. This strange phenomenon was simple in its design, yet it represented a lifetime of sorrow. The phenomenon that I speak of was a small, perfectly formed tear which rested permanently in the corner of Connie's right eye and was there for all to see.

It was as if this tear was there to remind both Connie and the world of her great loss and her untold suffering. I have now met Connie on nine occasions up to this point and each time we met that perfect little tear was always there. Connie never made any attempt to clear it from her eye nor did it seem to cause her any annoyance what so ever. Connie now lives alone in a small run-down terraced house on Wolf Street in East Belfast. In her tiny, cramped sitting room, she is surrounded by a small collection of memories from her past life. Instantly my eye was drawn to a collection of old photographs that were neatly laid out on top of an old mahogany sideboard. These photographs numbered eight in all, each photograph of a young man in military uniform. I discovered later that the photographs were of Connie's husband and her seven sons. As I began to chat with this lady it became clear to me that at one time in her life, this wonderful, charming, elderly lady was used to a much higher standard of living than that which she was now experiencing. It was easy to deduce that this lady had breeding, style and sophistication in abundance. Connie also possessed a kindness within herself that oozed from every pore in her body, a kindness hitched to an abundance of humility something that I had not witnessed before in anyone in my time as journalist. I clearly remember my first day with Connie and she has gripped me ever since.

FOOT NOTE...

It would seem that Colin Woodard had first became aware of Connie Gallagher when he stumbled across her existence by accident in the summer of 1991. Colin was the Belfast Telegraph's top investigative reporter and throughout his many years working for the newspaper he had uncovered and brought to light several tales of corruption and skulduggery that had been festering under the surface of Northern Ireland life. This latest investigation that Colin was vigorously perusing was a rather distasteful but a necessary inquiry into the alleged rape and abuse of thousands of children that had attended the Christian Brothers Schools throughout Ireland. Colin's investigations had discovered that Roman Catholic run institutions were guilty of terrible crimes towards children in their care. It was clear that Catholic priests and nuns had terrorised thousands of young boys and girls in workhouse-style schools for decades. It also appeared that the Catholic Church was unable or unwilling to stop the chronic beatings, rapes and humiliation that was being carried out on a daily basis within their schools. More than 30,000 children were deemed to be petty thieves, truants or from dysfunctional families.

For some reason also included in these categories were the unfortunate unmarried mothers of Ireland. These poor unfortunates were callously brought into the church and treated as either deviants, or lunatics, no matter which they were all classified as souls lost forever. Once under the control of the church they would then be dispatched to Ireland's austere network of industrial schools, reformatories, orphanages and hostels going back as far as the early 1930s and continuing right up to 1990s when the last of the church-run facilities was closed down.

Colin's investigations found that molestation and rape were "endemic" in boy's facilities, chiefly run by the Christian Brothers order and that the supervisors of these intuitions pursued policies that increased the danger to the children under their care. Girls were supervised by orders of nuns, chiefly the Sisters of Mercy. They suffered much less sexual abuse, although that kind of abuse wasn't totally unheard of. In the institutions that were run by orders of Nuns the abuse handed out to girls was more likely to be frequent assaults with canes or leather straps. Humiliation was widespread and was designed to make the girls feel worthless, making them easier to control. Colin discovered that in a few schools, a high level of ritualized beatings were routine. Girls would be struck repeatedly with implements designed to give maximise pain and these cruel and merciless blows would be administered repeatedly on all parts of the body. Colin stated in his findings that... Personal and family denigration was widespread.

Colin had spoken personally with some of the victims of this terrible abuse and each and every one of them were of the same mind. To a man or woman, all wanted the truth about their horrible experiences to be documented and made public so that children in Ireland never had to endure such suffering ever again. So their willingness to talk about their experiences made Colin's efforts to gather his information an easier task than he had first thought. But most leaders of religious orders in Ireland rejected all of Colin's allegations as exaggerations and lies. When they were confronted by Colin, they argued that any abuses were the responsibility of often long-dead individuals. Colin's investigations sided with former student's accounts of what really took place in these horrifying religious institutions. Colin concluded in his findings that church officials made every effort to shield their holy orders from ridicule. Thus allowing paedophiles within their ranks to escape arrest amid a culture of self-serving secrecy.

Colin also found that a climate of fear created by pervasive, excessive and arbitrary punishment permeated most of the institutions and all those run for young boys. Children lived with the daily terror of not knowing where or when their next beating was to come, but knowing that it would surely come sooner rather than later.

Colin Woodard's report concluded that he found overwhelming consistent testimony from still-traumatized men and women, now in their 50s, 60s, 70s and even 80s, that demonstrated beyond any doubt in his mind that the entire system treated children more like prison inmates and slaves, rather than people with legal rights and human potential. It was during Colin's investigations into historical abuse by the Roman Catholic Church in Northern Ireland that time after time the same compassionate story was to be heard from different people.

This was a tale of a wealthy lady from East Belfast, who had founded, built and financially supported her own orphanages in the seaside towns of Bangor and Holywood just after the Second World War had ended. This story was to be told on more than one occasion, arousing Colin's interest in this mystery lady. Also to Colin's great surprise and his undoubted admiration for this lady's forethought he discovered that her orphanages were non-denominational, open to all, something unheard of in Northern Ireland in the early 1900s. It was in the middle of his investigation into the catholic run orphanages that he decided that, when he had concluded this investigation, he would make it his business to find this lady from East Belfast, a lady by the name of Mrs Connie Gallagher. Once Colin Woodard had concluded his investigations into the schools and orphanages that had been run by the Catholic Church and had handed his report into his editor, Colin began his search for Connie Gallagher, wondering if indeed this lady was still alive.

9

Months upon months of reading through old copy from the newspaper now followed for Colin, eventually leading him to a story about a lady from East Belfast by the same name. This story told of a Connie Gallagher who lived in one of the most fashionable houses ever built in Belfast and that she was at the centre of Belfast's social and business world in the early 1900s. This was to be Colin's starting point in his search for this mysterious lady. It took Colin over a year of meticulous and laborious probing before he discovered that this lady was last heard off living in Wolf Street in East Belfast. So, on a bright Monday morning in 1995, Colin set out for Wolf Street, hoping to finally meet this legendary lady. Colin arrived at the front door of this small terraced house in Wolf Street at around 10 o'clock on a Monday morning. He stood silently outside number 88. Wolf Street, wondering if his quest to find Connie Gallagher was to come to a satisfactory conclusion on this fine morning. After taking a deep breath, Colin knocked softly on the old weather-beaten door and waited expectantly for a response. Several long seconds passed before the door was opened somewhat gingerly by a frail elderly lady. As Colin looked at the lady in the doorway he couldn't help but notice the kind and welcoming smile that she carried on her face.

"Are you Mrs Connie Gallagher?" asked Colin.

"Yes, I am young man. Can I help you with anything?" replied the elderly lady with a smile.

Colin returned Connie's smile and replied respectfully,

"My name is Colin Woodard. I work for the Belfast Telegraph and I would like to talk to you about your life if I may Mrs Gallagher."

"Come inside young man, please, come in and take a seat," replied Connie.

It was at this point that Colin realized that he was now face to face with the real Mrs Connie Gallagher, a lady he had spent a long time tracking down and now he had eventually found her and his quest was now almost complete. Connie moved to one side, inviting Colin into her home. Once inside Colin realized that this elderly lady was not living at the top end of life, but his instinct told him that once upon a time this lady surly dined only at the top table of life. After only a few minutes chatting with Connie, Colin quickly recognised the fact that he was in the presence of someone really special. Every time that Colin called upon Connie, she always had that welcoming smile on her face and of course that small tear in the corner of her right eye. Colin would listen intensely as Connie told her story.

MRS CONNIE KEAN, BORN IN BELFAST ON THE 22-3-1899.
MR BOBBY GALLAGHER, BORN IN BELFAST ON THE 15-6-1898.

CHAPTER 3

It was in the year of 1915 when Bobby Gallagher signed his name on a sheet of paper and joined up for the great adventure known as the Great War, or to give it its full title, The First World War. Bobby was only seventeen years old when he first put pen to paper in the recruiting tent that had been erected in the grounds of the Belfast City Hall. Six months after that day, Bobby was saying good-bye to his beautiful young raven haired colleen named Connie, as he set off on his big adventure. Connie was the great love of Bobby's young life and leaving her was not an easy thing for him to do, but like thousands of young men throughout N. Ireland he knew that his country needed him. Bobby stood at six foot two inches tall and was as handsome as handsome could be. He was a broad shouldered lad with the biggest, impish, eye-catching smile this side of the Irish Sea. His hair was thick and dark brown in colour and was always well groomed, as was the lad himself. As for Connie, well she was a real Irish beauty. The old women of East Belfast would talk of how she had been kissed at birth by the angels in heaven and smiled upon lovingly by the little people themselves. Connie was only sixteen years old and still a child some would say, but as she watched her man march bravely away that day into the unknown, in her head and deep within her heart she was truly a grown woman.

Connie had tear-filled eyes that day as she followed the procession of around fifty young men, each and every one of them marching proudly down the Newtownards Road towards the docks. There, a ship was waiting to ferry them across the Irish Sea to Liverpool and once there, their great adventure would begin for real. For Bobby, as well as most, if not all of the young men marching so proudly that day, this was to be their first excursion out of Belfast, never mind out of Ireland. The air around the marching men was thick with their excitement, each of them smiling bravely and taking every opportunity to wave their farewells to their loved ones that either lined the route, or like Connie were following the parades every step.

The closer the marching men came to the docks, the more animated their waves and smiles became as they marched further and further away from the safety of East Belfast. Soon the bracing smell of the sea began to fill the air as the docks and their ship neared with every forceful steep taken. Connie had now broke into a trot as she attempted to keep up with the young marching troops, jostling vigorously with the other younger women in the crowd, as they too tried to catch the eye of their lovers for one more loving moment. Connie eventually bumped her way through the throng of cheering women finding herself in a position close to her Bobby, so close she could almost reach out and touch him. Connie's eyes now remained firmly fixed on her Bobby. He looked so handsome in his new uniform, the buttons on his tunic shining brightly in the crisp morning sun, his head held high, his rifle resting military style on his manly shoulder, his chest pushed out like that of a strutting peacock. Bobby, although still only seventeen years old, looked every inch the man, the soldier. Bobby had told the recruiting Sergeant that he was nineteen years old and no one in the recruiting tent that day seemed to want to disbelieve him nor even question him nor ask for proof of his age. All they wanted from Bobby that day was for him to sign the papers, and that he did willingly.

Every now and then Bobby would glance in Connie's direction as if to make sure that she was still there with him and watching him. It would seem that Bobby was drawing a great strength and a sense of comfort from Connie's very presence. From time to time he would flash that cheeky, impish smile of his in Connie's direction. This was a smile that Connie loved to see. It always made her feel special and filled her with contentment. Sadly, from this day on until who knows when, Bobby's cheeky smile was now only to be seen when Connie would picture it in her thoughts and dreams. Connie could tell from Bobby's smile that he was saying...

> - I love you Connie, but I have to leave you now because I have to do this thing for my country and for the children we will have one day and for the children that they will have when all of this is over. -

Connie's heart was now beating faster and faster with every glance and every smile from her Bobby. Each time she would return his smile with one that was equally as warm, loving and tender as the one she had received from him. Connie, along with over a hundred other fretful women, continued to follow the young troops as they marched so proudly towards the docks. Connie had to increase her pace in order to keep up with the ever moving and increasingly restless band of well-wishers who were following their sons, husbands, brothers and lovers. Each and every one of them wondering if they would ever see their loved ones ever again. Connie's eyes moved slowly around the other young men who swelled the ranks that made up this fine group of marching men. At this point Connie realised that most of these young men were completely ignorant of just what lay in wait for them overseas, yet each one of them were only too willing to be marching off to fight for King and country. Connie looked on in a strange bewildering wonder, watching as the cold panting breath of the marching men, suddenly fused together in the salt filled morning air and forming a soft drifting cloud above their heads. In that chilled sobering moment, Connie's heart was filled with a sinking despair as she recognised the stark truth of what was taking place in front of her eyes.

Connie now realised that most of these brave young men would not be returning home when this great adventure had run its terrible course. Most of these young men would never have the opportunity to grow into adults nor experience the wonder of fathering their own children and in turn watch them mature and grow into adults. For some of these young men this was to be their last glimpse of happiness, because what lay in wait for them overseas would surely change their lives for ever, if not take it from them all together. This last display of pomp could well be the last joyful thing that they would ever witness. This would be their last remembrance of the smiling faces upon their wives, sisters, mothers and lovers. Was this really all that life had to offer these young men? Connie now knew that from that day forward all that they would ever know in their young lives would be unimaginable terror, hardship, brutality and cruelty. All that they would ever know from this point on, would be war. All that would surround them from that day forth would be death and destruction in every direction they looked.

Connie was being pushed from one side to the other as her eyes scanned the picture before her. Connie was suddenly left opened mouthed, her heart now pounding to a terrifying beat because she could now see past the waving flags, past the cheering women that filled the footpaths. No longer did the rousing, pulsating rhythm of the marching military band fill her with excitement. Connie could now see the reality of what was taking place before her very eyes. As she looked around at the faces of the mothers, wives, sisters and fiancées, she could see it as plain as day, every one of them with the same look of horror and fear in their eyes, each and every one of them burdened with the same look of uncertainty etched into their faces. Each and every one of them feeling and thinking identical thoughts. Will it be my husband, my son, my brother or my lover that will be one of the lucky ones to return home safely when this awful war is over?

Everywhere Connie looked, women clung tightly to each other, as if there was some comfort to be gained by their soulful togetherness. Each one of them fighting back the tears which filled their eyes, tears that constantly tried to force their way out into the chill of the morning air. Somehow these brave woman fought back these tears as they didn't want to let their men see them crying as they marched towards their parting. How could this valiant band of women send their men off to war with the shadow of sadness looming over their hearts? This band of wives, sisters and mothers knew only too well that their menfolk were going to have more than enough sadness and tears coming their way in the months and years to ahead?

Connie continued to follow the procession for another half an hour before the parade finally arrived at the docks. On arrival the young soldiers were promptly marched onto the waiting ship by a stern looking Sergeant Major. Most of the young soldiers managed at least one last wave to the cheering crowd before being ushered on board the ship. Once the soldiers were on board the ship, there was a scramble to find a place by the ships handrail, from where they could wave their last good-byes. All that remained now for Connie and the other woman was a heart-reaching wait for the ship to sail. Connie stood on the quay-side, her eyes glued on Bobby's position at the handrail, watching and waiting for his last wave goodbye. Although Connie's face was smiling broadly up at Bobby, her heart harboured a great fear and a deep sadness at his leaving. She could see that Bobby was trying to tell her something, but it was hard to make out his words through the din being created by the cheering crowd.

"What is it Bobby?" called Connie,

Again Bobby shouted loudly through the near deafening noise that now engulfed the quay-side, in an effort to make himself heard to Connie.

"Will you marry me, Connie?"

Connie still didn't totally understand just what Bobby had shouted to her but she thought, just for a fleeting second, that he had asked her to marry him.

Just then Connie was pushed to the side before she had a chance to reply to her Bobby. By the time she had regained her place in the over excited mass of heaving bodies that filled the dockside, Bobby was no longer standing at the handrail of the ship as he too had been pushed to one side. Other young soldiers who were jockeying for position to deliver their last waves to their loved ones, had replaced Bobby at the ship's handrail. As Connie struggled to once again find her Bobby, the ship slowly pulled away from the quayside, leaving Connie unable to answer Bobby's question, if indeed she had heard it the way she thought she had heard it. With Bobby now nowhere in sight, Connie simply whispered softly to herself,

- 'Be brave in all that you do Bobby... Keep safe in all that you
do Bobby... But above all, come home to me Bobby.' -

Connie remained standing by the harbour wall, watching Bobby's ship as it sailed down the Belfast Lough and disappeared from view. Connie was now standing alone by the harbour wall, everyone else had long since gone. She was now left with only her thoughts as company, thoughts that were still spinning around in her head, thoughts that were mixed with the last images of Bobby as he waved his last good-bye. As Connie stood alone at the docks on this cold Belfast winter's morning, there was one thought that refused to leave her, it was there in the front of her mind, nagging at her. That thought was this...

- Can this be right for ones so young? -

Connie turned and walked slowly from the Albert docks, Bobby's ship now long, long gone. As she left the harbour she glanced up at the Albert Clock and in a soft tender voice she whispered these words…

- Bobby left his home and everything he loved at nine-thirty on the morning of the 15th of February 1916. I shall remember this day and this time for the rest of my life.

Unhurried Connie began her long walk back home.

CHAPTER 4

Connie lived with her mother in a large 7 bed-roomed detached house in a very exclusive and fashionable area on the outskirts of East Belfast. Connie's father had been a very successful businessman and had left behind a thriving organization, which was now being overseen on a daily basis by Connie's mother Edwina and her godfather Mr Andy Powell. Edwina was thirty eight years old and still a very attractive and desirable woman, although since her husband Terry died she had shown no interest in other men whatsoever. Connie had loved her father very much and missed him terribly. If it hadn't have been for her mother and young Bobby showing her all the love and understanding that she needed, things might have turned out a lot worse for her after her father's death. After her father had passed away, Connie and her mother had become more than just mother and daughter. Her mother had become her friend and confident, talking over everything, no matter how small or how personal. A tight unbreakable bond now existed between mother and daughter as each adored the other more than life itself. When Connie returned home from the docks after saying her good-byes to Bobby, her mother was at home waiting to greet her young daughter. Edwina knew that Connie was going to be really upset at Bobby's leaving and was only too aware of the way both Connie and Bobby felt about each other and she approved. As Connie entered the house her mother flung her arms around her and hugged her tightly: after all Connie was still her little girl, no matter how grown up she thought she was.

"Tell me Connie," asked her mother, "How did Bobby look in his new uniform?" Connie looked straight at her mother with a pride filled smile and a tear in her eye.

"Handsome beyond compare, mother," was Connie's simple response. Edwina once again hugged her daughter tightly whilst stroking her long raven hair in an attempt to comfort her. Edwina could see just how proud Connie was of Bobby but she could also see the fear her daughter held in her soft brown eyes.

17

"Shall I ask Mary to make us a nice cup of tea, Connie?" asked Edwina

Mary was the house maid and had seen Connie returning home through the dining room window. Always one to keep one step ahead, Mary had anticipated the need for a freshly brewed tray of tea. Just as Edwina was about to call for Mary, she appeared suddenly in the hallway, carrying a tray of freshly brewed tea, accompanied by a selection of biscuits. Connie and Edwina both smiled at each other and then at Mary. Connie and her mother followed Mary into the sitting room where they had their tea. For the rest of that day Connie was pre-occupied with her thoughts of beloved Bobby. Edwina realised that her daughter needed to be alone with her deep and personal thoughts, so after instructing Mary to keep a close eye on her daughter, Edwina left the house and went to her office.

It was almost two weeks later before Connie received her first letter from Bobby, but from that day onwards she made a point of writing to Bobby every single day, Bobby replying to her letters when the war would allow. As the ensuing weeks turned painfully into months, Connie was finding it difficult adjusting to life without her Bobby, although he was never far from her thoughts, day or night. Not one day would go by without Connie praying for Bobby's safe return. It had now been four months since that memorable but sorrowful day when Bobby and the other young men marched down the Newtownards Road on their way to this great adventure. Bobby's mother, Margaret had not come to see her son march with the other boys. It was too upsetting for her to do so. She had said her goodbyes to her son that morning, before he left the house. No more than two months after Bobby's leaving, Margaret began feeling unwell. Connie would go and visit her almost every day but sadly her health was deteriorating daily. Edwina insisted that Margaret see a doctor and so one was called for and Margaret was sent to hospital. Several days later, Margaret was sadly diagnosed with lung cancer and was given but a few months to live. It was at this point that Edwina insisted that Margaret came to live with them.

Only three weeks into her stay at Edwina's house, Margaret's health began to decline rapidly and Margaret became bedridden. Edwina acted quickly to this unfortunate situation by employing two private nurses to attend to Margaret's every need, both day and night. Margaret had raised Bobby all by herself as there had been no father figure in Bobby's young life, Margaret had fallen pregnant with Bobby when in her early twenties. The identity of Bobby's father was never disclosed, not to anyone ever. The subject of who the father was remained clouded in mystery throughout Bobby's life. Bobby's mother would become angry and display signs of immense guilt every time Bobby, or anyone else would raise the subject. Margaret's mother, Ann was a softly spoken women who was ruled by her tyrant of a husband whose name was John. John was a successful businessman who owned a large gents outfitters in the centre of Belfast, situated on Royal Ave. It had been noted that from Margaret becoming a teenager she had shown little affection towards her father, but she had always adored her mother and now missed her terribly.

Unfortunately, from the early months of Margaret's pregnancy, her father John, who was known as a strong church going, God - fearing pious man throughout east Belfast, had turned his back on his daughter. The instant he had discovered that she was pregnant, he immediately disowned his only daughter, abandoning her and leaving her to find her own way in the outside world. Margaret was all alone now as well as being homeless and penniless. From that day onward Margaret struggled to survive, but survive she did, against all odds, as in Ireland in the year of 1898. A young women alone with a young child was something that was rarely seen and such women were inclined to be shunned by the surrounding community. Hard and uncaring yes, but people in these times were reluctant to show these fallen women any kind of kindness or compassion whatsoever, just in case they too were to fall foul of the lash of the scandalmonger's tongue.

Margaret had to find work when and wherever she could in order to keep a roof over her and young Bobby's heads. She insisted from the beginning that Bobby was to be raised with the manners and etiquette of the finest gentleman, insuring that he would grow up to be a decent and respectable member of society. From the day Bobby was born, Margaret had always loved and cared for her son to the utmost of her ability. So now, when the biggest part of her job of raising Bobby was almost over and her long struggle to provide for him had ended, it seemed unfair that she should now have to contend with this dreadful illness.

Connie was nervous inside on that Sunday morning when she left her home to go visit the home of Margaret's parents, in order to inform them of their daughter's illness. Standing alone on the threshold of this imposing, yet striking front door to Margaret's parents' house, Connie took a deep breath then slowly raised her hand and took a firm hold of the brass knocker and banged it three times as hard as she could, then waited for a response, but none was forth coming. Connie once again grasped hold of the brass knocker and again knocked three times, this time even harder than before. Suddenly the door was opened by a tall thin faced harsh looking man with a head of thick brown hair. Connie instantly took this to be Margaret's father.

"Are you Mr Gallagher?" enquired Connie nervously.

"Yes, I am girl, and who might you be?" came a snapped reply.

"My name is Connie Kean and I am here to tell you that your daughter Margaret..."

Connie was unable to finish her statement as she was rudely prevented from doing so by Mr Gallagher.

"Wrong house girl, I have no daughter. I did once, but no longer! Now please go away and leave us alone girl." rapped an angry Mr Gallagher.

"But you don't understand, Margaret is dying Mr Gallagher, and she wants to see her mother before she dies" said Connie.

There was a short pause, and then.

"I have told you once girl, wrong house! Now go away and leave me alone!" he barked.

Then from inside the house Connie heard a woman's voice calling out, "Who is it dear?"

The call was from Margaret's mother, who remained inside of the house.

Mr Gallagher turned inwards and shouted a sharp reply to his wife.

"It's nothing that concerns you my dear, it's just a silly girl that has come to the wrong house."

With that, Mr Gallagher slammed the door shut in Connie's face. Connie was so angry with his attitude towards his only daughter. She returned home but the episode that had taken place at Mr Gallagher's house lay heavy on her mind for several long days. Connie decided to go the following Sunday and try to talk to Mr Gallagher again. Once again Connie found herself standing outside Mr Gallagher's house, although sadly, since her last visit, Margaret had died. This time the news that Connie had to deliver was the worst kind. Connie truly believed that once she had told Mr Gallagher of the death of his daughter, that his attitude towards Margaret would surely change, after all, there were the funeral arrangements to be made. Connie also needed to let them know of the existence of their grandson, Bobby and how he was overseas fighting for his country.

Unfortunately, Connie couldn't have gotten it more wrong, as yet again the door was opened by Mr Gallagher and he was not pleased to see her standing at his front door yet again. Mr Gallagher began to scold Connie in a loud and frightening voice, ordering her to leave his doorstep instantly. This time Connie was not to be shouted down. She looked directly at Bobby's grandfather and standing her ground bravely informed Mr Gallagher that his daughter had died two days earlier, leaving behind a son named Bobby, his grandson. To Connie's shock and revulsion, this news was met with a cold and uncaring response from Mr Gallagher. Again his pompous attitude raised its ugly head as he began to quote scriptures and verses of damnation in a loud and chilling voice in young Connie's direction. Connie stood on Mr Gallagher's doorstep that Sunday, feeling nothing in her heart but contempt for this disgusting excuse for a father, a grandfather and even as a man. At that very moment, as she listened to the rantings of Mr Gallagher, Connie swore by all that was just, that as long as she took breath, Bobby would never have to meet this God awful man.

Connie turned and walked away from Mr Gallagher's house, leaving him to continue with his biblical rantings. No matter how hard Connie tried, she simply couldn't understand Mr Gallagher's spiteful standpoint. No matter what had happened in the past, Connie found it unbelievable that a man could show no interest whatsoever in the death of his only daughter. Even more shameful was his total rejection of the existence of his only grandson, regardless of the unfortunate circumstance surrounding his birth. Instead of showing compassion or some kind of forgiveness towards his dead daughter and his living grandson, this nasty abomination of a human being denied the very existence of both.

Connie returned home, her heart heavy and saddened by Mr Gallagher's complete lack of interest in his daughter's passing and the existence of his grandson. Again she made a promise to herself that Bobby would never have to meet this despicable creature who was his grandfather. After long and difficult consideration, Connie, with the help of her mother, came to the conclusion that it might be best if she didn't inform Bobby of his mother's passing by letter. She preferred instead to wait until Bobby's next leave when she could tell him in person the terrible news of his mother's passing. After long conversations with her mother, Connie thought this to be the best course of action. After all, Bobby had enough sorrow and pain to contend with as it was. Would it really serve any purpose to inform Bobby by letter of her death, knowing that this news would without doubt break his heart and him so far away from everyone he loved?

It was on the 18th of December 1916 when Bobby returned home on his first leave, ten long months after he had first marched along the Newtownards Road. Needless to say, Connie was there at the dockside to greet him as he disembarked. Connie's eyes watched closely as the returning soldiers began to make their way down the gangway towards the waiting crowd. She pushed her way through the cheering mass of women and girls who were all waiting for their first glimpse of their returning loved ones. Connie found herself nearing the front of the heaving crowd, her eyes constantly searching for her Bobby as line after line of troops were now coming in greater numbers. Then suddenly there he was at the top of the gangway. Connie could see that he too was frantically searching the quayside to see if his Connie was there to meet him.

"Bobby, I'm here. I'm over here Bobby," screamed Connie excitedly.

Because of the near deafening din that filled the quayside that morning, Bobby couldn't hear Connie's calls to him. She continued to push her way through the cheering throng until she was at the front of the crowd. Then suddenly Bobby saw her waving at him and he rushed down the gangway and began running towards her. As he got closer to her, Connie noticed that there was something different about him. Something had changed in his face and she could see it in his eyes. Somehow, they seemed fixed and without expression. Bobby's impish and pleasing smile had gone from his face and in its place was an emptiness, a nothing. Bobby's beautiful bright eyes no longer sparkled and instead now appeared to burn with an unforgiving anger. Bobby's mouth was shut tight, his lips hidden, making his mouth look wrinkled and unwelcoming. It would seem that this great adventure had taken a terrible toll on her Bobby. He dropped his holdall on the ground and flung his arms around Connie, holding her tight in his arms, lifting her slender body several inches of the ground and spinning her around.

Connie could feel the side of her face becoming damp as Bobby's tears fell from his eyes and trickled down onto her cheeks. Bobby held Connie tight in his arms but yet not a word had passed his lips. Bobby's lips began to gently caress the soft flesh of Connie's beautiful face, his arms still holding her fast. Connie made an attempt to speak but Bobby stopped her saying…

"Please don't say a word, not just yet. I just want to hold you close to me for a few more minutes."

Connie slowly pressed her slender body closer to her precious Bobby and its very closeness caused his body to quake at her very touch. This close embrace that they both shared together on this cold December morning would remain planted in Connie's thoughts for years to come. Connie whispered softly in Bobby's ear,

"I love you, Bobby and I have missed you so much."

Bobby's response was to clutch Connie's body even tighter to his. The two young lovers stood wrapped together in silence for several minutes. No mind was paid to the cold winter's wind that blew in from the Lough and was now biting angrily at both of their bodies. All that mattered on this bitter December morning was that they were once again together in each other's arms, held in an embrace that neither of them wanted to end. Most had now left the dockside, leaving Connie and Bobby alone, as soft snow flakes began to tumble down from the sky above, many coming to rest on Bobby and Connie's faces.

The Albert Clock which stood proudly but a short walk away from the docks was heard to strike twelve times.

"Shall we go home now Bobby?" asked Connie.

Bobby picked up his holdall and he and Connie walked slowly from the docks, their hands held together in a tight grip, their eyes fixed on each other.

"Shall we stop at Molly's tearooms before we go home Bobby? I don't really want to go home just yet. In any case, Bobby, I need to talk to you. There's something important you need to know." explained Connie as she kissed Bobby on the cheek.

Bobby's eyes suddenly opened wide with fear because these words were no stranger to his ears. These words had been said to many a soldier fighting in the trenches. These very words had troubled many of his comrades, leading many a good man to his death, when unable to face that his lover back home had found someone new. Bobby stopped instantly and stood directly in front of Connie blocking her path. Then he said nervously,

"No! Please Connie no, if it's what I think it is! Please don't tell me until tomorrow. For now please just allow me this one last day with you before I have to return to that hell in France, just one more day then you can tell me that it's over."

Connie smiled warmly at her Bobby then slowly she raised her hand softly, touching his shivering face with her long slender fingers.

"No. It's not what you think, Bobby, I would never leave you. What I must talk to you about is regarding our mother," whispered Connie.

"My mother!" exclaimed Bobby loudly. "What about my mother Connie?"

Bobby truly loved his mother and would have done anything for her, but now the deep fear that something might have happened to her worried him deeply.

"What is it Connie, what's happened to my mother? Please tell me!" He pleaded.

"Not here, Bobby. Let's go to Molly's tearooms and I will tell you when we get inside."

Molly's tearooms was but a few minutes' walk from the docks. When they arrived there Bobby found an empty table at the far end of the tearooms. He pulled out a chair for Connie to sit on, then he ordered tea and sandwiches for both of them.

"Please tell me Connie. What's happened to my mother?" asked Bobby.

Connie took hold of Bobby's hand and squeezed it tightly as she said,

"Your mother took ill some weeks after you left Bobby. I'm afraid you mother had cancer. She fought it bravely for some time, but in the end she lost her battle and she passed away."

This tragic news was devastating for Bobby after everything he had been through, and of everything that he had witnessed in the past months at the Front, this was one death he had not foreseen nor did he want to accept it.

"Was she in great pain Connie?" asked Bobby.

"Some, but thank the Lord, not a lot." replied Connie.

"Was she alone through her illness?" he asked.

"No, my mother brought Margaret to live with us, Bobby," answered Connie.

Bobby lowered his head into his hands and began to weep into his opened palms. Again Connie raised her slender hand and lovingly touched the side of Bobby's face. He raised his head and took Connie's hand in his and he kissed it softly as one tear after another rolled from his eyes onto his cheeks. Then he said softly,

"I am glad that my mother was not alone when her time came to leave us Connie. For that I thank you and your mother."

Connie looked into Bobby's eyes as she held his hands tightly in hers. She noticed the faint glitter of the tearoom lights reflecting on his tear-filled eyes. Her heart began to quicken and thud with a painful beat at the thought of what Bobby was going through, after all she had experienced the same thing when her father had died. Connie's heart went out to her Bobby as she thought within herself. How much more does this young man have to suffer before this is all over? Connie looked into her Bobby's eyes and was now convinced that she had made the right decision not to tell Bobby this dreadful news by letter.

Bobby suddenly raised his head and smiled at Connie, but this was not a smile of pleasure. It was a smile of acceptance and it was a smile of the celebration of his mother's life because he would always remember her as the smiling beautiful caring women he saw every morning of his young life.

"I don't know what I would do if you were not here for me this day, Connie. I really do need to have you in my life for ever."

"I will always be in your life, Bobby, for as long as you want me to be" whispered Connie softy.

Bobby took another sip from his cup of tea, then he asked,

"When did it happen, Connie?"

Connie told Bobby the day and time of his mother's death. She also informed him that he had just left for France a few weeks before his mother took ill and that it had been impossible to contact him in time. By the time we found out where you were Bobby, your mother was already dead. Connie then explained how she thought it best to wait until he came home to tell him the sad news in person, rather than just tell him in a letter.

Bobby sat in silence for over a minute, his mind racing, filled with past memories, thoughts and images of his mother. Then, lifting his head to look at Connie, he said,

"I thank you for looking after my mother in her time of need, Connie. I know that it would have meant a lot to her as she thought the world of you, as do I Connie."

The next few minutes passed in total silence, Connie thinking it better for now to leave Bobby with his thoughts of his mother in quietness. Minutes later Bobby said,

"Please tell me everything of my mother's last days Connie, I need to know."

Bobby thought for a moment, then he said,

"It's going to be strange going back to an empty house. I've never been in the house without my mother being there too."

"There's something I haven't told you yet Bobby," said Connie in a soft voice.

Bobby realised from Connie's tone that there was more bad news on its way.

"Oh good God Connie, what more bad news is there for me to come?" He groaned, fearing the worst.

"It's your mother's house, Bobby," said Connie.

"My mother's house!" exclaimed Bobby. "What's wrong with my Mother's house?" he added sharply.

Connie took a deep breath and began to tell Bobby what had happened to his mother's house.

"When your mother died Bobby, the landlord took possession of your mother's house. He said that he needed it for businesses reasons. My mother went to meet with him and assured him that she would continue to pay the rent until the war was over and you had returned home, Bobby. But he wouldn't listen to my mother's offer and he dismissed it out of hand, insisting that he had plans for the house. My mother then offered to buy the house off him, but again he refused. Later we found out that he had moved two young women into the house, much to the annoyance of the neighbours. It would seem that the businesses he had in mind for your mother's house was not a pleasant, nor honourable one, I'm sorry to say Bobby."

Bobby sat in silence, staggered to hear this dreadful news about his mother's house.

"I'm so, so sorry that you had to come home to all of this, Bobby, after everything that you have been through, this just isn't right." said Connie.

"What happened to my mother's belongings, Connie, are they safe?" asked Bobby.

Connie noticed that Bobby's eyes were glazed and red as she answered softly.

"All of your mother's belongings are safe Bobby, my mother has stored everything from your mother's house in the basement of our house. Everything is there for you whenever you want them."

"Where am I to go now Connie?" said Bobby.

Bobby had the look of total despair etched across his face and it was as if his whole world had collapsed around him.

"I know there is nothing we can do to make up for the loss of your mother's house but my mother insists that you come and stay with us whenever you are home on leave," replied Connie.

Bobby raised his head and looked at Connie with tearful eyes and said,

"It would seem that there is as much pain and torment for me here in Belfast as there was back in France."

Bobby picked up both of Connie's hands and kissed them softly, then he said,

"When this dreadful war is over Connie and if I am fortunate enough to return home, I am going to try and find my grandparents. They must live in Belfast somewhere, don't you think Connie?"

Connie sat silent, reluctant to pass any kind of comment on this particular subject knowing what she did about Bobby's grandfather.

"I think it's only right that they are told of my mother's death, and of course of my existence. If it takes me the rest of my life I will find them Connie," added Bobby.

Yet again Connie made no attempt to answer but instead just smiled and took a deep breath as she prayed inwardly for God's guidance and forgiveness in this matter. Although Bobby had no idea who or where his grandparents were, Connie did. This Knowledge was not an easy thing to bury out of sight but she had promised herself after meeting Bobby's grandfather that she would never have any part in this ghastly man ever meting Bobby. All that interested Connie at this moment was that she had Bobby all to herself for the next two weeks over

Christmas. This one thought warmed Connie's young heart and pleased her no end. Connie looked at her Bobby and said,

"Let's go home, Bobby and tomorrow I will take you to your mother's grave."

Later that evening after the best dinner Bobby had eaten in a very long time, Connie, Edwina and Bobby sat by the raging fire in Edwina's sitting room and talked for hours. Bobby slowly began to realise that despite everything that had happened to him since his return, he was in fact thankful to be back home in Belfast. He was even more thankful to be once again reunited with his beloved Connie. It was midnight before everyone retired for the evening, but it was to be a long restless night of tossing and turning for Bobby. A night spent grappling with the dark thoughts that haunted his mind meant sleep was to elude Bobby that restless night. Again and again this one distressing thought would continually return to disturb and haunt Bobby's mind, the thought of how hard his mother had worked throughout her entire life to provide a safe and clean home for him, filled his every waking hour. Now he was never going to get the chance to repay her for all that she had done for him throughout his life. Never would he have the opportunity to look after his mother in her advancing years, like she had done for him as a child. Never would he be allowed to give his mother the life she so richly deserved.

Early the next morning, both Bobby and Connie set out to visit Margaret's grave at Knock Cemetery. Their journey on that bitter, cold winter's morning was to be a long and silent one. Connie noticed that Booby had a cold and distant look in his eyes as they both huddled together for warmth on the old draughty tram as it creaked its way slowly through the snow. Connie could see that Bobby was fidgeting nervously the closer the old tram came to the cemetery and his mother's final resting place. Connie remained silent as she sat beside this saddened figure that Bobby had become, because deep within her heart she knew that words were of little importance to him right now. All he needed to know was that she was with him, close to him in his time of need. The old tram began to slow, then grind to a halt outside the large black iron gates of Knock Cemetery. Bobby and Connie climbed down from the tram and started their walk to Margaret's grave. Bobby placed both hands on the big black gates and pushed them wide open. He then stepped inside the gates and stretched out his hand towards Connie, inviting her to make this next step of the journey with him. For the first time since they had boarded the old tram, Bobby broke his silence when he said,

"Please come with me Connie."

Connie stepped forward and took hold of Bobby's hand, then both set off towards Margaret's grave, carefully picking every small but deliberate step as they made their way up the icy slope that led to Margaret's final resting place. Several minutes later Connie stopped beside a snow covered mound of earth.

"We are here Bobby," she said softly. "This is your mother's grave."

Bobby stared in silence at his mother's grave for several minutes as the icy wind bit relentlessly at his face. Then he took a few steps forward until he was level with his mother's headstone. One tear after another began to fall from Bobby's freezing face and slowly he removed the glove from his right hand and reached out and gently touched the icy cold granite which marked his mother's final resting place. Bobby's tears now fell to the ground with such regularity that they began to make small indentations in the soft, fluffy white blanket of snow which covered Margaret's grave. Seeing this took Bobby's thoughts back to his childhood as he remembered how his mother would lovingly cover him with a white fluffy blanket on those long freezing winter nights long ago. Bobby knelt down to place the flowers that he had brought with him in the small black receptacle which sat directly in front of Margaret's headstone. Bobby remained kneeling on both knees on this cold blanket of snow which now covered his mother. Bobby's eyes remained fastened tight as he lovingly remembered better times spent with his loving mother. Connie stepped back from Margaret's grave, deciding to allow Bobby keep this tender, but also mournful occasion to himself. Connie watched Bobby's every movement, keeping herself in readiness as she was well aware that sooner or later Bobby was going to be in need of love and attention. Suddenly Bobby got to his feet and turned towards Connie and with eyes that seemed to be looking for some kind of answer and he asked,

"Why her, Connie, and why now?"

Connie had no answer to give to Bobby. All she could do for him now was to be by his side and show him all the love and kindness that she could. Bobby said his last goodbyes to his mother and both he and Connie left Knock Cemetery and went home to Connie's house.

CHAPTER 5

That evening Connie and Bobby were to have dinner alone as Edwina and Mr Powell were attending a cocktail party at Belfast City Hall, hosted by the Chambers of Commerce. After dinner, Connie and Bobby were sitting by the raging fire in the front sitting room. Mary, the house maid, had brought them a tray of tea before retiring for the evening. Connie was gazing into the flames that were dancing around the hearth when she suddenly looked at Bobby and said,

"What is it really like over there Bobby?"

Bobby looked straight back at Connie and from the look of fear in his eyes Connie quickly realised that if Bobby wanted to talk about what he had been through at the Somme, then it was not going to be pleasant listening at all.

"It's just that you never mention too much about it in your letters," added Connie.

"Do you really want to know about it Connie?" ask Bobby.

"Yes I do, Bobby. I want to share in your pain with you, if you will allow me too. I don't want you to keep it all locked up inside yourself. Share it with me, please Bobby," she suggested.

"As you know, Connie," he began, "I have been at the Somme and this is the most terrifying and God-forsaken place on this earth. It was the beginning of May when we first arrived and immediately we set about digging our trenches."

At this point Bobby's voice was light and quick, portraying the excitement that the young men had experienced at this time.

"It was all very light hearted at first," continued Bobby, "the mood amongst the men was really good. Jokes and pranks seemed to be the order of the day and light was made about the amount of work we all had to carry out each day. But in the evenings, Connie, whilst it was still light, we played football or cricket, all of us to a man looked forward to the evenings. Sometimes in the afternoons, if we got a few hours off duty, small groups of us would go into one of the several small villages that were to the rear of our positions. Most of the villages were no more than a few miles away from us and if the weather was nice, as it always seem to be, we would walk to the village that we had picked out to visit that day. Once there our first job would be to find what the French called a café, then we would have lunch. At these cafés they would serve us our food at tables out in the open air. Think of it Connie, tables outside in the streets with people sitting eating at them. Along with our lunch which consisted of things we had never seen or heard of in our lives, they would serve us wine, both red and white. Sometimes, if the owner was in a good mood he would serve us with what they called champagne, a strange drink, Connie. It was full of bubbles that made us all burp for hours afterwards. At this time everything was wonderful. By the middle of June it had become so hot in the daytime that we all had to remove our shirts. Connie, you should have seen us, the sun was so hot on our backs as we worked that we all had to strip down to our shorts and boots.

Most of us had never seen anything like it in our lives before. Yes, we had all seen sunny summer days back home but never anything like this, Connie. The heat was so humid that we found even the smallest of tasks exhausting. By the end of the third week of June, everything was ready in our trenches that were also going to be our homes for as long as we were there, including our field hospitals. Please don't get me wrong Connie, it wasn't all fun and sports we worked hard and trained for long hours in all kinds of things, each and every day. We even constructed new roads leading in and out of our positions."

Bobby stopped for a second and picked up his cup and took a short sip before replacing it back in its saucer. He then continued with his story, but as he did so, Connie noticed that his voice had changed. This time Bobby's voice was low and unsettling. His facial expression had also changed and appeared now twisted in pain and anguish. His eyes darkened and had the look of terror deep within them. Connie was shocked and somewhat alarmed by the unearthly glare that had now appeared on Bobby's face. It was as if he had been confronted by Lucifer himself. Connie braced herself for what was about to come her way. Bobby continued in this vein for the rest of his story.

"I can still remember the morning that our bombardment of the German lines began, Connie. It was relentless, day and night our artillery blasted their positions. We all sat quietly in our trench, eyes fixed firmly on the ground between our legs, all of us wishing that we were somewhere else. The only sound to be heard in the air above our heads was the awful whistling sound of our shells as they passed over our trenches on their way to the German positions that were but a Sunday walk in front of us. This terrifying whistling sound that was constantly whizzing over our heads, would always be followed a few seconds later by the loudest of explosions. After a time we were sending so many shells in their direction that one sound melted into the other, until it was just one big cacophony of ear splitting eruptions all around us. This was the only sound to be heard anywhere; this was the sound of war Connie, and it frightened each and every one of us.

At its height this ear-busting noise was so loud that you couldn't even hear a word the man next to you was saying, if indeed he was saying anything at all. Little did we know at the time, Connie, that all of this was going to get a lot worse for each and every one of us. Our shelling of the German lines lasted for seven days and nights, then suddenly and without warning, it all stopped just as quickly as it had started. To a man we all thought the same thing Connie,

- Surely there can be nothing left of the German trenches! -

We all believed deeply that no one could have survived such a devastating onslaught but Oh my God, Connie, how wrong we all were! On the last day of June, suddenly everything changed. First it began to rain, rain like you have never seen the likes of before, Connie. It fell from the sky with such velocity that within a few hours everything around us had turned to thick putrid mud. The trenches we lived in were now flooded with this dirty brown rancid water. In some places the water was so deep that it splashed up to our knees, making even a few steps difficult to take. This was our first taste of what was to come for all of us, Connie. I remember on one occasion a few of us looked out over the top of our trench and there through the haze of the rain we saw something even if you had been told of, you wouldn't believe a word of it, Connie.

To the front of us was a large expanse of land which was completely barren except for rolls and rolls of barbed wire that had been placed some 100 yards in the distance. These evil, malicious rolls of razor-sharp wire had been previously placed there as part of the German defences. They seemed to stretch for ever, Connie, even further than an eye could see. Beyond this barbed wired covered ground lay another expanse of land, roughly of the same size as the first, this was to become known as:

No Man's Land.

At the end of this, No Man's Land, were the German defences. From the German lines and beyond to some of the German held villages, all we could see were large clouds of smoke and fierce flames of such magnitude that they leapt up so high that they coloured the sky, crimson red. If the reality hadn't have been so terrifying then it would have been a beautiful sight to see, Connie. Sadly, this was the devastating aftermath of our ruthless and relentless bombardment.

Although no one ever said it out loud, but it could be seen in each of our faces, we all felt it in one way or another, a strange kind of sympathy for the poor bastards at the receiving end of our big guns. But believe me Connie, this sympathy for the enemy was to be very short lived indeed. I've told you what was in front of us, now for what was either side of us. For as far as the eye could see, Connie, the ground was covered with more and more trenches, just like the one

31

we were living in. Each and every one of them filled with young men just like us. The strangest thing was this, Connie, I never once saw anyone who had out-lived their twenties and that included the officers.

We were all now members of the combined British and French forces. I found out later that the trenches on our side that I told you we saw from our trench, stretched for over sixteen miles. Think of it if you can Connie, sixteen miles of trenches all filled with young men just like me. Young men that had no idea of what lay ahead of them, young men away from home for the first time in their lives. Young men that had quickly discovered the reality of war after witnessing our bombardment of the German lines. The rain continued to fall, making conditions within the trenches intolerable. Movement around the trench was now impossible due to the flooding or the thick mud. That night we all knew that when the morning came this war would begin in earnest for us all. The mood amongst the men had now changed drastically, a cloud of fear now hung over the trenches, we sat around in small groups trying to keep warm as we wrote down what we hoped would not be our last thoughts in this world and recording our last messages to our loved ones. Every one of us would secretly wish that we were somewhere else, anywhere but there, Connie. Trust me when I say this, we were all really frightened young men because we all now realised that a large number of us would never see our homes or our families ever again. That night we all went to sleep wondering the same thing: was tomorrow going to be our last day on this earth?"

Bobby slowly reached into his pocket and pulled out a sheet of wrinkled, mud stained paper.

"This is mine," he said softly, as he held it out for Connie to see. "I still have it all these months later, most of us still do. We keep them as a reminder of that fear filled night, the night before it all began."

Bobby paused for a second as his eyes slowly closed as if in remembrance for fallen comrades. Then he continued.

"My good friend, Tommy Pollock, a lad I had come to know really well over the many weeks we had spent together in this miserable trench we called home. Tommy was a boy from Liverpool. He was as funny as funny could be, Connie, always had a joke. We were both sitting side by side in the pouring rain as we wrote down our thoughts and our hopes in a letter."

Suddenly a great sadness filled Bobby's face as he took a deep breath, then he said in a soft, but troubled voice,

"I delivered Tommy's letter to his tearful mother in Liverpool before boarding the ship to come home, Connie. Young Tommy was killed the next morning as we went over the top for the first time. He was only seventeen years old. After all of his hard work and all the hours of training he had done, Tommy's war lasted but fifteen minutes, then it was all over for him, Connie."

Bobby's eyes were now red and swollen and filling with tears. Connie reached out and took hold of Bobby's hand as she too could now feel her Bobby's pain. Bobby tightened his grip on Connie's soft feminine hand, his eyes remaining tight shut in remembrance of young Tommy.

"Was your letter for me Bobby?" asked Connie.

Bobby nodded his head to indicate that it was.

"May I read it Bobby please?" asked Connie.

Bobby opened his eyes slowly and answered,

"Yes, if you want too Connie."

Bobby placed his mud stained letter into Connie's hand, his eyes became fixed in a downward position as Connie opened up his letter. She straightened the crumpled grubby sheet of paper and began to read it in a low gentle voice.

> Dearest Connie,
>
> It is now the end of June and I am writing you this letter from a mud filled trench that has become my home. I am at a place they call the Somme, my good friend Tommy Pollack is here beside me, he is writing his letter to his mother. I am writing my letter to you Connie. I only tell you of his presences because he is sniggering and poking his tongue out at me in an attempt to lighten the quiet eerie mood that tonight fills our trench. Tommy knows only too well that he has the ability to make me laugh out loud any time he wishes to do so. But on this occasion, Tommy's fooling is not for pleasure or for fun, it is an attempt to mask the fear that he and the rest of us are feeling. As I look around this damp dismal place, which in truth is no more than a hole in the ground, I see that my comrades all have the same idea as Tommy and myself, they are all busy scribbling down on paper what might turn out to be their last thoughts on this earth. It might also be their last chance to say their good-byes to their loved ones. This is without a doubt the saddest sight I have ever seen Connie. The silence is all around us and it's deafening. As far as my eyes can see there are thousands of young men here all concentrating intensely on what they should say in what could be their last dispatch home? Because tomorrow morning Connie, we all go over the top for the first time and we know only too well that many of us will not be returning home to our hole in the ground at the end of the day. We are all frightened here Connie, but what can we do about our situation? We can't simply pack a bag and return home now can we Connie.

We can do nothing Connie nothing at all but to do as we are told to do by our Officers.

I pray to the almighty God above this night that he grants me the strength to carry out my duties when it comes my time to go over the top. Like most of the men here with me tonight Connie, I fear that the morning will bring something that this world has never seen the likes of before, nor I suspect will never witness the likes of ever again. Yes I am afraid Connie, terribly afraid that I might never see you again, I am afraid that I may never hold you in my arms again, I am afraid that my lips will never kiss your soft lips ever again, I am afraid that I may never set eyes on your beautiful face again, I am afraid I will never touch your soft long raven hair. As I write you this letter I hold your photograph out in front of me. Although it is now beginning to crack and split from me looking at it so often, it still shows me just how beautiful you really are and every time I hold it in my hands I truly marvel at your beauty.

I don't know what I would do without your photograph Connie, every night I hold it close to my heart and pray that one day, with the grace of the almighty God, I will see you once again. I hope that on this night of the 30th. Of June, that as you prepare for bed, that you have prayed for my safety harder than you have ever done before because I fear I will need all of your prayers come the morning. Tommy is waving to me now, as he has made a pot of tea for the both of us, I can see him smiling in the dim glow of the fires that are raging in the distance and I know he is smiling at me because he knows that I am talking to you. One day I hope you will meet him, because I am sure you will like him Connie. For now I will say good-night to you and I hope to see you soon, if God willing. God bless and keep you Connie.

Thinking of you always... Love Bobby.

Tears now filled Connie's eyes as she folded Bobby's letter and placed it on the wooden table to the side of her.

"My God, Bobby, I had no idea that it was this bad over there," whispered Connie. What on earth are they doing to you boys over there, Bobby and where will it all end?"

"I want to tell you everything, Connie, if you would like me to, "said Bobby.

"I want to know everything. I want to hear of all the horrors that you have suffered overseas Bobby," replied Connie.

Bobby looked at Connie and said,

"Then you shall hear everything, Connie, every last horrifying act that I have witnessed in that hell-hole called The Somme."

Bobby continued with his story.

"After both Tommy and I had finished writing our letters to our loved ones, we both huddled together in an effort to keep warm as we sipped at our cups of lukewarm tea. I swear to you, Connie, the rain was now so heavy, that it's constant pounding on the corrugated-iron roof of the officer's make-shift shelter, that it reminded me of the sound of the drums on a 12th. Of July Orange day parade. It's funny, considering everything that was going on all around me to think that this sound made my mind drift back to a sunny Belfast morning in July. I had become so engrossed in my thoughts of home that I hadn't noticed that Tommy had left the corner of the trench that we called home. I knew that he wouldn't have gone far but knowing Tommy like I did, something told me that he was up to some kind of mischief. Suddenly he reappeared with a kit-bag tucked under his arm.

"What you got there, Tommy?"

I asked him. Tommy smiled as he opened the kit-bag and produced two large canvas sheets.

"Here, Bobby," he said as he handed one of them to me. "Take hold of one of these mate, it might help to keep you a little dryer on this hellish night."

"Where on earth did you get these Tommy?" I asked curiously, knowing that it was only the officers that had been issued with these canvas sheets.

Tommy smiled that cheeky smile of his and replied boldly,

"Never mind where I got them, Bobby, just get under one of them."

This I did instantly and that's when Tommy turned to me with a huge smile across his face and said,

"You asked me where I got these canvas sheets that you don't need to know. But I will tell you this, Bobby, I know of two officers that are going to get rather wet tonight."

I had to laugh at his nerve, then pulling the canvas sheets over us we both huddled together once again under our newly found shelter and tried to get some sleep.

The rest of that night proved to be a restless one, at best a few cat-naps was all that, myself, Tommy and most of the men achieved that night. We were all far too nervous to sleep, Connie, knowing what the morning was to bring for us all. I awoke from one of my cat-naps to find that the morning light had arrived but still the rain continued to pound hard, turning the ground beneath out feet into a swamp. I looked at my watch, it was 5-30. In the morning of the 1st. of July, in the year of our lord 1916. Just a few hours to go until it would be zero hour. Tommy was already up and had yet again made a pot of tea for the both of us.

"Come on you sleepy head," he shouted as he handed me a cup of tea.

We both sat in the early morning mist drinking our tea, the silence that filled the trench seem to cast an eerie sensation over us all. As I looked around the trench a strange feeling griped me, I watched men that only a day before were laughing loudly and chatting openly with their comrades, their faces bright and smiling. But now these same men couldn't even bring themselves to look each other in the eye, never mind chat to one and other. Tommy too had now fallen silent, just like the others. I noticed that if the eyes of one man should happen to make contact with the eyes of another, then all that would be exchanged between them was a simple nod of the head, then both men would turn away as quickly as possible.

I can also remember, as the time approached six o'clock, the trench was filled with a strange putrid smell. It wasn't the smell of the stale mud that slapped around beneath our feet, no, this smell was different altogether. This smell seemed to float in the air above our heads, filling our nostrils and gripping the back of our throats as though it were coarse sand, making even a short breath hard to take. To this day none of us ever found out just what that horrendous smell actually was, but every time after that first day, whenever we would prepare ourselves to go over the top, this God awful smell would return and hang over us like a blanket of decaying flesh. I don't think I shall ever be able to forget that throat gripping smell, Connie.

By 7-00am. We had all made ready because it was about to begin for real. The idea was that we would go over the top in waves. Tommy and I were to go on the sixth wave. I looked at my watch, it was 7-28.am, two minutes to go to zero hour. Tommy and I moved into position in our trench and waited for it all to begin. We stood in line in silence, no man speaking to another. Tommy looked at me and held out his hand towards me and said softly,

"Take care, Bobby and, if God willing, I will see you at the end of this day."

I could feel Tommy's hand shaking as I held it tightly in mine. I could see his fear in his eyes and I knew then that Tommy didn't want to do this thing that we were all about to do. Tommy's bottom lip began to shake as badly as his hand was shaking, Connie.

'I need to tell you something Bobby,' said Tommy as a tear fell from his eye.

"What is it, Tommy?"

"I really shouldn't be here Bobby. I am only fifteen years old."

I flung my arm around him and pulled him close to me and said,

"Stay close behind me, Tommy and only go where I go and you'll see, everything will be alright, we'll make it through this day, Tommy, trust me. Just stay behind me, Tommy."

Tommy shook his head and replied,

"No, Bobby, please let me go first because with you behind me I know I won't stop, I know I will keep going Bobby. Knowing that you are behind me I will be able to make it out of this fucking trench, then no one will be able to call me a coward, will they Bobby?"

"No one will ever call you a coward to me, Tommy!"

"Please just keep me moving Bobby, don't let me stop, keep me going Bobby."

Tears began to bugle in Tommy's eyes, just as the officer blew his whistle for the first wave to go. The officer's whistle was a sound we all came to hate as the weeks went by. Both Tommy and I stood silent at the bottom of the ladder, waiting for our turn to go over the top, the noise of the gun-fire and the smell of burning raged from the outside of the trench. Tommy looked at me as the sound of men shouting and screaming in pain began to echo loudly in our ears. Tommy's eyes were now filled with tears and his body was shaking with fear. He looked at me as if he wanted me to tell him that he didn't have to go, but go he had to do. I placed my hand on his shoulder, but before I could say anything, Tommy said in a low voice.

"I don't' want to go Bobby, I'm afraid."

"No you're not Tommy," I replied, "Just stay close to me and everything will be alright. I promise you, Tommy."

Tommy looked at me and said,

"Will it, Bobby, will it really be alright?"

I told him that it would, but no sooner had I said it, than Tommy was off up the ladder. He was moving so fast that he was over the top before I had even put my foot on the first rung. By the time I reached the top, Tommy was long gone. I looked all around for him, but it was pointless because I couldn't see more than a few feet in front of myself. Men all around me were running, some even in the wrong direction because we could hardly see more than a few feet in front of us for the thick smoke from the shelling we were receiving from the German's heavy guns. All around the noise was deafening, Connie, thousands of guns all firing at once, hundreds of shells exploding both near and far. The worst sound of all was the screams of wounded and dying men, their screams of pain filled the air in every direction. I began to run forward along with the other men, but my advance was suddenly halted when I fell over something laying on the ground that sent me tumbling until I too was face down in the mud. When I picked myself up, I could see that it was our sergeant, Connie. He was lying dead in the thick mud with the lower half of his body missing. This was the first person I had ever seen dead in my entire life, Connie, but it wasn't to be my last.

I began running forward again with the other men around me, then suddenly, just for a second, the smoke cleared and I was able to see the reality of what was happening all around me. I tell you, Connie, for as far as the eye could see the ground was thick with the dead, the dying and wounded. Their agonizing groans and terrifying cries for help was almost as loud as the German guns, then just as quickly as it cleared, the air was again filled with thick choking smoke. Like the other men, I continued my attack on the German defences, screaming at the top of my voice as I went. Somehow this seemed to help as I found myself leaping over my dead and wounded comrades who lay in the mud beneath my feet.

I managed to stay on my feet as I moved forward for at least ten minutes, then once again tumbling over yet another of my comrades laying on the ground. I pulled myself to my feet and bent down to pick up my rifle and to my horror I discovered just who it was that had caused me to take the tumble. It was my good friend, Tommy. He was laying on his back in the sticky French mud with a hole in his chest so big I could have pushed my fist into the middle of it.

"Is that you, Bobby?" croaked Tommy painfully as he realised that it was me.

"Yes it's me Tommy," I replied.

I put my hand on his head and stroked his face gently, then I turned and shouted as loud as I could…

"Medic, medic, for the love of God will somebody help my friend, Tommy?"

But no one came to help poor Tommy, the medics were being overwhelmed, Connie. There were so many solders needing their help and all at the same time.

I turned my attention back to Tommy. He was holding on tightly to my hand and I could see that his pain was biting hard. If ever a man knew that his time on this earth was up, Tommy did that day as he lay in the mud. Tommy, now struggling to even take a short breath, looked up at me and said,

"Bobby, please will you take my letter to my mother and tell her that she can be proud of her only son, tell her that I didn't let her down, Bobby. Let her know that she was right, Bobby and that she mustn't cry at my passing. Tell my mother that I died bravely like a man, but above all tell her that I love her deeply, please, do this for me."

Tommy's eyes slowly faded and then closed, his grip on my hand weakened and in the blink of an eye Tommy was gone from this world for ever. I put my hand into Tommy's pocket and took his letter and placed it in the pocket of my tunic. I bent down and kissed my good friend Tommy on his brow and whispered softly,

"I think all of our mothers were right, Tommy, we are all too young for this and none of us have been prepared to be part of the savage atrocity that is taking place here on this hell called the Somme."

I closed Tommy's eyes and placed his helmet over his face, I looked sky-ward and asked God to embrace my good friend, Tommy. I stood up and with my eyes still looking sky-ward, I prayed that God would forgive us all for what we were about to do this day, then I said my last goodbye to Tommy and began running forward with the rest of the young men that found themselves in the middle of this carnage.

I discovered later that on that first day of the fighting we suffered 60,000 casualties, 20,000 of which were killed, Connie. Just think of it if you can, try and grasp the enormity of this terrifying thing that took place there that day. Think of it in these terms, then you begin to understand, Connie. In one day everyone who lives in East Belfast, disappeared overnight, never to be seen again. We all fought hard and long that day, and the next and the next. On the morning of the seventh day I remember being told that we were going over the top again that day. I looked around the trench at my comrades, each one of them to a man, cut a lonely sad figure as they stood silently in the thick mud that filled our trenches. But something was different that morning, uI could see it in their young faces. They all had the same look, it was a look that painted a gloomy picture. It was easy to see that all of the men were thinking the same thing:

- We don't want to do this thing again this day. –

Although the men had this one thought in their heads, there was no thought of insurrection in their minds. Nor any word of mutiny on their lips. We all knew deep down exactly what was expected of us and that it was our duty to go again that day and the next day and the one after that, no matter if we wanted to or not. We all wanted to know one thing, Connie and that was, who is responsible for this madness, because madness is surely what it is. This place is undoubtedly hell itself, Connie, the Somme is a judgement day for us all, a time when man was being held to account for all of the wrongs of his past. I can remember thinking to myself,

- We're all going to die here in this God-forsaken place and those that follow us here in the months and years that come, will surely suffer the same fate, for this place will be the end for us all, because this place is indeed the gateway to hell itself. -

Then it was time, the officer's whistle blew loud and clear in our ears telling us that it was time to once again go over the top. To a man we took up our rifles, fastened the straps on our helmets and went over the top for the umpteenth time. This daily ritual continued for over four and a half months, day after day we left out trenches and went into combat with the enemy. We had more than one hundred and forty days of continuous fighting, Connie, day after day we faced the same plight, kill or be killed, and day after day, when the fighting had ended, smaller numbers of us returned to our hole in the ground than had left it at the beginning of the day.

The ground in front of every trench was littered with the dead bodies of our fallen comrades, some of them had lay there so long that their bodies had begun to decompose, the smell of their putrefied flesh drifted towards out trenches on the evening breeze. This smell, along with thick black smoke from the many burning villages that lay in the distance, filled the air with a sickening choking mixture, causing us to be violently ill as every breath we took almost ripped our throats apart and sickened us to the pits of our stomachs. At times we even had to sit and eat our food amongst the dead bodies of our fallen friends, because to have buried them would have been a dangerous exercise for all concerned, suicide of the highest level. The German snipers would have seen to that.

On good days we would push the Germans back, and make up ground on their defences, sometimes we would push them back for days on end. But then they would regroup and mount a counter attack and push us all the way back to our trenches. Right back to where we started from, Connie. All that would have been achieved after days of fierce fighting, would be that there was now a few thousand less of us than when we started. Madness, Connie, shear bloody madness.

Sometimes at night small groups of men would be sent out to search amongst the bodies that littered the ground in front of our trench in the hopes that some of our comrades might still be alive. A lot of the time the search parties themselves never returned, as they too had fallen foul of the German snipers. I was now becoming like most of the other soldiers in my trench, reluctant to make friends with the new replacements that arrived weekly. The reason for this standoffish attitude was simple, no sooner would you get to know them, than they would be killed and replaced by other boys just as wet behind the ears as the ones that they had come to replace. You see, these replacements were raw, Connie, under trained, because there was simply no time to train them properly. At first those of us that had been there from the beginning tried to help these young lads through their first few weeks, but to be honest Connie, things were getting worse by the day. I saw hundreds of young men, all of them too young to even be there, die the most terrifying deaths day by day and it was the same in every trench along the line.

One of the most horrifying things that I witnessed, and I witnessed a lot, was when we were being pushed back towards our trenches, things would get a bit chaotic in the rush to reach the safety of our trench. Some of the men in their haste would get tangled up in the barbed-wire that covered no-man's land. At times they would hang, tangled in the wire for hours, helpless, calling out for us to come and free them, but it was hopeless Connie, how could we help them. The whole place was crawling with German snipers, and it wasn't difficult for them to keep us at bay. The poor bastards that had gotten themselves tangled up on the barbed-wire, would know that they would have to remain there until dusk. Then, maybe, we might be able to reach them to free them. But until dusk would arrive, these men would become target practise for the German snipers, not killing them right off, but slowly and brutally. Their game would be to pick on one of them, then first shoot him in the arm, then the other arm, then in the leg, and so on and so on, Connie, until he was dead. Then they would move on to the next man, then the next. We had to sit in our trench and listen to our friends scream out in pain and terror, then they would call to us, pleading for one of us to end their pain. This was the hardest thing to witness for all.

We would have to listen to the German snipers calling and cheering to each other every time one of them found their target. The sound of the German snipers calling out and the sound of our trapped comrades pleading for one of us to end their misery was too much for some of us to take. These terrifying sounds seem to reach out and torment us. When the German snipers had their fill of fun they would disappear like rats back to their own trenches, knowing that our comrades had suffered the most horrible painful deaths. I am loathed to say it Connie, but some of us couldn't take it no longer, we would take our rifles and climb to the top of our trench, then we would take aim and pray to God to forgive us for what we were about to do. Then, with a volley of shots, we would end their misery. For some reason the German snipers would find this act of mercy, a source of fun and would cheer wildly. Ending the misery of our comrades wasn't an easy thing to do and it wasn't without its own risks. Some of the German snipers would hang around and wait until we climbed to the top of the trench, then they would try to pick us off before we could do what we had to do. I have to admit that on many occasions they were successful in this.

By the middle of October the fighting had changed, because we were now beginning to make inroads into the German defences, and as a result there was now a lot of hand to hand fighting almost every day. As you can imagine, this type of warfare was even more barbaric than anything that had gone before, because now Connie, for the first time, we could see the look of panic and fear in their eyes, and the terror in their screams, as we took their lives from them. I remember one morning in particular, it was late October, just before daylight. Four of us had been out on a reconnaissance patrol and were returning to our lines, there was big Jim Campbell, Steve Waterman, Sergeant Albert Brown and myself. We were returning across no-man's land, after carrying out a night raid on a German machine-gun post. The incident that took place in the early hours of the morning, will stay lodged in my mind and haunt me for the rest of my life. The four of us stumbled across a clearing on the top of a small hill. This clearing was surrounded by several small, badly burnt trees. We began to carefully pick our way through a wood filled with still smouldering, motionless trees, we all became aware of this horrible, sickening stench.

"What the fuck is that horrible smell?" whispered Sergeant Brown.

The three of us just screwed up our faces and covered our mouths. This truly was the most sickening pong we had ever come across, Connie.

As we came closer to the clearing, the source of this revolting stench was revealed to us and it made us sick to the pits of our stomachs.

The four of us stood in the middle of the clearing, almost not believing what our eyes were telling us, Connie. At one end of the clearing we could see six British army rifles and six British army helmets. Which were neatly stacked in an orderly pile and placed by a burnt out tree stump. In the middle of this clearing we saw something that made all four of us be physically sick. Laying on the ground in front of us were the smouldering remains of six of our comrades. They were all victims of a new terrifying German weapon, called a flame-thrower. We had seen the results of its use before, but only on buildings or to clear scrubland. This was the first time we had seen it used on human beings and I can tell you, no one should meet their end in this fashion. We knew that this new weapon could turn everything in its path into a raging inferno. It can shoot out flames at an unbelievable speed, leaving nothing standing in its wake. But to deliberately use it on men, that can't be right, but these poor men had been murdered in cold blood, Connie. Their rifles and their helmets had been taken from them after they had surrendered, then they were made to group together in this once serene clearing, and then they were brutally murdered, burnt alive, Connie. We must have stood looking at this terrifying scene for over ten minutes in disbelief. We just couldn't get the choking stench of burnt flesh out of our noses and throats. Ones by one we turned away and were again physically ill. This new weapon that the Germans had invented, would frighten even the most hardened of soldiers because there was no defence against it.

Suddenly, Sergeant Brown ordered us to hit the ground and stay still and not make a sound. This we did as once. Within seconds of hearing Sergeant Brown's order, we could hear German voices in the distance and they were coming closer by the second. I was able to peep out from behind the rock that I was using as cover and that's when I saw them, a band of German raiders, numbering seven in total. It appeared that, like us, they were returning back to their lines after carrying out raids on a few of our outposts. Again Sergeant Brown gestured to us with his hands to keep still and remain quiet. We had become somewhat scattered about the outer ring of the small glade as we had taken cover where we could find it, some of us behind the burnt out trees, others behind rocks that were positioned at the edge of the clearing. None of us were really in close contact with each other, in truth we were all hoping that the Germans would pass us by. But they didn't, Connie, instead they came back into the clearing and from their actions that followed, they had come back to admire their handy work.

One of the Germans pointed to the remains of the six British soldiers and began laughing loudly, the others joined in without much encouragement. Two of them moved forward and opened up their trousers and relieved themselves on the burnt remains of the six British soldiers. This too was thought to be hilarious as the rest of the German soldiers burst into loud laughter. We all noticed that the youngish man in the raiding party, a man looking no more than twenty years old, had the flame-thrower strapped to his back. Sergeant Brown and Big Jim Campbell were positioned behind the Germans, Steve Waterman was behind a badly burnt tree trunk in front of them, as for myself, I was behind a rock to the left of them. The Germans were getting ready to move on, unfortunately, they were going in the direction of the tree trunk where Steve Waterman was hiding. We all knew that the Germans were going to see him, as he wasn't that well-hidden. What happened next is really hard to explain, because it all happened so quickly and without anyone giving the order.

In one quick movement, Sergeant Brown and Big Jim jumped to their feet, seeing this I did the same, it all happened so quickly, Connie. The three of us screamed loudly as we charged the Germans, hoping to draw them away from where Steve was hiding, this we succeeded in doing. As the Germans turned towards us, Steve then jumped to his feet and charged them from behind, running one of them through with his bayonet in a matter of seconds. A fierce hand to hand fight took place that misty morning in this small clearing. I can remember thrusting my bayonet deep into a tall blonde haired German, he must have been in his mid-twenties. As I twisted my bayonet in his gut his eyes seemed to pop out of his head, and his mouth lay open wide as his screams bellowed chillingly in my ears. I just stared into his eyes as he took his last breath, then he fell to his knees. I swear I saw tears bulging in his eyes as he crumpled in a heap on the ground. I quickly turned and attacked another German, this time piercing him through the back if his neck with my bayonet, just as he was about to slaughter Sergeant Brown.

I shall never forget the frightening sounds that were made by us all that morning, never before have I heard such shrilling screams in my life, Connie, not even as a young boy when I witnessed a pack of dogs fighting over some old bones that had been put in a bin outside Mr Tate's butchers shop. Suddenly I felt a blow to the back of my head and I fell to the ground. As I looked up dazed and unsure of what was happening to me, I saw a large German soldier standing over me, he was about to thrust his bayonet into my chest, I was dazed and powerless to stop him, Connie. I remember that he spit in my face and screamed something in German, and that's what saved my life, because before he could finish whatever it was he was shouting at me, a shot rang out and blood began to squirt from his head and he fell to the ground on top of me. I pushed him off me and got to my feet and looked around. I saw Big Jim, standing only a few feet away from me with a German officer's pistol in his hand, he smiled at me and said,

"Close one there, Bobby boy!"

"I just nodded and smiled at big Jim in response, then I picked up my rifle and with the cuff of my tunic I wiped away the dead Germans blood which had splattered over my face. I quickly gathered my senses and began to take stock of what was happened around me. To my relief, littering the ground around me I saw five dead German soldiers and one dead German officer. He still had Big Jim's bayonet sticking out of his chest. The seventh German soldier, the youngest of them all and the one with the flame-thrower strapped to his back, was on his knees on the ground sobbing like a frightened child, with Sergeant Brown standing over him. This violent encounter lasted only a matter of a few minutes, and we had won, or had we merely survived to fight another day? Big Jim and myself walked across the small clearing towards Sergeant Brown and the last remaining German soldier.

-Steve. - I shouted, as I couldn't see him anywhere, but there was no reply. My eyes scanned every inch of this blood stained dell, where this brutal struggle had taken place, but I couldn't see Steve anywhere. I remember thinking to myself, he must be here somewhere, but only Sergeant Brown, both Big Jim and myself remained standing. Then I saw Steve at the far end of the clearing, one of the

German soldiers was lying on top of him, his bayonet plunged deep into Steve's chest, he was dead, Connie, but he had taken his assassin with him.

I turned back towards Sergeant Brown and the one remaining German. Sergeant Brown had now christened this German Heinz, who was still on his knees with his face buried in his hands sobbing and muttering something in German. None of us knew for sure just what it was he was saying, but we all knew that he was pleading for his life. Sergeant Brown moved to the side of the German soldier, his face snarled and twisted in anger, suddenly he yelled at the top of his voice."

"Try this one on for size Heinz!" Then with the toe of his boot he kicked the German on the side of his head, knocking him off his knees onto the flat of his back.

"Sergeant, No:" I shouted. "What the hell do you think you are doing Sergeant?"

Sergeant Brown just looked at me, his face bitter and twisted with rage, as he pointed to the flame-thrower on the ground. The look in Sergeant Brown's face sent a chill running through my body. Believe me, Connie, I had no love for this German, or the weapon he carried, but I couldn't stand by and watch him murdered in cold blood.

"No Sergeant, don't do it!" I screamed as I ran forward in an attempt to stop him from doing something he might regret later. But he knocked me to the ground and continued continuously kicking the German soldier in the head. None of us understood German, but we all knew just what it was the German was screaming at the top of his voice, again he was pleading for his life, Connie. Again I tried to stop Sergeant Brown from this insanity, but he wasn't to be deterred from this madness that had now gripped him. Then both myself and Big Jim tried to stop him once again, but this time Sergeant Brown pulled out his pistol and pointed it at Big Jim and said,

"You're far too big for me to fight, Jim, but if your or you Bobby try to stop me I will shoot the both of you, do you both understand me?"

"Both Big Jim and myself took a step back as we could see that the Sergeant had completely lost all sense of reality. He was in such a rage, Connie, a rage that no one was going to drag him out of, I swear to this day that Sergeant Brown had been struck with a kind of madness. We watched as Sergeant Brown hauled the German soldier to his feet and grabbed him around his throat with both hands. He then pinned the German soldier to the stump of a burnt out tree. Again Big Jim and myself called for Sergeant Brown to stop before he went any further; his answer was to again point his revolver at the both us. Within a few seconds Sergeant Brown had tightened his grip around the German soldier's throat and had squeezed the last breath from his young body. Sergeant Brown had murdered him before our eyes, Connie. Both Big Jim and I stood in silence with our heads slumped in disbelief at what had just happened. There we stood for well over a minute, both of us sickened by Sergeant Brown's merciless act, but also sickened by our own lack of effort to stop this terrible thing taking place. We really should have done something to stop him, Connie, but we didn't. Big Jim was one of the older men amongst us. He was in his late thirties and was built like a tank, but I will always be thankful that he saved my life that day. From that day onward, Big Jim and I became really good friends, but our friendship was to be short lived Connie. Less than three weeks later Big Jim was killed when out on another night raid on German out-posts. As for Sergeant Brown, well he was never the same man after that day, and he himself was killed, burnt to death six days later, when he came across yet another German with a flame-thrower.

By now it was mid-November and the morale amongst the men was at an all-time low. There were only two things we all knew for sure, and they were that come the next day, it would rain, and once again we would be ask to go over the top and do it all over again. Our troubles seem to worsen by the day, now to add to the thick mud which was everywhere, we had to contend with an icy wind that bit bitterly at our faces, hands and toes. The cold was becoming insufferable in the extreme, our feet and hands were frozen, much like the surface of the water which filled our trenches. The cold made it imposable to even hold our rifles, never mind fire the damned things. By late November the Germans had begun to shell our positions, heavy shelling, Connie. Those of us that were there from the beginning now knew just how the Germans must have felt when it was our big guns shelling them. For now there was nothing for us to do but to curl up in our trenches with our helmets on and pray to God that we would see this bombardment through safely.

In these fear filled days I thought of you constantly, Connie, and I held your picture in front of me every night as I prayed for the day when I could hold you in my arms once again. I remember I wrote you a letter at this time, but for some reason I never sent it to you.

Connie slowly raised her hand and cleared several tears from her swollen eyes, then she placed her hand in Bobby's and asked softly…

"Do you still have it Bobby?"

"Yes I do," replied Bobby, as he pulled a small scrap of paper from his pocket and handed it to Connie.

"Silly I know, but I keep them with me always, no matter where I go, I always have them with me," said Bobby.

Connie reached out and took this second letter out of Bobby's hand, opened it up and began to read. It simply read…

> Dearest Connie
> This place is Hell.
> Love Bobby.

Connie folded the letter and placed it lovingly alongside the previous letter that Bobby had given her.

"May I keep them please, Bobby?" asked Connie.

Bobby smiled and said,

"Yes you can if you want to, Connie."

Connie simply smiled at her Bobby.

Bobby continued,

"Two weeks after I wrote that letter, I was on my way home to you, Connie, and for now at least, my war was over and I had survived… THE SOMME.

They say that this war is the war to end all wars, Connie, they say that this war will make this world a safer place for us all to live in and this which we do now, we do for the children that come after us, and their children that come after them. I tell you this, Connie, I must believe this to be true, for if not, then I could never return to that hell they call… THE SOMME.

What I believe to be true, I do with the thought that I do it for you and our children that will follow in the future, in the hopes that the world will be a better place for us all."

Tears welled in Bobby's eyes as he sat looking lovingly at Connie.

"I love you so much Bobby," said Connie,

Bobby reached out and took Connie's hand in his and pressed it to his lips and kissed it as he answered.

"I shall always love you, Connie, no matter what."

With the hours passing quickly and the rigors of the day now catching up with Connie and Bobby, both retired for the evening.

CHAPTER 6

The next morning was the 23rd. of December, the day before Christmas Eve and when Bobby arrived in the dining room for breakfast his mood had totally changed from that of the previous day. Gone was the disturbing stare from his eyes. It had been replaced by the brightest sparkle, just like it was before he had gone off to war. Gone too was the troubled frown that he carried upon his face as that too had been replaced with biggest, broadest smile. This was truly the Bobby that Connie had always known.

"Good morning Bobby, did you sleep well?" asked Connie.

"Good morning Connie and no I didn't sleep well at first. Then, at 3, o'clock in the morning it struck me, my mother always loved Christmas and as she is not here for this Christmas, then I must enjoy it for her and every Christmas that follows." replied Bobby with a gusto that brought a smile to Connie's young eyes.

Connie got up from the breakfast table and flung her arms around Bobby and hugged him as tight as she could. Then she said,

"And I will help you celebrate every Christmas from this year to my last year on this earth, Bobby. Each and every single Christmas will be made extra special, this I promise you, Bobby."

Bobby looked into Connie's eyes and with a more serious tone to his voice he said,

"If this war should prevent me from keeping this promise that I have made here this day, then you must keep it for me Connie, year after year. Because I know that you will live to be one hundred years old, of this I am sure, because a long and rewarding life will be your reward for the goodness and kindness that you have brought into this troubled world. I say it now, you are surely the nearest thing to an angel that this world have ever seen, Connie"

Once again Bobby put his arms around Connie and pulled her close to him, because he knew deep within himself that in his arms he held someone very special. He was convinced that Connie was truly the most wonderful human being that had ever walked God's green earth.

From that moment on, except for their sleeping hours, Bobby and Connie were inseparable throughout the rest of Bobby's leave. The Christmas of 1916, along with the new year of 1917 remained firmly locked in the strong-box of Connie's thoughts for the rest of her life. You see if there had been any doubts in her mind of her love for Bobby, or his love for her, these amazing days that they had spent together had vanquished any doubts for ever. Shortly into the new year of 1917, just as their enjoyment of each other was reaching its height, the time came for Bobby to return to his regiment. Bobby must once again take up arms in the defence of his country and play his part in this God awful war. For the second time Connie found herself standing on a cold Belfast quayside waving good-bye to her Bobby. As he made ready to board his ship, he said these words to Connie, words that echoed softly in her ears and filled her young heart with a pleasure that only lovers ever experience.

"If God willing, Connie, and I am lucky enough to survive this hell which I now return to, then I will take you to the most beautiful place that Ulster has to offer. A place that will forever remain special to the both of us. Once there I will ask you something that will change both of our lives. Until that day arrives, Connie, I will dream of it each and every day I spend fighting in the hell that for now has become my life. Throughout these dark days, Connie, I will hold this thought, along with the image of your entrancing beauty close to my heart. These thoughts and images of you will help me through the long tormented nights that I must spend in that hole in the ground that is now my home. I know that this above all else, will keep me sane until the day I am able to return home to you, Connie. This dream will surely keep me alive. I am sure of it, Connie."

Connie kissed Bobby for one last time, then she watched tearfully as he walked up the gang-plank. That's when she noticed that the bright, welcoming smile that had returned to his face before Christmas, had now once again brutally abandoned him. His handsome face now looked harsh and hostile to the eye. This time Connie's goodbye to Bobby was harder for her to endure than the first time he left because she now knew what Bobby was returning to in France. In Bobby's own words, this place is surely hell, and Bobby was going back to it in the full knowledge that there was every chance that he may not return from it. All of the horrors, all of the brutality, all of the killing, day after day, Bobby did willingly, in the name of freedom for us all. As Connie watched his ship sail away, she cleared the tears from her eyes, and whispered softly to herself, as if in silent and private prayer,

"Please God, I ask you here this day, please bring Bobby safely home to me when all of the horrors that are taking place in this wicked world have run their evil course."

Connie pulled her overcoat tightly around her shivering body and with a heavy foot, she trudged slowly away from the docks and continued on her homeward journey. A journey that she was not making alone, as she was one of many mothers, wives, sisters and lovers, who, like Connie herself, had just said their goodbyes to their brave young men that left with the uncertainty, of knowing whether they would ever be back home ever again.

It was now the 6th of January, and beneath Connie's feet fresh snow carpeted the ground in all directions. Connie could hear the crunch of her boots as they crushed deep into the brittle snow underfoot. This was the only sound that penetrated Connie's frozen ears, as she trod her way home that miserable day. She turned around and looked back to where she had just come from, all that remained to remind her of the journey she had just taken was the indentations that her boots had made in the soft fluffy snow she had just trodden on. There was nothing else to be seen anywhere that would have marked what had just taken place that day.

In the weeks that followed Bobby's departure, Connie had received no less than five letters from him, sending ten in replay. Bobby was still fighting on the Western Front, and life there was just as intolerable now for the young soldiers as it had always been. As January turned into February, Bobby tried his best to keep Connie updated with his situation in France. This was not an easy thing to do, as establishing communication from the Front at this time was an almost impossible task. By early March the battle of The Somme was over, but that wasn't to be the end of the Hell the soldiers had to live through. Oh no, because Bobby and his comrades' Hell was to continue for a long, long time on the Western Front. At this time most of Bobby's letters never reached Connie, nor did Connie's letters reach Bobby in France. But this fact didn't deter Connie from writing a letter each and every day to Bobby, in the hopes that one day he would receive them all and that they would be of some comfort to him. It was on the last day of April when Connie received her first correspondence in months from Bobby. As she sat on her bed reading his letter, her heart became heavy, and her torment at Bobby's plight now returned with a cruel vengeance, because unfortunately this letter was to confirm Connie's worst fears. It read…

> Dearest Connie,
>
> By the time you receive this letter, all that I am telling you will have long since passed, and I, along with the rest of my comrades will have moved on to our next objective.
>
> It has begun all over again, Connie, our heavy artillery is pounding the German lines once again and just like before our bombardment is relentless. Their front line troops at Arras are taking a terrible beating from our big guns, but there are so many German soldiers here, that we are all convinced, that

when our time comes to attack, there will be plenty of them left for us to fight. Our Captain tell us that our bombardment will continue for between twelve to fourteen days, Connie. So our attack on their lines is scheduled to begin around the 9th. of April 1917.

Early this morning, on the sixth day of our bombardment, my new friend Paddy O'Connor and myself took a look out over the top of this new trench we now live in. We both gazed dumbfounded at the German lines. Paddy is someone I have come to respect greatly these past few months. We are both of the same age, and yes you would be right to think that Paddy is a Roman Catholic. Paddy was born on the Falls Road. I will admit that Paddy is the first man of that persuasion that I have ever really gotten to know. I have to say that we get on together so well, Connie. What I have discovered Qis that Paddy is really no different than me, he's not one of those evil beings that we have all been told that Catholic's are. Funnily, Paddy says the same about me. We laugh about it now, but that's just us Connie, because this religious divide which we lived by in N. Ireland, seems to have followed us all the way here to France. It would seem that even in Hell we Irish have our differences.

In all the months that we have been here and after all that we have been through, the two sides of this strange divide that we have back home, continue to keep to their own. When in our trenches, no more than a nod of the head is given to those from the other side of the divide. Even then, this is done with eyes turned downwards, eye to eye contact with one the opposite sect, is never made Connie. Although, when the fighting starts, Connie, all differences are put to one side and we all look out for one another. Each one of us willing to stare danger in the eye, to help a comrade, no matter what side of the divide he belongs to, to make it back to our trenches at the end of the day. We are truly a strange bunch, we Irish, Connie.

As Paddy and myself peered out over the top of our trench that morning, what met our eyes, when the smoke would clear, was truly frightening, Connie. For as far as the eye could see, and beyond, all that lay stretched out before us was total devastation, nothing but waste land to be seen everywhere, Connie. Where once a thick fertile woodland stood, now nothing remained, nothing but burnt-out tree stumps littered the landscape. These stumps covered the ground like half used sticks of discarded charcoal that had been recklessly abandoned by a group of disillusioned artist. Nothing lives in this place anymore, Connie, not so much as a blade of grass can be seen growing here. It is now early spring and I have yet to hear a bird sing here, Connie, nor have I seen a clear blue sky overhead. Whole villages have been laid to waste, Connie, people's homes along with their worldly goods have been crumpled into the earth with the same ease as a discarded cigarette under a drunken sergeant's boot.

The people who live in the villages from behind our lines, who's homes and workplaces have been destroyed by the German guns, can be seen walking around in what can only be described as a confused stupor, as they set about the daily business of burying their dead. Yet they look upon us as their saviours, Connie, but we are powerless to prevent what is happening to these poor people. Children who once played their noisy, but innocent games in the streets and squares of the villages, now lie dead in the scorched earth, their young mangled bodies partly exposed, partly buried under the tumbled down houses that were once their homes. Now these crushed dwellings only mar the landscape that was once the playground of these blameless children. It just gets worse by the day here, Connie. I don't know how successful our next attack will be, but one thing we all know for sure and that is that many of us will not be alive when it is all over. In the evenings Paddy and I sit in our trench talking about Belfast and how we long to be back there, even with all of its faults, it is our home. I hold your photograph in front of me as I dare to dream of the day I can hold you in my arms and kiss your soft lips once again. I pray every night that this dream will one day become a reality, because it is this thought and this thought alone that keeps me sane in the midst of this madness that is all around me. I show your picture to my friend Paddy, and I tell him all about you, Connie, as we sit huddled together in this miserable trench, passing away the dark idle hours, as sleep is something that seems to elude us all. Paddy now jokes with me that he is not sure if you are his girlfriend or mine, but I am so glad that I have him as a friend, Connie. If both Paddy and I are fortunate enough to survive this terrible war, then I will take great pleasure in introducing my good friend Paddy to you, Connie.

So until then, I will leave you for now, but…
One day I will hold you tightly in my arms once again…
One day Connie…One day.

All My Love…
Bobby.

Connie neatly folded Bobby's letter and placed it with the others in a small wooden box that she kept in a blanket chest at the foot of her bed. It was mid-June before Connie received her next correspondence from Bobby. He had survived the fierce fighting at Arras, and his spirit seemed to be holding, but only just. In the following letters Connie received from Bobby, he talked at length about his good friend Paddy. He also talked of how he and the others were preparing themselves for their next attack, this time it was to be at a place called Messines. Bobby tells how each attack has now become more violent and more merciless than the previous one. He also speaks of how they are pushing the Germans back, although sometimes only as much as a few feet at a time, but for every few feet gained, a terrible price was having to be paid, in terms of young lives lost. The fighting most of the time was now fierce and savage and hand to hand combat was now a daily occurrence. Each day before they would go over the top, that putrid smell would once again descend upon them, filling the trench and chocking at their throats, as the sergeant would stand before them and scream loudly, - Remember boys… It's kill or be killed out there. –

Then the sound of that bloody whistle would blast in their ears, and yet another attack would begin.

Connie missed Bobby terribly, and sometimes in the evenings she would spread all of his letters out on her bed and spend hours reading them one after the other, time and time again. As Connie read through Bobby's letters, she would dream of the day when he would return home to her. On theses occasions, Connie would remain locked away in her bedroom with Bobby's letters until the new morning would break through the gap in the thick curtains, interrupting her solitude and reminding her that the world outside had begun a new day. Connie's mother, Edwina, found such evenings most upsetting, as she could clearly hear her daughter's forlorn sobbing for most of the night. Edwina realised that her daughter had now created a union with Bobby that was so strong, so solid that only this dreadful war had the power to break it.

CHAPTER 7

Mid-summer was now upon us, and due to rationing, daily living had become extremely difficult for everyone in N. Ireland, but Ulster people are a strong breed and each and every one of them were well aware that life had to go on. Everyday tasks had to be performed and dealt with in order that people were able to survive this dreadful war. Connie's mother, Edwina, was now working long hours at the bakery she owned along with Connie's godfather, Mr Andrew Powell. Mr Powell had started up the bakery many years before along with Edwina's late husband Terry. After Terry's death, Connie decided to take her husband's place at the helm. The bakery was the biggest in all of Ireland, manufacturing baked goods on an industrial scale. It was also, after heavy industry, the largest employer in East Belfast, and it's importance at this time was immeasurable, not only providing work for the families of East Belfast, but also the baked goods that it made were one of the few foods not to be rationed by the government. Yes, there was a shortage of grain at this time, and so the bread baked at the bakery was no longer white, but was now a little darker in appearance. Colour aside, this new type of bread was proved to be very popular with the people and had become a main part of their diet at this time. Edwina herself was a kind, caring lady, with an understanding of the plight of the poorer people that lived in the community.

Edwina was still a relatively young woman, she was only thirty-eight years old, and was a sophisticated, well-educated lady that had retained much of her youthful beauty. It was easy to see from whom young Connie had inherited her beauty and charm. Edwina had made a point of knowing most, if not all, of her employees by name, and would stop and chat with them each time she would cross the bakery floor. There were over two hundred people working at the bakery, but due to most of the men in East Belfast joining the army to go and fight in the war, the workforce was mostly made up of women and young girls.

In fact, 85% of the workers were female, leaving 15% male, all of them over the age for war. All that is except one, a Scotsman by the name of Alex Brown.

Alex Brown was thirty-two years old, a tall man of around six foot, with thick red hair, which was attached to a perfectly manicured red beard. Alex Brown had been working at the bakery as a night manager for almost a year. It has to be noted that Edwina found his manner somewhat off-putting, and had remarked on this fact on several occasions to Mr Powell. In truth Edwina found him the most obnoxious man she had ever come across in her life. There had also been whispers from the bakery floor that the ladies within the night workforce didn't have a good word to say about our Mr Alex Brown. It would seem that he tended to treat them with contempt and rudeness and stories of bullying had also been mooted. Unfortunately, as he was the night manager, Edwina didn't have that much contact with him on a daily basis and was unaware of his ill treatment of the ladies under his supervision. It would be discovered later that these ladies working on the night shift, were so intimidated and frightened by Mr Alex Brown, that they were reluctant to say a word against him.

From the very first day Edwina's husband, Terry and Mr Powell, had started the bakery, it had always been their policy to care for their workers, and to treat them with the respect that they deserved. This work ethic was something that Edwina was determined to continue with. As a result of this caring attitude over the years, first from Terry and Mr Powell, and now Edwina, they were and had been, held in high regard by, not only their workers, but also the people of East Belfast. So it was understandable that from the beginning the bakery grew in popularity, and flourished as a business. Then in 1899, the year of Connie's birth, the bakery was proving to be so successful that it moved location to the much larger premises that it still occupies today. Sadly, Edwina's husband, Terry died from a heart attack in late 1913, His death not only devastated Edwina and his daughter, Connie, but also his loyal workers as well as the people of East Belfast. Terry was only thirty-five years old when he sadly passed away. Only two months before his death, Terry had announced at a commerce dinner held at the Grand Central Hotel...

> - That he put the success of the bakery down to two things, one, the hard work and dedication of the workforce, and two, the loyalty shown to the bakery by the good people of East Belfast, and for both of these things, I thank you all. -

Apart from heavy industry in East Belfast, such as...

Harland & Wolf Shipyard, Sirocco Engineering Works and Short Brothers Aviation Company, the bakery and its many shops throughout Belfast and the surrounding district were now the biggest employer in the East of the City. Each morning, bright and early, the daily deliveries to the bakery's shops would take place at around 6am. A convoy of large four wheeled carriages, each one being pulled by a team of four of the most magnificent black shire horses. Their manes and tails plaited with bright red and blue ribbons, the highly polished horse brasses, reflected brightly in the early summer sun. Added to the appearance of these dazzling beasts, were a pair of fine coachmen perched proudly on top of each carriage. Both men dressed in bright red waistcoats, crisp white shirts, with black neck-ties and highly polished black riding boots that shone almost as brightly as the horse brasses. All this fine attire was topped off with black bowler hats. Truly a splendid sight to behold each and every morning. Although that wasn't the end of this daily experience, added to this splendour, the enticing aroma of freshly baked bread that wafted teasingly on the early morning air. This was more than the beginning of a working day, this was an event not to be missed. Mothers would gather in great numbers with their children just to watch this spectacle each morning, because in these dark days of war, splendour and the sense of occasion such as this, brought a little happiness to everyone's otherwise dismal lives.

Edwina and her daughter Connie lived in the very fashionable Knock area, on the outskirts of East Belfast. Connie's father, Terry, had commissioned the building of this splendid seven bed-roomed house to celebrate the launch of the Titanic in Belfast in 1912. The Titanic was hailed as the most luxurious cruise Liner ever built and was a ship that the whole of Belfast was extremely proud of. Yet, even after the sad demise of this great ship on its maiden voyage, Connie's Father still heralded its construction as one of the greatest achievements of our times. This house that Terry had built for his family was a grand residence to behold, the house reflecting the splendour of the Titanic itself. Spacious, well-manicured gardens ringed the house on all sides. The house itself stood four storeys high and boasted, amongst its many attributes, a magnificent entrance hall adorned with the most majestic swirling staircase. This excellence was overseen by two spectacular crystal chandelier which held your gaze as you entered through the large double doors at the front of the house. To one side of this staircase was the most breath-taking dining room imaginable and beyond that was an impressive music room housing a black grand piano. To the other side of this eye catching staircase was a large lavishly furnished parlour, adjacent to the parlour was a luxurious second sitting-room. To the rear of the house was a fully equipped kitchen. The upper floors were just as impressive. The first floor housed three double bedrooms and two large bathrooms. The second floor consisted of a further four bedrooms plus three more bathrooms. Above the third floor at the top of the house were three large attics. This was truly a magnificent dwelling! The gardens to the rear of the house trapped the sun for most of the day in the summer months, allowing the Kean family to host some of the most enviable garden parties ever seen in Belfast.

One morning in mid-October in the year of 1917, Edwina arrived at the bakery to find Mr Powell waiting outside the main gates for her arrival. He had been a life-long friend of Edwina's husband, Terry and he was also Connie's godfather. Mr Powell was a man of forty-eight years old and was, in appearance, of muscular build, standing at over six feet tall. He was also a man who likes to keep himself in top physical condition. Mr Powell and Edwina's departed husband, Terry had been like brothers and had been friends ever since they was small boys. Mr Powell lived alone in a large house that had belonged to his parents as, being an only child, the house reverted to him after their death. Mr Powell continued to live in the house with only his housekeeper as company. The housekeeper, a spinster by the name of Miss Reen, had been with Mr Powell for over twenty five years. After Terry's death, Mr Powell took it upon himself to take on the role of guardian to both Edwina and little Connie, looking out for them at all times.

"Good-morning, Andy." said Edwina as she approached Mr Powell.

Edwina was more than a little surprised to see him standing outside the gates of the bakery as normally he would be in his office by this time. She then noticed the strange look that Mr Powell had on his face.

"Is everything alright, Andy?" inquired Edwina inquisitively.

Mr Powell looked all around in a somewhat sinister manner. It appeared to Edwina that he was making sure that no one was watching them. Suddenly Mr Powell took Edwina by the arm and pulled her behind a small wall that ran alongside the bakery, ensuring that they were both well hidden from any prying eyes.

"What on earth is it, Andy?" asked a worried Edwina.

Mr Powell looked worried as he took yet another good look around, making sure that no one was watching them, then he said,

"Something has gone badly wrong in the bakery last night, Edwina."

"Gone wrong Andy, what on earth do you mean, something has gone wrong?" enquired Edwina.

"I'm not quite sure yet, Edwina, but something took place here last night that was unsavoury, I do know that much." replied Mr Powell.

He reached out and took Edwina's small briefcase from her and said,

"Let's go to the office and I will tell you everything I know but we will go the long way round, Edwina. We will walk across the bakery floor."

"Why?" asked Edwina, somewhat puzzled by Mr Powell's strange behaviour.

"I want to gage the mood of our ladies this morning." he said with a raised eyebrow.

Edwina looked at Mr Powell as if he had gone mad, then she said,

"Alright, Andy, if that's what you wish, then let's do it. Then maybe you can tell me what's going on."

Both Mr Powell and Edwina walked briskly across the courtyard which stretched out in front of the bakery building, eventually arriving on the bakery floor itself. By now Edwina was confused and more than a little worried by Mr Powell's extraordinary behaviour. As they began their journey through the bakery, a strange eerie sense of unease suddenly hit them. As they approached several young ladies who were stacking bread onto wooden racks, Edwina addressed them with her usual welcoming smile.

"Good morning girls, and how are you all this morning?"

"Good morning Mam." came a rather subdued answer from the group of girls.

More of a worry than the way their answer was delivered was the fact that not one of them raised their eyes in Edwina's direction. Edwina was shocked by their response because this wasn't the customary jolly, happy, smiling reaction that she would normally receive from the young ladies.

Edwina quickly turned to Mr Powell with a startled look in her eye. Again Mr Powell simply raised an eyebrow as if to say, I told you so. Edwina and Andy slowly continued their way through the bakery, moving towards their offices. As they did so they were met with the same subdued almost alarming atmosphere every step of the way. When they finally reached the staircase that led from the bakery floor up to the second floor where the offices were situated, both Mr Powell and Edwina stopped and looked around the bakery floor. Yes, all of the young ladies were getting on with their work, but something was different. There just wasn't the usual clanger of happy chatter going on between the girls. The customary sound of the young ladies frivolous giggling that would normal be echoing around the bakery was strangely absent. It looked to all intents and purposes that this normally happy bunch of young ladies had been beaten into submission, as if in fear of something, or someone.

"My good God, Andy, what on earth had happened here?"

Edwina and Mr Powell quickly turned and continued on their way towards the office and when inside Mr Powell sat down behind his large oak desk. Edwina made herself comfortable in a large leather armchair on the opposite side of the desk.

"You'd better tell me what you know, Andy!" demanded Edwina.

Mr Powell sat forward in his chair as he prepared to inform Edwina what he had witnessed earlier that morning.

"I might be wrong, Edwina but I believe we may have a big problem on our hands with Alex Brown."

"Brown!" exclaimed Edwina, "What on earth could he have done to cause this kind of reaction from the girls on the bakery floor?"

Edwina's dislike for Alex Brown was beginning to surface. Mr Powell was just about to continue with his account of what he had witnessed earlier that morning when a knock was heard on his office door. He quickly put his finger to his mouth, gesturing to Edwina that they should both say no more for now.

"Yes, who is it?" called Mr Powell sharply.

"It's Alex Brown, night manager, Mr Powell. I really need to speak with you."

Both Edwina and Mr Powell looked a little shocked at this point, not expecting the object of their pending conversation to arrive at the office door.

"Ah…Okay, Alex you best come in," answered Mr Powell.

The door was suddenly flung open with the force and arrogance of a man who was neither fearful, nor respectful of anyone, giving the appearance of a man who deemed himself untouchable. In the blink of an eye Mr Alex Brown was standing by the side of Mr Powell's desk, next to Edwina.

"Good-morning, Mr Powell." grinned Alex Brown.

He then turned his attention towards Edwina and with a lateritious smile struck menacingly across his face, he smirked.

"Good morning Mrs Kean, and please allow me to say how wonderful you are looking this fine morning."

Alex Brown had the knack of making women feel very uncomfortable when he was around them. He gave off the impression that in his view, women were there for his amusement and he made no attempt to hide this fact. In truth, he showed them little or no respect whatsoever. Edwina didn't respond to his unwarranted nor welcomed complement, instead she cringed in her chair, turning her head away from his glare. Mr Powell then intervened sharply saying…

"What is it I can do for you, Alex?"

Alex Brown then turned his attention back to Mr Powell. His voice was now a little deeper and harsher than when he had addressed Edwina and the reason for this was simple. Alex was well aware that Mr Powell didn't like him all that much and this was his way of showing strength and attempting to gain the upper hand in the conversation that was to follow.

"I thought I should let you know, Mr Powell, I had a little trouble with one of the girls in last night's shift. I am afraid to say that I had to let her go, Mr Powell." Although he was talking to Mr Powell, his eyes never strayed far from Edwina. The self-serving smile that filled his face portrayed a man that was proud of what he had done the night before and was more than willing to let everyone know about it.

"What do you mean you had to let one of my girls go? I sincerely hope that you have a very good explanation for this action, Mr Brown," interrupted Edwina angrily.

"Trust me, I have Mrs Kean. I found that she was stealing stock from the extra rations racks that had been earmarked for the poor and needy in the community. I know just how dear this project is to you, Mrs Kean. So you see, I had no alternative but to let her go as this wasn't the first time I caught her doing it." replied Alex Brown with an over confident grin.

"Which of the young ladies are we talking about, Mr Brown." inquired Edwina.

"It was young Sylvia Haggerty, Mrs Kean, that's who," he sneered rudely.

Edwina sat back in her chair flabbergasted by Alex Brown's revelations about young Sylvia because Edwina didn't really believe a word of what he had just told her. Edwina had known the Haggerty family for many years and knew them to be a God fearing family with strong morals and a deep sense of justice that their father had installed in each of his children. Before the war, Sylvia's father and her two brothers had worked at the bakery. Her father, Wilfred, was a member of the same Orange Lodge as Edwina's husband, Terry had been a member of. But thieves the Haggerty family certainly were not.

"I find that extremely hard to believe, Mr Brown." said Edwina crossly.

"Yes, I thought you might, Mrs Kean, but I am afraid it is the truth. You can read all of the details in my report which I am about to place on Mr Powell's desk, "he added defiantly, as he slammed his report down on the desk.

Mr Powell tapped Alex Brown's report lightly with his fingers, as he thought for a few seconds, then he said,

"I tend to agree with Mrs Kean on this affair Mr Brown, but both Mrs Kean and I will read your report carefully before jumping to any conclusions."

"It's all in there, Mr Powell, you both might just find it interesting reading." said Alex Brown with a sly smirk etched on his face.

Mr Powell pushed Alex Brown's report to one side as he said firmly,

"I think that will be all for now, Mr Brown, but thank you for bringing this matter to our attention."

"As you wish, Mr Powell." grinned Alex Brown.

Alex then turned to leave Mr Powell's office, but before he did, he turned his attention towards Edwina. He stood no more than two foot away from where she was sitting. Slowly and with a lustful glare his eyes he explored at full length Edwina's slender body, then for the second time in a matter of minutes Alex Brown delivered his unsolicited and sinister remark.

"If I may say so yet again, Mrs Kean, you are looking exceptionally fetching this morning."

To be in the same room as Alex Brown made Edwina feel extremely uneasy and so she began to fidget in her chair. Then suddenly Edwina looked directly at Mr Alex Brown and said abruptly,

"I really do not think that you have the right to pass comment of any kind on my appearance, Mr Brown. So kindly refrain from doing so in the future if you please."

Before Alex Brown had the chance to replay to Edwina's rebuke, Mr Powell jumped to the fore saying,

"I said that will be all for now, Mr Brown."

It would seem that Mr Powell's tolerance was wearing thin when it came to Mr Alex Brown's insulting behaviour towards Edwina.

Even after Mr Powell's intervention, he made no immediate attempt to leave the office. Instead he stood defiant, allowed his eyes to linger for a few further seconds on Edwina, then he said with innuendo in his voice,

"It's been a very long, tiring night and although my bed will be empty and cold, I really should go home to it, don't you think, Mrs Kean?"

With that last remark he turned around and left Mr Powell's office.

"I really can't stand that dreadful man, Andy!" blasted Edwina angrily.

Mr Powell tossed Alex's report on young Sylvia straight into the paper bin by the side of his desk.

"This is all nonsense Edwina, I am of a mind like yourself, I don't believe a word of it." Said Mr Powell.

Edwina got to her feet and began pacing up and down Mr Powell's office.

"I find all this really hard to believe, Andy. I have known the Haggerty family for many years and they are a good God fearing family, not thieves. There's only Sylvia, her young sister and their mother at home now. Sylvia's father and her two brothers are away fighting in France and all three of them are supporting the family so Sylvia had no need to be stealing from the bakers!" growled Edwina, her rage building by the second.

"I totally agree with you Edwina, now please sit down and allow me to explain what I witnessed this morning, because I now believe that something really serious took place here last night." said Mr Powell.

Edwina sat down at his desk again.

"I think you better tell me what you saw, Andy." said Edwina

Mr Powell began to inform Edwina of what he had witnessed that morning.

"I had the need to come into the office earlier than usual this morning, Edwina, as I had a lot of paper work to catch up with. I arrived just before seven o'clock. Knowing that the main entrance wouldn't be opened at that time, I entered via the back gates, the entrance the shift workers use. That's when I heard loud sobbing coming from Alex Brown's office. I immediately set about investigating who it was that was crying. I discovered that it was one of our young ladies. I was unable to see her face so I couldn't identify just who the young lady was. Although, after hearing Alex Brown's fairy-tale this morning, it is a safe bet that it was young Silvia that was in Mr Brown's office crying. What struck me was that this was not the sobbing of someone that was simply upset, it was more akin to someone that had just experienced a traumatic episode. The girl was hysterical, almost out of control. The closer I got to Alex Brown's office, the clearer things became to me. Alex Brown was in the middle of, what appeared to be, a threatening, even bullying rant. I quickly concealed myself behind some old boxes that were stacked one on top of the other at the end of the corridor.

I was no more than ten feet from the door of Alex's office. From my position I had a good view of what was taking place, although even now I didn't have a good view of the young ladies face. Suddenly the young lady came stumbling out of Alex's office into the doorway. Although it looked to me that her stumbling was more likely to have been caused by a push. It appeared to me that our Mr Brown had physically shoved the young lady out of his office into the corridor. To me this young lady looked as though she was in a severe state of distress. I noticed what looked like dried blood clinging to the side of her hair. By now she was crying loudly and cowering in terror in the door-way. She was just like a frightened rabbit caught in the beam of the poacher's night light. Then I saw Alex stand over her with the most sickening, gloating smile on his face, Edwina. Then he reached out and caught hold of the girl by the throat. At this point I wanted to rush in and intervene, but I thought it best to wait and try to find out more of what was going on. The girl simply stood cowering in a corner and sobbing deeply, her body limp and her arms tightly wrapped around her upper body. It was as if she was trying to protect that part of her body from Alex Brown's touch. The girl's clothes look somewhat dishevelled, I formed the opinion that her clothing had been altered in some way. I then listened carefully as Alex moved closer to the girl and began to speak to her.

All of a sudden, Alex pulled Sylvia roughly towards him, she was so close to him at this point that her small frightened face was pressed tightly against his. Now you listen to me, Sylvia, he said, If you know what's good for you and that young sister of yours, you will get out of here and keep your bloody mouth shut, do you understand me you little slut? At this point he pushed young Sylvia away from him, she was crying loudly and looked as though she had been to hell and back. The expression on her young face was frightening, Edwina. It was all I could do to stay where I was as all I wanted to do was to rush in and beat the living daylights out of that thug, Brown. Alex continued to shout at Sylvia as she tried desperately to clear the tears and dried blood from her face with the back of her hand. Now remember slut, I never want to see you anywhere near this bakery again, you got that girl, because if you do you know what will happen, don't you girl? Also if I ever hear that you have been talking to anyone, even your mother of what took place here then our friend Spike will be forced to pay a visit to that young sister of yours girl, do you understand? Alex was yelling at her by now, the girls on the bakery floor must have heard him, I'm sure of it. After that Alex pushed young Sylvia all the way down the corridor and out into the courtyard and eventually out of the gate finally returning to his office. I had followed them to the courtyard and after Sylvia had left the bakery grounds, I remained in the courtyard."

Edwina looked at Mr Powell, stunned, shocked and extremely furious by his appalling revelations. After a few seconds of staggered silence, Edwina said,

"Good God, Andy, I dread to think what took place here last night! I think we both should go to young Sylvia's house immediately and try to get to the bottom of this once and for all, don't you?"

"Yes, Edwina, I couldn't agree more," said Mr Powell.

CHAPTER 8

Both Edwina and Mr Powell waited until mid-morning, just after ten thirty in fact, before leaving the bakery in Mr Powell's motor car and heading for the Haggerty household. As they drove through the streets of small terraced houses which made up this part of East Belfast, they were both well aware that this meeting with young Sylvia was not going to be a particularly pleasant one. Never the less, they were both well aware that this was one meeting that had to take place. Edwina just couldn't get the idea out of her head that something dreadful had undoubtedly taken place at the bakery the previous evening. Sylvia lived with her mother and younger sister in one of the small terraced houses on Central Street off the Newtownards Road. For as long as Edwina had known Sylvia, she has always found her to be a shy, quiet girl, timid and innocent were words that would spring to mind when describing this pretty young girl. But just like the rest of her family, Sylvia was a good hard working girl and Edwina believed her to be as honest as the day was long.

At this point there is one thing that you must understand, and that is…

That this was Ireland in 1917 and young girls like Sylvia, working class girls that were badly educated, seemed to carry a natural fear of anyone in authority. All young working class girls would always feel inferior to people that they saw as someone from a higher station than themselves. Many adults amongst the working class of the day would also harbour thoughts of inferiority. Rightly or wrongly, the working class had been brought up to know their place in the scheme of things and to show respect their betters. So this attitude made young girls like Sylvia easy pray for men like Alex Brown because he knew that it would be most unlikely that she would tell anyone what had happened to her. What's more, even if she did gather the courage to tell of her abuse, who would believe the word of an uneducated working class girl who had been branded a thief, over the word of an educated semi-professional man like Alex Brown? Mr Brown and others like him were well aware that they would always hold the upper hand. After all, would young Sylvia's family really want their good name dragged through the gutter and be branded as thieves in a fight that they were unlikely to win?

Mr Powell turned his black shinny ford automobile into the noisy street where Sylvia lived. The long narrow street was filled with young children, all playing happily in the middle of the road. Most children at this time would use the road as their playground because, to see an automobile in these streets was a rarity to say the least. The news of Mr Powell's motor car arriving in their street quickly spread. Small groups of mothers began to gather up and down the street, all chatting and pointing towards his automobile. Within a few seconds of Mr Powell and Edwina exiting the vehicle, a respectful silence descended upon this small back street of East Belfast. Everyone's attention was now turned towards the big black automobile that had stopped outside Mrs Haggerty's house. Mr Powell tipped his hat in respect towards the watching ladies of Central Street.

Edwina's unexpected appearance in Central Street had created something of a stir amongst the groups of watching mothers. Mr Powell knocked twice on the old weather-beaten front door of Mrs Haggerty's house, then waited patiently for a response. Only a matter of seconds had passed before the door was opened no more than half way and Mrs Haggerty peered out nervously from behind the old wooden door.

"Good day, Mrs Haggerty," said Mr Powell, as he again tipped his hat. I'm sorry to arrive unannounced," he continued, "But Mrs Kean and I would like to speak with you and your daughter Sylvia if that would be convenient Mrs Haggerty."

Mrs Haggerty was more than a little shocked to see both Mr Powell and Mrs Kean standing at her front door, she began to fidget nervous in the doorway. Noticing Mrs Haggerty's uneasiness at their presents at her front door, Mr Powell said,

"We wish you no harm Mrs Haggerty, in fact it's the opposite."

Mrs Haggerty tried to regain her composure as she opened the front door to her house fully.

"Please, please, do come in." she offered nervously.

Mrs Haggerty then made a feeble attempt at a curtsy before moving to one side allowing Mr Powell and Mrs Kean to pass her and enter the house.

"Please, Mrs Haggerty there's no need for you to curtsy, not to us." aid Mr Powell as he took Mrs Haggerty by the arm and smiled kindly at her.

"Please, come in, come in." said Mrs Haggerty, as she led both of her distinguished guests down the narrow hallway into the parlour at the rear of this small terraced house.

"Please do sit down," said Mrs Haggerty.

Immediately Edwina noticed that Mrs Haggerty's eyes were reddened and swollen from crying, indicating that young Sylvia must have told her Mother something of what had gone on the previous evening. As Mrs Haggerty took her seat she became flustered and her hands began to tremble uncontrollably.

"Please Mrs Haggerty, you must relax, please calm down, both Mr Powell and myself are only to help, believe me." said Edwina trying to reassure the stricken woman.

Sylvia's mother took a deep breath and sat back in her chair hoping to overcome her fear and uneasiness of this strange situation, but also knowing only too well that she would have to compose herself if her daughter's story was to be told and, more importantly, believed if justice was ever to be done.

Suddenly Mrs Haggerty jumped forward in her chair and blurted out nervously...

"It's all lies, Mrs Kean, my Sylvia wouldn't do the things he says she did, my Sylvia is a good girl!" again Mrs Haggerty burst into tears.

Edwina now sat forward in her chair and moved a little closer to this distraught woman, then resting her hand on Mrs Haggerty's, she said,

"Would you like to tell us what happened, Mrs Haggerty?"

Mrs Haggerty lifted her eyes towards Edwina and in a voice that, although filled with anger, was also tinged with pain and fear, she declared,

"If Sylvia's father and brothers were here he wouldn't get away with this, I can tell you that, Mrs Kean."

"If he has wronged your daughter, Mrs Haggerty, then trust me he won't get away with anything, I can assure you of that, but you must tell us what it is he has done to your daughter, Mrs Haggerty," said Edwina.

Mrs Haggerty looked first at Mr Powell, then at Mrs Kean, her expression displayed all of the pain that she was obviously fighting with.

"Please Mrs Haggerty, you must tell us what happened," pleaded Edwina.

"Are you really here to help us, Mrs Kean or to have Sylvia arrested?" asked Mrs Haggerty.

Edwina smiled at Sylvia's mother saying...

"Arrested, good God no, Mrs Haggerty, both Mr Powell and myself have too much respect for your family to even think that Sylvia was stealing from the bakery. We don't believe Alex Brown's story for a second but we do need to find out what really happened."

Mrs Haggerty began to relax after hearing Edwina's words of comfort and reassurance, her crying now also ceased.

"Sylvia wouldn't take anything from your bakery Mrs Kean, we might not have much in this world but we do have our good name and out dignity. But now this man is trying to take that away from us, but it's all lies, Mrs Kean, it is he who is the wrong doer, not my Sylvia." said Mrs Haggerty.

"We know Sylvia is innocent in all of this, but we must discover the truth Mrs Haggerty, so please tell us." pleaded Edwina once again.

A short silence followed as Mrs Haggerty grappled with the situation she found herself in, unsure if she should make known the serious accusations that young Silvia was placing at the feet of Mr Alex Brown.

"Please, Mrs Haggerty," said Edwina, "Please tell us everything, we only want to help."

Mrs Haggerty raised her handkerchief and dried her eyes from the tears that were falling with such regularity.

"Please tell us, Mr Haggerty and please tell us how is young Sylvia?"

Mrs Haggerty lowered her sodden handkerchief and replied.

"Thank the Lord the child is sleeping at the moment, Mrs Kean, and for the first time since her return home she has stopped crying."

"Will you tell us what it was that Mr Brown did to her please, Mrs Haggerty?" asked Edwina once again.

Mrs Haggerty looked at Edwina then said,

"Yes, I will, Mrs Kean and I pray to the Lord above that you believe me and help my Sylvia."

"We will, if we can Mrs Haggerty." replied Edwina.

Mrs Haggerty then began to tell young Sylvia's side of the story.

"About an hour before Sylvia's shift was due to end, she felt a little unwell so Ann Jackson, Sylvia's line leader told her to go out to the courtyard to get some fresh air and this she did. Sylvia was walking across the courtyard towards the stables when she stopped beside the old gates at the back of the bakery and sat down on some old wooden cases that were piled on top of each other. That's when my Sylvia saw something she shouldn't have seen, Mrs Kean."

Mrs Haggerty was familiar with the bakery's layout, as she herself had worked there a few years before, but nowadays her health was failing and she was no longer fit for work. She continued with Sylvia's story…

"Mr Brown was in the courtyard with two men, one Sylvia recognised to be Mr Anderson who used to work at the bakery as a coachmen. The other was unknown to my Sylvia. To my daughter's misfortune, she found out later that this other man went by the name of Spike. All three were loading boxes of freshly baked goods onto a small cart which was being pulled by two small ponies. Sylvia realised instantly that what she was witnessing wasn't right and she tried to turn and leave, but the man called Spike saw her and came running after her, shouting…

- Stop right there, bitch. -

Sylvia was terrified, Mrs Kean, she didn't know what to do for the best, so she stopped still where she stood, frozen with fear. The man Spike came running up to her and caught her roughly by the arm, then he spun her around to face Mr Brown saying…

- What the hell are we going to do with this one, Alex? -

That's when Mr Brown came over to my Sylvia. He was in a rage, Mrs Kean, my Sylvia said that she thought he was going to kill her and now she wishes that he had. When he got to where Sylvia was standing he slapped her hard in the face. Then he began shouting at her. Sylvia says he was getting more and more angry, his face was red with fury! She was terrified, Mrs Kean, really terrified. He told her that he was going to teach her a lesion that she would never forget, a lesson that will teach her to mind your own bloody business in future. That's when both Mr Brown and the man Spike dragged Sylvia into one of the stables. Before Mr Brown had closed the stable doors, he turned to Mr Anderson, who was now sitting on top of the cart, and told him to be on his way. Mr Brown slammed shut the stable doors and walked to where the man, Spike was holding my Sylvia."

At this point Mrs Haggerty broke down in floods of tears. She was finding it almost impossible to keep control of her emotions and even harder to continue with Sylvia's story. Edwina now got to her feet and went to Mrs Haggerty's side, putting her arm around the distraught woman in an attempt to comfort her because Edwina now believed that she knew the horrors that were about to unfold in this frightful tale.

"I know that this must be difficult for you, Mrs Haggerty, but please continue, we need to know just what took place in that stable," said Edwina softly.

Mrs Haggerty took several deep breaths as she tried to compose herself to carry on telling her daughter's terrifying tale.

"The man, Spike then pushed Sylvia to the ground," continued Mrs Haggerty. "Mr Brown then told him to keep a close eye on her until he returned.

Sylvia was forced to lay on top of some old hay which had been gathered up in a small heap at the far end of the stable. The man, Spike was standing over her and smiling down at her. He told her that soon it would be play time and then he laughed out loud, mocking her as she lay helpless on the ground. Sylvia said that no more than ten minutes passed before Mr Brown returned and he was smiling as he entered the stable.

There now, he said. Everyone thinks that you have gone home because you are feeling unwell, Sylvia because that's what I have told them, girlie. Of course you do know just what that's means don't you little girl? Sylvia shook her head, indicating that she didn't. Then I will tell you, what it means, girly. Alex Brown then looked at his friend, Spike and both men laughed out loud. Well it means that you are here with Spike and myself, all alone, no one will give a second thought to your whereabouts now, girlie they all think that you have gone home, so no one is going to come looking for you, now are they? Mr Brown again looked at Spike and said, "I think it might be play time, don't you, Spike?" Both men laughed out loud, as they leered down at my Sylvia. Sylvia curled up into a tight ball in the hay and began to cry, she was so frightened, Mrs Kean.

Mr Brown then came and stood over her, he knelt down and took hold of my Sylvia by the throat, he then slapped her several times in the face. Sylvia pleaded with him not to hurt her but he just laughed at her and pushed her face into the hay. Sylvia told me that the man, Spike became very excited at this point, she said that he kept on shouting,

Go on Alex, do it to her, do it Alex.-

Sylvia pleaded with them to leave her alone and not to hurt her but both men again just laughed in her face."

Again Mrs Haggerty broke down in tears, the strain of telling Sylvia's story beginning to take its toll on her.

"It's okay, Mrs Haggerty, there's no need for you to continue, I think we know what took place in that stable last night!" said Edwina.

Edwina was feeling great sympathy for young Sylvia, and disgusted that such a terrible thing could have been allowed to take place at her bakery.

A wounded silence now filled the room as both Edwina and Mr Powell tried to take in what Mrs Haggerty was in the middle of telling them. It seemed, at this moment, that no one in the room was willing to interrupt the troubled stillness that now existed within Mrs Haggerty's small back parlour. Then something happened that was to break this unsettling silence. Suddenly the door to the small parlour was inched open slowly, all heads quickly turned in the direction of the parlour door. Slowly, but surely the parlour door was opened to its full and there standing in the doorway was Sylvia. Her appearance reflecting the terrible ordeal that she had suffered at the hands of Mr Alex Brown and the man called Spike. Sylvia's hair was wet and hanging loose around her shoulders as she had washed out the dried blood that had earlier stained her beautiful long blonde hair. Sylvia's arms remained tightly wrapped around her upper body as if to protect herself from another assault. It would seem that Sylvia had been outside the door listening to her mother telling her distressing tale. Sylvia's eyes looked blurred and puffed from crying, the soft skin of her young face marred and mottled from the rough treatment she had endured at the hands of Alex Brown and the man called Spike.

Upon seeing Sylvia in the doorway, Edwina jumped to her feet and crossed the small room towards the open doorway where Sylvia was standing.

"No, please, Mrs Kean, please don't come any closer," sobbed Sylvia.

Edwina realised as a mother herself, that Sylvia's eyes were saying something totally different than the words that had come from her mouth. Edwina could see as clear as day, that the child's eyes were calling out for some kind of help and an explanation for what had happened to her. After all, she was at work and should have been safe, shouldn't she?

"How are you Sylvia?" asked Mrs Kean softly. "Is there anything you need Sylvia? If so please don't hesitate to ask," added Edwina.

Young Sylvia entered the room and rested her trembling body against the large wooden sideboard which sat neatly along the wall just inside the door. Sylvia's arms remained tightly wrapped around her upper body as she looked right at Edwina and said,

"Yes, there is something you can do for me, Mrs Kean."

"Anything, Sylvia, just name it." said Edwina.

"I want you to hear what those two brutes did to me, Mrs Kean, and then I want you to make them pay for what they did." Sylvia's voice sounded weak and frightened.

"If you want to tell me, Sylvia, then I will listen to what they did to you and believe me I will make sure that they both pay for what they have done." said Edwina, taking her seat once again.

Edwina couldn't take her eyes off young Sylvia, her gaze was filled with compassion and understanding of the personal strength needed for her to continue with her story. Edwina could still see the youthful innocence in Sylvia's face, as it tried to push its way past the torment that had sadly disfigured this brave young girl's youthful charm. Edwina couldn't help but think, what if this was my child that was made to live through this dreadful experience? This thought sent a chill charging through Edwina's very being.

Mrs Haggerty now sat with her head buried deep in her hands as her beautiful young daughter prepared to tell the rest of her story. Mr Powell remained quiet throughout, listening carefully to young Sylvia's story, his fists clenched in anger, seeking revenge from beginning to end.

"As I lay frightened on the ground," began Sylvia, "I pleaded with Mr Brown not to hurt me anymore and asked him to let me go, but he just laughed and mocked me. Then he came and stood over me, the man, Spike became excited and began to shout loudly, - Go on Alex, give it to her, let's have a little fun with this noisy bitch -

Mr Brown then got on top of me, he pinned my arms to the ground, I couldn't move or fight him off because he was so strong, I did try, I really did try to stop him, but I couldn't. That's when Mr Brown began kissing me, again. I tried to struggle and push him off me but he was too strong for me. The more I struggled the angrier he became and he began to slap my face. He told me not to be such a tiresome little girl, if I knew what was good for me. As he began kissing me again. I could feel his hot sour breath panting on my face. I turned my head away from him, but he didn't like that. He told me to be a good little girl and play nice or he would have to hurt me again. All the time he was doing this to me I could hear the rough croaking voice of the man, Spike shouting over and over again,

- Go on Alex, do it to her. -

By now I was so frightened that I couldn't speak, no matter how hard I tried, but not a word would pass my lips. I tried to scream out, God knows I tried hard, Mrs Kean, but nothing would come out of my mouth. I closed my eyes and prayed to the almighty God in heaven to help me. I told our Lord in Heaven that I didn't want to die because I was sure that when they had finished with me they would surely kill me, Mrs Kean."

At this point Sylvia paused for a second, then she said softly,

"Maybe it would have been better if they had killed me, Mrs Kean." Sylvia continued with her story.

"I could feel his hands all over my body, touching me, Mrs Kean, touching me in places where only a husband should touch a woman's body. I could feel like a savage as he ripped off my under clothes. He began panting heavily as he struggled to undo his trousers, I was unable to stop him, I just couldn't stop him." Sylvia was now becoming a little agitated as she recanted the most distressing part of her story.

"I shut my eyes as tight as I could, I could feel him, Mrs Kean, I could feel what he was doing to me."

Sylvia turned and looked at her distraught mother who still had her head buried deep in her hands and was sobbing loudly. Tears now filled young Sylvia's eyes as she said the words that no one in the small room wanted to hear, but hear them they must.

"He raped me, Ma, he hurt me, Ma, and I couldn't stop him. I hated it, Ma, I hated every second of it. I could feel my tears run down my face but I was unable to make a sound of any kind. As I lay there in the hay unable to make him stop, I prayed to the almighty God to help me, but he never did, Ma, he never did, Ma. Why didn't he help me, Ma tell me please, why did he not make it stop, Ma. I don't know how long I lay there with him on top of me, listening to him grunting loudly as he took his pleasure on me, but I do know that he hurt me, Ma, it hurt really bad, Ma.

Suddenly he gave a groan and then a loud shout and it was all over. I lay there thinking to myself, what have I done to deserve this, I asked God to tell me what I had done that was so bad that I deserved what had just happened to me. I got no answer, Ma, no answer at all. Mr Brown then got to his feet, he looked down at me he was laughing at me as he said. There now little girl, that wasn't so bad now was it?

I curled up in a tight ball and pulled some of the hay that lay on the ground over my half naked body. I just wanted to cover myself from the view of the on looking man called Spike. I was terrified, I didn't know what they were going to do next. I was sure they were going to kill me, Ma. I could feel the hay between my fingers as I clinched my hands tightly in fear. I can still remember the strong smell of the horses, their smell was everywhere. It was so strong all around me that it nearly made me sick."

Again Sylvia halted her story for a few seconds, as she wiped several tears from her bloated eyes, Sylvia then raised her hand to her nose as if to confirm that the smell of the stable was still on her body, even though she had scrubbed herself from head to toe. Sylvia took a deep breath and continued.

"After a minute or so I sat up and tried to reach for my clothes because I now realised that I was completely naked, that's when I heard Mr Brown say to the man, Spike, Look, Spike she thinks it's all over and she's going home.

Both the man, Spike and Mr Brown laughed out loudly, then Mr Brown told the man called Spike, You best hurry up, Spike or you will miss your turn, she wants to go home now.

Again both men laughed loudly as they mocked me. I clutched the hay between my fingers as the man, Spike approached me with his trousers opened. I cringed and shut my eyes as I felt him climb on top of me. I could smell his hot sweaty body next to me, his smell was even worse than that of the horses. I don't know why or how, but for the first time throughout the whole horrible ordeal, my voice allowed me to speak. I began to pray out loud for the almighty God to put an end to my misery, I asked him to help me. My prayer was quickly halted as the man Spike slapped my face hard, he then he grabbed my face in his rough dirty hands and shouted,

"You can stop that for a start girlie, it's putting me off!"

The man, Spike continued with what he was doing to me, I will never forget his foul breath as he tried to kiss me, I could feel his tongue all over my face and into my mouth. I will never forget the feel of his hot wet body on top of me, his damp skin sticking to my skin.

I lay on the stable floor with my eyes shut tight, my face hurting from the slaps I had received, my body trembling from the repulsive touch from both these men. Again I don't know just how long I lay there with this disgusting man on top of me but just like before it all ended with a loud groan of pleasure from him. Then he got to his feet and both he and Mr Brown stood there looking at me as I lay naked in the hay. I reached out and pulled as much hay as I could over my naked body. Both Mr Brown, and the man, Spike were now standing by the stable door, they were muttering and looking in my direction, I turned away too afraid to look at them. I lay there on my back, my eyes looking skywards, I saw two big shire horses looking down at me from over the top of their stalls. My naked body hidden from their view, by what they simply saw as breakfast. I felt so alone and frightened, I felt that I had been abandoned by all that was good in this world."

Sylvia turned towards Mrs Kean and said,

"I felt that God had forsaken me, and I didn't know why, Mrs Kean. Suddenly Mr Brown came towards me, he picked up my clothes and throw them at me and told me to get dressed. This I did. Mr Brown looked at his watch and then said to me, "Your shift will be finished in another forty minutes then the morning shift will take over, that gives me enough time to make sure that everything is in place for the morning shift manager."

Mr Brown then turned to the man, Spike telling him to bring me to his office in ten minutes time and not to let anyone see him or me. The man, Spike told Mr Brown that he understood. Mr Brown then left the stables and I got myself dressed. Once I was dressed the man, Spike came over to me, he pulled me by the back of my hair and said to me, "Remember girlie, I can always pay you a visit at any time I like because I know where you live and you are more beautiful than all of the others." Then he laughed at me.

When I was dressed Spike took me to Mr Brown's office, there he told me that I was sacked for stealing from my employers. That's when he caught hold of me and pushed me against the closed door of his office and told me never to tell anyone what had happened nor was I to ever to talk to anyone from the bakery ever again or he would send Spike to pay me and maybe my young sister a playful visit."

Mr Powell now intervened saying,

"Yes I witnessed that, Sylvia. I was outside Mr Brown's office, but I didn't want to intercede at that point as I wanted to find out more but I had no idea what had taken place in the stables, please believe me Sylvia."

Edwina got to her feet and crossed the room and held young Sylvia tightly in her arms, then she said,

"He will never hurt you, nor anyone else ever again Sylvia, this I promise you."

Suddenly Sylvia's arms tightened around Edwina's body as she was now feeling a little unsteady on her feet. It would seem that Sylvia's telling of the traumatic episode that she had endured was now taking its toll on her. Mrs Kean then assisted Sylvia's mother to take young Sylvia up the stairs to her bed so she could rest. Sylvia's mother lovingly covered her child with the top quilt, wanting to make her daughter as comfortable as she could. Mrs Haggerty then kissed her beautiful daughter on the forehead and stroked her hair softly until the child had fallen fast asleep.

CHAPTER 9

With young Sylvia now peacefully resting, both Mrs Haggerty and Edwina returned to the parlour to find Mr Powell standing by the black cast-iron fire place, his right arm resting on the edge of the mantelpiece. Mr Powell's face was twisted in anger at the horrifying story that had just unfolded before him.

"How is the child now?" enquired Mr Powell, as Edwina and Mrs Haggerty entered the parlour.

"Sleeping well, thank The Lord," answered Edwina.

Mr Powell then took Mrs Haggerty by the arm and guided her to her seat.

"We will not allow this monstrous deed to go unpunished, be assured of that Mrs Haggerty. Neither myself nor Mrs Kean will rest until retribution has been taken on these beasts for what they did to your daughter!" raged Mr Powell furiously.

Edwina crossed the room to where Mrs Haggerty was sitting, and said softly,

"There are no words of comfort that I can say to you that will make any difference to the pain that you are going through right now, Mrs Haggerty. Please trust me when I say that I know what has to be done and rest assured, Mrs Haggerty, as God in heaven is my witness, I will not rest until it is done."

Edwina slowly knelt down beside Mrs Haggerty's chair and gently took hold of her hand as she continued,

"I can only apologise for the trouble you and your family now find yourself in at this time. This terrible thing should never have happened to you daughter, Mrs Haggerty, not during her working hours at our bakery."

Edwina slowly got to her feet and embraced Sylvia's distraught mother in an attempt to offer some kind of comfort and ease her troubled thoughts. Edwina then turned to Mr Powell and said,

"I think it would be best if we got Mrs Haggerty and her two daughters out of Belfast this very day. We need to know that the family are safe before we begin our investigation into this dreadful business."

"I think that is a good idea, Edwina. Where did you have in mind for them to go?" asked Mr Powell.

"My house at Kilkeel, they will be safe there and the sea air will do them a power of good. My housekeeper at Kilkeel, Mrs Hogan, will look after them and I would rest easy knowing that they were out of Belfast and safe at this time, Mr Powell," said Edwina.

Edwina turned to Mrs Haggerty and asked,

"Would you and your daughters like to go to Kilkeel for a few weeks, Mrs Haggerty, or even longer, depending on how long it takes to bring this dreadful business to a satisfactory end?"

Mrs Haggerty slowly lifted her head and looked at Edwina and said,

"We would like that very much, Mrs Kean. I think getting out of Belfast would be the best thing to do at this moment. I just want to keep my daughters out of the grasp of those two monsters. Myself and my girls thank you for your kindness, Mrs Kean."

"Good," said Mr Powell, "It's settled then. I shall take you and your daughters there myself this very afternoon. Can you all be ready to leave by four o'clock this afternoon, Mrs Haggerty?"

Mrs Haggerty assured Mr Powell that her family would be ready to leave by four o'clock that afternoon.

"Then I shall come for you all then, Mrs Haggerty," he said.

"We will go now, Mrs Haggerty. I will make all the arrangements for your arrival at Kilkeel and Mr Powell will be back to collect you and your daughters at four o'clock this afternoon. Mrs Hogan, my housekeeper at the cottage will take good care of you when you get there, Mrs Haggerty," said Edwina.

Later that evening, as Edwina and her daughter, Connie sat down for dinner, an eerie silence, slowly but surely, began to enclose around them. Connie was puzzled to why such a strange and unsettling mood should exist at the dinner table. This strange, sinister silence made Connie feel very uncomfortable indeed because she had never seen her mother in such a depressive mood before and it troubled her. At first Connie was unwilling to quiz her mother about what the cause could be that had put her into such a bleak mood. Throughout dinner Edwina's mood didn't change one little bit, Connie watched as her mother pushed her food around the plate without ever eating any of it. Connie noticed that her mother would from time to time steal a quick glance in her direction. After dinner as Edwina and her daughter sipped at their hot coffee, Connie could resist no longer,

"What on earth is the matter mother?" she asked worriedly.

"It's nothing for you to worry yourself about, Connie." answered Edwina in a low shaky voice.

This answer did nothing to convince Connie that all was well and that there was nothing to worry about. Connie was not to be deterred that easily and again posed the question to her mother.

"Please mother, I know that something is seriously wrong. I have never seen you like this before, please tell me what is troubling you," she pleaded.

Edwina sat in silence at the opposite end of the dinner table to her daughter, her eyes fixed on her beautiful young Connie. At times Edwina would catch fleeting glimpses of the childlike innocence that sparkled within her daughter's deep blue eyes. Edwina slowly closed her eyes and inwardly prayed that no one would ever take that look away from her beautiful daughter in the same way as these two beasts did to young Sylvia. Edwina straightened herself in her chair and took several deep breaths, then in a soft lamenting voice she said,

"If anything bad should ever happen to you, Connie, I don't think I could bare it, I think it would kill me."

A lone tear trickled down Edwina's cheek and fell to the floor.

Connie, seeing that her mother was in some distress, got to her feet and rushed to her mother's side and instantly putting her arms around her and hugged her tightly. Then with concern in her voice she asked,

"Please mother, tell me, what on earth is the matter, what has happened to upset you so?"

Edwina took hold of her daughter's hand and kissed it lovingly, then, in a tender voice she said,

"Come Connie, sit with me by the fire, and I will tell you everything."

Connie and her mother then left the dinner room and slowly made their way into the sitting room. Once there, both Edwina and her daughter sat in each of the two black leather armchairs that were positioned on either side of the raging fire that burned brightly in the hearth. For a few seconds Edwina stared deep into the raging fire, watching as the flames appeared to be dancing wildly around the hearth. Connie looked at her mother in silent trepidation, waiting for her to begin telling what had upset her so much. Suddenly Edwina lifted her gaze from the dancing flames and looked lovingly at her young daughter, then she said,

"Do you remember the Haggerty family Connie, they all worked at the bakery before the war started?"

"Yes I do mother, their daughter Sylvia is around the same age as me, she used to come to the house with her older brother at weekends when he looked after the garden for us. Yes of course I remember Sylvia. We used to play together along with Bobby when he would be here at the same time. I really liked Sylvia, she was good fun, but she stopped coming when the war started as her two brothers along with her father went off to fight in France. I don't understand mother, what have the Haggerty family got to do with you being so upset?"

Connie paused for a second, then as though she had been struck by lightning, she said loudly,

"Please don't tell me that something terrible has happened to Mr Haggerty or any of his sons?"

"No Connie, it's not Mr Haggerty or any of his sons. As far as we know they are all fine," answered Edwina.

"Well what is it mother, what has happened to the Haggerty family to make you feel so distressed?" inquired Connie.

Edwina braced herself in readiness to tell Connie the whole disgraceful story of what had happened to young Sylvia at the hands of Alex Brown and his friend, Spike.

"It's young Sylvia, Connie," began Edwina.

When Edwina had concluded the dreadful saga of Sylvia's living nightmare at the hands of Alex Brown and the man, Spike, Connie sat in silence, her eyes looking deep into the raging fire, just like her mother had done before revealing Sylvia's terrible ordeal. Dazed and shocked at what her mother had just told to her, Connie's body remained as still as the night, not so much as an eye flickered in the stony expression that was now etched into Connie's face.

"Are you alright Connie?" asked Edwina, fearing that the horrifying event that she had just spoken off might have been too much for her young daughter to take in. Connie looked at her mother with a tearful eye and said,

"Say it isn't so mother, please say it isn't so."

"I am so sorry that I had to tell you such a thing, Connie, but I am afraid that it is so, my darling," replied Edwina,

Slowly Connie got to her feet and stood beside the fireplace, her right arm resting on the edge of the mantelpiece, her eyes fixed on the rampant bright red flames which now raged angrily against the darkness of the back of the hearth. Connie remained as still as a statue just glaring into the raging fire for several long hushed minutes. Edwina sat back in her armchair with her eyes firmly shut it would seem, for now at least, neither of these two ladies wished to break this sorrowful silence. Instead both ladies welcomed this silence because they both realised and understood the full extent and the consequences that would surely follow the actions of these two beasts. As women, they both know that young Sylvia might never recover fully from what had been done to her.

Connie eventually broke the silence when she said in a low but determined voice,

"You must do something about these worthless men mother. They must not be allowed to get away with this appalling attack on young Sylvia."

"Believe me, Connie, I have no intentions of letting them get away with this. I will make sure that they pay dearly for what they have done to Sylvia," fumed a defiant Edwina.

"How is Sylvia?" asked Connie.

"I won't say that she is as well as can be expected because she isn't. The child is not good at all, Connie. It has torn her apart, leaving her confused and bewildered why such a thing could happen to her when at her place of work. We have arranged for Mr Powell to take the family to our cottage in Kilkeel this very evening. There they will remain until this dreadful business with Alex Brown and the man, Spike has come to a satisfactory conclusion. By a satisfactory conclusion, I mean that I will not rest until both men are behind bars."

"Good," said Connie. "I hope that the family all can find some comfort and some much needed rest in Kilkeel," added Connie.

"It's a dreadful business altogether, Connie," said Edwina as she cleared a tear from her eye.

"What about Mrs Haggerty, how is she coping?" asked Connie.

"The woman is devastated Connie. I have never seen such torment in one person's eyes like I saw in Mrs Haggerty's this very day," said Edwina.

"What has happened to Sylvia must be ripping her apart," said Connie

"The image of that poor women looking on helplessly as her daughter told the distressing account of her ordeal at the hands of those two men will be with me for ever, Connie. The woman is crushed, Connie, drained of all hope, her world is in tatters around her. I can't help but think what I would do if it were you in the same situation as young Sylvia. I think I would kill those men with my own two hands, Connie. It just doesn't bear thinking about. I tell you now, Connie, I shall not rest until I make both of them pay for this despicable deed."

Edwina stood by the raging fire and took her young daughter in her arms, hugging her as tightly as she could. With tears in her eyes Edwina began to stroke her daughter's long raven hair with the loving touch of a protective mother.

The next morning Mr Powell arrived at Edwina's house bright and early, as per arrangements, the purpose of this meeting was to formulate a plan of investigation into the atrocity that had taken place the day before. Mr Powell's first duty of the day was to inform Edwina that he had delivered the Haggerty family safely to the cottage in Kilkeel. Also that Mrs Hogan had agreed to keep a close eye on the Haggerty family, making sure that they were in need of nothing during their stay.

This news alone made Edwina feel a little more at ease, knowing that Mrs Hogan along with her husband, Herbert, would never allow anything bad to happen to anyone left in their care. Mrs Hogan is a kind God fearing woman who had been born and raised in the small fishing town of Kilkeel. She had been in the Kean family's employment for many, many years. When the cottage was not in use, Mrs Hogan would act as its custodian and when the Kean family were in residence, Mrs Hogan would act as housekeeper, looking after the family.

Mrs Hogan lived in a small stone built cottage in the next road to where the Kean cottage was situated no more than a ten minute walk from Edwina's larger cottage. Mrs Hogan lived with her husband, Herbert, who was a fisherman by profession, just like his father before him and his father before him. Mr and Mrs Hogan had four sons, each one of them was away fighting in France. Herbert Hogan hoped that one day he would pass on his fishing boat to his sons, should they return from the war. Edwina's stone built cottage was picturesque in appearance. Inside was a large sitting room, a well equipped kitchen, a dining room, three large double bedrooms and two bathrooms. A small white-washed wall surrounded the well-manicured rose gardens that ran all the way around the cottage. On a hot summer's day there was nothing more relaxing than to sit in the back rose garden taking in the hypnotic aroma of the fresh, embracing sea air which wafted in on the breeze from the harbour and merged with the sweet perfumed fragrance of the many roses which filled the garden. As a way of creating more income, Mrs Hogan's husband, Herbert would, at weekends, tend to the gardens keeping them and the cottage itself in tip top condition.

As the large grandfather clock that stood in Edwina's large hallway struck seven o'clock, both she and Mr Powell left for the bakery. Stepping outside into the early morning autumn air, Edwina couldn't stop herself from casting her eyes skyward, as if forced to do so. Edwina held this pose for several seconds, watching as the early morning sun begin its daily climb to its rightful position high above this place we call earth. Edwina looked on in silence, as if spellbound as this burning blaze of intense power moved across the sky. She slowly turned to Mr Powell and said in a soft voice,

"No matter what happens in this miserable world of ours, Andy, no matter what kind of evil man inflicts upon his fellow man, that bright sphere of energy forgives us all of our transgression and continues to make its daily climb to its position high above us, sending down that life giving light that we so depend on. But for how much longer, Andy? Because one day I fear that man will go too far and the sun's forgiveness will be withdrawn from us for ever, leaving us abandoned to our own devices. No longer will it make its daily climb to lighten up this earth, because one day, Andy, we will have gone too far and there will be no earth in need of any kind."

"You might just be right, Edwina," said Mr Powell.

It was seven thirty when both Mr Powell and Edwina arrived at the bakery but Mr Powell didn't make his way to the front entrance, no, instead he led Edwina towards a shabbily paint-striped red coloured door which was situated at the end of a narrow passageway at the side of the bakery. As they approached this old door, Mr Powell produced three very large keys from his coat pocket. Edwina looked on in some amazement because in truth, these keys wouldn't look out of place in the hands of a jailer. Edwina looked at Mr Powell with a wry smile and said,

"What on earth are they, Andy?" referring to the keys in Mr Powell's hand.

"You'll see Edwina," replied Mr Powell.

"More to the point, Andy, what on earth are we doing here in this alleyway?" added Edwina,

Mr Powell smiled as he placed one of the large keys in the lock on the old door, at first it was something of a struggle, as the old lock had rusted over the years. Then suddenly the large key turned in the lock and the old door opened.

"No one will see us entering through this door, Edwina and to be honest I think I am the only one that knows of its existence. I am most certainly the only one with a key that fits the lock."

"Again, Andy, Why?" asked Edwina.

Mr Powell gave Edwina a smile, then he said,

"Many years ago, Edwina, Terry and myself had this entrance built here, so we could come and go without anyone knowing."

Edwina looked at Mr Powell feeling really confused.

"But why?" she asked.

You see the thought of her husband Terry and Andy Powell being involved in any kind of mysterious goings on would have never crossed her mind. It just wasn't in their personality. Yet here they were!

"We did have need of it when we first opened the bakery, trust me Edwina," answered Mr Powell as he pushed open the old door, allowing Edwina and himself to pass through it. Mr Powell then slammed the door shut before locking it safely behind him. Edwina and Andy Powell were now standing in a dimly lit corridor which stretched out for about ten yards in front of them. At the far end of this miserable and neglected passage was yet another cracked and paint stripped door. Mr Powell pushed yet another large key into yet another rusted old lock on this second door. As with the first door, this too was a bit of a struggle to get the key to turn in the lock, but in the end turn it did. Once on the other side of this second door both Edwina and Mr Powell found themselves in yet another shabby, darkened hallway.

"Are you kidding me, Andy?" asked Edwina.

"No, not at all, Edwina." answered Andy Powell, "all will become clear in a few seconds."

This hallway was darker than the last and the only light that intruded was from small rays of sun-light that filtered in from a broken sky-light at the far end of the passageway. Stagnant water covered the floor underfoot, leftovers from the rain storm from five or six weeks ago that had leaked in through the many holes that peppered the overhanging ceiling above. This unwelcomed dampness was giving off the most unpleasant smell and was making Edwina feel really unwell. Edwina hurriedly pulled a handkerchief from her pocket and raise it to her mouth, as she held her breath. She hurriedly, but carefully picked her way along this dismal passage following but only a few steps behind Mr Powell until they reached the end of this appalling smelling corridor. Mr Powell took hold of Edwina's hand and led her up a narrow stone staircase. Once at the top they were faced with yet another door, it too had flakes of old perished paint clinging desperately to its withered wood.

This third door, although shabby in appearance, behaved much better than the other two had done. Mr Powell simply inserted the key turned it once and the door opened without effort. Edwina and Andy Powell now found themselves in a small, brightly lit and carpeted hallway and in front of them were two small empty offices.

"We are here, Edwina," said Mr Powell

Edwina looked at Andy Powell with some amazement and said,

"And pray tell, where is here, Andy?"

He gave a short chuckle as he said,

"This small office here on the right looks out over the back courtyard where the old gates are Edwina. That's the gate that Alex Brown has been using to move out the goods he has been stealing from us."

Edwina looked at Andy Powell and said jokingly,

"Your talents never cease to amaze me, Andy."

Mr Powell simply smiled in response as he opened the door of the small office to their right. Mr Powell hastily made his way to the far end of the small office to where the bank of windows were situated. He then wasted no time in opening two of the windows half way. This he did for two reasons, first, the office had not been used for several years and the smell within was almost as bad as the passageway they had just come from. Secondly, if they were in luck and Alex Brown was to continue with his black-market trading that morning, then with the windows already opened, both Andy and Edwina would be able to hear what was being said.

Beyond the courtyard and the old gates was a narrow cobbled-stoned road, completely devoid of buildings of any kind. This old cobbled-stone road, along with the old set of iron gates at the far end of the courtyard had long since been forsaken. Running alongside of the old road was a large, although abandoned and overgrown field. In happier times, before the outbreak of war, this neglected field would have been regularly used by the young men of East Belfast. Here was a place where young men would bring their sweethearts on long summer Sunday afternoons for picnics. Sadly, due to the war, these gentler of times were now a thing of the past, just like the field itself.

"Come, look here, Connie." requested Mr Powell politely, as he peered out of his office window at the court-yard below.

Edwina crossed the short distance from where she was standing to Mr Powell's position by the large cluster of windows.

"What is it, Andy?" asked Edwina curiously.

"Look." answered Mr Powell, "We can clearly monitor most of the court-yard and stables from here, Edwina, as well as those old iron gates that Mr Alex Brown has saw fit to re-commission," he added.

Edwina looked pleased with Mr Powell's discovery, and with a smirk on her face she replied,

"Yes, you're right Andy, we can see everything from here, and with these two small side windows opened, I dare to suggest that we could almost certainly hear everything as well, Andy."

Until now, Mr Powell was of the opinion that these old iron gates had been decommissioned a long time ago when the Bakery had switched to using the new and much larger gates at the other side. The reason for the switch was because it was easier for the coachmen to manoeuvre the team of shire-horses in and out of the courtyard.

As Mr Powell and Edwina stood by the windows observing the court-yard below, suddenly, Mr Alex Brown appeared in their eye line. At first he was moving slowly from their right across the courtyard, looking all around as if to make sure that he wasn't being observed by anyone. After a few seconds of scanning the courtyard Mr Alex Brown eventually came to a halt in the centre of the courtyard. After yet another quick scan of the courtyard, he then lit up a cigarette, taking no more than four quick puffs from it before tossing it to the ground. Once again he carefully looked all around the court-yard as if to confirm to himself that he was alone and safe from any prying eyes. Mr Brown then took his pocket watch from his waistcoat and looked carefully at the time before replacing it into his waistcoat. With the time now lodged, Alex Brown then moved swiftly towards the old iron gates. Digging deep into his trouser pocket, he pulled out a large old rusting key and proceeded to open the old gates wide to the wall. Mr Powell and Edwina looked at each other in surprised disbelief at their good fortune.

"I think that our friend, Mr Alex Brown is about to hang himself, Edwina," grinned Mr Powell in a low voice.

Now that the gates were opened to their fullest, Alex Brown returned to the centre of the courtyard, positioning himself on several bales of hay which were resting against the wall outside the stables. Alex lit yet another cigarette and waited. After only a matter of minutes had passed, a faint scraping, clattering sound could be heard in the distance.

"Listen," whispered Edwina. "Can you hear it, Andy?" Edwina's voice low, as she didn't wish Alex Brown to accidently overhear her.

Mr Powell smiled smugly in Edwina's direction, as he replied calmly,

"I can hear it, Edwina"

The sound was getting louder by the second as it drifted towards them on the early morning breeze. After only a few more seconds had passed, this strange sound became easily identifiable. It was the clip-clapping of small pony's hooves, mixed with the grinding of the iron trim of a cartwheels as they made contact with the cobbled-stone road at the back of the bakery. Suddenly Alex Brown jumped down from his perch on top of the bales of hay and again he scanned the court-yard carefully to ensure that it was free from any uninvited guests. Alex Brown then quickly moved towards the middle of the courtyard and waited. Mr Powell and Edwina listened quietly as the grinding, clip-clapping sound was drawing nearer by the second. Then there it was coming through the old iron gates, a small wooden cart that was being pulled by two small ponies.

The cart came to a standstill beside Alex Brown. It was being driven by a small overweight man dressed in a shabby black sweater and brown corduroy trousers. On his head was a dark cloth cap. By his side sat another man, dressed in a pair of old black trousers, the front of which were covered in greasy stains, as was the old grey ripped shirt he wore. Like the first man, this man too wore a black cloth cap upon his head. This second man bore a striking resemblance to the man Sylvia had described as the man called Spike. Now there he was in full view, the man called Spike that along with Alex Brown had so brutally attacked and raped young Sylvia in the bakery's stables.

Edwina and Mr Powell moved closer to the window in order to gain a better view and to hear what was being said a little more clearly. It was then that Mr Powell recognised the man driving the small cart as a man called Mr Anderson, a man that had worked as a coachman for the bakery until recently. It had been Mr Powell himself that had the pleasure to dismiss this Mr Anderson some months before for mistreating and roughly manhandling the horses under his care. It didn't take long for Edwina and Mr Powell's suspicions of the identity of the second man on the cart to be confirmed. When Alex Brown moved forward to greet both men he said,

"On time as usual, Spike."

The man, Spike was laughing out aloud as he climbed down from the small cart and with a distasteful smirk on his face he quipped,

"What's this Alex, no little play things for us to amuse ourselves with today?"

"Sadly not, Spike." replied a smiling Alex Brown, "but don't give up all hope I am sure that there will be another little play thing coming along before too long," added Alex Brown, with a menacing leer carved into his face.

"Well then, Alex, it looks like today won't be as much fun as yesterday, will it?" sneered Spike.

Both Alex and Spike walked away from the cart towards the bakery, leaving Mr Anderson sitting alone on the cart. Both Alex and Spike were now out of Edwina and Mr Powell's vision but it was only a matter of minutes before they reappeared in the courtyard both men pushing handcarts filled with boxes of freshly baked goods. Both handcarts were quickly loaded onto Mr Anderson's cart, and Spike and Alex returned to the bakery to refill their handcarts. This they did six times.

"Got them now, Edwina!" smiled Mr Powell in a low voice tinged with a sense of satisfaction.

"That we have, Andy," said Edwina.

"Now no one can harbour any reservations about Sylvia's version of the event what so ever because these two unspeakable rascals have now just hung themselves with their own words and their own actions, Edwina," added a contented Mr Powell.

Edwina looked at Mr Powell and said confidently,

"I never had any misgivings about what Sylvia had told us from the beginning, Andy."

"No, nor did I, Edwina, but we did need proof and now we have it!" replied Mr Powell,

Both Mr Powell and Edwina remained crouched behind the small interior wall underneath the cluster of windows silently observing the activities that were taking place in the courtyard below. After loading Mr Anderson's cart with yet more boxes of goods the man, Spike took Alex Brown by the arm and pulled him to one side. Both men were now standing directly below the windows where Mr Powell and Edwina were positioned.

"On a more serious note, Alex," said the man, Spike, "were you able to smooth over our little problem about that girl Sylvia with Mrs Kean. Did the lady accept your reason for why you had to sack the little bitch? It's just that I have been wondering about it all night."

Alex sniggered smugly as he placed his arm around Spike and said boorishly,

"Ah Spike my friend, the lovely Mrs Kean, what can I say, except that you can relax and forget all about that little interfering bitch. She's history, Spike. I don't think that the desirable Mrs Kean will be giving us any trouble in the near future over that little cow. You see, Spike I can read women like a book and I have noticed the lovely Mrs Kean's reaction to me whenever I am in her presence. It's there for all to see, Spike, you can see it in her stunning blue eyes every time she looks at me. The woman simply finds it hard to resist me. You see, Spike I have the ability to charm the lovely lady. I can make her believe whatever I want her to believe. Because, Spike, the lady has a secret yearning for me. Oh yes sure, she tries to hide it but it is most certainly there for all to see."

Spike looked a little shocked at Alex Brown's revelations about Mrs Kean.

"Really, Alex," he said, "do you really think the lady has a liking for you?"

"Oh yes, believe it, Spike and one day I will prove it to you," grinned Alex.

Then Spike added crudely,

"Maybe a quick visit to the stables with both you and myself is what the lady is in need of, Alex, what do you think?"

Both men laughed loudly before Alex added,

"Maybe you're right, Spike. We will have to look into that one of these days."

Spike's face suddenly changed from one of humour to one of worry as he asked,

"What of Sylvia herself, will she keep her mouth shut Alex?"

"Oh don't worry yourself about that little cow, Spike," sneered Alex, "I've put the fear of God into that meddling little slut. She will react just like all of the others did. Trust me, Spike, she won't breath a word of what happened to her to anyone. After all, who is going to believe an uneducated tramp like Sylvia, who had been branded a thief over someone in my position?"

Both men then shook hands firmly and laughed the laugh of arrogant complacency.

"That's okay then," replied Spike, "If you're sure that is, Alex?"

"Don't worry, Spike," said Alex, again putting his arm around Spike, "I know their kind, trust me everything will be fine but if you are worried about her then maybe you should go and pay our little play friend a quick visit and remind her to keep her mouth shut or we might have to have a little chat with her younger sister," added Alex with a sadistic snigger.

Spike then turned and climbed up onto the cart beside Mr Anderson, with a broad smile on his face as he said,

"Now that might not be such a bad idea Alex, and it might also be fun."

With that last despicable insult, Mr Anderson flicked the thin leather reins that controlled the two small ponies causing them to begin their homeward trot and within a few seconds, Mr Anderson, Spike and the cart had left the courtyard, leaving Alex Brown alone to close the old iron gates before returning to the bakery.

Once the unsavoury business had been concluded in the courtyard below and all participants had gone their separate ways both Edwina and Mr Powell got to their feet and left the seclusion of their hiding place under the cluster of windows. Mr Powell and Edwina then made their way to Mr Powell's office. Mr Powell sat down behind his large oak desk and Edwina rested herself in one of the two leather armchairs that were positioned on the other side of his desk, her teeth clenched in anger. Edwina suddenly banged hard on Mr Powell's desk top with her fists before exploding furiously.

"I really can't believe the conceit and contempt for women shown by those two scoundrels, Andy, and as for that man Brown's opinion of me, well never, Andy, never, as long as I live that would never happen! If you ask me, Andy the man is an abomination."

"I agree, Edwina, but you mustn't upset yourself on account of those two rogues because their time will come of that I am sure."

Edwina looked troubled as she continued.

"The most worrying thing that we have discovered from what we have heard here this morning is not their confessions, Andy. It is the fact that neither of those two men showed any kind of remorse whatsoever for their shameful actions. In fact, the opposite is the case, they seemed to get some kind of self-gratification from talking about the whole sordid episode."

Mr Powell nodded his head in agreement saying,

"Yes, Edwina, I agree. I have to say that I do find their attitude towards the whole affair somewhat distasteful."

CHAPTER 10

After a few short agonising minutes, Edwina got to her feet and looked at Mr Powell, a soft, thoughtful, muttered groan escaping from her lips as she reflected on what had just gone before. Slowly, she began to pace broodingly back and forth in front of Mr Powell's large oak desk, her head lowered in deep deliberation. Mr Powell looked on in silence having no wish to interrupt Edwina's deep sorrow and her regret at this tragic situation in which they both found themselves. After several pensive minutes had passed, Edwina ceased her pacing and looked expectantly at Mr Powell.

"Any thoughts about our next step, Andy?" said Edwina hopefully.

Andy Powell sat back in his leather armchair and began to stroke his chin thoughtfully with his middle finger. After a few hushed seconds he replied.

"I think we should tread most carefully at this point, Edwina, at least until we have thought the whole situation through thoroughly. I'm no expert in situations like this but I do think we need to make sure that our case against these two degenerates is more than watertight. Not just for the bakery's reputation, Edwina, but for young Sylvia and her family. Not to mention any of the other young girls that have yet to be identified that have also fallen foul of these two evil men. We owe them that at least, Edwina. We must be sure that the evidence we collect is strong enough to secure a conviction, mostly for the vicious rape of young Sylvia. Under no circumstances must both these men be allowed to escape the full vengeance of the law for what they did to that poor young innocent child."

At this point Mr Powell got to his feet and walked around to the front of his desk, perching himself on the corner of it in front of Edwina. Then he said

"Fortunately, Edwina, I have a friend at the lodge. His name is Hastings, William Hastings. He is a retired police inspector and was with the Royal Irish Constabulary for many years. I really do think that a few words with him would be our best plan of action as he will put us on the right road, make no mistake, Edwina."

The lodge which Mr Powell referred to was of course his Orange Lodge, the lodge formed in the Knock area of East Belfast in 1898 by Edwina's Father and his brother. Edwina's late husband had joined the Knock Lodge shortly after marrying her and that's where he met and became friends with Andy Powell. Over the years both men had become a well-respected members of the Grand Orange Lodge of Ireland, of which Andy Powell was still a strong and active member and a past Grand Master.

Again Edwina took her seat and looked at Mr Powell.

"Do you think this William Hastings will help us, Andy?" asked Edwina.

"I'm sure of it," replied Mr Powell. "Look," he continued, as he removed his pocket watch from his waistcoat and checked the time.

"It's only just after seven thirty so let's get out of here and clear our heads. Let me take you to the Grand for breakfast." The Grand Mr Powell referred to was of course The Grand Central Hotel in Royal Avenue, the best Hotel in Belfast and a place where it was good to be seen by Belfast's high society.

"Yes," replied Edwina getting to her feet. "That sounds like a good idea, Andy, a little breakfast and a break from here might just be the best thing right now."

Later that afternoon, at around two thirty, Andy Powell arrived at the front door of Mr William Hastings' residence. William Hastings was a man in his late fifties, strong in build and standing tall at six foot three. William Hastings lived in a quiet leafy suburb in the small town of Hollywood, no more than ten miles from Belfast. The house itself was a large double fronted detached dwelling, with its façade and twin front gardens meeting the very highest standard of upkeep. The large and very impressive front door to this house was painted bright red. Situated in the centre of this door and positioned at eyelevel was a big brass lion's head door knocker. Mr Powell took hold of the knocker in his right hand and gave it three firm knocks, then he took one step back and waited. Within a few seconds the door slowly opened, revealing a middle-aged, grey haired lady standing squarely in the opening. Knowing that William Hastings was a bachelor, Mr Powell took this lady to be William's housekeeper.

"Good afternoon, Sir. May I help you?" she enquired respectfully.

"Good afternoon to you, madam," replied Mr Powell, tilting his hat in respect as he did so.

"My name is Andy Powell. I am a member of the same Orange Lodge as William. May I talk with him if he is at home?" continued Mr Powell.

"Please, do come in Mr Powell," replied the quietly spoken lady, as she moved to one side, allowing Mr Powell to enter the house and move past her in the hallway.

"Mr Hastings is in the drawing-room, please follow me, Mr Powell." said the housekeeper.

Gracefully, this middle-aged lady moved to one side to allow Mr Powell to pass. Once Mr Powell had entered the house, the housekeeper closed the front door and slowly made her way down the long hallway, with Mr Powell following close behind. She stopped outside a highly polished mahogany door which was located some fifteen foot along a large entrance hall. The housekeeper then twice tapped softly on the door and waited until she heard a response from inside the room, then slowly she opened the door and entered the drawing-room.

"There's a Mr Powell from your Orange Lodge here to see you sir," announced the house-keeper.

She then led Mr Powell into a large, elegant drawing-room which had two large bay window at the far end of the room allowing the sun-light to flood the room. Upon hearing his housekeeper announce the arrival of Mr Powell, William Hastings got sharply to his feet, folding and placing the newspaper he was reading on a small table by the side of his large armchair.

"Andy!" he exclaimed loudly, somewhat surprised to see Mr Powell standing in his drawing-room as he and Andy Powell were not what you would call social friends, more associates through the Lodge.

"Please do come in, Andy and take a seat."

Mr Powell moved further into the room and sat in one of four large black leather armchairs that were positioned in the room. William turned to his housekeeper and said,

"Thank you, Mrs Birch, maybe a pot of tea for our guest...tea Andy?" William enquired.

"Tea would be most welcome," replied Mr Powell.

With this, Mrs Birch left the room, returning moments later with a tray of tea and biscuits.

"Now then, Andy, to what do I owe this pleasure?" asked William inquisitively.

Mr Powell sat back in his chair and with a troubled look on his face he began to tell William his loathsome tale. By the time Mr Powell had finished telling William the dreadful saga of what had taken place at the bakery, William was somewhat lost for words. William picked up his cup of tea slowly but he stopped short of taking a drink from the cup.

"No," he snarled angrily, placing his tea cup back into its saucer.

"No more tea I think, Andy, not after what you have just told me."

William's voice showed that he was completely repulsed by what he had just been told.

"Clearly something a little stronger is needed now I think, Andy, don't you agree?"

Mr Powell nodded in agreement as he too replaced his tea cup to its saucer. Then he replied,

"Yes I think I am more than ready for something stronger, William."

"Would a stiff Black Bush hit the spot, Andy?" asked William.

89

"Fine, thank you William." answered Mr Powell.

William poured out two more than ample glasses of Black Bush whisky.

"Water or as it comes, Andy?" enquired William.

"A little water please, William, just about half again would be fine thank you William," answered Mr Powell.

Both men sat in silence for a few moments, savouring their welcome Irish, their reflecting moments only interrupted when William said,

"I take it, Andy that you are telling me this because you would like my assistance in this dreadful matter?"

"Your help would be greatly appreciated, William," replied Mr Powell.

"I will be more than happy to help you put both these frightful men where they belong, Andy, whatever it takes I will do it. I have come across men like these before and trust me they sicken me to the pit of my stomach."

"Thank you, William, your help will be most welcome, I can assure you."

"Think nothing of it, Andy," replied William strongly,

William took a sip of his whisky then he continued,

"What I need from you now, Andy is how I can meet with the young girl, Sylvia and also I will need the names of any other young girls that have left or been sacked in the last year. How I may get in touch with them without raising any suspicions?"

"Consider it done, William. I will have everything you require ready for you by the end of the week," confirmed Mr Powell.

Both men then swiftly dispatched the remainder of their Irish, then placing their empty glasses on the small table in the centre of the room they both got to their feet, shook hands firmly and parted.

True to his word, William made contact with Mr Powell on the Thursday, setting up a meeting between the two men on the Friday afternoon. The meeting was to take place in the Lounge bar at the Grand Central Hotel, Belfast at two thirty. Of course, in the end, the choice of meeting place was of course William's idea as he did not want to be seen with Andy anywhere near the bakery nor indeed anywhere in East Belfast. Best to stay away from prying eyes at this stage of the game was William's thinking. After the meeting, William informed Mr Powell that he might not be in contact for some time, saying that the less the two men were seen together the better. Just leave the investigations to me, Andy. You and Edwina take no further action on this subject. Do nothing until you hear from me. The less Alex and Spike suspect at this point the better.

CHAPTER 11

In the weeks that followed, nothing was heard from William Hastings and life went on very much as usual at the bakery. Connie continued to write to Bobby every day, although it would be weeks before she would receive any letters in return from him, not that he didn't answer her letters as soon as possible It was just that it took such a long time for letters from the front to find their way back home. But when they would eventually arrive, Connie would have a delivery of up to fifteen to twenty letters at a time. This event would certainly brighten Connie's day and would see her remove herself from her daily routine and take refuge in her bedroom for hours at a time. Connie would simply spread herself out on top of her bed and read Bobby's letters time and time again. Although most of what Bobby had to say would lay heavy on Connie's heart, forcing more than a few tears to fall from her fretful eyes. These reading sessions would always be followed by a short pleading prayer offered up for Bobby's quick and safe return.

It had been several weeks since Mr Powell had heard anything from William Hastings and in truth Andy Powell was becoming more than a little anxious. He was sitting in his office one Friday morning, pondering whether or not to make contact with William, when, at around ten thirty, a telegram boy arrived at his office door.

"Morning Sir," said the telegram boy, "are you Mr Andy Powell?" he enquired politely.

Mr Powell looked up at the young man and replied smartly.

"Yes that would be me, young man, please do come in."

The boy entered the office and promptly delivered the telegram into Mr Powell's waiting hand. This was the news that Mr Powell had been waiting for, contact being made with William Hastings. Mr Powell promptly opened William's telegram to find that the message inside was short and to the point. The telegram read,

"Time we talked. Both you and Edwina meet me at the Grand for lunch on Sunday at twelve thirty." My best regards William Hastings."

Mr Powell immediately rushed to inform Edwina that William had made contact and that they were to meet with him for lunch that Sunday at the Grand. On the following Sunday both Mr Powell and Edwina arrived at the lounge bar of the Grand Central Hotel, the time being just before twelve thirty. William Hastings was sitting at the far end of the bar at a table adjacent to the large double doors leading to the restaurant.

"There he is, Edwina, over there," said Mr Powell, indicating to Edwina where William was sitting. Both Mr Powell and Edwina quickly made their way across the busy bar to William's table.

"Good afternoon William, it's good to hear from you," said Mr Powell, as both he and Edwina reached the table.

"Good afternoon to you both," replied William. "Please…do take a seat."

"William…May I introduce you to Edwina Keane?" said Mr Powell as Edwina was about to take her seat.

"It would be a pleasure, Andy." replied William,

Getting to his feet and respectfully tilting his head in Edwina's direction. William offered his hand in welcome to Edwina and after a gentile hand-shake had taken place, Edwina and Mr Powell took their seats.

"I knew your late husband Edwina, from the lodge that is," said William, "so to meet you after all these years is a joy, Mrs Keane, although the circumstances might have been a little happier," he added.

"Thank you, William," replied Edwina, "and yes, the circumstances could certainly be happier."

William then ask both Edwina and Mr Powell if they would like a drink and both said that they would. William called for the drinks waiter to come to the table.

"I think a drink first to ready ourselves," said William, "then we can talk about this wretched business over lunch," he continued.

"Yes, a splendid idea, William," was Mr Powell's response.

The waiter took the order and left the table. But not before looking long and hard at William.

After drinks, William called the waiter back to the table.

"Would you find out if the table I have reserved for lunch is ready please?" William asked politely.

"Certainly Sir…your name please, Sir?" enquired the waiter.

"Hastings, Mr William Hastings," William answered.

Over lunch, William began to inform Andy and Edwina about what he had discovered following his thorough investigations, also he wanted to inform them both of the plans he had made to bring this appalling saga to an end.

"I have visited and talked with the young girl, Sylvia. She concurred with everything you told me, Andy, as of course I knew she would. I have also met and talked with another four young girls whom you informed me had left the bakery rather suddenly. It took a lot of persuading to get them to talk to me as these girls are so frightened of these two men it is beyond belief. I have never known anything like this level of fear in anyone in all my time in the Constabulary. I informed them how both of you are looking after Sylvia and her family, keeping them safe, although I didn't say where. This news seemed to ease their fears a tad. I then promised them that we would protect them and their families in the same way, should they wish to help with our investigations. When I informed these young ladies and their families, that both you, Andy and you, Mrs Keane are behind the efforts to catch these two men and put them behind bars, well they were more than willing to help."

"Fantastic news, William and of course we will look after and protect all of the families involved. Whatever it takes, William," pledged Mr Powell instantly.

William continued.

"All four girls confirmed that they had seen Alex and the man, Spike stealing from the bakery. One, a girl called Mary Riley, aged sixteen, told me that she had been badly beaten by Alex, as the man, Spike watched on. Both men then threatened further violence towards her and her family if she didn't leave the bakery there and then. They also told her that if she was ever to tell anyone about what had happened to her, or what she had seen at the bakery, then they would find her and make her very sorry indeed. Young Mary Riley also told me that the man, Spike paid her several visits just to remind her to keep quiet about her ordeal. Although what happened to Mary Riley was terrible and disgusting, she was one of the lucky ones, I am loathed to have to inform you both. As far as the other three girls are concerned, Margaret O'Brian, aged sixteen, Bridgette Kelly, aged also sixteen, and Theresa Campbell, aged seventeen, I am sorry to have to inform you both, but they all met with the same brutal fate as young Sylvia.

All three young girls were viciously beaten and then raped in the stables by both men. The whole ordeal got even worse for the girl Margaret O'Brian, as she found herself pregnant as a result of the rape and is due to give birth within the next few weeks. This girl has been frightened out of her wits by the man, Spike. He stopped her in the street a few days after the attack and told her that if she ever told of what had happened to her, then her mother and her younger sister would get the same treatment. The saddest thing about Margaret's situation is that until the day I spoke with her and her family, she hadn't told her mother what had happened to her, fearing that the man, Spike might come after her mother and her younger sister. This meant that her family, including her mother, her aunts and the neighbours, had all thought her to be nothing but a common slut, a tart. As a result young Margaret has been living her life facing ridicule from all in sundry on a daily basis. Every time she would leave her house, she would be the target of insulting mutterings and dirty looks, ever since her pregnancy became evident."

"My God, this gets worse by the minute!" blasted Edwina.

The mood around the table was now at an all-time low as both Edwina and Mr Powell digested this latest bombshell delivered by William.

"But strangely enough," continued William, "when the girl's mother discovered the truth about her daughter's pregnancy, although devastated at the thought of her daughter's ordeal, it did seem to come as some kind of relief to learn that her daughter was not the common tart everyone thought her to be."

Edwina face suddenly changed to one of anger to one of muddled confusion.

"Oddly enough," she muttered softly, "I kind if understand the mother's thinking, strange as it sounds, but I do."

"I have to say," added William, "Margaret was not alone in her silence. As none of the other girls had ever disclosed to their families what they had gone through at the hands of Alex and Spike. The fear that had been installed into these young girls by Alex and Spike, the likes of which I have never known before in my life. These young girls to a one kept their silence, thinking that they were protecting their mothers and their younger sisters from reprisals from these two loathsome men. Sadly in each case, none of the families have men over the age of sixteen living at home, due to the fact that they are all off fighting for King and country. Only snakes like these two men are left at home to do as they please. Men like them know only too well that these poor girls have no fathers or brothers to defend them, making them easy prey. I must tell you both that now the truth is out, the revelation of what happened to their girls has devastated the families. In my opinion, I do believe that these girls and their families will need all of the help that we can give to them. Not only for the now but also in the future when all of this dreadful business is over."

"Dear God," winched Edwina, "we will most certainly do whatever is needed and we will provide everything that these families require to get their lives back to something like it was before Alex Brown and that man, Spike tore their lives apart. If you would please inform the families that they will have our full support for as long as they need it."

William nodded his head in appreciation, then went on to say.

"I am sorry to have to tell you this information, but I think its best you know everything there is to know."

"Yes of course we must know everything, William, please do continue." replied Mr Powell,

William continued.

"I introduced a friend of mine to each of the girls and their families. He is an old colleague of mine from my days with the Constabulary. His name is Inspector Albert Nabney and is one of the best Inspectors that the constabulary has ever had. Inspector Nabney has talked at length with the girls and their families and they have all agreed to make statements to him and they have also agreed that they will testify in court when the time comes. But only on the condition that they have the protection of both you, Andy and you, Edwina."

"By God, they have it, William, trust me they have it!" responded Edwina swiftly.

"What do you suggest we do to help the families now, William." asked Mr Powell.

"First we need to remove them from Belfast as their safety is now paramount because without their cooperation we don't have as strong a case against both Alex Brown and the man, Spike. With your approval I have found a very nice secluded hotel in the Antrim hills, which is just big enough to hold all of the families together. I have also hand-picked three good men as minders to keep the families safe. These three men I would trust with my life. Also I have selected a nurse who will look after Margaret and the others if needed. This nurse I have known for many years and like the three minders, her too I would trust her with my life. There will be no one else staying in the hotel, just the families, so no one will even know they are there. All you both need to do is pick up the bill when this is all over."

"Of course, William, whatever it takes, you just let us know if you need anything," replied Edwina.

"Good…Just as I thought!" said William, "As we speak the families are being transported to the hotel and they will all be there by late afternoon. Everything is in place for their arrival."

"Thank you for everything, William, we couldn't have done this without your considerable assistance," declared Mr Powell.

"Only too willing to help on this occasion, Andy," replied William.

"Now," he continued sternly, "there is something more I must tell you, something I think you will find very interesting. During my investigation of Alex Brown, I discovered that he is not all that he appears to be and s in fact an army deserter. Our Mr Brown was conscripted into the Black Watch in October 1915, but absconded two weeks before Christmas. The army have been looking for him ever since."

"My good God!" erupted Mr Powell, "What more can this man be guilty of?"

Mr Powell's anger and loathing for this man, Alex Brown plain for all to see on his face.

"He will answer for it all believe me, Andy but for now the army will have to wait," declared William.

"Is that wise?" asked Edwina.

"For now it is, Edwina." William then continued," Also in my conversations with Inspector Nabney, he informed me that Alex Brown and the man, Spike have been under investigation for some time. This is due to their activities in the black market and their links with the Dublin based Irish Brotherhood. This group that call themselves the Irish Brotherhood have some dangerous ideas of one day creating an independent Ireland, by fair means or foul. Inspector Nabney is of the opinion that by using these two scoundrels the Constabulary have a good chance of breaking up and arresting a large number of members of the outlawed band called the Irish Brotherhood. The Constabulary are convinced that this Irish Brotherhood are behind several murders that have been committed here in Ulster as well as in Dublin itself. After a long conversation with Inspector Nabney, I have assured him that we will indulge him with his request in return for his help and support when the time comes to arrest both Alex Brown and the man, Spike."

"If you think it best, William, then we will work with Inspector Nabney," said Mr Powell.

"On this occasion I think it's the road best suited to us, Andy," answered William.

Mr Powell nodded his head in agreement as William then continued.

"My first step was to make contact with the man, Spike. I met him by accident of course, two Friday nights ago in a bar in east Belfast called the First & Last. The bar is situated on the Newtownards Road. Spike now knows me as Sam Wallwin. My investigations led me to believe that he can be found in this bar on most evenings and I also discovered that he likes to think that he is a bit more important than he really is. This is a man who is a little too full of himself, who appears to have more cash to splash around than the average drinker in the bar and he likes them all to know it.

He also has this nasty habit of talking down to other drinkers in the bar, the more Guinness he brutishly empties down his throat. Thankfully, this fact is not lost on the other drinkers in the bar. In short, although the man, Spike is too stupid to realise it, most of the other drinkers don't have much time for him. In fact most of the men in the bar would be more than happy to see him brought down a peg or two. Plus the other men in the bar are much older and look at him with some contempt as they dislike the fact that a man of his age is not away fighting for King and country like most of their sons are doing. One thing is to our advantage after he has downed several pints of Guinness, his tongue then becomes a little too loose for his own good. If you get my meaning."

"Isn't you're meeting with this man, Spike a little dangerous William?" enquired Edwina tentatively.

William gave a dry smile answering,

"Well it would be if I were a helpless teenage girl, Edwina, but thankfully I'm not."

William slowly levered open the top of his jacket revealing a holstered hand gun strapped to the side of his chest just below his shoulder.

"It's okay Edwina, don't worry so," said William smartly after noticing the shocked and worried expression that had suddenly flashed across Edwina's face.

"As a retired police Inspector I am legally allowed to arm myself at all times. You must understand, Edwina that my whole working life was spent putting men like Spike behind bars where they belonged. Some of these men that I have arrested over the years have been behind bars for a very long time and I can tell you that most of them don't have me on their Christmas card list," continued William.

Edwina gracefully acknowledged William explanation with a wry smile and a slight nod of her head. William continued.

"After several conversations with Spike it became apparent to me that greed, as well as stupidity play a large part in his life and it would seem that the same may be said for his friend and colleague, Alex Brown. So with this in mind, I began to put my plan into operation. First I let it be known to Spike that I was not hostile to the idea of making a few pounds under the table. I had to convince him that I was more than just a little shady in my dealings when it came to making a little money. It didn't take long for Spike to swallow the bait. Without missing a breath he eagerly agreed with my way of thinking and confirmed that he was also of the same persuasion. That's when I let him know that I could get my hands on as much under the counter Irish Whisky as I could get customers for. This brought a twinkle to his eye. He looked right at me and said, well now, is that a fact? I assured him that it was a fact.

I could sense his hunger to know more and I could see his greed bulging in his eyes with every passing second. That's when he said to me, do you think that we could do a little business together then, Sam. Don't see why not, Spike. I told him. He was now becoming more and more interested in getting his hands on the Whisky. Then he said, Okay, sounds good to me, Sam. Can you leave it with me, I'm sure I will be able to relieve you of a few cases of that Irish you are talking about. Just let me talk it over with a friend of mine first. I smiled and told him. Sure take your time, just let me know if you are really interested, Spike. He then said, Meet me here on Tuesday night, I will have some news for you by then. You sure? I ask. More than sure. He answered. At that point I got to my feet and left the bar.

Come Tuesday evening I made my way to the First and Last bar. To my surprise, when I arrived for my arranged meeting with the man, Spike, he wasn't alone, but was accompanied by none other than Mr Alex Brown. We sat in one of the booths at the far end of the bar, just far enough away from the other drinkers, who prefer to congregate around the bar counter, rather than sit down. Spike introduced me to Alex Brown as Sam Wallwin. We exchanged pleasantries for only a few seconds as Mr Alex Brown seemed impatient to get down to business. Straight away he said, how much Whisky can you get your hands on by next Friday night? I smiled and replied, how many cases do you want? Can you get three cases by Friday?" he asked. I laughed out loudly in his face just to gage his reaction, you understand. Why the laughter? he snarled. Easy to see that Mr Brown doesn't take kindly to people laughing at him.

I looked him in the eye and replied sternly. Are you here to waste my time, Alex, three cases, really!! I wouldn't bother the sweat on my brow to deliver three cases of Whisky to anyone, never mind for a first order. If that's the best you can come up with, then I think it best I go and not waste any more of each other's valuable time. Alex sat back in his seat at this rebuff, then he said, almost apologetically. Well then, Sam Wallwin, how many cases are we talking about before the sweat on your brow is justified?" Alex asked. I sat forward and softly told him, Got to be at least fifteen cases to make it worth my while. I'm not into supplying people with their own personal stock. Fifteen cases is the least I will move, preferably more if you have the outlets to shift it."

This took Alex a little by surprise. I knew then that he was out of his depth and would have to take this offer to someone higher up the pyramid than either him or Spike and that's just what I wanted him to do. I also knew that his greed would push him on. I could see the pound signs beginning to shining bright in his eyes. Then he said, "Okay, Okay, Get me fifteen cases by Friday, I will have sorted out my end by then. You meet Spike here at the bar on Thursday night, at eight-thirty, Spike will tell you where and when okay, Sam?" We then agreed a price for the Whisky and I left. I met with Spike on the Thursday evening and he told me I was to bring the whisky to the back gates of your bakery at 3am Saturday morning. I agreed and we parted.

Myself, along with a retired colleague of mine from the constabulary, Sargent Rigby, brought the whisky on a small horse-drawn cart to the back of the bakery at the allotted time. We were met at the gates by Spike, Alex Brown and two other men. One was called Paddy Murphy the other called himself Shaun O'Brian, both men spoke with a strong Dublin twang. From listening to them I formed the opinion that these two men were based on the other side of town, the Falls Road area I believe. So I had Inspector Nabney do a little digging and his investigations confirmed that both men were well known to the Constabulary as activists in the Nationalist Dunlin centred Organisation, The Irish Brotherhood. It is also believed that these two men were heavily involved in the Easter Rising of 1916. In Dublin."

> (- The Irish Brotherhood was later to become the I.R.A. - From this point on Connie always referred to the Brotherhood as the I.R.A. saying… that's the name that everyone would know them by.)

"The I.R.A." said a shocked Mr Powell.

"Afraid so, Andy," replied William.

"I didn't think they were still active these days," said Mr Powell anxiously.

"Trust me, Andy they are. The Constabulary has suspected I.R.A involvement in Black Market activities for some time now," added William.

"Good God, what next?" muttered Mr Powell under his breath.

William continued with the outline of his plan.

"Alex and Spike loaded the whisky from my cart onto a rickety old hay cart which was pulled by a small black pony that the two Dubliners had arrived on. Then the man called Paddy paid me the fee for the whisky that I had agreed with Alex. The man, Shaun O'Brian climbed up onto the cart and took the reins in his hand. Nice to do business with you I told them. Then the man called Paddy approached me, he took hold of my arm and took me to one side and whispered, Look Sam, both you and I know that we don't need these two jokers in this deal anymore, now do we. I played along, if you say so Paddy. I replied, adding, it makes no difference to me one way or the other, both Alex and Spike are in this on your side not mine. True he replied, then he said, I think that they have outlived their usefulness to the both of us, so here's the thing, Sam, I want you to meet me later today, at around three this afternoon in the Kitchen bar in Belfast. Do you know where it is Sam? I told him that I did, then he said, excellent, be there. There are a few some people I want you to meet, okay Sam?"

I assured Paddy that I would be there, Paddy smiled and said, good man, Sam. At that I climbed up on my cart and left the back yard of your bakery, Edwina. That afternoon, after a few hours' sleep, I made my way into the centre of Belfast and arrived at the Kitchen Bar just after three. There, sitting at a table to the back of the bar and to the right of the bar counter, I saw Paddy and Shaun sitting at a table, they were with two other men. I I approached their table slowly. Paddy saw me and called out, Come Sam, join us. Paddy pulled out a chair from the table as I neared the group of men. I sat down beside Paddy facing the bar counter, I removed my hat, placing it on the table in front of me. Paddy then began to introduce me to the two other men that were sitting at the table. Paddy pointed to the man on his right and said, "This is Cornelius O'Hanlon." Then pointing to the other man he said," And this is Finbarr O'Leary." Both men were siting with their backs turned towards the wall.

Paddy introduced me to both men saying, this is the Sam Wallwin, the man I have been telling you about. Both men extended their hands towards me and one after the other shook my hand firmly, delivering their greeting in the strongest Dublin brogue. Finbarr was a big man, over six foot tall with a grim look about his face, Cornelius on the other hand was a small man in stature and was wearing rimless glasses, he looked more like my bank manager, than an I.R.A. Commander. Paddy, said Finbarr, order pints of Guinness for everyone. I sat there exchanging polite pleasantries with these three Dubliners until Paddy returned with a tray of Guinness. I decided to make a determined effort to take in my surroundings, as I needed to make sure that there was no one in the bar that might recognise me from my days with the Constabulary. Immediately my attention was drawn to four men directly to our left, two of the men were standing with their backs resting against the bar counter, the other two men had placed themselves at the opposite end of the bar counter. Every few seconds these men would glance in our direction, then quickly diverting their gaze to other areas of the bar room, as if studying the other drinkers. Each time the bar door would open, all four men would instantly turn their heads to see who it was that had entered the bar. This activity brought me to the conclusion that these four men were in fact bodyguards for both Cornelius and Finbarr. This being true, then Finbarr and Cornelius would be placed higher up the pyramid than I had first thought, in fact this would place them somewhere in the region of local battalion Commanders of the I.R.A."

"Really William!" said a shocked Andy Powell loudly.

"Yes really, Andy, we are talking top of the tree here," added William

He continued with his story.

"After ten minutes or so of idle chit-chat, the man, Cornelius decided to get down to business. We were very pleased, if somewhat surprised, by the swiftness in which you were able to deliver the whisky, Sam. I try to please, you know what they say, always keep the customer happy. I replied calmly. Both Finbarr and Cornelius quickly exchanged glances, then Cornelius said, I have to say Sam, we were very impressed with the standard of the merchandise, it was excellent, not like some of the goods we have received in the past. At this point the man, Finbarr joined in the conversation, explaining. A lot of the whisky we have acquired recently has not been in the best of condition, the bottles tend to be water damaged, or fire damaged, or both, labels ripped, some labels half missing, or in fact no labels at all at times, but we can still find ways of shifting the stock. So when Paddy and Shaun told us about you, we were very interested in meeting you indeed, Sam. The only problem that we have is this, Sam, the price you want for the Whisky. We think it a bit high, a little off putting, shall we say. The only thing that has held our interest is the fact that you tell us that the quantity you can deliver is large, really large. That fact alone makes us very interested indeed, Sam. Cornelius then paused for a few seconds, then he asked me, I take it that the quantity and quality won't be an issue.

Not in the least Cornelius, as much as you can shift. I replied. Finbarr then entered the conversation. Can I ask you how it is that you can get your hands on so much whisky and in such pristine condition? Tell me, where does it come from, Sam? The last delivery was excellent, not even as much as the slightest damage on the boxes? How is that Sam? I wasn't fooled by his friendly, but inquisitive approach. I smiled broadly and replied, well now Finbarr, if I were to tell you that, then you wouldn't need me, now would you? He smiled back at me saying, now that's very true, Sam. Again I smiled confidently, letting them know that they were not going to intimidate me in any way. Finbarr continued, you can guarantee us the quantity and quality can you then, Sam? Like I said before, not a problem. I told him bullishly. Good, said Finbarr, Just what we wanted to hear, Sam. I think it's looking like we are going to have a long and profitable alliance, don't you think, Sam. I picked up my pint and held it high towards the four Dubliners saying, here's to our new profitable alliance then boys, then I took a long drink from my glass of Guinness. We then came to an agreement on the amount and price of the next delivery, one hundred cases of whisky they wanted and they wanted it delivered by next Saturday.

The time of delivery is to be 3am. I told them that I would only hand over the whisky on my side of the Queens Bridge, as for me it was safer than going across town, this being my first big exchange with them. They reluctantly agreed. So I arranged to make the delivery to them on a patch of wasteland by the deep water near the East Slipway of the Harland & Wolf Shipyard. I told them it would be a quiet and secluded place to conclude our business, no prying eyes wondering what we were up to. I went on to tell them that I would be using five small horse drawn hay carts to deliver the goods, each cart would be manned by two men.

I explained that by using this method of transport, rather than motorised trucks, there would be less chance of drawing interest from prying eyes. I also told them that the carts would arrive at the drop zone at fifteen minute intervals, avoiding the creation of a convoy. They agreed and decided that they would use the same transport system when they picked up the goods. Finbarr then asked me if I would be there in person on the night to seal the deal. I told him that I would and that I would be on the fourth Hay Cart. I then finished my Guinness, made my farewells and left.

Obviously I will need a few good men to man my hay-carts for the delivery, that's where Inspector Nabney comes in. He has assured me that he will arrange for men from his unit to man the hay carts for the delivery. Also Inspector Nabney will have extra men hidden around the drop area waiting to move in once the exchange has been made. He expects to make multiple arrests on the evening, hopefully ending the activities of this I.R.A. Battalion for good. Needless to say we will all be armed on the evening, as we know only too well that they will all be armed. I have also made arrangements to meet with Alex and Spike in the First & Last Bar on the Friday evening before the drop. Inspector Nabney has agreed to place four of his men in the bar and that's when Alex and Spike will be arrested. Inspector Nabney feels that in addition to the multiple rape, assault and larceny charges on Alex and Spike he can also get them both on Black Market activities and colluding with an illegal organisation i.e. The I.R.A. thus making sure that they both go away for a very long time."

"Well you seem to have got everything under control, William," announced Mr Powell confidently.

"I think everything is covered, Andy," answered William. "Next time we meet, Andy this dreadful business will have been concluded satisfactorily."

"Thank God for that!' interjected Edwina.

With those last words from Edwina, and all business concluded, all three conspirators parted.

CHAPTER 12

On the Wednesday morning, directly after the Sunday lunch date of Edwina, Andy Powell and William Hastings, the man, Spike unexpectedly turned up at the bakery, just as Alex Brown was finishing his night shift.

"Spike!" Alex exclaimed loudly, "what the hell are you doing here?"

"We need to talk, Alex," said a worried Spike, as he took Alex by the arm, pulling him forcefully towards the middle of the courtyard.

"What is it Spike?" enquired Alex.

Spike looked all around nervously, then he said,

"Not here, Alex."

Both men then moved quickly away from the bakery gates to a more secluded spot at the end of the bakery wall, adjacent to an old disused paddock where the bakery shire horses at one time were put out to pasture.

"Come on, Spike, spit it out!" snapped Alex rudely, as he really didn't want to be seen with Spike anywhere the bakery.

"Look, Alex, something isn't right, there's something strange going on and your bosses Powell and the bitch Edwina are behind it."

"Something strange like what, Spike, what do you know?" roared Alex,

Alex began to fidget nervously, worried what it was that Spike had to tell him, because judging by Spike's uneasy behaviour, something must be very wrong.

"Listen, Alex, I went to look up our little play friend, Sylvia on Sunday afternoon, just to let her know that I was still keeping an eye on her and to make sure that she was keeping her mouth firmly shut. But their house was empty. Sylvia, her sister and her mother all gone. It would seem that they have vanished off the face of the earth. They are nowhere to be seen and even the neighbours say that they haven't seen them for some time. But the puzzle thickens, Alex. I just couldn't understand why Sylvia's family were not at home, where can they possibly be? This raised my curiosity, so I went to check on the other girls that we had a little fun with, Alex. Believe it or not, the same situation has repeated itself at all of the other houses that I went to observe. Mary Riley and her family, Margaret O'Brian and her family, Bridgette Kelly and her family, also Theresa Campbell and her family, they are all in the land of the missing, Alex, none of them are anywhere to be found or seen."

"Christ, Spike, that's very odd, why should they all vanish at the same time? Do you have any idea where they have all gone?" asked Alex, his concern now growing.

"None at all Alex," answered Spike, "but that's not the end of the mystery either, Alex."

"No?" asked Alex uneasily.

"No." answered Spike, "I made a few inquiries, I chatted to several of the neighbours, but mostly they said that they had no idea where they had gone. One lady did however tell me that she saw Bridgette Kelly's family get into a large black motor car that was being driven by a well-dressed man. I asked her if they saw what this man looked like. The description she gave me matches that of our new friend, Sam Wallwin, but more on him later, Alex. The lady told me that this man first came earlier in the day and that he stayed for an hour or more before he left. She said that he came back later that day and that the family left in his car with their bags fully packed. As far as Sylvia is concerned, Alex, I got lucky there, although none of the neighbours would tell my anything about the family's sudden disappearance, but as I was about to leave the area, a young boy approached me. He told me that Sylvia and her family had left with their bags packed several weeks ago, after a visit from Mr Powell and Edwina no less."

"Damn it, Spike, this doesn't sound good, sounds like those bitches have opened their bloody mouths and told Edwina and Powell everything."

Alex anger was now reaching boiling point.

"It gets worse, Alex," continued Spike, "I have a friend that I see sometimes in the First and Last bar, well he's more of an acquaintance than a friend."

"Get on with it, Spike, who cares what he is to you, what did he tell you?"

"My friend's name is Albert Wright, he works as a drinks waiter in the lounge bar of the Grand Central Hotel. He was working at lunch time one Sunday a few weeks ago, when our friend Sam Wallwin came in to the hotel bar. Albert recognised him instantly, as he had seen him with me in the First and Last bar and knew that he was called Sam Wallwin. Albert told me that Sam was joined in the lounge bar by a man and a woman. He told me that he overheard the woman being introduced to Sam as Edwina Keane. The man that made the introduction was a man that Sam Wallwin called Andy. Albert didn't get his second name, but if he was with Edwina, then it's a safe bet that this man Andy, is none other than Andy Powell."

Alex's expression quickly changed to one of panic.

"What the hell is Edwina and Andy Powell doing meeting with Sam Wallwin in the Grand?" snarled Alex sharply.

"There's more, Alex," added Spike, "our friend Sam Wallwin is a fake, because he had booked the table for lunch in the name of William Hastings and that's our friend Sam Wallwin's real name."

"This isn't good, Spike. Why would he pretend to be called Sam Wallwin and be holding meetings with Powell and Edwina?" seethed Alex,

"Still more I'm afraid, Alex," added Spike, "my informant tells me that another waiter at the Grand recognised William Hastings and he told Albert that he knows our friend Sam only too well, but not as Sam Wallwin. This second waiter knew him by his real name, Inspector William Hastings. He's a fucking retired Peeler, Alex."

"Shit, Spike, is this waiter sure it's him?"

"Oh he's sure alright, Alex, because Inspector William Hastings arrested him several years ago putting him behind bars."

"Jesus Christ, Spike and we have introduced him to the fucking I.R.A. This is bad, Spike, really bloody bad!" growled a frightened Alex.

"What can we do Alex?" snivelled Spike, as he wiped his nose with the back of his hand.

"We have to try to put things right, Spike. We must get hold of Paddy and Shaun as soon as we can. We must let them know what's going on, before things go too far. The last thing we need, Spike is the I.R.A. after us," moaned Alex.

Spike shuffled his feet anxiously and again wiped his nose with the back of his hand, then he said,

"I know where we can find both Paddy and Shaun. They are always in the Crown bar in town on Thursday afternoons."

Spike's throat was now getting dryer with every word that fell from his lips.

"Okay, Spike meet me there tomorrow at one thirty, but let's not take any chances until then. It would be best if you moved out of your house and stay out of sight as we don't know if the law are out to lift us before they go for the big boys," said Alex.

"I know what you are saying, Alex," said Spike. "I spoke to Sam on Saturday night in the First and Last bar and he arranged for us to meet him there this Friday evening. I now understand why. That's when they are going to lift us, Alex."

"Maybe, Spike, but let's not take any chances. Best thing to do is for the both of us to disappear until we meet with Paddy and Shaun on Thursday," said Alex.

"Sure, Alex, no problem, I'm gone, trust me, I'm well gone!" said Spike.

"The same goes for me, Spike. It's best no one sees us for the next few days. Don't try to contact me ok, Spike? Now go and I'll see you on Thursday," said Alex.

On the Thursday afternoon Spike arrived at the Crown bar in the centre of Belfast just before one thirty in the afternoon, sheepishly he prised opened the door to the bar and glanced inside. There sat at the bar were Paddy and Shaun, but there was no sign of Alex. Spike quickly closed the bar door and decided to wait outside until Alex turned up. He held no desire to face Paddy and Shaun on his own, not with the news that had to be delivered to them that day. Spike rested his back against the bars outside wall and waited for Alex to arrive. Some ten very anxious minutes had passed before Spike saw Alex walking towards the bar.

"Both Paddy and Shaun are inside, Alex," said Spike in a low voice as Alex approached.

"Okay, Spike, let's face the music, let's see if we can put this mess right before things get beyond redemption," replied Alex with some uncertainty.

Both men nervously entered the bar and slowly approached Paddy and Shaun. As they came closer to where they were sitting, Paddy spotted them coming out of the corner of his eye. Immediately Paddy swivelled around on his barstool until he was facing in their direction.

"To what do we owe this pleasure then, boys? We don't often see you two this side of the Queen's Bridge," joked Paddy.

"We need to talk," replied Alex in a soft passive voice.

"Okay, talk away, boys," added Paddy, not realising that anything was amiss.

Alex took a deep breath, braced himself and said,

"Have you arranged to do any more business with Sam?"

Paddy laughed and looked at Shaun saying,

"Ah Jesus, Shaun, looks like the boys are feeling a little left out."

"It does that, Paddy," sniggered Shaun mockingly, before taking a large swallow of his Guinness.

"This is bloody serious, Paddy," fumed Alex. "Have you made any arrangements to do business with Sam?"

Alex's voice was now getting louder with every word. Paddy moved himself forward on his bar stool, his manner now changed to one of worried anger. Paddy looked straight into Alex's eyes and ask firmly.

"What's all this about, Alex, is there something I should know?"

"Christ, Paddy, just answer me, have you made a deal with Sam?"

Alex was now becoming more and more anxious,

Paddy now sensed that Alex was about to deliver the kind of news that he could well do without hearing. Paddy responded to Alex's question with a hint of uneasiness in his voice.

"Yes we have, Alex. I took Sam to meet the top brass and they were most impressed, so we did a deal and the whisky is being delivered early on Saturday morning. Does this create a problem somehow, Alex? I do hope not," added Paddy forcefully.

"Ah God, Paddy, you must believe, I didn't know about him, I swear it, Paddy. I didn't know!" said Alex.

Beads of sweat were now beginning to appear on his brow.

"Know what about him, Alex?" snapped Paddy worriedly.

Alex took a deep breath, steadied himself and replied.

"Sam's a fake, Paddy, his real name is William Hastings. He is, or was, a police inspector, we're not sure which, but we are sure that he is working for my boss, Edwina."

Paddy jumped to his feet and roughly grabbed Alex by the lapels of his jacket and promptly manhandled him across the bar room and into one of the booths opposite the bar counter. Alex ended up on his back on top of the table inside the booth. Both men were quickly followed into the booth by Shaun, who was holding Spike by the scruff of the neck, forcing him into the booth.

Paddy then asked Alex,

"Tell me why on earth would this Edwina have a police inspector investigating you, Alex? This Edwina of yours has not set a police Inspector onto you for just pilfering the few backed goods that you have been passing onto us every week. There's got to be more to it than that I'm thinking, Alex, so enlighten me if you will!" snapped Paddy furiously.

"There is, Paddy! Indeed there is." wheezed Alex because Paddy's hands were now pushing down hard on his throat.

"Talk quickly, Alex," ordered Paddy.

Alex made another loud wheezing sound, followed by uncontrollable coughing and spluttering as he struggled to get his words out. Paddy loosened his grip on Alex's throat, allowing his garbled speech to be understood. Paddy listened in disbelief as Alex told the loathsome story of what he and Spike had been up to at the Bakery with the young girls that worked there. On hearing the whole dreadful story from Alex, Paddy slowly released his grip on him and stood back looking down at him with revulsion, then turning towards Spike he asked angrily.

"Is this all bloody true?"

Spike shuffled his feet nervously and lowering his head he answered shamefaced,

"Yes, it's all true, Paddy. God forgive us, it's all true."

"Mother of God." gasped Paddy, "You two bloody disgust me."

Shaun then pushed Spike roughly with both hands, knocking him off his feet and unto the bench on the other side of the booth. Shaun then turned towards Paddy and said,

"Jesus, Mary and Joseph, Paddy! What the hell do we do with them now?"

Paddy sat on the edge of the small table inside the booth, plunging his head in his hands, masking the despondent look that was now firmly fixed on his face. After a few seconds he got to his feet and reached out towards Alex, pulling him onto his feet.

"Right you two," Paddy bellowed furiously, "only one thing for it, both of you will have to come with us, my Commanders will want to know what you both have been up to. Also you will need to explain to them the fucking hole that you have dropped them in as a consequence of your disgusting actions. Trust me when I tell you, Alex, my Commanders won't be best bloody pleased with you two. The last thing they wanted is to have the constabulary on their tail."

Both Alex and Spike dragged their pitiful bodies out of the booth, Alex adjusting his clothing back to some kind of normality. Within seconds the four men had left the Crown Bar and had set off for the Falls Road. For Alex and Spike this was a dangerous journey in more ways than one, as the Falls Road was a place that normally they would never go, as both men were Protestants and the Falls Road was the heartland of the republican community in Belfast.

It was around three in the afternoon when the tram reached the tram depot at the top of the Falls Road. Upon arrival Paddy and Shaun quickly ushered Alex and Spike off the tram. Once on the footpath, Paddy turned to Shaun telling him to go and fetch Finbarr and Cornelius and to bring them to Murphy's Bar.

"Tell them we have news they need to hear and nothing else for now, okay, Shaun?" said Paddy.

"Sure, Paddy, will you be alright with these two?" asked Shaun.

"Yes I'll be fine Shaun. I'll take these two to Murphy's and we will meet you there, in say, fifteen minutes. Now go!" ordered Paddy.

"Fifteen minutes it is then Paddy," replied Shaun.

Murphy's Bar at the top of Falls Road was a well-known meeting place for I.R.A. men in that particular part of Belfast. Paddy was well aware that Murphy's bar was a safe house and that they could carry out their business without worrying about any prying eyes. Murphy himself was also a Dublin man and a long time operative in the I.R.A. He was known to all as Spud. The bar was once owned outright by the I.R.A. and was used as a front for their activities but Spud Murphy took control of the bar a few years ago. It had been passed onto him as a thank you from the I.R.A. for services rendered over many years. Murphy's bar was only a short walk from the tram depot so it only took a few minutes for Paddy and his two charges to reach the place. Paddy entered the bar, pushing Alex and Spike through the door first. When all three men had entered the bar, Paddy immediately called out,

"Spud, we will need the back room for a bit. Finbarr and Cornelius are on their way."

"Oh Jesus, Paddy, things must be serious if the bosses are on their way," shouted Spud.

Spud was of course referring to Finbarr and Cornelius, Finbarr was the Commander in Chief of the first Battalion West Belfast Brigade and Cornelius was the Commander in Chief of the second Battalion West Belfast Brigade. These are men that you really don't want to cross or even upset, if you want to see the sun rise the next day. Spud replied to Paddy's request.

"Ah sure now, Paddy, the key is in the door, just help yourself to the back room. I'll wait for themselves to get here then I'll bring you all a drop of the black stuff through, okay Paddy?"

Paddy opened the door to the back room and pushed both Alex and Spike through the door before entering the room himself and closing the door behind him. It wasn't long before Shaun arrived at the bar with Finbarr, Cornelius and four other men. As the two Commanders entered through the double doors of Murphy's bar, the whole of the bar room immediately fell silent as a mark of respect. Spud smartly stepped forward from behind the bar to welcome both Commanders.

"Ah now to be sure, It's a huge pleasure to have you both here. Come right through to the back room. Paddy and two other men are already there waiting for you."

Spud's enthusiasm at having both of the West Belfast's Brigade Commanders in his bar was there for all to see.

"It's good to see you again too, Spud, it's been a while," said Cornelius as he shook Spud warmly by the hand.

"That it has, Sir," replied Spud,

Cornelius then said,

"It's looking more and more likely that we will be in need of your services very soon, Spud."

"Just say the word, Sir, you can depend on me."

"Good man, Spud," said Cornelius with a smile.

Spud then showed Cornelius, Finbarr, Shaun and the other four minders to the back room.

Cornelius, Finbarr, Shaun and two of the minders entered the back room closing the door behind them. The other two minders remained outside, standing either side of the doorway, their eyes fixed straight ahead, looking back into the bar room. The back room at Murphy's bar was a small room and was without windows. It was furnished only with an oblong wooden table and six wooden chairs. Alex and Spike were sat at the long side of the table with their backs towards the door. Cornelius and Finbarr were sat on the opposite side of the table to both Alex and Spike, facing the door. Paddy was positioned at the end of the table to Cornelius's right. Shaun was placed at the other end of the table to Finbarr's left. The two minders that had accompanied Shaun and the Commanders to the bar had placed themselves in the doorway inside the room.

"What's all this about, Paddy?" enquired Cornelius.

"It's not good, Sir, not bloody good at all." replied Paddy.

"Well then, Paddy, I think it best you bloody well fill me in about what's been going on," snapped Cornelius.

"I think you need to hear the full story from Alex, Sir," answered Paddy.

Cornelius's temper was rising by the second and he banged hard down on the wooden table, then roared loudly.

"Listen to me, Paddy, somebody better fill me in and fucking quickly!"

Paddy turned towards Alex and roughly pushed him on the arm prompting him to explain to the Commanders.

"Go on then, Alex, tell the Commanders what's been going on," ordered Paddy.

Alex took a deep breath and began to inform Cornelius and Finbarr what they had discovered about Sam Wallwin. Alex informed the Commanders that the man he had introduced to them as Sam Wallwin was or at one time had been a police Inspector by the name of Inspector William Hastings. Furthermore Alex went on to inform the Commanders the real reason why he and Spike were being investigated in the first place. Once Alex had concluded his despicable tale both Cornelius and Finbarr fell back in their chairs in disgust at what they had just heard. After a few strained seconds had past, Cornelius lunged forwards in his chair, saying,

"Jesus Christ almighty, Alex, are you bloody well serious? Are you really telling me that you and that low-life beside you had physically abused all these young girls? As a result of your depravity this woman, Edwina then got involved, subsequently getting you both investigated, Inspector Hastings to become implicated and now we have the constabulary sniffing around us like dogs after bones, something we could well do without, Alex"

Cornelius's temper was almost at breaking point as he continued his verbal rant on both Alex and Spike for several minutes.

"Not only have you brought the law down on us but you even introduced a bloody Inspector to Paddy resulting in said Inspector making contact with myself and Finbarr. I have to tell you, Alex, what you have done is unforgiveable and now you are going to have to put things right. That goes for this bloody woman, Edwina, whoever she is."

Alex sat in silence, his head drooped in shame, Spike, like the snake he is, slithered deeper into his chair, hiding his face from the glaring stare from both Cornelius and Finbarr.

"Mother of God, boys, this is an awful bloody mess you have dropped us in this day," growled Cornelius,

For a few chilling seconds the room fell silent, everyone waiting for Cornelius's next outburst. This chilling silence was suddenly broken when Cornelius lunged forward in his chair and said calmly,

"Damage limitation time I think boys. It's obvious that this bloody whisky exchange in the early hours of Saturday morning is a setup, a fucking Brit trap. You ask me this fucking Hastings man in conjunction with the Royal Irish Constabulary are out to rid the streets of Belfast of the Brotherhood (I.R.A.) but we can't allow that to happen, can we, Paddy?"

Paddy shook his head in agreement as Cornelius continued,

"Paddy, get yourself down to the place where the exchange is to take place, have a good look around and try to work out what they have in mind for us. Try to work out what you think their most likely trap would be and find a way for us to make a safe getaway because we have no choice. We have to show up on the day, there's no way we can run from this, we have to let the Constabulary know that we are here to stay. We will meet back here tonight at seven o'clock ok, Paddy?"

Again Paddy nodded in agreement and Cornelius then turned his attention towards Shaun, whilst at the same time pointing directly at Alex and Spike.

"Shaun take these two foul creatures to the safe house, keep them there until it's time to go to the exchange because they will be coming with us to the drop on Saturday morning."

Cornelius then promptly turned to face Finbarr and said,

"Finbarr, after Saturday morning has been dealt with we will all have to disappear back to Dublin for a while. It wouldn't be safe for any of us to remain in this city, not after what we have to do this Saturday morning, by then our time here will have come to an end. You need to inform the High Command in Dublin of our situation as soon as possible, Finbarr. Tell them that we intend to deal with this unforeseen setback in our own way and that once we have put it to bed we will have to return to Doblin and leave Belfast that very day.

"I'll get right on it, Cornelius," replied Finbarr as he got to his feet and left the room.

Cornelius then told Paddy and Shaun to keep a close eye on Alex and Spike because sooner rather than later, both men would have to make amends for their sickening behaviour at the bakery as well as their greed and stupidity. Once arrangements for them all to meet that evening back at Murphy's bar had been made, Cornelius and his minders left Murphy's bar.

Later that evening, Paddy returned to Murphy's bar with a full and detailed report from his inspection of the drop zone that William Hastings had picked out for the whisky exchange. Paddy explained to the others that the spot that Hastings had picked out was nothing more than a stony, rubble filled secluded patch of waste ground which was hidden from view, not only from the end of the road that steered you towards it, but also from the Queens Bridge itself. The reason for its seclusion and its obstructed view from all points, was that it was surrounded by several old and crumbling dockside boathouses.

This segment of forgotten land was adjacent to the river Lagan, situated half way down a small cobbled road on the East Belfast side of the Queens Bridge. This small road had only one way in and one way out and this fact made it impossible for the I.R.A. hay carts to withdraw from the exchange in any other way. Their only option was to travel back up the cobbled road then cross the Queens Bridge from the East Belfast side. Paddy informed everyone that in his opinion, the whole thing was nothing more than a set-up, a trap. He then told the meeting that he had followed the road to its end, eager to find alternative means of escape. At the end of this small road Paddy discovered a dilapidated old quay, saying that it looked as though it hadn't been used in a very long time. After some more investigation Paddy found out that this almost discarded minor quay was at one time used on occasions by tug boats working at the docks of Harland & Wolf, even then it was only used when all other docks and quays were fully in use, which wasn't that often.

Paddy informed his Commanders that in his opinion the Constabulary would place most of their officers across the Queens Bridge on the City side, cutting off their escape. That's when the officers that were manning Inspector Hastings hay carts would close in behind them, leaving the I.R.A.'s hay carts trapped in the middle of the Queen's Bridge with nowhere to go. The only option left to would be to shoot it out with the constabulary. Paddy's idea was this, for the I.R.A. party to go to the drop zone as normal, that way they wouldn't raise any cause for concern amongst the law officers that undoubtedly would be observing their every move from their hiding places. Then, after they had concluded the business that they had come for, the I.R.A. party would make good their escape by tug boat. Paddy had arranged for a tug boat Captain, who was sympathetic to the I.R.A. cause, to have his boat moored by the old quay at the end of the road, he was then to take the I.R.A. party down the river some distance then to turn and cross the river allowing them to disembark on the city side of the river. Paddy had also organised transport that would be waiting to transport them and the whisky back to the relative safety of the Falls Road. There they would remain until the time was right for them to begin their return to Dublin. Needless to say, Paddy's plan was welcomed by Cornelius. All that was left to be done now was to select the operatives that were to go on the mission.

It was now twelve, midnight on the Friday evening, just a few hours before the whisky exchange was to take place. The six I.R.A. foot-soldiers, including Spud Murphy himself that had been selected for the evenings undertaking had now arrived at Murphy's bar. Cornelius, Finbarr, Shaun, Paddy, Alex and Spike were already at the bar and were waiting in the back room. The minute the other five foot soldiers arrived at the bar, they were ushered swiftly into the back room of the bar by Spud Murphy. There they all remained until it was time to leave for their meeting with the forces of the Crown, it wasn't long before the appointed time of departure had arrived and the I.R.A. hit-squad clambered upon the truck that was to be used to transport them from the Falls Road to a quiet corner of the city. Once there they would take charge of the hay carts that would be waiting for them. The driver of the truck would then drive the truck to a pre-appointed place by the river. There he would wait for his comrades to return, after they had carried out their vengeful action upon the representatives of the Crown. Cornelius, Finbarr and the rest of the night party were soon on their way to pick up the three hay-carts. Cornelius had decided that afternoon that they would arrive at the appointed exchange area a lot earlier than they would have if this had been a normal transaction. Cornelius needed to have time to look around the area and convince himself that Paddy's plan was a good one. After Cornelius had surveyed the scene for himself and talked with the tug boat captain, he thanked Paddy for his well thought out plan. With everything now in place the night party prepared themselves for the events to come. Then suddenly breaking through the stillness and floating eerily towards them on the fresh early morning sea air, came the unmistakeable sound of the steady clip clop of a pony's hooves tapping gently on the old cobbles of the lonely road. This unmistakable sound had now merged with the grinding of the iron rims of the carts wheels as they crunched down heavily on the old cobbled road. Cornelius and the waiting I.R.A. operatives now knew that their quarry would soon be upon them.

"Get ready, boys. The first cart is on its way," smiled Cornelius callously.

It was only a few minutes later when the first of the hay carts pulled into the waste ground, it quickly positioned itself opposite Cornelius and his carts. Cornelius was eager not to raise any suspicions in the minds of the young undercover police officers, so he moved quickly toward them to welcome them. One thing that did shock him a little, was the young age of the officers.

"You've made it then, boys?" Cornelius said with a smile on his face.

"Yes, we're here alright," replied one of the young undercover constables.

Cornelius continued to make idol chit chat with the two young officers, trying his best to put them at ease. Then the sound of the second cart could be heard coming down the cobbled road. Cornelius stepped back as the second cart pulled into the clearing and came to a halt beside the first cart.

"And a good-morning to both you boys," joked Cornelius loudly.

Both officers on the second cart were just as young as the two on the first one, the youngest looking no more that nineteen, the oldest no more than twenty-two. Cornelius moved quickly forward towards the newly arrived hay-carts, clutching a packet of cigarettes in one hand and a small silver hip flask in the other, his intention to engage the officers, putting them at their ease and eventually encouraging them down from their carts.

"Come on, boys, climb down from there and have a smoke and a warming tot with us while we wait for the others to arrive," said Cornelius.

All four of the young officers glanced questioningly at each other, unsure of what to do. Their thinking was, if we refuse a smoke and a tot, will that make Cornelius think that we might be police officers?

"Come on, boys, climb down from there and take a smoke and a tot, after all we are all sort of business partners here, now aren't we?"

Cornelius continued to smile broadly at the officers, trying his best to make his approach seem calm and unthreatening. Suddenly one of the constables, not wishing to raise any concern in the mind of their hosts, jumped down from his cart and replied,

"I guess we are all partners here on this night and a smoke would be most welcome, so thank you for your kind invitation."

The young officer then turned towards the other officers and nodded to them to follow his lead and climb down from their carts, in order to join Cornelius for a welcome smoke and a tot of whisky. As the other constables were climbing down from their carts, the grinding sound of the next cart could be clearly heard approaching the waste ground where the drop was to be made. The next cart pulled up just as Cornelius was handing out his cigarettes to the young officers, who were now all standing in a group. The two officers who were in charge of the third cart, also climbed down from their cart and joined the group. Cornelius was quick to follow up his cigarette hand out with two hip-flasks filled with whisky.

"That's it, boys, light them up and take a stiff swig from the flask. Enjoy, boys, after all we're all friends here!" he said with a smile.

All six of the young officers began to relax and began to chat openly with the others that were stood around waiting for the rest of the hay carts to arrive.

Cornelius continued to chat with the group of constables and a relaxed atmosphere now existed between the Law Officers and the I.R.A. men. Sadly this air of contentment was to be short lived. Without making it look too obvious, Cornelius, Finbarr, Paddy, Shaun and Spud, had slowly moved themselves to a position behind the young Officers. Two of the I.R.A. operatives were in place in front of the Constables, chatting freely to them. Cornelius's men now surrounded the young Officers, then with a nod from Cornelius, all of the I.R.A. men pulled their revolvers from under their coats. Two of the Officers quickly realised what was happening and as they attempted to pull their revolvers from under their coats, they were quickly knocked to the ground by Spud Murphy and Paddy.

"Not a good idea, boys," declared Finbarr loudly.

Finbarr quickly instructed three of his men to take the carts that were loaded with the whisky and transfer the goods onto the tug boat. Cornelius then moved forward towards the young officers, who were now completely surrounded with nowhere to go.

"Ah, boys, what can I tell you?" Cornelius grinned tauntingly,

Cornelius then ordered Paddy to take the officers' firearms from them. Paddy wasted no time in disarming the young officers, six members of the Brotherhood (I.R.A.) then approached the young officers. Each one of the I.R.A. gun men quickly positioned themselves behind the young constables, binding the hands of each of them tightly behind their backs. Once their hands were secured safely they were moved to the centre of the clearing, positioned in a straight line and then forced onto their knees. Six of the I.R.A. gun men, Finbarr, Paddy, Shaun, Spud Murphy and two other operative stood behind each of the young officers, waiting for Cornelius's signal. It took but only a few seconds for Cornelius to give the nod to his six henchmen, prompting each one of the gun men to pull a large black cloth bag from their pocket and place it over the head of the officer in front of him. Each of the I.R.A. assassins then took hold of the left shoulder of the officer that knelt before him with their left hand. Gripping it tightly, forcing the young officers to maintain their position on their knees. In their right hand each of the I.R.A. assassins held a revolver. The heads of these young men were brutally forced to the downwards position. A revolver was then placed at the back of their heads, awaiting Cornelius's order.

All six of the young constables began to shake violently, their breathing became rapid and uncontrolled, and the cloth bags covering their heads were now being sucked deeper and deeper into their open mouths with every terrifying breath they took. To a man, the constables pleaded in vain for their lives to be spared, these pleas were met with cruel laughter. Suddenly the air was filled with the acid stench of human urine and faeces. One by one the young petrified and traumatised constables felt their bodies plummet into a violent feral shock, causing them to lose all control over their bodily functions. Garbled and mumbled prayers along with uncontrollable sobbing and the sound of vicious vomiting could be heard coming from under the cloth bags. Cornelius stepped forward and without showing remorse or compassion of any kind towards these six young men that he was about to have murdered, he said mockingly,

"Ah boys, what can I say? You have no one but yourselves to blame for the predicament you now find yourselves in. After all, no one forced you to take the King's shilling. Each of you did that willingly and I am sure that each of you had a smile on your faces as you did so. But by surrendering freedom to do the bidding of the King, then you have laughed in the face of every true Irishman that loves this Island. Sadly boys, the time is now for you to face the consequences of your actions. My condolences to your families and pray the Lord takes mercy on your souls"

Within a split second of these sickening words leaving Cornelius's mouth, he had nodded grimly in the direction of the six primed executioners, sanctioning the terrible deed that they were about to carry out. With this last act of heartless apathy six chilling shots instantly rang out in unison, disturbing the otherwise calm of this Belfast night. Before the ringing of the shots had faded the bodies of the young officers lay crumpled in a heap on the ground, wallowing in a pool of their own blood that was now mixed with the human waste that already had tainted the ground beneath them.

"Oh my good God, what's just happened here, what the hell has been done here this night?" called out Spike hysterically.

"Things not to your liking, Spike?" snarled Cornelius furiously.

"Was that really bloody necessary, why did we even have to come here this night, why didn't we all just fucking disappear?" Spike sobbed loudly.

"We all have to do what we have to do in this life, Spike, we all have to pay sooner or later for our actions carried out in this world. Sadly tonight was to be their time to pay the piper, that's all it was, Spike."

Cornelius stood upright, showing no emotion whatsoever in his stare which was firmly fixed on Spike.

"But now I would suggest to you, Spike that your time might also have arrived." grinned Cornelius cruelly.

While Cornelius had been debating the rights and wrongs of previous actions with Spike, unbeknownst to Spike three of Cornelius's men had edged slowly towards him, positioning themselves directly behind him, then with one wave of Cornelius's hand, they grabbed hold of Spike and roughly dragged him into the middle of the clearing, forcing him face down in the dirt, with his legs spread eagled. Two of the I.R.A. men held Spike firmly down on the ground, a gag was then vigorously pushed into his mouth, deadening any sound that he was sure to make. Paddy approached Spike and knelt down between Spike's opened legs, in each hand Paddy held a revolver. Paddy then placed a revolver at the back of both of Spike's knees. He then told Spike to count to three and on the count of two, Paddy pulled the trigger of both revolvers, blasting both of Spike's knee-caps into pieces. Again Cornelius showed no sympathy or remorse as he stood over Spike, who by now was lay in the dirt in horrendous pain. Cornelius put his boot on Spike's head and said callously,

"A little something to remember us by Spike, maybe you will think twice in the future, before you let your greed cloud your judgement. Now tell your friend Hastings when he gets here that he needn't waste his time and effort looking for us as we will be long gone from this city before he knows it."

Cornelius moved away from Spike leaving him slumped on the ground bleeding heavily from both legs. He turned his attention towards Alex, who was cowering nervously beside one of the hay carts.

"You look nervous, Alex," laughed Cornelius.

"Is it any wonder I do Cornelius, after witnessing the events of this horrifying evening?" replied a petrified Alex.

"I suppose you're wondering if you're next, is that it, Alex?" said Cornelius.

Alex's body was now visibly trembling, wondering if indeed if he was to be next to fall under Cornelius's sadistic will.

"Well the thought has crossed my mind," muttered Alex anxiously.

"Relax, Alex, we have something more interesting in line for you." smiled Cornelius.

"And that would be?" asked Alex as an uneasy feeling began to creep steadily throughout his body. Cornelius moved closer to Alex and smiled broadly at him saying,

"This woman, Edwina."

"Edwina, what about her?" asked Alex.

"You're going to kill her for us, and you're going to do it before Monday evening has passed," said Cornelius with a sadistic grin.

Alex was stunned, unable to respond to Cornelius's unforeseen proclamation, he just stood still and silent, his head hung, his body shaking with fear. Suddenly, the not so distant sound of police whistles could be heard coming from all directions. Finbarr moved forward and took hold of Cornelius's arm

"Sounds like they're closing in on us, Cornelius." he whispered calmly.

Cornelius nodded his head in agreement, then said,

"That's it, boys, we're done here this night, it's time to go."

The night party then quickly left the clearing and made their way to the waiting tug boat that was moored at the old quay at the end of the cobbled road. Within minutes they were underway, leaving the scene of their carnage far behind them.

CHAPTER 13

William Hastings, along with the other officers on duty that night were now in something of a panic, to a man they all knew that the sound of gunfire that they had heard coming from the direction of the arranged meeting place, could only mean one thing. Trouble, with a capital T. Officers who had been positioned on the East Belfast side of the Queens Bridge, were now rushing franticly towards the old cobbled road that would lead to the clearing. William Hastings, along with Sergeant Mullins and Constable Miller were first to arrive at the scene, sadly their haste to get to the clearing was brought to an abrupt halt as the horrifying scene of Cornelius's brutal mindless act was now only too evident. A sickened William stood in shock at the edge of the clearing as his eyes fell upon the bloodbath before him. William stood for only a few minutes before the rest of the police pack had reached the clearing. They too were stopped horror-struck in their tracks as they too saw the carnage before them. Several officers began to heave and vomit violently as their stomachs churned furiously inside them, their eyes fighting to accept the heartless cold-blooded slaughter of their colleagues. None of the attending officers had expected the night to end in this way. William moved to the centre of the clearing and stood in total silence, his revulsion at what he saw before him was overwhelming.

"Jesus Christ why? Why in the name of God has this happened?" lamented William loudly.

William's shocked mood was suddenly interrupted when one of the officers called out loudly,

"Sir…Sir…quickly over here, Sir. This one is still alive."

William turned instantly towards the officer who was knelt on one knee beside a man with blood-soaked legs, William immediately recognised this man as Spike. William rushed quickly across the clearing to where the officer and Spike were located. William then dropped down on one knee next to Spike's head and removed a vomit soaked gag from his mouth. Spike was at best only semi-conscious and was groaning painfully as he lay on the ground. William turned Spike's head towards him and said angrily,

"Where have they gone Spike, tell me where the hell they have gone. Tell me Spike and tell me now or so help me Spike I will leave you here to bleed to death."

Spike began to mumble faintly, but his garbled answer was barely lucid. William put his ear close to Spike's mouth and listened carefully as Spike once again attempted to give his answer.

"They had a tug boat moored at the end of the road, at the old quay. They've gone down and then across to the safer side of the river. They have a truck waiting for them on the city side of the Queen's Bridge," mumbled Spike in-between spurts of coughing up blood.

William could just about understanding what Spike was saying. William then asked,

"How did they know what we had planned, what alerted them to us?"

Spike was now drifting in and out of consciousness as his body slipped deeper into shock. The ground beneath his body was stained red as there was to be no slowing of his lifeblood that oozed freely from the wounds to his legs. Spike's condition continued to weaken by the second, but William was determined to get the answers he need from Spike.

"How did they know, Spike? Tell me now!" shouted William angrily,

"Help me please." pleaded Spike.

Spike's voice was weakening with every move of his lips, his eyes slowly rolling back in his head.

"You can have all of the help that you need, but not until you tell me how they knew we were the police," demanded William.

Sadly no answer was forthcoming from Spike, as he had once again lost consciousness, leaving him laying helpless on the ground.

At this point Inspector Tom Nabney arrived on the scene along with the ten officers that had been with him on the other side of the Queens Bridge. Their revulsion at the blood-bath before them was plain for all to see. Following closely behind Inspector Nabney's arrival at the incident, several ambulances could be heard noisily rushing along the cobbled road leading to the clearing. It didn't take long before the true picture of what had happened became sickeningly clear to the paramedics and that their haste to help was indeed futile. Apart from attending to the wounded man, Spike, there was nothing more for them to do but begin the messy and unpleasant business of clearing the bodies of the young officers from the murder scene. The two paramedics that were attending to Spike quickly loaded him onto a stretcher and lifted him into the back of an ambulance and rushed him straight to the Royal Victoria hospital. William and Inspector Nabney wasted no time in following the ambulance to the hospital, as both men were indeed keen to interview Spike as soon as possible.

On arrival at the hospital, Spike was immediately rushed into the operating theatre, leaving William and Inspector Nabney cooling their heels in the waiting room.

"What the hell went wrong, William?" asked Inspector Nabney

"I really don't know, Tom." replied William, "but I suspect that our friend Spike knows something about it," continued William.

I am inclined to agree with you, William," said Inspector Nabney.

"If you ask me, Tom, after witnessing the severity of the retribution handed out to Spike, he has undoubtedly done something to annoy them. Because that has all of the hall-marks of a punishment shooting if you ask me," said William.

"Yes I have to agree with you, William, it certainly looks that way," replied the Inspector.

William got up from the wooden bench he had been resting on and began to pace up and down, a confused look fixed on his face as he pondered the puzzle before him.

"What I also want to know from Spike is what has happened to Alex? I'm really interested to discover where he is and why wasn't he punished in the same way as Spike? Whatever it is that has annoyed Cornelius and Finbarr so much, the chances are that Spike wasn't in it alone. Alex Brown will have been mixed up in it somewhere along the line," said William.

Inspector Nabney nodded in agreement, adding,

"Yes, something must have taken place in the last few days, something that prevented them from keeping their meeting with you at the First and Last Bar on Friday, William, when we were all set to arrest them."

"Yes, but what happened to alter their plans Tom? There's no possible way they could have discovered that I was in league with you and the Constabulary," said William.

"That's the only answer to the puzzle, William, but how could they have discovered that you were working with the Constabulary? More of a puzzle William is why they have taken Alex Brown with them," continued Inspector Nabney.

"There's more going on here than meets the eye, believe me Tom. The only reason why they would have taken Alex with them is because they have something that they want him to do for them. That will be his punishment for his part in whatever it was that he and Spike did to annoy them. They must want him to do something really serious, judging by what they did to Spike. But what the Hell could it be?" quizzed William.

William and Inspector Tom Nabney waited in the hospital waiting room well into the afternoon on that sombre Saturday, hoping that someone from the hospital would tell them that they could now interview the man, Spike. Then suddenly a Doctor entered the waiting room.

"Any news, Doctor?" asked William as he hurriedly got to his feet.

"Good morning," said the doctor.

William and the inspector quickly introduced themselves to the doctor.

"I'm Mr Brookside, the Surgeon attending to the gunshot victim that was brought into the hospital last evening. I am sorry but at this point I do not have a name for the injured man."

Mr Brookside's demeanour was that of someone that considered himself superior to those around him.

"Well we only know him as Spike ourselves, Mr Brookside," replied William.

"Spike! Now that's an interesting name!" declared Mr Brookside. "Well! Spike is at best stable, he's recovering from a serious operation. I am sorry to have to tell you both that this man that you call Spike isn't out of the woods by a long way. He has lost a lot of blood and we are keeping him under sedation for at least the next few days," announced Mr Brookside.

"How long before we can talk to him?" enquired the Inspector?

"I cannot allow anyone to speak with him before Monday at the earliest," replied Mr Brookside sharply.

"That long?" snapped an irritated William.

"You must understand," continued Mr Brookside. "Like I said, he's been heavily sedated. So if you want to question him I would say Monday would be your first opportunity to do so. There would be little point in trying to talk to him before then. The answers that he would give to you wouldn't make any sense, all that you would hear would be the ramblings of a heavily drugged man. The reason for his heavy sedation is because we had to amputate both his legs above the knee. The man's injuries were most unpleasant when he arrived here last evening, both his knees were shattered beyond repair, the gun shots wounds had also created other complications and he had lost a lot of blood. Also infection had set in so we had no chose but to amputate."

"I see," said the Inspector, giving William a quick glance.

William then said,

"If you say Monday, Mr Brookside, then Monday it is."

"Like I said, no point before Monday," answered Mr Brookside.

"Thank you for your time, Mr Brookside," said William, "we won't detain you any longer."

Mr Brookside then shook both William and the Inspector firmly by the hand and left the waiting room. Both William and the Inspector were left somewhat annoyed at not being able to quiz Spike, knowing that precious time was being lost by having to wait until Monday to talk to him. The inspector then said,

"I'll get back to the station and set the wheels in motion. We just have to discover where these cold-hearted killers have gone, William. It won't be easy without Spike's input but we will try our best. I'll keep in touch, William. There's nothing more we can do here for now."

"Yes, of course," replied William. "I will meet you back here Monday morning around nine thirty, Tom."

With that both men left the hospital and went on their separate ways.

Later that Saturday afternoon at around four o'clock, Cornelius, Finbarr, Shaun, Paddy, Alex and another man, a stranger to all but Cornelius and Finbarr, were gathered around the wooden table in the back room of Murphy's Bar. They had gathered to finalise their plans to make good their exit from Belfast. Cornelius knocked firmly on the wooden table, drawing the full attention of all in the room.

"Well boys," he announced with some authority. "First can I thank and congratulate you all on a job well done last evening."

The assembled following collectively muttered their acknowledgement of Cornelius's appreciation.

"Now down to the business in hand boys," continued Cornelius, "getting us all safely back to Dublin without any fuss or interference from the bloody Constabulary. First of all allow me to introduce you all to Captain Kelly," said Cornelius.

Then turning to his right and pointing to the unknown man sitting at the table beside Finbarr he said,

"Now then, boys, Captain Kelly here is a good friend of the Republican movement. He's also the captain of the trawler, The Freedom Boys out of Donaghadee a small port but a few miles down the coast from here. So tonight myself, Finbarr and Shaun will sail on the evening tide to Ramsey in the Isle of Man. Paddy you will stay behind for now with Alex, I need you to make sure that he carries out my instructions to the letter and puts an end to this interfering bitch, Edwina."

Cornelius then addressed Alex.

"You do realise that in order for you to escape the punishment that you so deserve, Alex, you must do one thing for me, one thing and one thing only!"

"And that is what, Cornelius?" asked Alex nervously.

"You must go to the woman, Edwina's house and kill her. That's it, Alex, just kill that interfering bitch, Edwina. Do this one thing for me and you get your freedom? Are you ready to do this one little job for me, Alex? I do hope that you are," said Cornelius, showing no emotion on his face whatsoever.

Alex just nodded his head like a frightened boy standing in front of his headmaster in acceptance of his fate.

Cornelius then turned his attention towards Paddy, saying,

"This undertaking must be brought to a close by late Monday afternoon. Both you and Alex must be in Donaghadee by seven o' clock to meet with Captain Kelly because at ten o'clock you will both sail on the evening tide and join the rest of us in Ramsey. There we will all remain for a period of one month before once again teaming up with Captain Kelly and sailing to the port of Howth, ten miles north east of Dublin. There we will stay for a period of four weeks, by which time it will be safe for us all to return to Dublin. Any questions boys?"

There was no reaction from the others in the room.

"No? Good," said Cornelius sharply,

Cornelius then told Shaun to take Alex out of then room, this he did without delay.

"Paddy," said Cornelius, "I am depending on you to make sure that Alex sees his mission through to a satisfactory conclusion. I am also depending on you to clean up after the job has been concluded. Do you understand what I'm saying to you Paddy? We cannot allow any lose ends that could lead back to us, know what I am saying Paddy?"

Paddy nodded his head as he got to his feet, then he looked Cornelius straight in the eye and without showing emotion of any kind he said,

"Make no mistake, Cornelius, I understand everything that you're saying and I will not let you down. There will be no lose ends to come back to bite us, you can be sure of that!"

"Ah Jesus, Paddy, you're a good man, make no mistake." muttered Cornelius in a soft, withering voice as he griped Paddy's hand firmly and shook it with as much vigour as the grip he held it with.

Paddy then made his way towards the door and as he did so Cornelius called out,

"Send Spud in to me, Paddy if you will."

Paddy just nodded in response as he quickly left the room. A few seconds later Spud Murphy entered the room.

"You wanted me, Sir?" said Spud.

"Ah Jesus, its Spud, come sit here beside me," said Cornelius.

Spud Murphy quickly sat down in the chair that Cornelius had indicated to him.

"There is something that I need to let you know, Spud," said Cornelius, "and that is that myself, Finbarr and Shaun will be leaving Belfast tonight, as for Paddy, he will follow us in the next few days. So if there's anything he needs before he leaves, see to it Spud for me. Remember, anything he needs, ok, Spud? Although we are leaving, you must not worry yourself, because I tell you here and now, the Republican Movement isn't dead in this city just yet, Spud, not by a long way. Within the next week or so we will be being replaced and I am hoping that you will show the new Commanders the same loyalty that you have shown us these past few years, Spud. I am also depending on you to make sure that no one interferes with our departure, you understand, Spud?"

Spud looked at both Cornelius and Finbarr and said,

"Cornelius, you and Finbarr will be sorely missed around here that's for sure and you can put your trust in me to insure that your departure goes without a hitch."

Cornelius shook Spud Murphy warmly by the hand as he said,

"Good man, then all that's left to do is say our goodbyes and be on our way."

That evening Cornelius, Finbarr, Shaun and two minders left Belfast for Donaghadee and a meeting with Captain Kelly and his Trawler.

On the Monday morning at ten thirty, both William Hastings and Inspector Nabney arrived at the Hospital to keep their appointment with the man, Spike.

First they had to find Mr Brookside. After quizzing a passing nurse, both men were pointed in the direction of Mr Brookside's office. William knocked politely three times on his door.

"Come in!" came a shout from inside.

Both Tom and William entered Mr Brookside's office.

"Ah, you two again," muttered Mr Brookside, turning his attention back to the papers on his desk. It was obvious to both William and the Inspector that the weekend hadn't altered Mr Brookside's superior attitude.

"Yes, it's us again," retorted William angrily, "and this time we insist on speaking the man, Spike as soon as possible."

"I have just come from his bedside," replied Mr Brookside, without lifting his eyes from the papers he was studying.

"And?" asked Inspector Nabney impatiently.

"He's coming around slowly,"

"And that means?" snapped the Inspector.

"Maybe another hour or so before he would be lucid enough to answer any questions you might have for him. But you're more than welcome to wait by his bedside, if you so wish."

"Yes, we would like to be there when he becomes lucid enough to answer our questions," said William with some distain.

"In that case I will take you to him," replied Mr Brookside as he put his glasses down on his desk and got to his feet.

Spike was in a side room off one of the main wards, no more than 50 yards from Mr Brookside's office.

"Here you are gentlemen, in here if you please," said Mr Brookside as he opened the door to the side ward.

Both William and the Inspector entered the small room to find Spike laying on his back with a surgical cage in the centre of the bed and under the bed sheets. That was obviously there to both cover and protect Spike's stumps. There were tubes and lines entering his body from all directions, and as serious as Spike's condition looked and as pitiful as it obviously was, this pitiful image before William and the Inspector failed to draw a shred of compassion from either man. Both men approached Spike's bedside, but unfortunately for both William and the Inspector, Mr Brookside was right in his assessment of Spike's ability to answer any questions. Spike was still under the influence of the drugs he had received after both of his legs had been amputated. To even attempt to question Spike at this moment in time would be a futile exercise. All there was to do now was to wait.

"Like I said," muttered Mr Brookside, "He's not fully conscious yet, but give it an hour or maybe two and he will be able to answer all your questions. There is one thing that you both need to know. He doesn't know that we have amputated both of his legs. When he realizes what has happened to him, his response might not be what you are hoping for."

Mr Brookside looked straight at both men as he delivered his opinion on what Spike's state of mind might be when he would eventually came out from under the influence of the drugs.

"Well then gentlemen, I'll leave you to it," said Mr Brookside and he left the room.

William and the inspector made themselves comfortable and waited for Spike to regain his senses. This was to prove to be a longer and more irritating wait than both William and the Inspector had expected, in fact it took another three hours before Spike began to rouse from his enforced stupor. At first Spike was dazed and sluggish, his mind seemed confused, it appeared that he was unable to grasp any awareness of his surroundings or his whereabouts. His speech was garbled and jumbled, as one sentence seemed to drift aimlessly into another without the original sentence ever being completed.

"We best wait a little longer, Tom before we try to question him because this is getting us nowhere," groaned William impatiently.

The Inspector agreed and both he and William were forced to wait for another two hours before Spike was in any fit state to be questioned. Spike opened his eyes and when he saw William standing by his bedside he said,

"The bastard shot me in the legs!"

Spike's look of anger quickly changed to one of fear as he quickly realised that all was not as it should be. Suddenly his hands began to fumble frantically under the bed sheets as he searched for his legs. In that one desperate moment the stark realisation that Spike had lost both of his legs had hit home. Spike let out the most terrifying yell, a screech so chilling that it reverberated around the small room. William and the Inspector looked at each other with a cold uncaring stare. Neither man moved by Spike's chilling screams of reality, neither man feeling nor showing sympathy of any kind for the man laying helpless in the hospital bed before them.

"Where the hell are my legs, what have they done to my legs?" screamed Spike hysterically.

William moved closer to Spike and in a soft voice whispered,

"I'm sorry to have to tell you, Spike, but they had to amputate them, there was nothing else they could do."

This devastating news sent Spike into an uncontrollable rage. He began to scream and rant loudly as the reality of his situation hit home hard. This activity had now drawn the attention of a nurse who was on duty on the main ward and she called to one of her colleagues. Within seconds they were both rushing into the room and were quickly followed by Mr Brookside himself, who immediately ordered the Inspector and William to leave the room and wait outside while they settled Spike down.

Again, both William and the inspector found themselves waiting to interview Spike. Luckily on this occasion their wait was short lived, as within fifteen minutes Mr Brookside had been able to calm Spike down. William looked at his watch as Mr Brookside called them back into the room.

"It's now going on four o'clock, Tom, we need to get on with this as soon as possible," said William.

"Are we free to question him now?" William asked Mr Brookside.

"Yes, as far as I am concerned, he's all yours," replied Mr Brookside as he left the room.

William and the Inspector sat down on the seats provided, one on each side of Spike's bed. They were now ready to begin questioning Spike.

"How long have I been here?" asked Spike.

"A few days," answered William.

"So it's now Monday or is it Tuesday?" enquired spike.

"Its Monday afternoon now Spike," replied the Inspector.

William was first to begin questioning Spike, in order to discover everything that he knew as regards the events of the last few days. Bizarrely, Spike was more than willing to cooperate, this was not what William and the Inspector had anticipated at all. It would appear that Spike's willingness to help, was due to the legacy that the I.R.A. had left him with. You see Spike's full cooperation was being driven by revenge, he wanted each and every one of them to pay for what they had done to him. Needless to say, both William and the Inspector were more than happy with this unexpected turn in events. Spike told them everything, from the day his friend the waiter recognised William at the Grand with Edwina and Mr Powell, to the day when both Alex and himself went to inform Shaun and Paddy what they had discovered about William. Spike then went on to divulge everything that followed that meeting with Shaun and Paddy. Spike also informed both William and the Inspector that they were wasting their time looking for Cornelius and his crew in Belfast as they had undoubtedly already left the city.

"But why have they held onto Alex, what on earth do they want with him Spike?" quizzed William.

Spike looked shocked at this question.

"You mean she's not dead then?" spike responded with some dismay.

"Who's not dead, Spike?" asked William somewhat confused by Spike's response.

Spike's expression quickly changed as he raised himself up in the bed.

"Edwina of course, Cornelius wants Alex to kill Edwina and he wants it done by the end of the day, today. Cornelius, he holds Edwina responsible for involving you in all of this, William. Paddy was instructed to shadow Alex every minute of the day ever since the events of Saturday morning. Cornelius ordered it to be that way. Paddy is to make sure that Alex carries out Cornelius's orders no later than today."

This dramatic and unexpected revelation from Spike sent a chilling fear gushing through William's veins.

"My good God!" gasped William as he jumped to his feet. "I must get to Edwina's house and warn her without delay."

"Do you have her telephone number, William? If so we could alert her to the danger ahead," said the Inspector.

"I'm afraid not, Tom. I have never had the need to call her before, as I see her daily," answered William as he headed for the door.

"Go without delay, William, I will rouse a few good men and we'll meet you at Edwina's house," replied the Inspector.

It was now four forty on the Monday afternoon and a slow moving car had just pulled into the road where Edwin's house was situated. Edwina's house was a large imposing building set in its own grounds with a six foot wall inclosing both the house and gardens. The only entrance into the grounds was through a large set of double gates, which were always firmly shut. As the slow moving motor car came level with the double gates of Edwina's house it slowed down even more until it eventually came to a standstill. Here it held its position for a few minutes, then suddenly it speeded up and drove off at speed. As this motor car rounded the corner at the end of the outer wall that surrounded Edwina's house, it came to a halt. After a few minutes of inactivity had passed, the doors of the motor car opened and out got Paddy and Alex. Both men stood in silence by the side of the motor car for a few moments, just to compose themselves.

"Are you ready to do this, Alex?" asked Paddy firmly.

Alex took a deep breath then wiped a few beads of sweat from his brow.

"If I have to do this, Paddy, then I will," Alex replied nervously.

Paddy took a revolver from under his coat and handed it to Alex.

"Here, take this, Alex and remember what we talked about this morning. All you have to do is to get into the house without being seen. Once inside find Edwina as quickly as you can, whatever you do, don't allow her to enter into conversation with you, you understand me, Alex."

Alex apprehensively nodded his head in acknowledgement, his body trembling nervously as he griped the revolver that Paddy had given him with both of his hands.

"Ah Jesus Christ, Alex, try and relax or you'll end up bloody shooting yourself," quipped Paddy.

Alex nodded his head in response.

"Now remember," continued Paddy, "two quick shots to the head then get out of there as quick as you can. I will be outside the front of the house with the motor car revved and ready to go. Okay, Alex, have you got all that"

Alex's mouth was so dry that his tongue was beginning to stick to the roof of his mouth, all he could do to respond to Paddy's instructions was to nervously nod his head, indicating that he understood what Paddy had told him. Alex then left Paddy by the side of Edwina's house and made his way hurriedly towards the rear of the house.

Alex lurched his way down a small narrow passageway which lead to the back of Edwina's house and once there he was faced with an eight foot wall which ran all the way around it. Alex wasted no time in scaling the wall and was now standing at the end of Edwina's large garden. As quickly as he could, Alex made his way through the garden as he headed towards the doors at the back of house. He began to search frantically for a way to enter Edwina's home, but his search was suddenly made a lot easier when Edwina's housekeeper opened the kitchen door. This action forced Alex to take cover behind a large garden statue beside a row of three large rose bushes. Edwina's housekeeper came out of the house and made her way towards a group of bins that were situated no more than five yards from the house. In her hands she carried several bags of kitchen waste. As she tipped the waste bags into one of the bins, Alex hastily seized this unexpected opportunity with both hands as he crept up behind the housekeeper and delivered a swift blow to the back of her head with the butt of his revolver. This heavy blow to her head rendered the housekeeper unconscious and she fell to the ground. Alex then quickly entered the house through the open kitchen door. Cautiously, he made his way through the kitchen and into a long hallway which had several rooms leading off it. His search for the lady herself had now began in earnest.

Alex moved slowly along the hallway, listening carefully for any indication that would alert him to which room Edwina might be located in. Suddenly he heard a sound coming from one of the rooms. He listened carefully and there it was again, a soft, yet a distinct clinking sound, the kind of sound that a cup makes when coming into contact with its saucer. Alex was now convinced that the sound was coming from the room to his left. Slowly, Alex moved towards the door to the room where he had heard the clinking of china upon china. He stopped outside the door and listened once again, there it was, cup upon saucer. Taking a deep breath and then tightening his grip on his revolver, Alex slowly turned the handle on the door. When he had turned the handle to its full rotation, Alex pushed the door open to its widest and rushed inside. Edwina was sitting in an armchair next to the window and on hearing the door open with such force, she turned around quickly to see Alex standing in the doorway.

"What are you doing here and what do you want?" shouted Edwina angrily, as she jumped to her feet.

"I've come for you, Edwina," replied Alex,

"Whatever do you mean, you have come for me? Get out of my house this instant!" ordered Edwina angrily.

Alex raised his arm in Edwina's direction, his hand shaking as beads of sweat rolled off his brow as he pointed his revolver directly at her.

Edwina could now see the revolver twitching in Alex's hand.

"My God you're here to kill me aren't you?" said Edwina.

"It has to be this way, Edwina, I have no chose in the matter," said Alex, his voice now as shaky as his hand.

"You won't get away with this Alex, they will find you. Of that you can be sure."

Edwina was now sure that she was going to die within the next few minutes.

Alex moved menacingly closer to his quarry and was now standing only a matter of a few feet away from Edwina. He raised his revolver and pointed it at Edwina's head. She shut her eyes tight and began to pray openly for her mortal soul. Just as Edwina was uttering the last words of the Lord's Prayer, having accepted her fate, suddenly she heard the front door being opened and then closed. Edwina opened her eyes to see her daughter, Connie standing in the doorway. At first Connie didn't realise what was happening as yet she hadn't noticed the revolver in Alex's hand. Suddenly Alex turned towards Connie and grabbed her by the arm. With great force he swung her around knocking her off her feet, causing her to roll across the floor towards her mother.

"Mother!" screamed Connie loudly, "what's happening, who is he and what does he want with you?"

Edwina instantly helped Connie to her feet and placed her young daughter behind her, using her body to shield her child from any danger.

"Stay behind me Connie," pleaded Edwina, not wishing any harm to befall her only daughter.

With this unforeseen turn in events, Alex was thrown into a panic and was unsure of what to do next. He was more than aware that Connie's unexpected arrival meant that she could identify him. This fact was not lost on Edwina either. Reaching backwards Edwina caught hold of Connie's arm and whispered softly,

"Whatever happens in the next few minutes, Connie, when you get the chance to run, for the love of God take it without looking back. Do you hear me Connie?"

"Why mother, why is this happening?" asked Connie.

Edwina looked at Alex and said,

"Listen to me, Alex, it's me that you want, not my daughter. Just do to me whatever it was you came to do. But I beg of you, please, Alex let Connie go."

By now Alex was in a state of melt down, he might be many nasty things, but a seasoned killer he wasn't. In the midst of the turmoil that was raging in Alex's head, one question repeatedly pushed its way to the fore, what was he to do? Was he to simply kill Edwina and let Connie live, or was he to kill them both? Alex suddenly remembered Cornelius's last words to him. One thing and one thing only. It was only Edwina that Cornelius wanted killed, but if he was to spare Connie's life, she could identify him later. But if he was to kill them both, Cornelius would not be happy, because every newspaper in the land would then label the I.R.A as child killers. Alex then shouted,

"Bring your daughter out from behind you Edwina and tell her to come over here to my right. When you get here, girl I want you to go down on your knees and cover your face with your hands."

Alex continued to point his revolver in Connie's direction, his hand shaking and his body trembling with a mixture of fear and anxiety, again he shouted,

"Why is she here, no one told me she would be here, I thought it would be just you and me, Edwina. But your daughter knows who I am now. I have no choice, she has to die along with you. Now send her here right now, Edwina!"

"Leave her, Alex, let her go, please, Alex," begged Edwina.

"I can't do that, Edwina, send her here to me now!" yelled Alex, his gun hand now flapping about like a flag in a strong wind.

Edwina now realised that both her and her daughter could lose their lives to this man right here in their own sitting room if she didn't do something immediately. Without a thought for her own safety, Edwina suddenly lunged forward grabbing hold of Alex's gun hand. A violent tussle quickly ensued. Seeing that her mother was in danger, Connie rushed across the room in an effort to join in the struggle and help her. Before Connie had reached the scrimmage, a single shot rang out and Connie fell to the ground, hitting her head on a small wooden table as she crumpled in a heap on the floor. Edwina stopped her struggle with Alex and looked around to see her young daughter flat out on the floor with blood spurting from her shoulder as well as her head. Edwina screamed loudly as she looked in dismay at her daughter bleeding heavily on the sitting room floor.

With Edwina's attention momentarily distracted towards her fallen daughter, Alex was once again in control of the situation. Brutishly, he pushed Edwina to the floor next to her young daughter and stood over her with his revolver pointed at Edwina's head. Paddy's words of instructions on how the killing should be carried out now rang loudly in Alex's ears. Looking down at Edwina, Alex aimed his revolver directly at her head. Edwina was unconcerned for her own safety or by the situation in which she found herself, all of her thoughts and all of her attention was now focussed on her beautiful daughter who lay bleeding on the floor. In an effort to protect her daughter from any more harm, Edwina flung herself to the floor, shielding her bleeding daughter from whatever Alex Brown was about to do next. Edwina shut her eyes tight and said,

"Do you worst, Alex, but remember this, the deeds that you will do here this day, will see you burn in hell for all eternity."

With those last words from Edwina's mouth, a loud gunshot rang out. Alex stood motionless for several seconds in disbelief at the devastation he had just created. His eyes fixed in a downward position as he watched Edwina's life's blood gushing from his gunshot to the back of her head. As Alex watched the carpet beneath both Connie and Edwina turn red from their blood, he closed his eyes tight as he cried out in his shame.

"May God forgive me for what I have done here this day?"

Alex screamed loudly and then he ran from the room, making his way down the hallway towards the front door of the house. When he had reached the front door his hands were shaking so badly that he began to fumble clumsily with the brass handle on the inside of the big oak door. Finally he got to grips with it and he flung the door open wildly and ran outside to see Paddy standing just inside the gates to the garden.

"Is it done, Alex?" quizzed Paddy.

Alex stopped on the steps outside the front door, his body bent over his hand holding his chest as he tried to take several deep breaths in an attempt regain some kind of composure. But his heart was pounding so heavily and his mouth was so dry that each time he attempted to take in a gulp air it seemed like a life threatening struggle to do so. After several seconds, Alex straightened himself up and ran his hand despairingly through his hair as he took one more deep breath. Again Paddy asked,

"Is it done, Alex?"

"Yes…yes, I've fucking done as you told me, it's done and may God forgive me for my actions this day." moaned Alex loudly.

"Quickly, Alex, get over here to me," ordered Paddy.

Alex rushed down the steps and made his way sharply towards to the large gates where Paddy was standing.

"Give me the revolver," demanded Paddy.

Alex willingly handed it over. Paddy took the revolver in his right hand and checked the bullets inside.

"As I thought, Alex, more than one shot fired. Why more than the one shot when I told you one shot to the head and then get out of there as quickly as you can?" asked Paddy.

"Because her young daughter was at home, no one told me that she would be there Paddy!" grumbled Alex.

"You didn't kill her as well did you, Alex?" said Paddy.

"Yes I did, now can we go, Paddy, I just want to get as far away from here as I can and as soon as I can," moaned Alex, again running his hand wildly through his hair.

Paddy stood in the middle of the opened garden gates. He had positioned himself in such a way that he was blocking Alex's exit, preventing him from leaving the grounds of Edwina's house.

"What are you doing, Paddy, let's get out of here for God Sake. We have to be in Donaghadee by seven!" roared Alex as he tried to push past Paddy.

Paddy gave Alex a withering smile, as he forced him back inside the gates.

"Change of plan I'm afraid, Alex. I have to be in Donaghadee by seven o'clock, you on the other hand don't have to be anywhere, I'm sorry to say." grinned Paddy

"What do you mean, Paddy? I have done what Cornelius wanted me to do," whinged Alex, fearing that all wasn't how it should be.

"Yes, you have, Alex and Cornelius will be very pleased when I tell him, but now I have to do what Cornelius wants me to do," said Paddy curtly.

"No, no please, Paddy, don't do this, please, Paddy no!" pleaded Alex,

Paddy raised the revolver and pointed it at Alex's head. Alex took a step back away from Paddy and again pleaded for his life. Sadly, all of Alex's pleading was falling on deaf ears. Without uttering another word or showing any kind of compassion on his face, Paddy shot Alex twice in the head at close range. Leaving him lying on the ground and bleeding profusely from two holes, one to the side of his head and the other straight through his forehead.

Paddy put the revolver back inside his coat and turned around to leave through the opened gates at the front of Edwina's house. Unfortunately for Paddy his advance was halted by a loud shout from the other side of the road.

"That's far enough, Paddy," came a loud shout.

It was William who had now arrived on the scene and had positioned himself behind a small wall which ran alongside the open parkland opposite. Paddy jumped back behind one of the concrete pillars from which the large gates were suspended. Quickly he reloaded the revolver that he had taken off Alex a few seconds before. Paddy carefully peered outside the gates, hoping to find a way to escape. But things weren't looking good for Paddy, as what met his eyes was the sight of Inspector Nabney and four armed officers, all taking cover behind the parkland wall just a few feet down from where William had positioned himself. Paddy's attention quickly reverted back towards the house, thinking that he might be able to make good his escape through the back of the house, much in the same way that Alex had entered it.

Unfortunately, this idea was quickly made even more complicated when a chilling scream bellowing out from inside the house. It was the housekeeper, who, once she had regained consciousness, had entered the house only to stumble across her mistress lying dead on the sitting room floor. As Paddy made a move towards the house, suddenly the housekeeper appeared in the doorway. Seeing Paddy advancing towards the house with his revolver in hand, she quickly slammed the front door shut and bolted it from the inside. Paddy returned to his previous position behind one of the brick pillars that supported the large gates.

"Give it up, Paddy, you can't get out of this one, there's no escape. Just toss out your gun and come out with your hands in the air," called William loudly.

"Ah Jesus, William, or is it Sam, or whatever bloody name it is your going by this day, you know bloody well I can't do that," replied Paddy.

Paddy knew only too well that there was no possibility of allowing himself to be taken alive, not after the crimes he had committed. For him to spend many years in a British jail would be like going to a living hell.

"Then make your move whenever you think the time is right, Paddy," yelled Inspector Nabney.

Paddy pushed his back tight up against the brick pillar and took several deep breaths. First, Paddy checked the revolver that he had taken off Alex, making sure that it was fully loaded, it was. Paddy then checked his own revolver, it too was now fully loaded.

"Well then, boys," called Paddy loudly, "if you think that you are ready for me, then let's get this party started."

"Don't do it, Paddy, give yourself up and there's no need for anyone else to die here this day," shouted William.

"Ah Christ, boys, if I am going to do this, then there's no time like the present, what do you say boys?" shouted Paddy defiantly.

"Don't do it, Paddy." called William once again.

All of William's pleading was to be in vain, it would seem that Paddy had made up his mind and there was no changing it. In a flash Paddy turned and ran out of the large gates, his revolvers blazing wildly in the direction of William and the other police officers. Paddy was making one last desperate dash to reach his car that he had parked only a few feet away from the large gates of Edwina's house. Paddy's attempted escape was brought to an abrupt halt as William and the other police officers quickly returned fire and in a matter of seconds Paddy was cut down in a hail of gun fire. Some might say that the volume of fire returned from William and the other Police officers could be described as a little excessive. But once Paddy had opened fire on the police officers with his revolvers, his fate was well and truly sealed. It was later discovered that Paddy was hit with no less than twenty bullets. It would appear that Inspector Nabney and the Constabulary were determined to put an end to this man's activities once and for all.

All hell had been let lose outside Edwina's house that afternoon, all be it for only a matter of seconds and when it was all over, Paddy lay dead in a pool of blood in the gutter outside Edwina's house. Slowly, William and the police officers came out from behind the wall that had been their shield throughout the short gun battle, each one of them an eye witness to the brutal demise of a man that had played a big part in the deaths of so many of their comrades. William and the Inspector now rushed to the front door of Edwina's house. William banged hard on it with his fist, then he called out that it was the police that were at the door, knowing that the housekeeper was alone inside. Within seconds a distraught housekeeper opened the door.

William and the Inspector rushed inside followed by the other police officers. Inspector Nabney quickly ordered two of his officers to remove Alex's body from the pathway were it lay. The Inspector then instructed two other officers to attend to the distraught housekeeper. William and the Inspector then set about finding Edwina, hoping that they would find her alive. Suddenly both William and Inspector Nabney heard hysterical screaming coming from the room at the end of the hallway.

"Quickly," said William, "someone is still alive!"

William and the Inspector hurried down the hallway towards the room that they had heard the screaming coming from. Inspector Nabney was first into the room. There he saw a distraught young lady sitting on the floor cuddling the blood soaked body of another woman.

"Help my mother, please help her!" screamed the young lady loudly when she saw the Inspector and William standing in the doorway.

William could see instantly that the young lady had been shot in the shoulder, but he also knew that woman in her arms was dead. William quickly dashed across the sitting room towards the young lady and her dead mother in an effort to render his assistance and to try to calm the young lady. It was obvious that she was in a state of shock and deeply traumatised by the sight of her mother's horrendous wounds to her head. William knelt down beside Connie and put his arm around her in an attempt to comfort her. Connie looked at William with tear filled eyes and in a soft, pain filled voice said,

"Please help my mother."

William's response was sympathetic yet firm.

"You have to let go of your mother, there's nothing you can do for her now."

Slowly William began to remove Connie's arms from around her dead mother. Connie continued to weep uncontrollably as William took Edwina's body from her and laid it gently on the ground. William removed his top coat and covered Edwina's body with it. William then placed his arm compassionately around Connie and slowly raised her to her feet. William then beckoned to one of the police officers to take Connie out of the room and away from her mother's dead body.

Connie was somewhat unsteady on her feet as she crossed the sitting room assisted by the police officer. He took Connie and the housekeeper into the kitchen and away from the ugly scene that existed in the sitting room. Outside the house, three ambulances had now arrived, on board were several doctors and two of them were guided into the kitchen to attend to both Connie and the housekeeper. Two members of the ambulance crew, along with another doctor, entered the sitting room. The doctor removed William's coat from Edwina's body and after a few seconds of an examination he certified Edwina's death. Two members of the ambulance crew then covered Edwina's body with a blanket before removing her body from the house and placing her into the ambulance.

While the doctors were attending to the housekeeper and the gunshot wound to Connie's shoulder, the unpleasant business of removing the other two dead bodies from the outside of the property had taken place. The doctors who were with Connie and the housekeeper in the kitchen were informed that all of the dead bodies had been removed and that it was now acceptable for the ladies to leave the property without causing any further distress. One of the doctors then instructed the ambulance crew to take Connie and the housekeeper to the Royal Victoria Hospital for further treatment.

CHAPTER 14

Now that Connie and the housekeeper, along with all three corpses had been removed from Edwina's house and grounds, the police quickly set about the undertaking of securing the property. Two constables were left on duty outside the property, one at the front of the house, the other to the rear of the house. There really wasn't much more for Inspector Nabney and the other officers to do for now and so they left. Now the task of securing Edwina's house had been completed William also left the scene and quickly rushed to inform Mr Powell of the brutal murder of his good friend Edwina and the wounding of her daughter Connie.

It was early evening when William arrived at Andy Powell's house. William stood outside Mr Powell's front door for several long agonising seconds as he was not relishing having to tell Andy Powell that his friend Edwina had been shot dead by the I.R.A. Even harder was going to be telling him that his goddaughter, Connie had also been shot. William stood in silence on the doorstep, his hand raised in readiness to knock on the front door. But for some reason he couldn't bring himself to do so. William, inhaling deeply several times in an attempt to gather his thoughts, knowing that the devastating news he was about to divulge to Andy would not be easy for him to do. Then, on his forth inhale his hand suddenly moved towards the knocker and gripped it firmly and before he had realised what was happening, William had knocked vigorously three times on the large wooden door. Then he waited nervously for a reply. It wasn't long before the door was opened by Mr Powell's housekeeper.

"Good evening, Sir, may I help you?" enquired the housekeeper politely.

After clearing his dry throat loudly William replied as he removed his hat.

"Good evening too you, madam, may I speak with Mr Powell please?"

"Whom shall I say is calling please, Sir?" asked the housekeeper.

"My name is William, he will know who I am." William replied.

"Wait one moment please, Sir, said the housekeeper and closed the door.

After a few seconds she returned and admitted William into the house.

"This way please, Sir," said the housekeeper.

The housekeeper then led William to a sitting room at the back of the house where Mr Powell was waiting.

"William, to what do I owe this pleasure at this late hour?" asked Mr Powell.

"Please do come in and sit down, William," he added.

William placed himself in an armchair opposite to the one which William was occupying.

"Drink, William?" asked Andy Powell getting to his feet.

"Yes please, Andy, I do believe that would be a good idea. I have a feeling we are both going to need a stiff whisky before this night is done," answered William

Mr Powell looked slightly confused by William's seemingly dismal manner.

"Is there is something troubling you, William, has something happened?" asked Mr Powell anxiously,

Mr Powell handed William a large glass of Irish Bush whisky and sat back in his armchair. William thanked him for the whisky and sat forward in his armchair.

"Okay William let's hear whatever it is you have come here to tell me." said Andy Powell worriedly.

William then told Mr Powell the whole dreadful saga from beginning to end. When William finally came to the end of his tragic account of the events of the past few days, Mr Powell collapsed back in his armchair. This dreadful news had totally and utterly devastated him. Andy Powell remained slumped back in his chair for several minutes, not a sound coming from his lips then suddenly he sat forward in his chair and said,

"This can't be happening, not to Edwina and young Connie."

"Can I get you anything, Andy?" asked William.

"I think we both could do with another drink, William," said Andy Powell.

William walked across the room and began to pour out two whiskeys.

"Best make them large ones, William, very large ones!" said Andy Powell.

William handed Andy Powell his glass of whisky and returned to his armchair.

"How badly wounded is young Connie, William?" asked Mr Powell nervously.

Realising that Andy Powell was under the impression that young Connie was badly hurt and that he was fearing the worst, William moved quickly to reassure Mr Powell that Connie had only suffered a shoulder wound and that she was not that badly injured. William also informed Mr Powell that the doctor had assured him that Connie would make a full recovery within a matter of weeks and that she would be released from hospital within the next few days. William also informed Mr Powell that things might have been ever worse and that the killer might well have made good his escape but for the brave and quick thinking of Mrs O'Hara, the housekeeper.

Although Mr Powell was devastated by the news of Edwina's death, this welcome news about Connie's situation came as a great relief to him and went some way to putting his mind at ease. Once the initial shock at hearing William's shattering news eased somewhat, Mr Powell quickly realised that Connie was now going to need all of the help that he could give once she was discharged from hospital. Mr Powell got to his feet and put his hand on William's shoulder, thanking him for coming so promptly to inform him of this terrible news.

"Anything you need, Andy, just let me know," said William as he shook Mr Powell's hand warmly.

With that last act of friendship, this unpleasant and unsolicited conversation between the two men ended and both parted company.

First thing the next morning Mr Powell then made his way directly to Edwina's house. He was determined to see that no remnants of that frightful evening were left lingering to remind Connie of the dreadful events that had taken place in her mother's house. Mrs O'Hara, the housekeeper, was discharged from hospital later that day, returning to her duties at the house immediately in preparation for Connie's homecoming. Mr Powell had employed a team of cleaners to make sure that everything was as it should be. When Mrs O'Hara returned to the house to take up her duties, Mr Powell summoned her into the back sitting room. Mr Powell's first thoughts were to ask after Mrs O'Hara's wellbeing and if she felt well enough to carry on with her duties at the house. Mrs O'Hara assured Mr Powell most emphatically that she was feeling fine and was only too happy to return to work.

Mr Powell informed Mrs O'Hara that all he wanted her to do for now was to look after Connie's bedroom. As the cleaning team would be looking after the rest of the house. Mrs O'Hara assured Mr Powell that Connie's bedroom would be ready and waiting for her return. Mr Powell then asked Mrs O'Hara to sit down as there was something that he wanted to talk to her about. Mrs O'Hara sat on the long sofa next to the fireplace and waited for him to begin.

"I have a proposition to put to you, Mrs O'Hara, but I don't want you to think that you are under any obligation to accept it. Should you not wish to accept my proposition then things can continue as they are at this minute Mrs O'Hara," he said.

"I will listen to what you have to say, Mr Powell," replied Mrs O'Hara politely.

"This is what I had in mind, Mrs O'Hara," said Mr Powell. "I am aware that presently you are living with your niece, Mary in a lodging house in East Belfast."

Mary was also employed by the Kean family as a house maid and both these ladies shared the one large room at the lodging house, a room that was sparsely furnished, containing only two small beds, a dressing table and one small wardrobe. Mary was in fact the sixteen year old daughter of Mrs O'Hara's dead sister, Nula, who had died in childbirth. But because of the rumours surrounding the pregnancy, the O'Hara family wanted Nula to go and live with her Aunt in Cork until the child was born. Once the birth had taken place the child was to be placed in an orphanage as far away as possible from the small village in which they lived. The reason for this was that it the identity of the father should be made known, it would have caused such a scandal and that the repercussions of this would be unthinkable.

Thankfully, Mrs O'Hara, whose first name was Rosheen, had promised her frightened younger sister that come what may, she would always look after the both of them and that if she didn't wish to give her baby away she wouldn't have to. So when Nula died in childbirth, Mrs O'Hara kept to her word and took charge of the child, naming her Mary. The alternative to this action was to follow the family plan and place the child in the hands of an orphanage. The very thought of this happening repulsed Mrs O'Hara deeply, as she was well aware of the dreadful conditions that existed in Irish orphanages at the time. Needless to say, this decision caused a huge rift in the O'Hara family, causing Liam O'Hara, the father and head of the family, to tell Rosheen that if she insisted in her plan to take care of this child, then both she and the child would have to leave their village.

You see, although Rosheen O'Hara was now referred to as Mrs O'Hara by the Kean family, she was in fact a spinster, devoting her life to looking after her dead sister's child, Mary. Rosheen's sister Nula was only fifteen when she fell pregnant. Nula had left school at the age of thirteen in order to earn money to help support the family. She was given a job as a live-in housemaid to the local Priest, Father Kavanagh, a middle-aged over weight man who looked more than the age he professed to be. Although it was never talked about openly in the family circle, it was known to have been whispered with caution in lonely corners within the village. The truth is that everyone in the village knew that Father Kavanagh was the father of Nula's illegitimate child. The O'Hara family, not wishing to fall foul of the wrath of the Catholic Church, entered into a lengthy meeting with a delegation of senior Clerics from Dublin. At this meeting it was decided that it would be best all round to remove Rosheen and the child from the village. The thinking of the Dublin delegation was this, out of sight was out of mind.

Also the church's thinking on this matter was that if they removed the child from the village, it would go a long way to help stop the rumours and innuendos that were spreading throughout the village and beyond. As this scandal, if not halted quickly, was in danger of dragging the Holy Church into unwanted ridicule and humiliation. This thinking was made only too plain to Liam O'Hara at this meeting with the Dublin Clerics. So it was that Mrs O'Hara took the child, Mary and left her village and her family and came to Belfast. This story and the origin of Mary was known by the Kean family, as Mrs O'Hara had no option but to divulged her secret to Edwina several years before when she had applied for the position as housekeeper. Mary was only thirteen at the time and Edwina made arrangements for Mary to attend a local school until she was fourteen, at that time she could come and work at the house as a maid.

Mr Powell told Mr O'Hara that his idea was to have the four attic rooms transformed into living accommodation for both herself and Mary. Mr Powell told Mrs O'Hara that once the renovations were complete that herself and Mary could live there rent free. Mr Powell's reasoning was this, he didn't want Connie, at her young age, living alone in such a large big house. Mrs O'Hara was delighted to hear Mr Powell's plans and informed him that she and Mary would be only too happy and willing to accept his kind offer of accommodation at the big house, assuring him that she would keep a close eye on young Connie at all times. Mr Powell thanked Mrs O'Hara for her cooperation and told her that both herself and Mary could move into the big house right away, He then informed her that they could take charge of the two bedrooms on the second floor until such time as the attic rooms were completed. Again, Mrs O'Hara thanked Mr Powell warmly for his kindness.

"No need to thank me, Mrs O'Hara," he told her, "I am just so pleased that you will be here on hand to look after Connie, it means a lot to me Mrs O'Hara."

Now with the accommodation situation resolved to Mr Powell's satisfaction he could now turn his attention to the unpleasant task of making the arrangements for Edwina's funeral.

It was on the Thursday afternoon when Connie returned home from hospital looking pale and drawn, her eyes burnt red from crying. Her face looked sunken and troubled, her arm tied tightly in a white cloth sling to take the pressure off her wounded shoulder. Mr Powell told Connie the news that Mrs O'Hara and Mary would be living in the house from now on. Connie thought this was a good idea and thanked Mr Powell for making the arrangements. Although Connie didn't get over excited at hearing Mr Powell's news, deep inside she was more than pleased to hear that she would not be alone in the house. After having a pot of tea with Mr Powell, Connie retired to her bedroom to rest. Feeling saddened and deeply troubled at the brutal loss of her mother, Connie rested on her bed and began to read Bobby's letters. Each letter in turn would be read thoroughly and then folded and placed neatly in an orderly pile. The deep sadness that was consuming Connie's very being was made even more severe as she now feared that one day she might lose her Bobby too. With everything that had happened, young Connie was missing her Bobby more than ever before. Her heart ached almost to breaking point every time she thought of how her dear departed mother had been killed. These desperate and agonising thoughts would cause Connie to burst into a flood of tears and sob loudly in desperation. Mrs O'Hara, true to her word, was most attentive to Connie's every need, checking on her at regular intervals, but also knowing when to leave the child alone with her sorrow whilst always making sure that she had food and drinks at hand throughout the day.

Over the next few days Mr Powell busied himself making the arrangements for Edwina's funeral, which was now to take place on the Wednesday afternoon. A full service was to be held at St. Mark's Parish Church at Dondela at two thirty. Edwina's final resting place was to be at Dondonald Cemetery at Knock. After the interment, a funeral supper had been arranged at the Grand Central Hotel in the centre of the city.

On the day of Edwina's furneral in the year of our Lord 1917 at precisely one thirty, the mourners began to assemble outside Edwina's house. Mr Powell was in the sitting room with Connie, Mrs O'Hara and Mr Meredith, the undertaker. Edwina's coffin was placed in the centre of the room. Mr Powell took a gentle hold of Connie's arm and led her across the room to where her mother's open coffin had been placed. Connie wanted one final look at her beloved mother, as she stood tearful by the side of her mother's coffin, Connie raised her hand and kissed her middle two kissed fingers and then lovingly touched her mother's brow with her kissed fingers. Mr Powell was forced to take a firmer hold of young Connie's arm as she became unsteady on her feet as she gazed longingly at her departed mother for the last time ever. Mr Powell then took Connie from the sitting room as he didn't want her to see Mr Meredith fasten down the lid of Edwina's coffin. Once the lid had been fixed in place, Edwina's coffin was then festooned with the most fragrant and colourful floral arrangement imaginable. Mr Meredith had now made ready Edwina's coffin and everything was in place for the coffin to be taken from the house.

As Edwina's coffin was leaving the sitting room, a still cold silence suddenly filled the room. All that could be heard was the lonely and intrusive ticking of the long case clock which stood in the corner of the room, as if on sentry duty. Mr Powell and Connie followed Edwina's coffin out of the house and into the sunlight of this Belfast afternoon. Outside Edwina's house was gathered the largest member of distinguished and revered faces from Belfast's social, business, legal, political and heavy industry communities that had ever been seen in one place at the same time. Mr Powell could hardly believe his eyes as he looked at the assembled mourners that were mingling openly outside the gates of Edwina's house. Every one of them there to say their last goodbyes to a most wonderful lady. It would be safe to say that everyone who was anyone in Belfast had turned up to pay their respects to Edwina, including several reporters from different newspapers all across Ireland. At first Mr Powell was at a loss to understand why they had all turned up at Edwina's funeral in such numbers. Then it hit him.

If there is one thing that you have to understand, it is this. In Ireland at this particular time, the Roman Catholic population's support for nationalism was gaining momentum by the day. More and more Catholics across Ulster were joining the ranks of Sinn Fein and the I.R.A. swelling their ranks alarmingly. Talk of an independent Ireland had been openly discussed in Dublin for almost a full year. Worryingly, that talk had now left Dublin and was quickly spreading across the whole of Ireland. With the momentum growing with every week that passed, more and more sabre rattling could be heard coming from Sinn Fein and the I.R.A. in Dublin on a daily basis. Of course the protestant population in Ireland, who mainly living in Ulster, were totally against this idea as they remained loyal to the British Crown.

Everyone in the Unionist community was well aware of the circumstances surrounding the cold blooded murder of Edwina and the young constables. Mr Powell realised that this gathering of the most influential and powerful people in Ulster were not there to only say their goodbyes to Edwina. They were also there to make a strong and unmistakable statement to Sinn Fein and the I.R.A. in Dublin and in Belfast. What was actually taking place here this day was a show of strength, defiance and opposition to the leaders and to the rank and file of Sinn Fein and the I.R.A. This was a message that would yell out loud and clear across Ulster. A message and a warning to those who would promote the idea of an independent Ireland. A message telling all who would use force, intimidation and murder to reach their objectives. This gathering was to let them know that no longer can they operate without opposition to their ideology. This message is loud and clear. Ulster Unionists would meet force with force, the message was now clear. No Surrender.

Waiting outside the gates of Edwina's house was a magnificent black horse drawn funeral carriage, its glass sides glistening brightly in the summer sun. The four corners of the top of the carriage were ornamented with flowing black fathered plumage. The coach itself was pulled by four dazzling black stallions, the top of their heads also adorned with black plumage which fluttered gently in the summer breeze. The four stallions stood perfectly still, their heads lowered as if in respect for this mournful occasion. Not so much as a swish of their tails could be seen as they stood like statues waiting patiently for their most precious cargo to be placed inside the carriage.

An eerie silence instantly fell upon the gathered assembly as Edwina's coffin came into full view. Directly behind the coffin and walking unsteadily came Edwina's distraught daughter, Connie, who was being closely watched by Mr Powell who held tightly onto her arm. Connie's slow walk behind her mother's coffin was beginning to take its toll on her, her walk became unsteady, tears now flowed openly from her saddened eyes. It was clear to see that Connie was finding it hard to cope with the demands of this distressing day. After several short minutes had passed, the funeral procession was ready to leave for St Mark's Parish Church. This was a church that, over the years, had been well attended by not only the Kean family, but also Edwina's family before she was married to her late husband, Terry Kean. It was also the church where both Edwina and her daughter, Connie, had been christened. The funeral service was to be conducted by Reverend Copper, who had served as the local vicar there for over twenty years and was a close friend to the Kean family. Reverend Copper had also officiated at the marriage of Edwina to her late husband, Terry and had also conducted the service of Terry's funeral some years earlier. In addition, and on a brighter note, he had also celebrated the Christening of young Connie at St. Mark's, at which Mr Powell had stood as Connie's godfather.

As the funeral cortege made its way along the narrow country road that led to the church, its advance was somewhat hampered, slowing down to an almost standstill. It would seem that almost everyone from East Belfast had turned up to line the roads and fill the fields surrounding St. Mark's church. Each and every one of them keen to say their own goodbyes to Edwina. Eventually the cortege arrived at the entrance to the church, all be it fifteen minutes later than initially arranged. A respectful and deeply moving service was then conducted by Reverend Copper, with the gathering of people outside the church joining in whenever possible. Mostly it was the singing of the hymns that lent themselves to group participation. It was reported later that the sound of the hymn singing could be heard clearly over two miles away.

When the moving service had been concluded, Edwina's coffin was taken to the Dondonald Graveyard at Knock and there Edwina was laid to rest beside her loving husband, Terry. As you may expect, the sad mournful events of this tragic day were beginning to overwhelm young Connie as she broke down sobbing pitifully on several occasions. Mr Powell, with the help of Mrs O'Hara, did what they could to get Connie through this emotion sapping day. The most painful and deeply distressing part of the day was when Edwina's coffin was led to rest. As the mourners began to leave the graveside and make their way to the Grand Hotel for the funeral supper, Mr Powell instructed Mrs O'Hara and Mary to take Connie home, as in his opinion, she had been through enough for one day.

The following days saw little improvement in Connie's deep and warring torment. The combined efforts of Mr Powell and Mrs O'Hara to console and comfort her were failing miserably. Nothing seemed to snap her out of this web of saddened mourning that she now found herself imprisoned within. Day after day Connie remained locked away in her bedroom reading Bobby's letters over and over again, searching for some kind of solace. Alone in her bedroom she battled with her demons, as she tried to come to terms with the loss of her mother. Connie was yet to reach her seventeenth birthday and with her beloved Bobby so far away fighting in France and her mother now regrettably gone, there was only her godfather, Mr Powell left to look after her and give her guidance. The stark realisation that if something were to happen to Mr Powell and God forbid her Bobby who was so far away, then at her tender young age she would all alone in this world. Connie was unable to fight past this distressing thought and it weighed heavy on her young mind and tormented her deeply. The most frightening thing was not so much that she would be alone, but it was the worry that she might lose both her Bobby and her godfather, Mr Powell. Five days had passed since Edwina's funeral and Mr Powell thought it was now time for Connie to emerge from her bedroom and face up to her new life.

Mr Powell arrived at Connie's house just after two thirty on the Monday afternoon. Upon his arrival he instructed Mrs O'Hara to go to Connie's room and inform her that he wished to speak with her and would she join him in the front sitting room. Some ten minutes later Connie stood in the doorway of the bright, sunlit room looking tired and red eyed as she timidly passed through the open doorway.

"Please take a seat, Connie, I think we need to talk, don't you?" said Mr Powell in a soft caring voice.

Connie walked across the room and sat in an armchair by the window, at first seeming unwilling to look directly at Mr Powell. Connie was well aware of what he wanted to talk to her about, but this topic was one that Connie really didn't want to enter into. She sat perfectly still in her armchair, her gaze seemed mesmerizingly fixed on the brilliant sunlight that flooded into the room through the open curtains.

"Tell me, Connie, how are you feeling today?" enquired Mr Powell.

Connie raised her head slowly as she turned her body uneasily towards Mr Powell. In her hand was firmly held a white cotton handkerchief which from time to time and in turn she would dab lightly against her cheeks, as she delicately cleared away small teardrops as they rolled from her eyes.

"I think it's safe to say that I have felt better, Mr Powell," replied Connie in a soft quivering voice.

Mr Powell called for Mary, the house maid, and asked her to fetch a pot of tea for both Connie and himself and this Mary did without delay.

Over several cups of tea and almost two hours of meaningful conversation, Mr Powell finally convinced Connie that it was perfectly normal for her to think of her mother every day. Although she should not allow her grief to take over life. Hard as it may be, Connie needed to put the terrible events surrounding her mother's demise behind her and concentrate on getting on with her life. Mr Powell told Connie that she should never forget what had happened to her mother, but that she also had to control those thoughts and not allow them to control her. Mr Powell told Connie that Bobby must now become her main focus in life and that he would return home very soon. When that day came, Connie would need to be strong for her Bobby. Mr Powell assured Connie that he would always be on hand to talk with her or to help her in any way that she needed him too.

As the weeks passed, things improved greatly in Connie's life, although she thought of her mother on a daily basis she was now coping adequately with her loss. To add to the improving situation, Connie's shoulder wound had now healed fully and life was slowly returning to a kind of normality. Connie had now inherited all of her mother's wealth, including the house and her mother's half of the bakery. After a meeting with Mr Powell, they both agreed that Connie would take no part in the running of the business that would be left to Mr Powell to contend with. As the weeks turned into months, no word had been heard from Bobby and this was becoming a worry for Connie as she longed for the day when a letter would arrive from him. Every night Connie would offer up a prayer for the safe return of her beloved Bobby. It was now the second week in October, the time was five forty five in the afternoon. Mr Powell was with Connie in the front sitting room having tea when suddenly a knocking could be heard coming from the front door. Mrs O'Hara was quick to answer the call.

"Are you expecting anyone, Connie?" enquired Mr Powell.

"No, no one," answered Connie,

Connie was puzzled as to whom would be visiting her so late in the afternoon.

"Who is it, Mr O'Hara?" called Connie curiously.

There was no replay forthcoming from Mrs O'Hara. Connie then heard Mrs O'Hara close the front door and then there was silence. Again Connie called out,

"Who is it, Mrs O'Hara?"

A few seconds later, a troubled looking Mrs O'Hara appeared in the sitting room doorway.

"What is it, Mr O'Hara, is there something wrong?" enquired Connie getting to her feet.

Mrs O'Hara moved sheepishly towards Connie holding a telegram in her right hand.

"It's a telegram, Miss Connie. It's addressed to you," she said softly as she handed over the telegram to Connie.

Connie held the telegram tightly in her hand, her eyes staring down at it. She was well aware what was in this telegram as it was from the war office. Mr Powell walked across the room to be by Connie's side as he said,

"Shall I open it, Connie?"

Tears began to well in Connie's eyes as she handed the telegram to Mr Powell.

"Please, Mr Powell will you read it for me?" asked Connie.

In reality Connie never, ever wanted this dammed telegram to be opened, knowing only too well what it had to say. Mr Powell opened the telegram and began to inwardly read it. Connie watched to see if his expression changed and it did. A look of anguish now swept across his face, telling Connie everything she needed to know. She looked at Mr Powell with a hopeless stare, her eyes bulging, her chest heaving uncontrollable.

"Please read it out to me, Mr Powell," asked Connie with a look of dread across her face.

Mr Powell raised up the telegram and in a voice that was soft and filled with compassion he began to read aloud the short but devastating statement which was written inside.

146

"This is to notify Miss Connie Kean that Private Bobby Gallagher is missing in action, believed killed."

It would seem that after the death of his mother, Bobby had notified the army that Connie was now his next of kin. A tearful Connie reached out and took the telegram from Mr Powell. Her tears now fell freely to the ground as she crumpled the telegram in her hand and pressed it tightly to her heart. Connie turned and quickly ran from the sitting room to the sanctuary of her bedroom.

"Dear God above," groaned Mr Powell as he thumped the table in hopeless anger.

"She could have done without this news at this time in her young life!" he said.

"Shall I go after her, Mr Powell?" asked Mrs O'Hara.

Mr Powell thought for a second then he replied.

"No, I think it best not, Mrs O'Hara, it's probably better if we leave her for now to digest this tragic news on her own. Although I think that you might keep a close eye on her tonight, Mrs O'Hara," he suggested.

"Yes of course sir, I will keep a close eye on things here, don't you worry yourself," answered a tearful Mrs O'Hara.

Mr Powell thanked Mrs O'Hara for her kind diligence and left, telling her that he would return the next day to see how things were.

CHAPTER 15

For the rest of the day Connie remained dolefully entrenched in her bedroom yet again, refusing to see or speak to anyone. With Bobby's letters scattered around her she lay curled up on the top her bed like a frightened child who was craving the reassuring and warming embrace of its mother's loving arms. Reaching out Connie clutched wildly at her thick white eiderdown with both hands, pulling it tight around her cowering body. It was as if she was using the eiderdown as a surrogate mother to create a warm, calming safe haven in which she could snuggle into and rest. Once Connie had settled herself in this self-made comfort zone, she began to read through the mountain of old letters she had previously received from her dearest Bobby. The testing hours that followed were slow and painful in their passing for everyone. At regular intervals, Mrs O'Hara would ferrying trays of refreshments up to Connie's room but sadly, not once did Connie open her bedroom door in reply to Mrs O'Hara's knocking. Time and time again Mrs O'Hara would remove the previous untouched tray and replace it with a new one.

Each and every heart-breaking trip that was made to Connie's room by Mrs O'Hara would sadly end in failure as Connie never once yielded and opened her bedroom door to Mrs O'Hara. The longer this stand-off continued, the more concerned Mrs O'Hara became about young Connie's wellbeing. Sadly at this time it would appear that all Connie was interested in was to continue with her seclusion, reading through Bobby's old letters. From time to time Mrs O'Hara would listen intently at Connie's bedroom door, hoping to hear something that would reassure her than Connie was safe. Instead all that Mrs O'Hara could hear coming from Connie's bedroom was uncontrolled sobbing breaking through the soft voice of Connie reading Bobby's old letters aloud. This distressing day soon turned into a long sleepless night for Mrs O'Hara as she maintained the caring vigil of her young charge through the darkened hours. To Mrs O'Hara's great relief, the bright early morning sun had begun its long climb to its rightful place in the sky, thus ending the long night of forlorn lamenting for all within the house.

The time was now approaching seven o'clock on the Tuesday morning and as Mrs O'Hara descended the grand staircase, carrying yet another unused tray of food and drink, a loud knocking could be heard on the front door. Mrs O'Hara placed the unused tray of food on a small hall table and rushed to see who on earth was visiting at this early hour. Mrs O'Hara opened the door wide and to her surprise she saw Mr Powell standing on the doorstep.

"Mr Powell!" she exclaimed. "I didn't expect to see you this early."

Mrs O'Hara took one step back, allowing Mr Powell to pass through the opened door into the house.

"I do apologise for arriving at this ungodly hour, Mrs O'Hara, but I simply could not wait another minute, I needed to see if Connie's situation has improved." Mr Powell removed his hat and placed it on the hall table beside the unused tray of tea and sandwiches that Mrs O'Hara had placed there just seconds before.

"Please give that to me, Mr Powell," said Mrs O'Hara as she reached out and picked up Mr Powell's hat.

"How has Connie been, Mrs O'Hara?" asked Mr Powell.

Mrs O'Hara pointed to the untouched tray on the hall table and said,

"As you can see, Mr Powell, I have been unable to get Miss Connie to eat or drink anything throughout the day or throughout the night. I tried on numerous occasions to gain access to Miss Connie's bedroom since you left yesterday afternoon. Sadly I have been unsuccessful in doing so. I also made a point of knocking as well as listening at Miss Connie's bedroom door on several occasions throughout the night. The one notable change that did strike me was that her sorrowful sobbing seemed to stop just before the sunrise. I do believe that she may be through the worst of things now, Mr Powell and with the grace of God she will find the strength to carry on with her young life."

"Thank God for small mercies, Mrs O'Hara," sighed a relieved Mr Powell.

Mr Powell had never married so he had no children of his own, but he took his position as Connie's godfather very seriously indeed. From the day she was born he had treated her as if she had been his own daughter, something Terry had often teased him about. But one thing was sure, Terry never once regretted his decision in asking Mr Powell to be his daughter's godfather. Mr Powell placed his hand gently on Mrs O'Hara's shoulder and added gratefully.

"I can see that it has been a long sleepless and exhausting night for you Mrs O'Hara, so I suggest that now I am here you take this opportunity to catch up on some well-deserved sleep. After all, Mary will be on duty very soon and if Connie or I need anything, I am sure that Mary will be more than capable to look after us."

"Yes, Mr Powell, Mary will look after both you and Connie. In truth, I will be all the better for a few hours' sleep," said Mrs O'Hara.

"Once again we are indebted to you, Mrs O'Hara and I cannot thank you enough for your devotion to the family in this our time of need," smiled an appreciative Mr Powell.

Mrs O'Hara left Mr Powell standing in the hallway and began to make her way to her room for a well-earned rest. As she reached the top of the stairs she was met by Mary who was walking across the top landing heading towards the staircase in readiness to begin her daily duties. Mrs O'Hara stopped to have a few words with her niece before going to her rooms to rest. Mary continued to descend the winding staircase, making her way towards where Mr Powell was standing.

"Good morning, Mary," said Mr Powell.

"Good morning to you too, Sir," answered Mary politely.

"May I inquire, Sir, have you eaten breakfast yet this morning?" she asked him.

Mr Powell gave a broad thankful smile saying,

"As a matter of fact I haven't, Mary."

"Would you like me to make you something to eat, Sir?" asked Mary respectfully.

"Breakfast would be most welcomed, Mary, so I will graciously accept your most kind offer," replied Mr Powell,

"Breakfast it is then sir!" replied Mary.

"While you are in the kitchen preparing breakfast I will take the opportunity to go and check on Connie," said Mr Powell.

Just as the words had left his lips both he and Mary suddenly turned their eyes upwards as their attention was drawn to the top landing. There they saw Connie standing at the top of the staircase.

"Good morning," said Connie in a bright clear voice.

"Do you think I could join you for breakfast please, Mr Powell?"

It would appear that Connie's self-detention had come to a sudden end. Mr Powell watched open mouthed as Connie began her descent of the staircase, her step was lively and full of bounce, her expression bright and filled with fervour. Mr Powell looked on with great relief and some amazement as Connie approached the bottom of the staircase. The closer she came towards Mr Powell, the bigger her smile became. Mr Powell smiled and said,

"That will be breakfast for two if you please, Mary."

Mary smiled excitedly, happy to see Miss Connie feeling so much better.

"It will be my pleasure to cook you some breakfast, Miss Connie," she beamed.

Mr Powell offered Connie his arm as he escorted her into the dining room.

"I am so pleased that you are feeling better, Connie, although I am bound to ask why the sudden change in your outlook?" asked Mr Powell,

Connie smiled as she took hold of Mr Powell's hand and squeezed it gently as she began to explain her sudden change of heart.

"As I lay on my bed locked away from everyone who cares for my wellbeing, all I could think about was Bobby. Did he die alone, was he in pain at the end of his young life, was there anyone there to comfort him in his dying moments. I opened Bobby's letters and began to read them over and over again, hour after hour I read them.

Throughout the night I thought of nothing else but my Bobby, then as I lay on my bed weeping loudly, something really astonishing happened. It was just before the breaking of the down this morning. I was cowering miserably on my bed thinking of the hell that Bobby has been forced to live through since he first left to fight in this God awful war. That's when I suddenly felt something take over my whole being, as this feeling surged through my body I suddenly felt confident that my Bobby was still alive. I felt that he was telling me to pull myself out of this downward spiral into which I had fallen. This feeling was so robust, so forceful inside me that it convinced me that Bobby isn't dead and that he is trying so hard to get home to me. This extraordinary feeling seemed to gain in power the more I read through Bobby's old letters. As I continued with my reading the same words kept recurring in my mind. Again and again the same words would flash clearly in front of me, they were the words that were contained within the telegram. Missing in action, believed dead. That's it Mr Powell, can't you see. Believed dead, not dead!

Suddenly the realisation of those words hit me and I have to say, Mr Powell, my mindset quickly changed, my sadness, my despair, all began to fade. Think of it, Mr Powell, these few meaningful words that were contained within that telegram, they didn't say Bobby was dead, Mr Powell now did they? They only said, believed dead, not known to be dead, just believed dead, Mr Powell. So with these words etched into my mind I became comforted and I began to drift further into a clouded slumber. I was overcome with this enthusiastic sensation of contentment, I could feel it slowly filling my very being and that's when I saw her there in the room with me, Mr Powell. My beautiful, loving mother, she was there with me. I saw her as plain as plain could be, she gently lowered her head and kissed my brow softly. I then saw her raise her hand and tenderly stroke back my hair in the same way as she always did when I was a child. My eyes were wide as I gazed up at her, this was no sleepy deception, nor was it my mind playing games with me, Mr Powell. Make no mistake, my mother was there by the side of my bed. My beautiful mother was there standing over me and smiling that loving smile she always had for me. Then she lowered her head and she whispered these words of comfort softly in my ear.

- Bobby isn't here, Connie, he isn't with us, because it's not yet his time to be with us here. I am here with your father. He has told me to tell you that he loves you so much and that he wants you to keep on fighting and keep strong in your belief and to listen to what your heart tells you. Your father and I are both happy now, Connie, now that we are once again reunited. Bobby's mother is here with us and she knows only too well that her loving son is not here, as it is not his time yet, Connie. So I tell you now, Connie, no matter what the future might bring, we will both always be watching over you. -

Then she disappeared from view, leaving me convinced that my Bobby is still alive and that one day very soon he will return home to me."

Mr Powell sat back in his chair somewhat taken aback by Connie's ghostly revelations and he now found himself in something of a quandary. He didn't wish to upset Connie any further by pouring scorn on her new found contentment, but he also didn't want to encourage her in her misguided belief that her late mother had visited her and told her that Bobby was still alive. Because in the future, when this information was found not to be true, he feared that Connie's wellbeing would face serious consequences as a result of following this ethereal path. Mr Powell quickly decided to walk the road that he thought, at this moment in time, to be the lesser of the two evils. He got to his feet and hugged his goddaughter tightly, then he said,

"Yes, you are right, Connie, the telegram did say believed dead. It definitely didn't claim to have found any specific proof that Bobby is indeed dead. So for now..."

To Mr Powell's relief he was interrupted in mid-sentence by Mary as she entered the room carrying a tray of tea.

"Here's a nice fresh pot of tea to be going on with, Miss Connie, the breakfast won't be long now," she said as she placed the tray on the side table.

Connie smiled and thanked Mary, she then picked up the teapot and began to pour both herself and Mr Powell a well-deserved cup of tea. After Connie and Mr Powell had finished their breakfast they retired to the front sitting room where Mr Powell chatted freely with Connie in an attempt to discover if she was truly back to her bubbly best, or if her newly found enthusiasm was but a front. After more than an hour of revealing chat, Mr Powell had satisfied himself that Connie's recovery, although gained in a somewhat mystical manner, was in fact real. Well at least in Connie's mind it was real and to Mr Powell for now that was enough for him. He then asked Connie if she had any thoughts on what she might do in the near future. Connie's eyes lit up at this question and she sat forward excitedly in her chair.

"Yes, I do, Mr Powell, I have been thinking very seriously about this idea for some weeks now and as you have now raised the question I would appreciate your thoughts on my idea," responded Connie quickly.

Mr Powell was pleased that Connie was now at least thinking of the future, so he smiled then asked inquisitively,

"Please tell me your idea, Connie and if I can help in any way, then I will."

Connie straightened herself in her chair and began to explain her idea to Mr Powell.

"I have heard it mentioned there is a military hospital somewhere here in East Belfast, do you know anything of it, Mr Powell?"

"Yes, I know of it," replied Mr Powell. "It's situated on the Circular Road, just a short car ride from here as it happens. It's the Ulster Volunteer Force Hospital, they opened their doors to all wounded British soldiers a few months ago and since then it has become known as the Somme Nursing Home. Why do you ask, Connie?" enquired Mr Powell.

"Well," said Connie smartly, her enthusiasm plain to see, "I think I would like to work there as a volunteer nursing assistant. I think working there would make me feel that I am contributing something to this war. Also I believe that it will make me feel closer to Bobby, as I wait for his safe return."

Mr Powell deliberated for a few seconds on what Connie had just told him. But it didn't take him long to come to the conclusion that it might not be such a bad idea at all for Connie to go and work at the U.V.F. hospital. For one thing, it would keep her occupied and maybe in time all thoughts of Bobby's return would fade from her mind. Because without a doubt, sooner or later the cruel reality of this war would be sure to hit home. With an approving smile Mr Powell nodded his head, then asked bluntly,

"Are you sure this is what you want to do, Connie? You do realise that this won't be an easy task for you to undertake? I want you realise from the very beginning that all of the young men at this Hospital will be recovering from extremely serious war injuries. It won't be a pleasant experience having to tend to the mutilated bodies of these young men day after day, Connie. I need you to understand this before I consider helping you in this matter."

"I understand everything you are telling me, Mr Powell but I have thought hard and long about this and it's what I need to do. I am ready for this, trust me, Mr Powell, I really need to do this," enthused Connie eagerly.

"Well then, Connie," said Mr Powell, "If you're sure about this and it's definitely what you want to do, then I think I can help you with your quest."

"Really! Can you help me in this matter?" shouted Connie excitedly.

"Yes, really, Connie, I can help," quipped Mr Powell, "You see, the head of Medicine at the U.V.F. hospital is a friend of mine, as indeed he was a good friend of your late father. His name is Dr Roland Reynolds and he is a member of our Orange Lodge at Knock. If you like I will speak with him on your behalf, Connie. I'm sure he will be only too pleased to accommodate you in this issue."

Connie's eyes lit up like a beacon at Mr Powell's revelation that he was a friend of Mr Roland Reynolds.

"Please do speak with him about me Mr Powell, I would be most grateful to you if you would," beamed Connie excitedly.

Mr Powell smiled and said,

"Consider it done, Connie. I will go this very afternoon and talk to Roland on your behalf."

Mr Powell finished his breakfast and left Connie's house. That afternoon, true to his word, Mr Powell arrived at the U.V.F. hospital at two thirty. His meeting with Mr Roland Reynolds was a short one, as he was only too pleased to have Connie Kean volunteering at the hospital.

It was but ten days after Mr Powell's meeting with Mr Roland Reynolds when Connie began her voluntary work at the U.V.F. hospital. Several days before her start date, Connie held a meeting with the nursing administrator, Matron Gaskin, where Connie agreed to work on a voluntary basis on Mondays, Wednesdays and Fridays from eight in the morning until five in the evening. Connie arrived bright and early for her first day's work at the hospital, her enthusiasm for the work ahead couldn't have been higher. Then, as she made her way to the Administrator's Office, Connie quickly discovered that everything Mr Powell had told her about the hospital was indeed correct and then some. With her eyes opened wide, Connie saw for the first time the true horror of what these young men had gone through. As she trod the long chilling corridor leading to the Administrator's Office, Connie couldn't help but notice the string of open wards which lined both sides of the corridor. Connie's eyes moved in a wild frenzy flitting from one side of the corridor to the other. To her shock she observed that each and every one of these wards were filled to overflowing with young men with all kinds of horrifying injuries. Young men of roughly the same age as her Bobby, some without legs, some without arms, some with the most horrendous facial injuries, faces that had been burnt so badly that not even a mother would recognise them.

As Connie continued on her way to Matron Gaskin's office there was more than the gruesome injuries she had just witnessed to the young men to chill her blood, there was also the horrifying sound of young men screaming out in unimaginable pain. Screams so loud and so prolonged that Connie realised that every one of these young men had suffered terribly in this God awful war, some of them in body, they were the more obvious. Others were suffering in mind, not so obvious to see their injuries, but injured they were none the less. Connie's eyes sank almost as deep as her heart as she witnessed for the second time in her young life, man's cruelty to his fellow man. Here were young men who had seen and done things that no human being should ever see, or ever be asked to do. Sadly she now understood fully the horrifying truth behind the dreadful accounts of the war mentioned in Bobby's letters. Connie glared in abject disbelief at the horrendous injuries many of these young men had sustained. Slowly her eyes filled with anguished tears as her chest tighten and her heart began to pound in torment within her young body at the sights before her.

Through blurred eyes, Connie continued to scan the countless beds that filled the overcrowded wards lining both sides of the hallway. Suddenly Connie came across a most disturbing sight. She came to a halt outside a long narrow, dimly lit ward containing twenty or more beds. Connie moved slowly towards the open door and peered inside, what she saw made her wish that she had never stopped and looked inside the door to this ward. Connie's body suddenly began to shudder in horrifying disbelief as her eyes fell upon a host of the most devastatingly injured young men you could ever see, This ward was filled with young boys that had their youthful faces cruelly ripped apart by the horrors of this God forsaken war. Injuries that if you had not seen with your own eyes you would never believe, if told about them. Young men with their faces so badly melted that their facial features had become unrecognisable.

With a heavy heart and a tear filled eye, Connie continued to make her way to the Administrators office, as she turned yet another corner she was confronted by a sight that at first glance, confused her a little. Because now before her she saw two wards, both with large glass double doors at the far end, which were opened and led out into the gardens beyond. Connie stood looking inside the wards for a few seconds, to her it seemed that the patients inside didn't look to be injured in any way whatsoever. To a man they were all on their feet and walking around laughing and chatting to each other, but at closer inspection it quickly became clear that they were in fact just as much victims of this damned war as the rest. These young men, although seemingly sound in body, had been separated from the most brutally wounded and had been grouped together in wards at the far end of the hallway. The young men that filled these wards had injuries that at first sight were not obvious to the eye. These young men had different injuries, some had been blinded for life while others had lost their hearing, their eardrums being cruelly ruptured due to the constant loud thunderous pounding of the big field guns they had been operating. As Connie looked on she pondered with the thought that there didn't seem to be an end to the suffering created by, what these young men in the beginning understood to be ... THE GREAT ADVENTURE

It would be true to say that the first few weeks of Connie's volunteer work at the U.V.F. hospital came as something of a horrifying but sobering experience. Try as she might Connie found it extremely difficult in those first few traumatic weeks at the hospital to come to terms with the dreadful injuries these young men had suffered. Never before had she witnessed such human grief on such a large scale. Never before in her life had she seen or even heard such bone-chilling, heart-breaking sobbing from ones so young. Never before had she witnessed such demoralizing cries of pain, suffering and despair. Never before had she experienced such a feeling of total and utter hopelessness by ones so young. Their misery and their despair seemed so unstoppable that it swept through each of the wards within the hospital like a wild dog suddenly finding its freedom. From that first terrifying day, Connie was determined to work through the horror and torment that she faced each day as she entered through the hospital doors. This she did because at the end of the day she knew deep in her heart that these young men needed her to be strong for them. Connie knew only too well that they depended on someone just like her to help them in their everyday tasks, tasks the rest of us take for granted.

So it was that Connie diligently thrust herself into her work at the U.V.F. hospital and as the weeks quickly turned into months, Connie had become something of a favourite with the young soldiers under her care. This of course was understandable as Connie was a real Irish beauty. With her long thick curling raven hair that framed a face so beautiful and a smile so angelic that it could bring a tear to the eye of the hardest of men. Connie's beauty was perfectly matched with skin so flawless and smooth that it looked as though it was made of the finest porcelain. Some would say that the child had been kissed by the angels in heaven at birth. Connie also had an uncanny ability to make every one of the young men feel that she was there only to tend to their needs, theirs and theirs alone. She was always bright and cheerful around the young wounded men under her charge and she always showed a willingness to help with each and every task they would ask of her. Nothing was ever too much trouble for Connie and each and every day she spent at the Hospital, she spent trying her hardest to brighten the day for these brave young men that were under her care.

Sometimes, even at the end of a hard and strenuous day, Connie would stay behind and sit by the bedside of one or more of the young men, who for one reason or another, found themselves falling under the dark cloud of depression as they struggled in their battle to overcome their crippling injuries. So when Connie would see this powerful and distressing illness raising its ugly head and manifest itself deep within these young men, her heart told her that their need for her company was stronger than her need to go home. Connie wasn't able to administer medicines to the young men affected by this terrible sickness. Although sometimes medicines were not the answer, sometimes all that was required was for someone to be there with a warm compassionate smile. Sometimes a willing hand was enough to gently soothe their heated brow. Or maybe just a sympathetic ear was needed to listen to their deepest darkest thoughts. When situations like this would arise, Connie would happily stay behind talking with the young men in question, doing her very best to comfort them in their hour of need. This made Connie very popular with every patient in every ward she ever entered.

It was now late October 1917 and Connie had increased her work load at the hospital, now working five days a week from eight in the morning until five in the evening, only having the weekends to herself. Saturdays, Connie reserved for resting, often seeing her sleeping in until late in the afternoon. Sunday mornings continued much in the same vein as they had always done ever since Connie's childhood. The day would begin with Mrs O'Hara cooking an early breakfast for everyone. Once Mary had served Connie with her breakfast, both herself and Mrs O'Hara would leave for morning Mass at St. Matthew's Roman Catholic Chappell in East Belfast. Connie would ready herself and wait for Mr Powell to arrive and accompany her to St. Marks Church for morning worship. After Sunday service Mr Powell would then drive Connie back home and stay with her for lunch, this would give him the opportunity for a long chat with Connie, making sure that everything was right with her and that she was not experiencing any difficulties from her work at the U.V.F. hospital. Once Mr Powell had left for home and Mr O'Hara and Mary had cleared away the lunch dishes, they would have several hours to themselves. This was the time that Connie looked forward to the most, it was those few precious hours on a late Sunday afternoon, between lunch and a late supper, that would see Connie retire to the front sitting room to spend time alone with her most private thoughts. This alone time also gave Connie the opportunity to put pen to paper and wright several letters to her beloved Bobby.

Monday mornings would see Connie refreshed and eager to continue with her duties at the hospital. Although in reality Connie's daily duties rarely changed from one day to the next. To Connie's great credit this mundane daily routine that she faced never once discouraged nor dampened her enthusiasm for the tasks ahead. You see, deep within herself Connie knew that what she was doing in the hospital day after day was of immense importance and a tremendous help to the young men who found themselves recuperating within the confines of the hospital walls. In truth Connie had grown to really enjoy the time she was spending with this heroic group of young men. In a strange kind of way the courage that they showed in facing their individual and personal daily battles to come to terms with the horrendous disabilities, had begun to rub off on Connie herself. As she witnessed at first-hand how these brave young men were fighting hard to overcome their horrifying injuries that this dreadful war had inflicted upon them. This bravery shown and this bravery alone lifted Connie's heart and filled her with an enormous respect for the valour shown by these gutsy young men.

Any wayward thoughts of repetitious boredom that Connie found creeping into her head were quickly flushed away after spending just ten minutes in the company of these brave young soldiers. Connie would begin each day by helping to serve breakfast to the patients. Once this chore had been completed and the used dishes cleared away, Connie, along with the other nurses and volunteers, would then begin the daily task of toileting and then washing and dressing the young men in her care. Through no fault of their own most of these young men were unable to carry out these simplest of daily tasks for themselves, daily tasks that the rest of us carry out without a thought. Due to their injuries the majority of these young men were totally unable to toilet themselves, assistance was needed every step of the way. When all the patients had been attended to and all of the young men had been readied for the coming day, Connie along with the other nurses and volunteers were able to take a short break. When the weather allowed, the nurses and volunteers would steal a relaxing few minutes in the gardens of the hospital with a well-deserved cup of tea before once again returning to their duties.

Chapter 16

It was just after lunch on a bright but blustery Tuesday afternoon when the nursing Sister asked Connie if she would oblige her by going to work on ward E6, which was situated at the far end of the hallway. The reason for this request was that two of the volunteers had failed to report for duty that day and it had left the ward short staffed. Connie was only too willing to accommodate and instantly set off for ward E6 where she was needed. The ward in question was one of the wards that contained some of the more mobile soldiers, soldiers that were almost capable of looking after themselves and were really only recuperating before leaving the Hospital. Some of these patients in ward E6, although well on the road to recovery, were in some cases confined to wheelchairs until such time as the strength had fully returned to their injured bodies and a degree of sturdiness was felt in their legs. Each day these young men would be taken by a volunteer for a trip around the gardens, but today due to the shortage of volunteers, some of the young soldiers were unable to be taken into the garden and enjoy their daily excursion into the bright sunshine and feel the clean fresh air waft over their faces, hence the reason for Connie's transfer.

When Connie arrived at ward E6 the Sister in charge asked her if she would take one of the patients out for his daily outing around the gardens and Connie agreed. The nursing sister then pointed towards the glass double doors at the end of the ward, telling Connie that the soldier's name was Patrick. Connie quickly put on her cardigan and made her way across the large noisy bustling ward to where Paddy was waiting patiently in his wheelchair.

"Good morning," said Connie as she approached the young soldier. "I take it that you are Patrick?" she enquired politely.

Patrick was a young man of no more than twenty years of age, with bright red hair and a rosy complexion. At hearing Connie's voice he turned quickly in her direction, his huge smile seemed to light up his youthful face like a welcoming beacon. But then, as Connie came into his full vision, suddenly his expression

161

changed and he looked shocked. This was something that Connie picked up on immediately.

"Is everything alright, Patrick?" Connie asked, feeling a little shocked by the soldier's sudden reaction to her.

"Yes…yes, everything's fine, really," he answered.

Although Patrick tried to hide his shock at seeing Connie standing before him, Connie could tell that everything was not fine with this young soldier. His voice remained a little anxious and the shocked look that had arrived so quickly, still remained.

"Look, I'm really sorry if I frightened you by my sudden and cutting stare, but when I saw you it was as if I knew you, but I wasn't sure how or from where," continued Patrick.

Connie smiled forgivingly at the young soldier as she moved behind his wheelchair and took hold of the handles. She then began to push Patrick through the opened doors and out into the garden.

"It's okay Patrick, don't worry yourself so, you have probably seen me around the hospital from time to time, that's all it will be," said Connie

Patrick again looked puzzled as he replied,

"No…No! That's not it, that's not it at all!" he exclaimed.

Connie smiled to herself, knowing that is was highly unlikely that this young man had ever seen her outside of the hospital.

"Anyway, Patrick, let's just enjoy our walk in the garden on this fine autumn day. Let's not allow this quandary to worry us too much for now because, if indeed you do know me, it will all become clear in time," said Connie.

"Yes perhaps," replied Patrick, all be it unconvincingly.

"First of all, Patrick, allow me apologue to you for not introducing myself when we first met," said Connie.

Connie had now positioned herself to the front of Patrick's wheelchair with her hand held out in readiness to shake the young soldier's hand.

"My name is Connie and I am really pleased to meet you, Patrick," Connie said cheerfully.

Immediately on hearing Connie's name Patrick's expression once again changed, at first it was one of total shock, it was as if he had just seen a ghost. Connie was, not surprisingly, a little taken back by Patrick's reaction to her introduction. Feeling unsure to why the young soldier's reaction to her was so stark, Connie quickly took a few paces back from Patrick's wheelchair. Then just as quickly as Patrick's shocked expression had arrived, it swiftly changed yet again. This time it was one of clarity, Patrick now looked like a man that had suddenly solved a great puzzle, a puzzle that had been troubling him for many years. Suddenly Patrick smiled broadly and said with great feeling,

"No! Surely not? It can't be you? Can it?"

Connie looked confused and felt a little worried by Patrick's new found gusto.

"What can't be me, Patrick!?" asked Connie.

Again the young soldier smiled broadly his voice was now filled with a strange but excited enthusiasm as he replied,

"You're not Connie Kean, are you?"

Connie was shocked that this young man whom she had never met before today seemed to know who she was.

"I'm sorry, Patrick, but have we met before?"

"Are you Connie Kean?" enthused Patrick. "Please tell me that you are Connie Kean," he continued.

"Yes I am," replied Connie with a confused tone in her voice.

Patrick then gave a full and hardy belly laugh as he sat up straight in his wheelchair saying,

"No, Connie we have never met before, but I feel that I have known you all my life, for you have comforted me on many a long tormenting night as I sat in my damp cold trench, waited in dread for the dawn to break and the new days battle to begin."

Connie looked confused as she asked,

"But how did I do that?"

"As I said, Connie, night after night as I sat in that hell-hole that had become my home. Waiting in fear for the morning to come and we would again go over the top as our next attack would begin. I sat there Connie with my best friend, Bobby Gallagher. He would show me your photograph and tell me all about you. He would talk for hours and hours about you, Connie, keeping our attention focused on you well into the night and not on the hell that would occupy our lives when the morning would finally arrive. He would tell everyone that would listen that you were the most beautiful girl in Ireland and that the minute he returned home he was going to marry you. I have to say that now that I have seen you in person with my own eyes, I am bound to agree with every word Bobby ever spoke about you, Connie."

Connie stood in stunned silence, her eyes filled with tears as she moved forward and knelt down on her hunches in front of Patrick, then taking his hands in hers she ask fretfully,

"You really know my Bobby do you, Patrick?"

"Yes I do, Connie, we became very good friends," answered Patrick.

Instantly Connie raised her soft slender hand and pressed it tight to her open mouth as she gasped loudly in astonished disbelieve. Mixed tears of shocked surprise and elation quickly welled in her eyes at hearing Patrick's revelation of knowing Bobby. Connie remained in reflective silence for several seconds, before inquiring with hopeful anticipation.

"Tell me my Bobby is still alive, please, Patrick say it is so."

Connie raised her head slowly in anticipation, her eyes pleading for Patrick to give the answer that she so wanted to hear. Again Connie asked the question,

"Please tell me you know my Bobby is still alive and well, please, Patrick tell me it is so."

The young soldier placed his hand tenderly under Connie's chin and lifted her head gently until he was looking her straight in the eyes, then he said in a low reassuring voice,

"I know that you will have received a telegram telling you that Bobby is missing in action believed dead, Connie. I know this because our Captain that day said so in his's report, but I was with Bobby that day. I can verify that Bobby is indeed missing in action, but the last time I saw him he was still alive and I told Captain Goodman so, but he wouldn't listen to me, Connie, he put in his report regardless of what I told him I saw."

Connie got to her feet and looked up into the crisp clear autumnal sky above as she whispered softly with clenched hands,

"My dear God I thank you this day, I thank you for saving my Bobby. I know that he is still alive, I always have."

Connie's soft brown eyes were now filled with tears of joy, as she reached out and hugged Patrick firmly in both arms. Then she said,

"Then you must be Paddy O'Connor, my Bobby spoke of you many times in his letters."

Patrick replied with a smile,

"One and the same miss Connie and please can we drop the Patrick, call me Paddy, everyone else, but that nursing sister does."

"You must tell me everything, Paddy, I want to know what happened that day." said Connie with great relief.

Paddy looked up at Connie and smiled warmly, then he asked Connie to push him over to the big oak tree at the far end of the garden. This was something that Connie was only too willing to oblige. When they reached the oak tree Connie placed Paddy's wheelchair under the large overhanging branches. Connie then sat herself down on the wooden tree seat that surrounded the thick trunk of the tree. Once both were settled, Paddy began to tell Connie the full story of what had really happened on the day when he last saw Bobby.

"I don't know when you last heard from Bobby, Connie, but after we fought at Messines our regiment was moved across the French border into Flanders where we were to take part in the third attack at Ypres. Ypres was a small market town, really nothing to write home about, but apparently in the greater scheme of things it had now become one of the most important little towns in the whole of Europe. It was early in August when we arrived in Flanders, I have to tell you, Connie that the battles that followed outdone everything we went through at the Somme. It out played every horrifying or brutal action we witnessed anywhere throughout this bloody war, Connie. Even troops that had fought long and hard at the Somme and at Messines like both Bobby and myself found this hard going. So it was that on the 9th. of September that Bobby, myself, and three other boys from our platoon were sent out on a recognisances patrol, under the command of Captain Goodman. We were to gather as much information about the movement of the German forces as we could without actually crossing the Germen army's main lines.

The whole mission was to take no more than three or four hours, but Captain Goodman was a novice, this was his first time in action, as he had only arrived with us three day before. We set off at 3 o'clock in the afternoon and by 6 o'clock the same afternoon Captain Goodman had managed to get us lost. Both Bobby and I tried to tell him that we were going the wrong way but he just wouldn't listen. You see Captain Goodman was a real English toff, the kind of officer us regular soldiers hated to serve under. We all know that these kind of officers only get a commission because of the families that they come from. We also know that sooner or later they would drop us right in it, Connie. At first Goodman came across as a bit of a numskull, but it didn't take long for his arrogance towards the ranks to shine through. He had a superior attitude towards the ranks, thinking that we were all of limited intelligence. He had a high opinion of himself, Connie, a real know it all at only twenty one years old. We reluctantly followed Captain Goodman, knowing that we were drifting deeper and deeper into trouble as we neared the German lines. Suddenly we emerged from the thick wood that we had been aimlessly trudging through for the last few hours. That's when we saw straight in front of us a small farm-house and several barns, the farm itself ran along the edge of the wood. Captain Goodman suggested that we took a well-deserved rest in the large barn that was situated about 200 yards from the cover of the trees.

Much against both Bobby and my objections to this idea Captain Goodman insisted that we head for the shelter of the barn. Again we both told him that this wasn't a good idea as we would have to leave the cover of the woods and cross open land to reach the barn. We both told Captain Goodman that this was a very risky idea. Because we were unsure of our position and we couldn't be sure of what might be waiting for us once we left the cover of the thick wood. Goodman insisted and so we left the cover of the trees, exposing ourselves on open land. At this point both Bobby and myself realised that Captain Goodman was becoming flustered and more than a little frightened about the situation he had now put us in. Unfortunately for us Captain Goodman continued to make a succession of what were obvious blunders with the choices he was making. We moved quickly across the ground, Connie as we tried to reach the barn safely. We got no more than half way across the open ground when a German raiding party, that had positioned themselves on the edge of the wood just to the left of the barn, suddenly opened fire on us. Both Bobby and I estimated their numbers to be around twenty strong, although it was difficult to be sure as they were well concealed behind the thick trees and countless overgrown undergrowth. No matter their numbers, we all knew that they had the upper hand on us and they were undoubtedly a force to be reckoned with.

We realised that reaching the safety of the barn had become our priority as we were like sitting ducks out in the open. At first we tried to find cover wherever we could, but it wasn't long before we realised that our best bet was to reach the barn. We began to return fire as we rushed towards the barn, but before we were able to reach the safety of the barn two of our party had been killed. Two boys both aged nineteen, one called John Johnson and the other called George Gavin, both were Belfast lads just like Bobby and myself. Now there was only Bobby, myself, Captain Goodman and another lad, an English boy called Peter Walker, he was aged eighteen years. It was as plain as day that this boy was terrified with the situation he found himself in. You see, Connie this was all new to him as he had only arrived with us on the same day as Captain Goodman. Most of what happened next was just a blur, but somehow the four of us had reached the barn.

Captain Goodman stood in the centre of the barn and looked sheepish as he informed us that he thought it would be a good idea if we remained where we were for now. He was of the opinion that we would be safe there, as the barn provided us with cover should the Germens decide to attack. His expression was one of a man that was expecting us all to agree with his logic as you see, in his pathetic thinking, he thought he had done well in finding us this safe haven. But Bobby was of a totally different opinion and he was about to let Captain Goodman know it. Bobby furiously jumped to his feet and stood in front of Captain Goodman shouting really angrily at him. Stay here! he screamed, Bloody well stay here, Captain, what bloody choice do we have now that we are pinned down here in this bloody barn, we shouldn't damned well be here in the first place, Captain. That's enough, Gallagher, Goodman shouted back at Bobby.

But Bobby was determined to let Goodman know just what a fool he had been from start to finish. Bobby was really furious, Connie and again he shouted at Goodman. No it's not enough Captain, we told you from the start that we were going in the wrong direction, but you wouldn't listen, we told you that we shouldn't leave the cover of the woods, but again you wouldn't listen to us and now we are stuck here in this bloody barn with twenty or so German soldiers outside and us in here with no means of escape. Goodman replied angrily saying loudly, we have cover here Gallagher, what else do we need. Cover, Captain, bloody cover, screamed Bobby, Tell me, Captain just how long do you see us staying here in this damned barn, because sooner or later the Germans will attack us and they will keep on attacking us until we are all dead, Captain. The reason that they can't let us escape from here, Captain is because they can't be sure just how much of their troop movements we have seen. On the other hand,

Captain, the second we set foot outside this bloody barn they will cut us down like dogs in minutes, so then and only then will it be enough, Captain Goodman.

Goodman didn't answer Bobby, instead he walked across the barn to an open window and looked out at the German raiding party and yes he saw that they were slowly advancing towards the barn. Bobby looked straight at me, I had never seen such anger in his eyes, Connie. I think it was the realisation that he might never see you again, Connie that enraged him so much. Then he looked at me and said in a soft voice, we are not going to get out of this, Paddy, you do know that, don't you? I just nodded my head in agreement, because our chances of escape didn't look that good. I put my hand on Bobby's shoulder and he smiled at me and said, I'm glad that it's you that's with me on this day, Paddy. I replied, and you with me, Bobby. Bobby then took out his bayonet from its sheath and with its point he began to carve something into the thick wooden post that was supporting the roof. When he had finished he went to one of the other windows in the barn in readiness for the German attack. I looked to see what he had carved into the wooden post, it read:

Bobby loves Connie for ever.

I glanced over at Bobby as he waited by the open window for the German attack to begin. That's when it struck me, no matter what battle we found ourselves in the middle of in the past, no matter how fierce the fighting we had faced in the months in which I had known and fought alongside Bobby, never before had I seen him look so troubled before the beginning of a skirmish. I walked across the barn and joined Bobby at the window, we both smiled again at each other knowing that our time on this earth was about to end. We watched as the Germans manoeuvred themselves into position in readiness for the attack. Everything was still within the barn as we waited for them to make their move, we waited and watched for maybe fifteen minutes and in that time not a word was spoken between any of us. Then it began, the Germans opened fire on us as they began to advance across the farmyard. They were now no more than fifty yards away from the barn, we returned fire, although we knew it was a futile exercise because there was no way we could hold them of for long. Although it hadn't been said by anyone of us, we all knew that we were going to go down fighting and that was for sure. Suddenly Bobby looked at me and smiled broadly as he said, No Surrender Paddy, I smiled back and replied, No Surrender Bobby.

We exchanged fire for something like fifteen minutes, but they were making ground on us all the time, we knew that it wouldn't be long before they were close enough to start launching fire bombs at the barn, after all we were in a wooden shelter that was filled with hay. Once they had set the barn alight all they had to do then was to set back and wait, because it would then be an easy task for them to pick us off one by one as we ran from the burning barn. But just as we thought that our time was coming to an end, something happened that took us all by surprise. Suddenly we could hear gun fire coming from the woods to our left, both Bobby and I quickly looked in the direction of the gun fire. If you could have seen the size of the smiles that quickly filled our faces, Connie, because to our amazement coming out of the woods to our left were two groups of, what we took to be farmers and villagers, each group was about twenty strong and all were armed with rifles. They opened fire on the Germans forcing them to retreat and take cover behind some outbuildings close to the farmhouse. Two men from the group of farmers that was closest to the barn came to the edge of the wood and signalled for us to leave the barn and make for the woods. We couldn't make out what language they were speaking in, but they were able to make themselves understood. Captain Goodman was the first to run from the barn and head for the woods, this he did without a word to any of us. Bobby then told me to go next. I made it to the cover of the wood and returned fire towards the Germans. Peter was next to leave the barn, but by now some of the Germans had turned their guns in our direction. Peter was only twenty yards from the edge of the wood when he took several bullets to his back and legs. I watched as he dropped to the ground only a few agonising yards from where I was standing. Captain Goodman didn't stop to return fire, instead he was well into the woods. I called to him to come back and help us and he stopped running and looked back at me, but he didn't return. He just stood there looking at me, then he shouted,

Come on, Paddy get out of there!

No Captain, I shouted, Bobby is still in the barn and Peter is wounded, we must help them, but Captain Goodman just stood his ground looking at me. Then he shouted again, Get out of there, Paddy. Bobby and Peter are goners, save yourself! Then he turned and began running away from the barn, he did nothing to help. Suddenly Bobby appeared in the clearing running towards me. Come on Bobby, I shouted, run hard Bobby, for God sake run as hard as you can. I was screaming at him at the top of my voice. I think he would have made it too, Connie, but he stopped to help Peter who was screaming in pain as he lay on the ground. Bobby picked Peter up in his arms and began to run towards me again, but a volley of gun fire was aimed right at them. Peter was hit again and this time in the head. He was killed instantly. Bobby stopped and gently placed Peter's body on the ground, then he turned and ran towards me in an attempt to make it to the cover of the woods. He only advanced a few paces before another volley of gun fire came in his direction. I saw Bobby fall to the ground. At first I thought he was dead, then I could see him move. Bobby are you hurt bad mate? I called out to him. He waved to me and called back, I have been hit a few times in my right leg but I will be okay, just get yourself to hell out of her Paddy!

I was going to run into the clearing and help my friend, when two of the farmers came out of the wood no more than five yards from where Bobby was laying. The other farmers began firing constantly as one of them waved franticly for me to go, but I stayed to witness them load Bobby onto a handcart and disappear into the woods with him. I then turned and ran as fast as I could after Captain Goodman. It took us a full day to get back to our lines, I told Goodman what I saw, but he wouldn't listen to what I had to say. If you ask me, he didn't want to tell my version of events as too many questions would have been asked about his behaviour in the whole affair. If that had happened he would surely have been shown up to be the snivelling coward that he really is. So you see, Connie, yes Bobby is missing in action, but I don't believe for one minute that he's dead! The next day after Captain Goodman had handed in his report, I was moved to another platoon further down the line and it was three days after this when I was wounded myself. I took three bullets, two to my shoulder and back and one to my right leg. You know in a strange kind of way, I am so glad I was wounded, because it has given me the opportunity to meet you in person, Connie and tell you that Bobby is indeed still alive."

Connie remained perfectly still after Paddy had finished telling her his story, not a muscle in her young body as much as flinched. Her deep brown eyes were now completely veiled by the floods of tears that joyfully gushed down her young face.

"Are you alright, Connie?" enquired Paddy.

Connie turned her head towards Paddy and smiled broadly saying,

"Am I alright, Paddy? I'm more than alright thanks to you, Paddy."

Connie put both arms around Paddy and hugged him tightly for several long seconds, then she shouted loudly,

"By God I could kiss you, Paddy."

"Don't let me stop you then, Connie," laughed Paddy loudly.

Connie again put her arms around Paddy's neck and kissed him full on the lips in gratitude and celebration of the wonderful news he had delivered to her about her beloved Bobby.

Connie only ever worked on ward E6 for that one day as the next day she was moved back to the wards that she normally worked on. Before going home each day Connie would meet Paddy in the gardens and chat with him for as long as she could. As the weeks past, Paddy began to regain his strength and he was soon up on his feet and walking freely, which meant that his release date from the hospital grew closer by the day. It was on a Friday evening, just before Connie left for home, that she made her daily visit to see Paddy. As she entered his ward she saw a young woman by Paddy's bedside. They were talking but it didn't appear to be a friendly chat.

Connie, not wishing to interrupt their conversation waited by the door for them to conclude their dialogue. Suddenly the young woman gestured furiously towards Paddy with her hand, then she turned away in anger and quickly stormed from his bedside, pushing past Connie as she hurriedly left the ward. Connie could see that this visitor had upset Paddy and she slowly approached him with more than a little concern. As Connie drew closer to Paddy she couldn't help but notice that several small tears still lingered in his eyes.

"Is everything alright, Paddy?" Connie asked nervously.

Paddy turned slowly and looked at Connie with reddened eyes.

"My God, Paddy, what is it, have you received bad news?" enquired Connie.

Paddy just nodded his head.

"Who was that young woman and what has she said to upset you so?" asked Connie.

Paddy got to his feet and said,

"That was my older sister, Connie. I wrote to my family telling them that I was being released from hospital next week."

"Surely that's good news, Paddy?" said Connie.

"Well I thought it would be, Connie, but it seems it's not being as well received as I had anticipated," grumbled Paddy. "You see, I am not only being released from hospital, I was informed this morning that I am also being discharged from the army on health grounds," added Paddy.

Connie's expression was one of confusion as she sat down on the chair by Paddy's bedside, then somewhat perplexed she declared,

"I'm sorry, Paddy, but I don't understand, surely that has to be a good news, don't you think, Paddy?"

"You don't understand, Connie," replied Paddy, "you know that I am West Belfast, don't you?" he continued.

"Yes, I remember you saying once in conversation, but I still don't understand, Paddy," answered Connie.

"Well that would make me a Roman Catholic, Connie," said Paddy.

"Well yes, I guessed as much from our conversations, Paddy, as well as from Bobby's letters, but forgive me, I still don't understand," said a bemused Connie.

Paddy looked straight at Connie, his eyes saddened and regretful as he continued.

"Look Connie, Ireland is changing by the day and it seems to me that there is nothing anyone can do to stop what is taking place in Dublin, and in turn these newly formed thoughts are feverishly spreading throughout this land of ours. One day soon, Connie something is going to take hold of this country of ours by its throat and squeeze the life right out of it. When I joined up to go and fight in this bloody war, my father tried everything in his power to try to stop me. At the time I thought it was because he loved me and feared for my safety, I now know that I was deluding myself with that thought, Connie, because that thought could not be further from the truth. My sister was sent here today by my father and it appears that my whole family are nationalist. It would seem that they have all been swept along in this fanatical fervour of Irish republicanism that is being spouted all over Ireland by the many mouthpieces of Sinn Fein. Their doctrine is spreading rapidly throughout the Roman Catholic population of this Island, Connie. Each and every member of my family are willing to fight and die for a free Ireland. Trust me, Connie, trouble isn't too far away for us all in this Ireland.

My sister informs me that my father, no my whole family, see me as a turncoat and a traitor to Ireland because I dared to don this British uniform and go to fight for the British Crown. My father sent me a message via my sister. His message is simple and straight to the point. His message is this Connie, I am not now nor ever will be welcome back at the house where I was born and lived with my mother my father and my two sisters all of my life. It was also made plain to me that they never want to see nor hear from me ever again. As far as my family are concerned, I died in disgrace in the mud of the fields in France. Killed fighting for the Kings shilling and for a cause that had nothing to do with any true Irishman. Connie, I tell you I honestly. I fear for this Island of ours, ever since the Easter Rising in Dublin in 1916 things changed for everyone in Ireland and now there can be no going back. You will see, because it is coming, Connie, one day soon we will all have to take one side or the other in a conflict that will undoubtedly be thrust upon us all in the coming months and years. Neighbour will be set against neighbour, friend set against friend, fear, distrust and deception will scar all our lives for years to come Connie. But where will it all end? But what's even far more frightening to me is this, how and when will it all end?"

Connie looked fiscally shaken by what Paddy had just told her and she fell back in her chair in total disbelief. After a few seconds of complete silence, Connie responded in a voice that trembled with every word that left her lips.

"My good god, Paddy, I had no idea that all this unrest was going on in Ireland, are you really sure things are this bad."

"Yes, and things are going to get a lot worse, Connie," said Paddy as he took Connie's slender hand and kissed the back of it, then he said in sombre tones.

"One day very soon, Connie, you and I will not be able to stand face to face, chatting freely like we are here today. Even my friendship with Bobby would have to come to an end. It would be impossible to continue with a friendship that would be frowned upon and treated with the highest suspicion by all on both sides of the divide that will undoubtedly will be created in this Island of ours. When that day comes Connie, the consequences of a friendship such as the one that Bobby and myself have forged, would be unthinkable. Not just for myself and Bobby, but for our families too."

Connie looked disturbed by Paddy's forecast for the future of Ireland. She took Paddy by the hand and squeezed it tightly saying,

"Neither I, nor my Bobby would ever take any part in such wickedness, Paddy."

"You might not have a choice in the matter, Connie, one day we all might find ourselves doing things that we don't agree with, but do them we will, because to refuse would be seen as cowardly and treacherous and the retribution handed out for such a crime would be unthinkable, Connie. I really do hope I am wrong in all of this, Connie, but only time will tell and we shall all just have to wait and see," said Paddy dolefully.

Connie and Paddy then walked into the garden and headed towards the large oak tree at the far end of it, the oak tree where Paddy had told Connie the true story of Bobby's disappearance some weeks previously. This calm part of the garden had become a place where they both went when they wanted a relaxing chat.

"What are you going to do now, Paddy, have you made any plans for the future?" asked Connie.

"No plans, Connie and who knows what I will do when I leave here next week, you see there's nothing for me here now. I always thought that when the war was over I would work with my father in his joinery shop. Sadly that is not going to happen now, so I have no job, no family and nowhere to live."

Connie thought for several seconds, then she asked,

"Can you drive a motor car, Paddy?"

"Yes I can, I was taught to drive a motor vehicle when I first joined the army. Why?" asked Paddy.

"Tell me, Paddy, are you good with your hands when it comes to repairing and fixing things that are in need of mending around the house?"

Paddy looked confused, then he said,

"Yes I am, Connie, my father is a carpenter and I learnt a lot from him, but why do you want to know all these things, Connie?"

"What about maintaining a garden, Paddy, can you do that as well?"

Paddy was now really confused at Connie's strange questioning.

"Yes, I know a little about tending to a garden, but tell me, Connie, why do you want to know these things?" enquired a confused Paddy.

"Simple, Paddy, I need a man that can drive me when I need to be taken places, I also need him to tend to my gardens, as they have been badly neglected these past months, I also need him to mend things around the house when they need mending. Are you that man, Paddy?" asked Connie with a smile on her face.

"Are you offering me a job, Connie?" asked Paddy.

"I am, Paddy if you want it," answered Connie.

"First, I would have to find somewhere to live," replied Paddy.

"No need to worry, Paddy, I can sort that out for you as I own several lodging houses in East Belfast. I am sure that we can find something to suit you in one of them, Paddy," said Connie.

Paddy face lit up as he nodded his head wildly saying,

"If you are sure, Connie, then how can I refuse your kind offer?"

"Good," beamed Connie, "I'm really pleased that you are going to come and work for me, Paddy, because you will be close when my Bobby returns home and he would want it to be that way, I just know it," she smiled.

"I can't thank you enough for this, Connie, this means the world to me, and I will look forward to the day when Bobby returns home safe and well, then we can all celebrate together," said Paddy gratefully.

"It's settled then, Paddy and I will pay you the same wages as the British Army have been paying you, plus your acclamation will be without charge. If you find that agreeable of course, Paddy."

"Connie, that's more than agreeable to me!" replied Paddy with a broad smile.

Although she did not know it at this time, this act of kindness towards Paddy was to be Connie's first, but well deserved lifeline thrown to a lonely Irish Roman Catholic boy returning home after serving in the British army.

CHAPTER 17

The next morning saw Connie dispatching Mrs O'Hara to the house of her godfather and guardian, Mr Powell. Mrs O'Hara was delivering a request from Connie asking Mr Powell if he would be so kind as to visit her at her home that evening. Mr Powell informed Mrs O'Hara that he would be at Connie's house just after 6.30pm that very evening. In fact, Mr Powell arrived at Connie's house a little before 6.15pm. Mrs O'Hara opened the door and welcomed Mr Powell inside, then she escorted him to the back sitting room where Connie was waiting to receive him.

"Good evening, Connie," said Mr Powell as he entered through the door of the sitting room.

"I received your message from Mrs O'Hara earlier today, Connie and now I am here as requested," said Mr Powell.

"Thank you for coming Mr Powell," said Connie.

"I do hope that nothing is amiss with you, Connie," Mr Powell asked anxiously.

"Please take a seat, Mr Powell," said Connie, "and to ease your fears Mr Powell, nothing is amiss with me, so you can relax as there's no need for you to worry. In fact the opposite is the case, Mr Powell."

"Glad to hear it Connie." responded Mr Powell.

"Although I do have two issues I wish to talk over with you, Mr Powell?" Connie said nervously.

"Of course, Connie, I am always here to help you with any issues you wish to discuss with me," replied Mr Powell.

"First of all I want to inform you of some wonderful news that has come my way," said Connie smiling broadly.

"Really!" replied Mr Powell inquisitively as he sat down on one of the large armchairs next to the fireplace. "Judging from the expression on your face it must be something very interesting indeed, Connie," he continued.

"It is," replied Connie

"Please do enlighten me, Connie, I can't wait to hear this wonderful news that has so obviously lifted your spirit so. You are grinning like an expectant child on Christmas morning," quipped Mr Powell playfully.

Connie gave a humorous smile as she was somewhat amused by her godfather's droll response to her statement that she had good news to tell him. Connie readied herself to inform Mr Powell of the news that Paddy had told her about Bobby's disappearance. Mr Powell listened carefully to what Connie had to say. When she had finished telling Paddy's astonishing story of Bobby's disappearance, Mr Powell sat forward in his chair and thought in silence for a minute.

"Well?" said Connie enthusiastically, impatient for Mr Powell's response. "Isn't it wonderful news, Mr Powell?" she added quickly.

Mr Powell got to his feet and walked to the side of the fireplace, a concerned look set firmly on his face. Then he said thoughtfully,

"On the face of it Connie, it sounds like fantastic news, but we must be convinced that this young man is telling the truth, because it would be folly if we were to blindly believe his incredulous version of events without first seeking out some kind of verification that he did actually know Bobby. You must understand Connie, you are an extremely wealthy young woman. You have inherited your mother's half of a very successful bakery empire, along with several valuable properties scattered around Belfast. Not to mention this grand house you are presently living in, and then there are the sizeable bank accounts also left to you in your mother's will. You must be aware of and recognize the fact that it is not beyond the realms of possibility that some of these young men who have returned home from the war are returning home to nothing, Connie. Therefore it is understandable that some of them should seek to secure their future by befriending wealthy young woman like yourself."

Connie looked angered by Mr Powell's ostensibly heartless attempts to dampen her enthusiasm in her willingness to trust Paddy's version of events surrounding Bobby's disappearance.

"Paddy is not that kind of boy, Mr Powell, be assured," retorted Connie irritably, "He even recognized me the very first time we met. He identified me instantly, remembering me from my picture that Bobby had shown him. Trust me I have talked with him at length about Bobby and it is plain and obvious to me from our extensive conversations that he is indeed a good friend of Bobby. Another fact that proves to me that this young man is telling the truth and that he does indeed know Bobby is that Bobby talked often about him in his letters. I can show these letters to you if you wish, Mr Powell."

Mr Powell was a little shocked by Connie's aggressive response to his questioning of the validity of the boy, Paddy's account of Bobby's wounding and his subsequent disappearance. Although he would never do anything to distress or hurt Connie in any way, he had to be sure that this boy, Paddy posed no harm to his goddaughter.

"Maybe that would be a good idea, Connie. Then if I am convinced by what Bobby has written about this young man in his letters, then the next step would be for me to meet this Paddy for myself," said Mr Powell.

Connie turned around and quickly left the sitting room and rushed up to her bedroom to fetch Bobby's letters. She had gone but a few short minutes before returning with a bundle of Bobby's letters clutched tightly in her hand. The girl's stride was quick and purposeful as she stamped across the room, eventually stopping at the side of the Grand Piano. Connie immediately disseminated Bobby's letters along the highly polished lid of the Grand Piano.

"Pick one, any one," Connie stormed irritably.

"Very well, Connie," replied Mr Powell as he pointed to one of the letters.

Connie picked it up and opened it, then finding the appropriate text she handed the letter to Mr Powell to read. In it Bobby did indeed talk openly about his friendship with a boy called Paddy O'Connor. After reading the letter Mr Powell handed it back to Connie.

"Pick another one," ordered Connie crossly.

Mr Powell then pointed to another of Bobby's letters, the same procedure followed with the same outcome being attained. This process was replicated several more times, each time the same result was achieved. In one of Bobby's letters he even gave a short description of the boy Paddy O'Connor, a description that Connie was able to assure Mr Powell compared favourably to the boy in question.

When Mr Powell had concluded his reading of the forth letter, he placed it alongside all the others on the lid of the Grand Piano and moved away saying,

"Okay, Connie, you have convinced me that this boy, Paddy does indeed know Bobby, so I would still like to meet him in person, if you have no objections that is, Connie".

Mr Powell looked a little sheepish as he now realised that he had managed to upset his godchild and that was the last thing in the world he would ever wish to do. He once again took his seat by the fireplace then he said,

"It would seem on the face of it that there is every chance that this boy, Paddy is indeed telling the truth. If after I have talked with him I am sure that what he tells us is indeed true, then I will be greatly pleased for you, Connie."

"Good," said Connie. "I will arrange a meeting for you with Paddy."

Mr Powell now returned to his armchair and then asked politely,

"What was the other subject you wished to discuss with me, Connie?"

Mr Powell was keen to move the conversation on as quickly as possible, as he didn't want to pursue the matter of Paddy's story further at this time. Not that he thought this boy, Paddy was intentionally being untruthful, but he was aware that in the heat of battle things have a tendency to get muddled. But at this point in time Mr Powell had no intentions of telling Connie that he remained sceptical about Bobby's chances of still being alive. Mr Powell realised that such a conversation with Connie at this time would be futile.

Connie proceeded to inform Mr Powell how Paddy's family were now treating him as an outcast and traitor. After explaining in full Paddy's depressing domestic situation, Connie then continued to inform Mr, Powell of Paddy's disturbing thoughts on the future of Ireland and how he had told her that after the Easter Rising in Dublin things could never be the same again in Ireland. Mr Powell told Connie that this boy, Paddy was an astute young man indeed, as Mr Powell himself had to agree with the young soldier's foresight of the future of Ireland. Mr Powell then explained the situation in more detail to, Connie, saying that it wasn't so much the Easter Rising that was the problem, as most of the people of Dublin were opposed to the Rebellion taking place at all. The one event that will forever change the minds and hearts of the Catholic in Ireland and shape the future of this Island of ours, Connie, was the stupidity of the British Government when they rounded up and executed the fifteen leaders of the Rebellion. In the group arrested there were the two well thought of leaders, Patrick Pearse and James Connolly. All fifteen of them were secretly tried by a British military court and quickly found guilty, their secret executions followed without delay, the people of Ireland only being informed of the Rebels demise after their executions had been carried out. Thereafter, even the people of the southern counties, the Irish Catholics, who had opposed the Rising in the first place, now saw these executed rebels as martyrs to the Irish Republican cause and now they flock in huge numbers to side with and even join the Republican movement. Connie was shocked to hear Mr Powell's expansion on Paddy's thoughts on the Easter Rising and its consequences on the future of Ireland.

"Good God! Where will it all end?" exclaimed Connie.

"Things could well get a lot worse, Connie before it is all over," sighed Mr Powell.

"It would seem that Paddy's grasp of the situation was not that far from the truth, Mr Powell," declared Connie.

"Yes it would appear so, Connie," concurred Mr Powell.

Connie then sat forward in her armchair and looking straight at Mr Powell as she announced,

"After considering Paddy's situation, Mr Powell, I decided that I was going to help him, so I have offered him a job. I informed Paddy yesterday that he can come and work for me. I believe it is time I bought myself a motor car, Mr Powell as travelling back and forth each day by tram to the Nursing Home is becoming something of an tiresome chore and as Paddy knows how to drive a motor car I have told him that I will employ him as my driver. I also informed him that his duties will include him tending to my gardens, as they are becoming neglected and overgrown. With summer approaching fast the sooner he starts the better, also he will be attending to minor repairs around the house, under the instructions and guidance of Mrs O'Hara of course."

"Mr Powell suddenly looked rather perplexed at Connie's latest declaration. The one thing that worried him the most was where this young man was going to live, so wasting no time he quickly asked the question.

"Tell me, Connie, where do you intend for this young man to live, surely not here at the house?"

"No of course not," snapped Connie, "it would be most improper to have a young man living here with three unmarried ladies. So I intend to make arrangements for him to stay at one of the lodging houses that I own. One that is a suitable distance from the house of course," added Connie.

Mr Powell's relief was plain to see and now that his accommodation concerns had been clarified he realised that this wasn't such a silly idea after all.

"Perhaps Mrs O'Hara's old lodging house would serve the purpose, do you think Connie?" injected Mr Powell firmly.

"I think that would be a suitable answer to Paddy's housing requirements Mr Powell," replied Connie.

"It's settled then," said Mr Powell, "I shall make the arrangements at the lodging house first thing in the morning. I shall also arrange for a car to be delivered to your house within the next few days, Connie, if that is agreeable to you?" said Mr Powell.

"It is, Mr Powell and I thank you for your kind assistance in these matters," answered Connie.

Several days after Mr Powell's lively exchange with his goddaughter, he had finally set everything in place for Paddy's release from hospital. Paddy was on his way to the big house to take up his position as handyman-driver in Connie's employ. Upon arriving for his first day's work at the big house Mrs O'Hara took Paddy into the kitchen and sat him down at the large wooden kitchen. Mrs O'Hara then set about informing Paddy that although he was a friend of Bobby's, he must not consider himself to be a friend of Miss Commie. He was an employee and should show Miss Connie the respect that her position commands. Mrs O'Hara then stressed in the most strongest of terms that when he was addressing the Mistress he must always refer to her as Miss Connie, in the same way as both herself and Mary did. Without a query of any kind, Paddy willingly agreed to Mrs O'Hara's decree.

Over the next few weeks this arrangement between Connie and Paddy blossomed, as Paddy was a hard working young man and did everything in his powder to please in all of the duties that he undertook. As for Mr Powell, well needless to say he kept a close eye on Paddy's performance in carrying out his daily duties. Mr Powell also closely monitored Paddy's manner as well as his behaviour when he was in Connie's company. After several weeks of this close scrutiny Mr Powell had to admit to himself that Paddy's attitude towards Connie and his dedication towards his duties were found to be faultless. As a result of his observations Mr Powell was now willing to except that young Paddy was not trying to dupe Connie in any way over his account of what had happened to Bobby. In fact Mr Powell was now beginning to believe that this young man just might be telling the truth and that Bobby just might well be still alive.

Although things were going along smoothly at the big house and Paddy was proving to be something of an asset to Connie, the same could not be said for the rest of Ireland. Tensions between nationalist and agents of the crown were growing by the day and the breaking out of violence was becoming common place in many parts of Ireland, mostly in the southern counties it has to be said. Everything Paddy had predicted in his conversation with Connie was now worryingly beginning to come to pass. What's more, Paddy's disquieting declaration that after the Easter Rising at the Post Office in O'Connell Street in Dublin on the 24th, April 1916, things in Ireland could never go back as they once were, was now becoming blatantly obvious to everyone.

The violence that was being witnessed in places like Dublin, Cork and Tipperary hadn't yet manifested itself in quite the same way in the six northern counties, known collectively as Ulster. The situation in Ulster was totally different. The main reason for this was that in Ulster the population was mainly Protestant Unionists, who outnumbered the Roman Catholic Nationalists by more than five to one. Ulster Unionists saw themselves as British and on the side of the Crown, therefore they had no need to attack agents of the Crown as the Nationalists were doing all over the rest of Ireland. But the more the Nationalists continued with their urban war against the forces of the Crown, the more the Ulster Unionists and the Irish Nationalists became segregated. This standoff resulted in a huge chasm being forged in both thought and deed between the people of the two ideologies. Although Home Rule was first talked about in British Politics in 1885. The subject was brought to the fore again in 1910, promoted by Herbert Asquith's Liberal Government, after they narrowly won the Westminster election and only held onto power by joining forces with John Redmond's Irish Nationalist Party. In return for their support, the Nationalists wanted Asquith's backing for the Home rule Bill.

Needless to say the Ulster Unionists were vehemently against Home rule, as they saw this as the beginning of the breakup of the United Kingdom, something they were bitterly opposed too. Some Unionists like George Wyndham believed that the country had every right to use any means at its disposal to stop Asquith and his Home rule Bill in its tracks and that included using the Army. But as it turned out, Asquith and Redmond Home rule Bill was halted by the outbreak of World War 1. in 1914. Earlier in 1912, Conservative Leader Andrew Bonar had actively encouraged the Unionists of Ulster to forcefully oppose Home rule. Ulster Protestants led by Lord Carson and Sir James Craig signed on mass a document that was known as the - Ulster Covenant - a document which stated clearly that Ulster Unionists would oppose any form of Home Rule whilst also promising total loyalty to the King. Due to the threat of the Home rule Bill being pushed through by Asquith and his cronies, in 1912 Lord Carson formed the Ulster Volunteer Force. (U.V.F.) to oppose Home Rule and the threat of James Connolly's newly formed Irish Citizens Army, (I.R.A.) The armed Nationalist at this time were known by several different names, the, Irish Republican Brotherhood, the, Irish Citizens Army, even the, Irish Volunteer Force, but they soon became known only as the Irish Republican Army. (I.R.A.) the name most of the world knows them by. After the outbreak of war in 1914, the home Rule Bill was suspended and the U.V.F. was integrated into the British Army, fighting with distinction at the Somme and the many Battles that followed.

Meanwhile, the Christmas of 1917 was something of a sombre affair for young Connie, as it was her first Christmas without her loving mother. In addition to this distressing situation was the fact that Connie had still not received any news whatsoever of Bobby's whereabouts nor of his homecoming. But throughout these dark reflective days, Connie never once relinquished here resolute belief that one day soon her Bobby would return home to her safe and well.

As the war overseas showed no signs of ending, more and more of the young soldiers that had been released from the army, there fighting days in this God awful war now over, due to the injuries they had received, began to flood back home to Belfast. But unfortunately it has to be noted that it had become something of a common occurrence in Belfast to see large numbers of young Catholic soldiers being disowned and abandoned by their families and ostracized by their communities upon their repatriation. This problem seemed to be largely ignored by the protestant community, their focus being centred entirely on the wellbeing of the returning protestant soldiers.

So what were these young Catholic boys to do? To their own they were seen as turncoats and traitors even by members of their own family. The communities that they had been born and brought up in now thought of them as untrustworthy and shunned them. The Unionists also spurned these young soldiers, thinking that they were probably Nationalist conspirators, there to spy on them. Work was almost impossible for these young Catholic boys to find, hence they found it extremely difficult to feed themselves or even to put a roof over their heads. Many of these young boys tragically found themselves destitute, cold and hungry and could be discovered sleeping rough in the streets of Belfast on any given night. But as time went by the Armed Nationalists (I.R.A.) decided to take advantage of this appalling situation. Suddenly these young men were offered a get out to the predicament in which they found themselves. A get out that many refused to take up it must be said. For those young men who decided to courageously reject the advances of the I.R.A. often suffered terrible public beatings at the hands of I.R.A. thugs. These public beatings were intended to be seen as a lesson to others. In several cases some of these unfortunate young men were even beaten to death by the I.R.A. Regrettably a lot of the Catholic boys who had shunned all Nationalists attempts to recruit them now found that life in Belfast didn't have a lot to offer them. Finding work and a place to live was proving to be almost an impossibility for these young Catholic boys and with no other way of feeding themselves, many of them ending up in prison as common criminals.

As for those young returning Catholic soldiers who did indeed accept the offer from the I.R.A. to re-establish themselves within their former communities, they found that the price that had to be paid for such benevolence was indeed a high one. First, the community would be gathered in the street to watch as the young returning soldiers would be forced to strip off his British Army uniform until they stood naked in the street. Then item by item of their British Army uniform they would hold aloft in front of them and set it alight. As each item was burned, the young soldier would be forcefully encouraged to publicly denounce the British Crown, much to the hysteria of the gathered crowd. Following this humiliation the young soldier would then endure a public beating, although not as brutal as the beating handed out to the young soldiers that had the effrontery to decline the offer presented them by the I.R.A. This beating was seen more as retribution for what was perceived to be the young man's treachery against the Nation of Ireland. Once he had been accepted back into the fold by all, he would then be forced to take part in some kind of military assignment on behalf of the I.R.A. against the agents of the Crown.

It was now January 1917 and the worrying situation in Ireland was gaining momentum at an alarming rate. A group of Nationalists under the banner of Sinn Fein and led by Eamon de Valera swept to success in four Westminster by-elections. This dramatic and totally unexpected event sent shock waves crashing through the protestant communities in the Northern Counties, resulting in severe repercussions throughout the whole of Ulster. The Unionists now feared that Home rule was about to raise its ugly head once again. What was of some encouragement to the Ulster Unionists was that they enjoyed some support from several leading British politicians who also opposed the home rule Bill, politicians such as Sir Winston Churchill and Lloyd George who thought that there were far more important issues to be dealt with, than what had become known as the Irish problem.

As tensions grew in Ulster the two communities were being pushed further and further apart by the actions of the Catholic Nationalists in other parts of Ireland. The Unionist also feared that should the Nationalists decide to perpetuate this sectarian violence in Ulster, then they might be at something of a disadvantage as most of their young men were away fighting for King and country in France and Belgium. This worry was a real concern to the Ulster Unionists, as now throughout Ulster fear and distrust raged between both opposing sections of the community.

The spring of 1918 was now upon us and it was the Monday morning in the second week in April. Paddy was returning to the big house after carrying out his daily duty of driving Miss Connie to her volunteer work at the Somme Nursing Home. Paddy was in no rush to get back to the big house as the day ahead was not one that was filled with a long list of things to do. So he was enjoying the leisurely drive back, humming happily to himself, as the bright early morning spring sunshine shimmered through the automobile's windscreen, casting a distracting glare unto his eyes. The time was now just past eight thirty in the morning and as Paddy turned the motor car onto the road which led to Connie's house, in the distance he noticed a lonely figure coming towards him, this lone figure was carrying an army knapsack, which was slung over his left shoulder. The figure was dressed in full British Army uniform.

At first glance Paddy didn't devote too much of his attention to this lone soldier, as to see a lone soldiers returning from the war was now a common sight on the streets of Belfast at this time. But the further Paddy travelled down the long road heading towards Connie's house, the more his interest in this lone soldier began to grow. Paddy's attention was suddenly drawn to the fact that this lone soldier had a limp and needed the assistance of a walking cane. For some unknown reason, Paddy slowed the motor car right down then squinting his eyes from the bright sunshine he quickly focused his full attention on the limping soldier. As the two parties came into closer view, Paddy suddenly sat forward, again he shielded his eyes from the bright sunlight with his hand as he peered intently through the windscreen in ecstatic disbelief. Instantly Paddy slammed on the breaks bringing the motor car to an abrupt halt. He quickly realised that in fact he knew this limping soldier only too well, because he now realised that the lone soldier coming towards him, was in fact his good friend, Bobby. In a flash, Paddy flung open the car door and jumped out onto the footpath. He was now standing directly in the path of the limping soldier.

"My good god it is you, Bobby!" exclaimed Paddy loudly as he grabbed his old friend and hugged him warmly.

My God it is you, Paddy?" said Bobby.

"When did you get back to Belfast?" asked Paddy.

"I got off the Liverpool boat this morning, Paddy and I have to say, you are a sight for sore eyes. I can't believe how good you are looking mate!" declared Bobby.

Both men hugged each other once again, then Bobby said,

"Not wanting to sound too rude mate, but what the fucking hell are you doing in this part of town?"

Bobby's question wasn't such a strange one to ask, as the part of town Bobby was referring to was a very affluent corner of East Belfast. An area much sought after by the very rich, an area consisting of only a few well-appointed houses, fringed with picturesque open fields and manicured parklands. Before Paddy had a chance to reply to his old friend's question, Bobby was already firing more and more questions in his direction.

"Come on, Paddy tell me, what have you been up to since you got home and what's more, when did you get home?" asked Bobby.

Paddy shuffled a little to his left, leaning his body up against a very expensive looking motor car.

"Well Bobby," said Paddy, "Less than a week after our disastrous episode with Captain Goodman and your subsequent disappearance, I was moved to another unit. Once again I was sent out on night patrol, we ran into a German raiding party and I was wounded and sent back home to the Somme Nursing Home here in Belfast in early September. I was only released from both the army and the nursing home two months ago," explained Paddy.

"God, mate," gasped Bobby, "I'm glad you made it back home."

"True and I thank God for that, Bobby." said Paddy.

"But what are you doing here in this part of East Belfast, Paddy? And driving such a motor car as this one, Things must be on the up for you, Paddy," teased Bobby.

Paddy laughed out aloud in response to his old mate's misguided assumption.

"Not mine, Bobby, I'm sorry to say," sniggered Paddy.

"Who's then?" enquired Bobby curiously.

"Listen Bobby, you're not going to believe what I am going to tell you, but the motor car belongs to an amazing young lady. I only work for her. In fact you might even know her Bobby," quipped Paddy giving his friend a broad smile.

"I might know her?" queried Bobby.

"Yes, I think you just might know her, Bobby, her name is Miss Connie Kean." sniggered Paddy.

Bobby was taken a little by surprise by Paddy's revelation that he was now working for Connie.

"How do you know my Connie, Paddy?" asked Bobby, looking a little confused.

"We met when I was recovering from my wounds in the nursing home. Then when it came time for me to leave the nursing home, Connie offered me a job as her driver, her handyman and her gardener," replied Paddy.

Bobby screwed up his eyes in a puzzled look, wondering what on earth Connie was doing at the Somme Nursing Home in the first place.

"What was Connie doing in the nursing home?" asked Bobby.

"Connie works as a volunteer there, Bobby, you can find her there five days a week. In fact I have just left her there this very morning," said Paddy.

"Do you drive Edwina around as well as Connie?" quizzed Bobby.

"Who?" asked Paddy, slightly baffled by the question?

"Edwina," replied Bobby, "Connie's mother, Edwina, do you drive her around as well as Connie?"

Paddy furrowed, looking a little bewildered because he had no idea who this Edwina was.

"I sorry Bobby but I don't know anyone called Edwina, there's only Connie, the housekeeper Mrs O'Hara and Mary the house maid living at the big house and may I say that I find the girl Mary very good-looking indeed," replied Paddy with a cheeky smile.

"Do you live in the big house too, Paddy?" asked Bobby.

"No not me, Bobby, I live in a lodging house not too far from here," answered Paddy.

"Doesn't make any sense, Paddy, where's Edwina gone then?" asked Bobby.

Bobby was becoming more confused the longer his conversation with his old friend continued.

"Listen, Paddy," said Bobby, anxious to get to the bottom of this puzzle. "Take me to Connie's house, maybe Mrs O'Hara can shed some light as to where Connie's mother, Edwina has gone."

"Okay, get into the motor car, Bobby," said Paddy.

Bobby and Paddy got into the automobile and headed for Connie's house which was in fact only at the end of the road. Paddy proceeded to tell Bobby that he had told Connie the real story of his disappearance and that she had always refused to believe that he was dead. Bobby looked at Paddy and said,

"You have really no idea who Edwina is, Paddy?" asked Bobby.

"None what so ever, Bobby, but I am sure that Mrs O'Hara will be able to explain everything to you. Plus if we speak nicely to her she will make the both of us one of her famous big Irish breakfasts."

Both men laughed loudly, then Bobby said,

"You're right, Paddy, Mrs O'Hara will surely be able to sort out this quandary, I'm sure of it."

Paddy brought the motor car to a halt by the side of the big house. Both men got out of the car and as they did so, Paddy took hold of Bobby's knapsack and slung it over his shoulder.

"Okay, Bobby, let me go in first, then I will give both Mrs O'Hara and Mary the big surprise."

Bobby agreed and rested his back against the wall by the kitchen door in readiness for his surprise entrance.

CHAPTER 18

Paddy quickly jumped the two steps outside of the kitchen door into the kitchen. Mrs O'Hara was at the stove and Mary was sitting at the big wooden table in the centre of the kitchen. Paddy carefully positioning himself just inside the doorway. Mrs O'Hara and Mary were just finishing their breakfast.

"Morning Mrs O'Hara," quipped Paddy in a jovially voice.

"Good morning to you, Paddy and how are you this morning?" responded Mrs O'Hara cheerfully.

"Fine thank you, Mrs O'Hara," replied Paddy, then quickly turning his attention towards young Mary and aiming a devilish smile accompanied by a playful wink in her direction he asked, "And how is the world treating you today, Mary?"

Mary was embarrassed by Paddy's obvious flirting and she quickly lowered her head looking rather coy, her face instantly beginning to blush as her bright red glow tried unsuccessfully to mask the impish smile she returned in Paddy's direction.

"I'm good, thank you, Paddy," she answered modestly.

"Come in, Paddy," ordered Mrs O'Hara, "Why are you standing there in the doorway? Come in I say, come in boy this instant and I will make you some breakfast."

Paddy smiled broadly as he moved father into the kitchen, then he announced bravely,

"I think on this occasion you better make it breakfast for two, if you don't mind that is Mrs O'Hara."

"For two?" shrieked Mrs O'Hara, "Why breakfast for two, Paddy? Don't you think I have enough to do without you bringing your friends here to eat as well?" growled Mrs O'Hara, although if the truth be told Mrs O'Hara's crankiness was really meant in jest.

"Ah, don't be like that now, Mrs O'Hara," joked Paddy. "Because I think you just might be only too pleased to make breakfast for this particular friend of mine this fine morning, Mrs O'Hara," he added as he steeped smartly to one side allowing Bobby to enter the kitchen.

In an instant a thunderous ear-splitting scream echoed loudly around the kitchen as Mrs O'Hara immediately jumped to her feet and scampered feverishly across the kitchen to where Bobby was standing.

"The Lord be prised, you've come home safe to us, Bobby!" roared an excited Mrs O'Hara,

She flung her arms around Bobby, hugging him tightly. Mary also got to her feet and turned herself towards Bobby to welcome him home, but unlike her Aunt's greeting, Mary's welcome was a little more sedate and was conducted in a more controlled manner. This was because for her to act in a more familiar manner would be thought to be unseemly for one of her age and position within the household.

"Welcome home, Mr Bobby, it's so good to have you back with us safely. Miss Connie will be so thrilled to see you." Mary's voice was soft and nervous.

Bobby smiled broadly at young Mary and replied,

"Thank you, Mary, it's really good to see you all once again."

Bobby then walked smartly across the kitchen to where young Mary was standing, then without a second thought Bobby grabbed hold of Mary and hugged her warmly.

Mrs O'Hara then asked,

"Does Miss Connie know that your home, Bobby?"

"No one but the three of you know that I have returned home, Mrs O'Hara, as I only arrived on the Liverpool boat this morning," answered Bobby.

"By God, Miss Connie will be overjoyed to know you're home safe, Bobby. Ah God bless the child, be sure, Bobby that not for one minute of any day did she ever gave up hope of your safe homecoming. Not even when everyone around her doubted if you were ever going to return home, Bobby but the child, God bless her just kept on believing that you would return to her one day. Ahh, enough talk for now, you two boys get yourselves sat down and I will fix you both a breakfast fit for the King himself!" said Mrs O'Hara.

Bobby and Paddy took their seats at the large wooden kitchen table in readiness for Mrs O'Hara's big Irish breakfast. Over breakfast, Paddy explained to Bobby in more detail how he had met Connie when he was a patient at the Somme Nursing Home. Paddy then informed Bobby that he had explained to Connie what had happened the day he and Bobby got separated after the skirmish with the German patrol. He then told Bobby that he had told Connie that in his opinion he had every reason to believe that Bobby was indeed still alive. This information had put Connie's mind at ease and strengthened her resolve and belief that you would indeed one day return home safely to her. Later we talked openly about my own situation and that's when Connie offered me the position as her driver, gardener and odd job man. Paddy then asked Bobby to tell his story of what had happened to him in the days following the skirmish with the Germans.

Bobby began to tell his story. I remember running towards the trees where you were waiting for me, Paddy, that's when I got wounded in both of my legs. I remember laying on the ground unable to move. I began thinking to myself, looks like your time is finally up, Bobby boy. Then suddenly I felt several hands pulling at me, it was a few of the farmers, they had left the cover of the trees and had come to rescue me. I remember that they pulled me across the open ground back into the woods, whilst we were still coming under fire from the Germans. Three of the farmers then loaded me onto a cart pulled by a small pony, they then rushed me away to safety through the wood, while the larger group of farmers continued their gun battle with the Germans. They took me to a farm on the other side of the valley where they kept me hidden from the Germans for weeks. They brought a doctor to tend to my wounds and he returned to the farmhouse several times to make sure that my wounds were healing and not getting infected. As the weeks passed, the British forces began to pushed the Germans back, the farmers eventually handed me over to a Canadian regiment and they in turn transported me back to the British lines. A few weeks later I was strong enough to be shipped back to Liverpool where I stayed for a week, then in their wisdom the British army discharged me on medical grounds and sent me back home to Belfast.

"And we are all thankful for it," sobbed Mrs O'Hara as she clutched Bobby's hand, squeezing it tightly.

Bobby then asked,

"Tell me, Mrs O'Hara, how come Paddy here doesn't know who Edwina is; has he never met her?"

It was now Mrs O'Hara's sad and regrettable duty to enlighten Bobby about the heart-breaking events that had taken place at the big house whilst he had been away fighting in the war. Mrs O'Hara explained in full gory detail the shocking events surrounding Edwina's death and of Connie's wounding.

"My God!" said a shocked Bobby at hearing Mrs O'Hara's account of the brutal attack on Edwina. "Connie must have been devastated!" added Bobby.

"She was, Bobby, it hit her very hard indeed," said Mrs O'Hara.

"How is she now?" asked Bobby.

Mrs O'Hara picked up the large white teapot from the centre of the table and poured everyone a fresh cup of tea and then she said,

"Thanks be to God that the child is coping better now than she was when it first happened, Bobby, but seeing you will help with her healing I'm sure."

An eerie and uncomfortable silence now hung over the small gathering around the kitchen table, no one really knowing what to say. Paddy, being Paddy then took it upon himself to breach this awkward silence.

"Bobby," he asked, "would you like me to take you in the motor car to the Nursing Home to see Connie?"

Immediately upon hearing Paddy's suggestion, Mrs O'Hara added her support to Paddy's proposal by saying excitedly,

"Oh yes, Bobby, what a good idea Paddy has just had. I know Connie would be really delighted to see you and it would make her day, Bobby. No, in fact it would make the child's year."

Bobby sat in silent thought for several long seconds, then without saying a word he reaching into his tunic pocket he pulled out a small velvet covered box, which he placed on the table for all to see. Bobby then cast an enquiring eye over the expectant faces that were sitting around the kitchen table and then he said,

"No thanks, Paddy, that won't be necessary. You see when I first got off the boat this morning I could not wait to see Connie once again but now, after hearing all that she has been through, I think not, Paddy. You see, I now realise that the first time Connie sets her eyes on me has to be something extra special. Something that will take her breath away, something that will stay with her for the rest of her life. Because as you all can tell from the little box that I have placed on this kitchen table, I intend to ask Connie to marry me."

Bobby then picked up the small box and placed it in the middle of the table for all to see. Slowly Bobby opened the small box to reveal a sparkling diamond engagement ring inside. Mrs O'Hara gasped loudly, before once again flinging her arms around Bobby and hugging him tightly saying,

"Dear God above, I have wanted for this day for Miss Connie for such a long time and now it's finally here."

"Any thoughts on how you intend to do this, Bobby?" asked Paddy eagerly.

Bobby closed the small box and put it back into his tunic pocket and then he said, "Yes, as a matter of fact I do, Paddy, I want to propose to Connie in a place that I know she holds dearly in her heart. A place I have heard her talk fondly about on many occasions. A place that she wanted to take me to see one day but sadly the war prevented that from ever happening. This is a special place in Connie's life, this is a place where she often went as a child with her late father. This is a place where we both must be when Connie sets her eyes on me for the first time since my return. This place is called Tollymore Forest and it is situated but a few miles outside of Newcastle Co. Down. Connie has told me on many occasions that she believes this place to be the most stunning, peaceful forest anywhere in the world. She told me that this forest is filled with undisturbed scenic beauty. Connie often talked of the many crystal clear streams that wind their way through the forest. All this and more is set in the shadows of the magnificent Mourne Mountains. I can't think of a more appropriate place anywhere in Ireland to ask the most beautiful girl that Ireland has ever known to become my wife."

"Oh, Bobby it sounds so, so wonderful," sighed Mrs O'Hara with a tear in her eye.

Bobby smiled as he looked at the gathering around the kitchen table and then he said,

"One thing more, I may well need the help of you all if I am to pull this off, so first of all, can I relay on you all to keep my homecoming a closely guarded secret?"

All were quick to agree. Bobby then added,

"Also, I am thinking that I am going to need the help of you all in this secret undertaking."

Mrs O'Hara was first to voice her support, quickly followed by Paddy and young Mary. All three had now agreed to help Bobby in any way they could, as well as in keeping his homecoming a secret from Miss Connie.

Bobby then got to his feet and said,

"My first job is to find somewhere to stay because I am now homeless as my mother's old house is sadly long gone and no longer an option for me," said Bobby.

"Well now," interrupted Mrs O'Hara, "why don't you go and talk to Mr Powell. I'm sure he will be only too pleased to have you stay with him, Bobby, until such times that you can find other accommodation."

"Yes, you're right Mrs O'Hara, that's a very good idea!" replied Bobby.

"Shall I take you in the motor car to Mr Powell's office, Bobby?" asked Paddy.

"Yes, thank you, Paddy, that would be most appreciated," answered Bobby.

"Any time," said Paddy.

"Maybe tomorrow you and I can take a trip to Tollymore Forest to see if I can find the ideal spot for me to meet with Connie."

"Good idea, Bobby and it will be like old times, you and me out on a reconnaissance," joked Paddy.

Bobby smiled and then he said,

"I do believe that this proposal is going to take a good bit of organising, Paddy. I really do want everything to be just perfect when I show myself to Connie for the first time. I am hoping that you all will help me in this?" asked Bobby.

"Whatever you need us to do Bobby, you only have to ask," said Mrs O'Hara.

"Thanks to you all!" said Bobby.

"Okay then, Bobby, let's go see Mr Powell," said Paddy

Paddy and Bobby left the kitchen and made their way to the bakery to talk with Mr Powell.

Mr Powell was working alone in his office when he heard a firm knock on his office door.

"Yes?" called out Mr Powell.

Strangely no answer was forthcoming. Again Mr Powell called out,
"Yes, who's there"?

Still there was no answer, but the knocking continued. Mr Powell was now becoming a little short tempered and again he called out,

"Yes, who's there?" and yet again there was no replay. Just another loud knock on the office door.

Mr Powell's patience was now beginning to wear rather thin, as he was busy man and didn't have time waste on Tom-foolery.

"Yes," he roared angrily, "just open the door and come in, but please stop thumping on the damn door."

In an instant Mr Powell's office door was dynamically thrown wide to the wall and there in the office doorway, with the broadest of mischievous smiles fixed impishly on his face, stood Bobby Gallagher. Mr Powell quickly scrambled to his feet, almost falling over twice in shocked disbelief at who he was seeing in his office doorway.

"My good God!" he exclaimed loudly, "can it really be you, Bobby?"

"I think you will find that it is me, Mr Powell," joked Bobby.

Mr Powell rushed towards Bobby and embraced him warmly.

"Come in, Bobby, good God, come in boy," yelled an ecstatic Mr Powell.

"How…" he continued, "When…good God boy it's really you, I can't believe it, it's really you, Bobby. The child was right all alone and I didn't believe her. Shame on me for not listening to Connie. Not once did she waver in her belief that you would one day return to her, Bobby and now you have. Does Connie know that your home safe, Bobby?"

"No, not as yet, Mr Powell and that's how I want it to stay, for now at least," said Bobby.

Mr Powell looked confused by Bobby's statement, then he asked curiously as he sat down behind his desk,

"Why don't you want her to know that you are home safely, Bobby? I really don't understand."

Bobby then pulled one of two leather armchairs closer to Mr Powell's desk and sat down on it. He told Mr Powell that Mrs O'Hara had told him of Edwina's murder by the I.R.A. and that Mr Powell was now Connie's legal Guardian. Bobby continued to explain that he had come to see Mr Powell for two reasons. First and most importantly, Bobby told Mr Powell was his proposal idea and to ask for his approval. Luckily Mr Powell was in no doubt that his goddaughter's potential engagement to young Bobby was indeed the best thing that could happen to her. Mr Powell held no reservations about his goddaughter's marriage and was well aware of Edwina's thoughts on the matter when she was alive. Mr Powell could easily recall that on several occasions both himself and Edwina had discussed the possibility of this very event taking place. Edwina had always indicated that she was more than willing to offer her blessing upon their union.

With the question of Mr Powell's blessing now received both men shook hands firmly.

Bobby then informed Mr Powell that he had nowhere to live at the moment and that Mrs O'Hara had suggested that he ask Mr Powell if it would be possible if he could stay with him until he found somewhere more permanent. Mr Powell quickly put Bobby's mind at ease, telling him that he could stay with him until such time as he and Connie got married. For this kindness, Bobby thanked Mr Powell wholeheartedly. Then in a totally uncharacteristic and unexpected impulse Mr Powell decided to conclude his work for the day, he hastily shuffled the papers in front of him into a neat pile and placed them in the middle of his desk, then he looked Bobby in the eye and said boldly,

"I would like to lay a bet that that friend of yours, Paddy, is lurking about outside somewhere, Bobby?"

Bobby sniggered as he replied,

"He is that, Mr Powell, he's outside waiting in the motor car."

"Thought so," jibed Mr Powell. "Then first let's get you settled into my house, then allow me to take both of you two boys into Belfast for a few celebratory glasses of porter at an old haunt of mine, The Duke of York, where in my opinion, they serve the best porter in the whole of Belfast."

"We would be only too pleased to accompany you on the mission, Mr Powell," joked Bobby as both men left the office.

Over the next few days, to everyone at the big house, it seemed that they were all walking on eggshells, as no one wanted to give Miss Connie any inclination that something exciting was afoot. After breakfast had been eaten on the Sunday morning, Connie continued with her usual preparation for her weekly trip to St. Mark's church for Morning Song. Each Sunday Connie would be escorted to church by her godfather Mr Powell. Although Connie was now in possession of her own automobile and driver, she still preferred to be accompanied to church each week by her godfather, allowing Paddy to use the vehicle each Sunday in order to take himself, Mrs O'Hara and Mary to morning Mass at St. Matthew's chapel in East Belfast.

But this Sunday was to be different to all the others, the instant Connie and Mr Powell had departed for church, Paddy arrived at the house in Connie's motor car. Mrs O'Hara and Mary could be seen carrying two large baskets, one covered with a thick tartan blanket from the house and with Paddy's help they loaded both into the back of the vehicle. The moment this chore had been completed, Mrs O'Hara and Mary clambered into the back of the motor car and were ready to leave for Morning Mass. Upon arrival at St. Matthew's Roman Catholic chapel, Paddy brought the automobile to a halt outside the chapel gates, allowing Mrs O'Hara and Mary to get out of the motor car, but on this occasion Paddy remained in the vehicle as there was to be no Sunday Mass for him this day.

"Good luck Paddy," called Mrs O'Hara, as Paddy drove away from the chapel gates.

Meanwhile, back at St. Mark's Church, Morning Service had just ended and Mr Powell and Connie were going through their customary after Service ritual of exchanging pleasantries with other members of the congregation in the grounds of the church. Although Connie was well aware that Mr Powell wasn't one given to idle chitchat as a rule, she had always believed that on occasions such as this, he enjoyed the informal weekly gatherings in the church grounds along with all of the other parishioners. So it came as something of a puzzle to Connie as she observed her godfather's impatient fidgeting and his lack of interest in all conversation. What could be the cause of his irritation? Connie thought to herself. After all, it's not as though it was an unpleasant day, far from it, today was a beautiful, sunny spring morning, with the sun shining brightly in a blue cloudless sky. The more Connie monitored her godfather's bizarre behaviour, the more it became clear to her that his attention was undoubtedly focused elsewhere. It occurred to Connie that others may well have become alerted to Mr Powell's, shall we say, unusual, even rude manner. Connie looked on in dazed amazement as it became more and more evident that her godfather was itching to get away as soon as possible.

Suddenly and without warning Mr Powell removed his gold hunter from his waistcoat pocket and with a hurried but calculated glance he logged the time, before quickly replacing the watch back in his waistcoat pocket. Almost to the second that his hunter watch had disappeared into his waistcoat pocket, Mr Powell announced restlessly,

"I really think we should be making a move, Connie, it's now gone eleven fifteen."

Connie looked at her godfather in mystified dismay, not quite understanding his reasoning for wanting to leave the church so quickly.

"If you think it's time to go, then go we shall, Mr Powell," answered Connie sharply, feeling completely baffled by her guardian's unexpected haste to depart.

Mr Powell then extended his arm as he beckoned his goddaughter towards him and once she was by his side she promptly placed her hand on his arm, giving him a sideways stare in disbelief at his atypical conduct. Without more a do, Mr Powell instantly set in motion the process of saying their goodbyes to the assembled worshippers. Once this task had been somewhat hurriedly carried out, both Connie and her godfather took their leave and quickly made their way to Mr Powell's motor car.

As they drove away from the church, Connie turned to Mr Powell and enquired curiously,

"Don't you think our departure from church today was just a little abrupt?"

"Really Connie!" snapped Mr Powell, "Did you really think so, I have to say I wasn't aware of it being like that at all," scoffed Mr Powell dismissively.

"Well it seemed that way to me, Mr Powell and I couldn't help but notice that we received quite a few unpleasant glances as we left." said Connie.

"Well I do apologise if I made you feel uncomfortable, Connie." said Mr Powell. "It wasn't done intentionally, I assure you."

"I really don't think that it is me that you need to be concerned about, Mr Powell."

"Who then?" enquired Mr Powell curiously, not really understanding what it was that he had done wrong.

"Maybe a few of your fellow parishioners might feel that they are due an explanation for your undoubted sullen performance in the churchyard this morning, Mr Powell," replied Connie sharply.

"Well, again I do apologise if I was anything else but civil this morning Connie. It's just that I have a lot on my mind today," replied Mr Powell apologetically.

For good reason, Connie remained unconvinced about her godfather's explanations about his conduct at church that morning because he still seemed to be preoccupied with something, but what? Connie decided not to say anymore on the subject, thinking it best not to force the issue.

Connie sat back in her seat and opened the passenger's side window of the motor car. This allowed the fresh spring morning air to burst into the vehicle, whilst at the same time, allowing the airless heat that had built up from the bright sunshine to escape into the outside air. After a time, Connie looked at her godfather and said in a soft relaxing voice,

"It really is a wonderful morning, don't you think, Mr Powell?"

"Yes it is, Connie," replied Mr Powell, "I don't think we could have planned it for a better day!" he added.

Connie's attention was quickly drawn towards her godfather after his latest puzzling statement.

"What do you mean you couldn't have planned it for a better day, Mr Powell, planned what?" asked Connie curiously.

Mr Powell instantly realised that he had almost let the cat out of the bag by his unthinking tongue, which he now wished he had bitten off. All he could do for now was to try his best to back track as quickly as possible. Hoping to avoid raising Connie's suspicions any further.

"No...no plans at all, Connie and the fact that I said we couldn't have had a better day for it, was said for no particular reason, only that..."

Mr Powell didn't get to finish his sentence because he was rudely interrupted by his goddaughter as she glared with some suspicion in his direction. Not only for what he had just said, but she now noticed that they were going in the opposite direction to where Connie's house was situated.

"Hmm, no plans then, Mr Powell," muttered Connie.

"No, No plans at all, Connie." Mr Powell quickly replied.

"Then, if you don't mind me asking, why are we travailing in the opposite direction from my house? inquired Connie curiously.

Mr Powell gave a nervous grin, then he said calmly,

"Just relax and enjoy the journey, Connie."

"What journey, Mr Powell. Where are we going?" inquired Connie once again. Connie was now becoming worried and confused by her godfather's continuing bizarre behaviour.

"I just thought as it is such a beautiful day that we might go for a drive in the countryside before lunch, that's all, Connie," answered Mr Powell.

"Won't Mrs O'Hara be a little put out if we are back late for lunch?" ask Connie.

"I shouldn't think she will be too annoyed with us, Connie, not once I explain to her that I thought you were in need of a nice day in the country, just so you could get away from it all for an hour or two," said Mr Powell.

Although she didn't say it out loud, Connie wasn't as confident as Mr Powell seemed to be about Mrs O'Hara's reaction to them being late for lunch. Although on the brighter side, it was Mrs Powell's idea to go on this little jaunt, so at least Connie considered herself to be in the clear. As time passed, Connie became more relaxed and exceptive of the situation she now found herself in. In truth she was beginning to actually enjoying this leisurely drive in the countryside. With a few miles travelled, Connie suddenly sat forward in her seat, because she now realised where they were heading. More and more familiar landmarks were being passed more frequently as Mr Powell's automobile went on its way. Again Connie's excitement was beginning to rise.

"I know where we are going, Mr Powell," she shouted eagerly."

"Do you?" he asked.

"I do," said Connie, "we are heading towards Newcastle Co. Down, so that means we are going to my favourite place in all of Ireland. We are going to Tollymore Forest."

Tollymore Forest was a place close to Connie's heart and it was her favourite place in all of Ireland for the simple reason that it was the place where her father would bring her for long picnics in the heat of the summer when she was a little girl. As Mr Powell's motorcar travelled nearer and nearer to its destination, Connie's mind took her back to happier days when her loving father was still in her life. With eyes firmly shut she recalled how her father would set a treasure trail for her to follow. Clue after clue would be thoughtfully laid out for her to find. At the end of the hunt there would always be a surprise for her to find and keep. A small tear trickled down Connie's cheek, not so much a tear of sadness, more a tear of reflective joy, as she pictured both her and her father strolling through the tree covered pathways, as the hot sun burned down on them through the forest canopy.

Connie's face was now glowing brightly from the sunshine that was beating its way through the windscreen of Mr Powell's motorcar. Connie's excitement at once again visiting the forest quickly began to bubble up inside her young body. More and more happy memories of times spent at the forest with her loving father came flooding back to her. Mr Powell could see in Connie's face that she was really excited about this trip to the forest. He smiled at his goddaughter in the knowledge that this trip into the forest would hold much more than his young charge could ever have expected it to.

"How did you know what this place means to me, Mr Powell?" asked Connie.

"Your father would tell me about your trips to the Forest on long summer Sunday afternoons Connie. He would come into the office on a Monday morning still bubbling with the excitement of the adventures you both had the previous day. He would talk at length of how much you enjoyed your visits here and how your face would light up the closer you both came to the entrance of the forest, just as it is this very minute, Connie."

Connie gave her godfather the biggest smile she could muster, then she said,

"I can't thank you enough for this Mr Powell, I am so pleased that you have brought me here today." Connie gave him the biggest smile and then squeezed his hand tightly in a gesture of thanks.

In time, they were at the entrance to the forest, both Mr Powell and his young passenger got out of the motorcar and walked slowly into the forest.

Connie's eyes were big and bright as she gazed all around, taking in all the wonderful sights that this enchanting place had to offer. Both Connie and Mr Powell made their way along the dirt track path travelling deeper into the forest. Suddenly Connie took flight, leaving her godfather some distance behind as she ran forward shouting excitedly.

"Look, Mr Powell, someone has set a trail to follow."

Connie stood in the middle of the narrow pathway pointing franticly at a bunch of broken branches that had been laid out in the shape of an arrow. This bunch of sticks had been carefully arranged as an indicator that needed to be followed.

"What do you think, Connie?" asked a slightly puffed Mr Powell, who was trying hard to keep up with his young energetic companion, "Shall we follow it?

"Oh Yes please, let's do it, Mr Powell," beamed an animated Connie.

With no time to waist, Connie set off running down the narrow dirt track leading her deeper into the forest. Mr Powell followed behind her, although this time he was making less of an effort to keep up with young Connie. Connie forged quickly ahead in the direction that the makeshift arrow pointer was showing her to go. She had travelled only a short distance when she came to a fork in the path. Connie gestured franticly to Mr Powell to hurry, as he was now falling even further behind with every passing minute. As for Connie, well she was now becoming even more excited as she had discovered yet another arrow shaped pointer on the ground. This one was different from the first one, this time the marker was made from small stones and was telling whoever was following to travel down the path to the right. This Connie did, but not before calling out to Mr Powell.

"This way, Mr Powell, quickly follow me"

Connie eagerly ran further down the path of choice, which was taking her deeper into the forest. Mr Powell was so far behind young Connie that she was now out of sight. After a few minutes of travelling eagerly along the track Connie had found the next direction guide, it was boldly displayed on the ground in the middle of the pathway. This time the indicator was a little more elaborate in its invention and its appearance. Spread out on the ground was a collection of coloured rags that had been shaped into an arrow and had been fixed to the ground with tiny sharpened sticks. Connie continued on her mysterious journey, following the course that had been laid out in front of her. Suddenly the path that Connie had been following for some time seemed to come to an abrupt dead end. Connie stood perfectly still in the middle of the pathway, confused as to why the trail had come to such an unexpected end. It now seemed to Connie that there was nowhere left to go. She stood looking at the small thorny coppice which was blocking off the pathway. Unable to see anyway past this considerate growth with its thick menacing thorns protruding from every branch.

Connie was now stopped in her tracks and her enthusiasm for the hunt had taken a sharp downward turn. Connie was unsure of what she should do next, should she give up the hunt and go back to where she had left Mr Powell? As Connie stood staring angrily into the thorny bush that had stunted her advancement, something deep inside her told her that she must go on, but how? There has to be a way past this, Connie announced aloud, whilst her mind was still working hard trying to fathom why she had been trapped in this way. The trail she had been following had most certainly been set by someone for a reason, so why would it end in this most unacceptable way? Connie was at a loss as she pondered over her hapless situation, with no answer to the puzzle in sight, Connie was about to give up the hunt. Just then, as Connie turned to make her way back along the trail, something happened to reignite her passion for the quest.

Just to the right of this annoying hindrance that had halted her advance, Connie heard something moving in the bush by her right hand side. Connie quickly moved in the direction of where the rustling sound was coming from. With closer investigation Connie heard the sound again, it seemed to be coming from a thick clump of river reeds only a few feet away from her.

Connie remained perfectly still as she looked directly into the clump of river reeds, her ears pricked as she listened carefully for the sound she had heard a few seconds before. Suddenly and without warning, out of this matted clump of tall river reeds, bounced a large grey rabbit, quickly flowered by a much smaller grey rabbit. Connie smiled as she watched the two mammals scampering as fast as they could down the path behind her. Connie quickly moved towards this unassuming cluster of reeds, then raising both her hands she took a firm hold of them. This riverside growth felt rough and damp to her touch, but Connie was determined to find a way past them, knowing deep inside that this was going to be her only way to pass this thorny barrier. With one stroke of her hand, Connie forced the reeds apart, revealing a narrow line of large steppingstones, each one neatly placed in the shallow stream which seemed to be meandering its way slowly around the thorny bush.

Connie smiled as she carefully made her way through the coarse reeds and onto the steppingstones on the other side. Connie cautiously picked her way along the flattened stones which rested firmly in the shallows of the river. When Connie reached the end of the line of steppingstones, she was confronted by a steep incline which sloped upwards from the river to a pinnacle of around six or seven feet. Conveniently for Connie, this incline had small indentations cut into its side that were set out in a ladder pattern and were just big enough to fit a human foot into. The thought struck Connie that these indentations appeared as though they had been put there deliberately to help whoever had been following the trail. For by these indentations, there were also several large overhanging branches that could be used as leverage in the climb. Connie smiled broadly as she hitched up her skirt, just like she use to as a child when exploring the forest with her father and began her climb.

Once Connie had reached the top of the rise, to her surprise and delight, she found herself standing in a small secluded glade. Connie walked to the middle of this beautiful little clearing, her eyes filled with the astounding and natural beauty that now surrounded her. Turning back towards the river from where she had just come, Connie noticed that the glade was surrounded on three sides by the river. It was then that Connie realised that the only way to reach this beautiful little dell, was to pass through the reeds and climb the incline just like she had done. For some reason Connie's eyes became transfixed on the shallow crystal clear stream which flowed gently around this little peninsula. To Connie it felt as though she was in the most magical place she had ever seen, she was simply spellbound by the sheer beauty and tranquillity of this place. Standing alone in this sleepy hollow, she was gripped by its enchanted charm. Connie stood in silence just listening to the rhythmic sound of the river as it gently rippled over the steppingstones that had brought her to this magical place. The soft gentle breeze that drifted across the river created the most mystic of sounds as it echoed rhythmically through the leaves and branches of the surrounding trees.

As Connie looked upwards she became completely mesmerised by the dense, dazzling, multi-coloured canopy above. This natural formation was only encroached upon further by the intensity of the sunbeams that forced their way through the tiny gaps between the leaves of the canopy thus allowing them to begin their fairylike dance on the surface of the gentle rolling water, which cast an enchanted spell upon anyone who's eyes should happened to fall upon this charmed spectacle of nature.

Connie was truly captivated by this spiritual place. She gazed deep into the hypnotic rolling waters in front of her and as she did so, one magical thought occurred to her. That if the leprechauns of Ireland that everyone talked about did actually exist, then this would surely be the place where they would choose to live.

It was at this point that Connie realised that she was now all alone in this beautiful place, with no idea where her godfather had ended up, but Connie held no fear of being alone here, none whatsoever. Connie's eyes moved slowly around the clearing and to her disbelief, under the shade of a large tree at the back of the glade and next to a large fallen tree trunk, there laid out on the ground was a tartan blanket. Resting on top of this blanket was a rather large picnic basket.

'I didn't notice that picnic-basket being there before,' muttered Connie under her breath.

Connie walked the few paces towards the fallen tree trunk which was conveniently providing some natural seating should anyone wish to make use of it. As Connie approached the picnic basket she noticed that a note had been fixed to the lid by a small twig. Connie picked up the note and read it out loud, it read:

Take the twig in one hand and hold it tight, then walk to the edge of the river and gaze deep into the water for just a few seconds. Then you must shut your eyes as tight as you can, the river will then allow you one wish. As soon as you have made your wish, you must then toss the twig into the rolling water. Then, and only then, may you open your eyes in order that you can watch the little twig carefully as the river takes it away. You must keep your eyes firmly fixed on the twig until it is out of sight, if you want your wish to come true. Once the twig is completely out of your sight, you can return to the blanket and the picnic basket. If you do all this, then the river will grant you your wish.

Connie looked all around the clearing carefully, unsure of what to make of this strange note that she had found on top of the mysterious picnic basket. There was nothing to be seen anywhere that really looked out of place, blanket and picnic basket apart. The only sound to be heard was the gentle flow of the water over the stepping stones in the river. This captivating rhythm was only matched by the sweet harmonious springtime chirping of a small flock of tiny birds that had now assembled in the outreaching branches of the surrounding trees.

Connie walked to the edge of the stream and looked deep into its clear, glimmering waters and she then began to follow the instructions that had been laid out in the note attached to the picnic basket. Connie closed her eyes tightly whilst holding the twig firmly in her right hand, then she whispered in a soft trembling voice,

My wish is this and only this...

Please bring my Bobby back home to me safe and well.

Connie then opened her eyes and tossed the small twig into the river's softly rippling water, her eyes fixed upon this small twig, as she watched it closely on its journey down the river. Not once did Connie's eyes flinch from the task that the note had laid out for her, at all times Connie's eyes watched until the small twig had disappeared from her view. Connie then pulled a white handkerchief from the small bag that she was carrying across her shoulders and dabbed several tears from her eyes. Slowly she turned back in the direction of the picnic basket, the sun was now really strong as it broke through the canopy above. So bright was the sun in Connie's eyes that she was forced to squint and raise her hand to shield her eyes from the blazing sun. That's when she thought she had seen a figure moving just to the right of the picnic basket and in front of a large hedge that filled the back end of this beautiful little glade. Connie took a step forward in an attempt to identify this figure who had now moved away from the hedgerow and was now standing by the side the picnic basket, but the sun was so strong in her eyes that she could not clearly see just who it was that had joined her in this little glade.

"Is that you, Mr Powell?" called Connie.

"No." was the short answer that came back.

Connie moved cautiously towards the unidentified man, as she did so her eyes were slowly beginning to adjust to the bright sunlight. Connie could now make out that this unidentified man was dressed in a British Army uniform.

"Who are you and what are you doing here?"

Connie was becoming a little nervous with the situation she now found herself in.

"Don't think that I am not alone here, because I'm not," added Connie quickly.

The soldier, realising that Connie was becoming frightened quickly said,

"Don't be afraid, Connie, I am here to meet you, you have nothing to fear from me."

"Who are you?" asked Connie.

"Don't you know who I am, Connie?" said the soldier.

Connie moved closer to the soldier, her eyes now fully adjusted to the sunlight, although at first she thought that her eyes were playing tricks on her. All of a sudden Connie gasped loudly as the realisation of who the British soldier really was. Connie's heart began to beat at a frightening rate, her mouth became dry and she felt the blood run cold in her young body. Connie's chest began to fall and rise in time with her racing heart, causing her breathing to become erratic. The soldier moved out of the sunlight and into the shade of one of the large trees that surrounded the clearing.

"My good God!" exclaimed Connie loudly, "It really is you, Bobby."

Bobby smiled as he ventured forward towards his only love.

"Yes, it's me Connie, I have come home to you at last," Bobby whispered softly.

Connie turned her head back towards the river and as she looked in disbelief into its rolling waters, she whispered just three small word in grateful gratitude,

-Thank you, river.-

Within an instant Connie had run across this magical glade to where Bobby was standing, both young lovers then fell into an emotional embrace as they hugged and kissed each other passionately for several long minutes.

"When, how?" stuttered Connie.

Bobby tenderly placed his finger to Connie's lips, stopping her from saying any more, then with a smile he whispered softly in her ear.

"Time for explanations later, Connie, I promise I will tell you everything, but for now, please come with me."

Bobby took a gentle hold of Connie's hand as he escorted her across the small glade to where the fallen tree trunk was placed. Bobby, still holding Connie's hand, lovingly sat her down on the seat that nature had so graciously provided for them. Within seconds of Connie making herself comfortable on the fallen log, Bobby had fallen on one knee. Still holding Connie's hand Bobby reached into the pocket of his army tunic with his other hand and pulled out a small box. Connie's young body began to shake, was Bobby really going to propose to her. Slowly Bobby raised the small box upwards until it was at Connie's eye level. Connie's eyes suddenly became animated and were as wide as the headlamps on Mr Powell's automobile as Bobby slowly opened the small box. Inside was revealed a sparkling gold and diamond engagement ring. Bobby's beautiful smile was never bigger and never more handsome to Connie as it was at this very minute. Bobby looked deep into Connie's big blue eyes and said boldly,

"Miss Connie Kean, would you do me, Mr Robert Gallagher, the greatest honour of all by agreeing to spend the rest of your life with me by accepting my proposal of marriage and becoming my wife."

Connie's lower lip began to quiver uncontrollably the instance she heard Bobby's marriage proposal leave his lips. Although Connie had dreamt of this moment for years, because of the war she had unwillingly tempered her enthusiasm for the idea of becoming Bobby's wife. But now that the moment was actually here, Connie found herself so taken back by the excitement of the situation, that she could only gawp opened mouthed at her Bobby. Connie now found herself stuck in the middle of an unwelcomed stupor and to make things even worse her voice for some reason had decided to forsake her. Connie's mouth quickly became as dry as the desert sands, causing it to move without releasing any sound. Connie tried unsuccessfully several times to answer Bobby, but her voice still refused to cooperate. Again Bobby looked up at his Connie and squeezing her slight feminine hand a little tighter, again he whispered in a soft tender voice,

"Marry me Connie, please say yes and marry me."

Tears rolled slowly down Connie's face as she took several deep breaths, hoping that on this occasion her voice would show her a kindness and give the answer she wanted Bobby to hear, then suddenly she heard the words leave her lips.

"Yes Bobby, of course I will marry you."

Bobby's infectious smile was as broad as the glade that they were standing in as he lovingly slipped the engagement ring onto Connie's slender finger, then getting to his feet, he wrapped his arms around his one love and kissed her adoringly. When all kisses and hugs had ended, Bobby took hold of Connie's hand and said,

"Shall we enjoy this glorious forest for the rest of the afternoon and indulge ourselves in this wonderful picnic that Mrs O'Hara's has lovingly prepared for us, Connie?"

Connie placed her hand across her mouth and giggled like a school girl, as the thought of everyone knowing what was about to happen in the forest that day, both tickled and amused her. Connie took yet another look at her newly acquired diamond ring and said,

"So everyone knew about this did they, Bobby?

Bobby smiled and simply nodded his head as he began to set out the picnic.

"It all makes sense to me now, all the strange things that have gone on this day," smiled Connie.

Again Bobby nodded his head and smiled broadly as the two young lovers settled down to enjoy their picnic in the woods.

CHAPTER 19

Connie watched as Bobby emptied the picnic basket. First to be placed on the tartan blanket was a large white dinner plate containing four thick slices of Mrs O'Hara's famous rabbit and leek terrine. This was followed by a small platter of cucumber and mint sandwiches, several slices of cold baked ham, a selection of small coronation tarts, one small apple & blackberry pie, a cluster of assorted biscuits, one small block of cheese and, for their thirst, Mrs O'Hara had packed two large bottles of ginger beer. Once all the refreshments had been unloaded and displayed on the ground both Bobby and Connie then relaxed in the warming afternoon spring sunshine, both enjoying the splendid fare Mrs O'Hara had lovingly provided for them.

That's when a thought suddenly sprang into Connie's mind and she instantly turned to Bobby and asked curiously,

"Tell me, Bobby, how on earth did you get here today?"

Bobby smiled at Connie as he answered with an impish grin,

"Paddy brought me here in your newly acquired motor car, Connie."

Connie smiled, then asked.

"Don't you think we should try to find both Paddy and my godfather and ask them if they would like to share in this wonderful lunch with us, Bobby?"

"No need, Connie." replied Bobby. "You see Mrs O'Hara had the good sense to make up two picnic baskets, so as we speak both Paddy and your godfather are somewhere in this wonderful forest having their own picnic lunch."

"Really!" exclaimed Connie.

"Really." replied Bobby,

Both he and Connie then laughed at the idea of Paddy and Mr Powell sitting down together in a forest eating lunch.

"One more thing, Bobby," sniggered Connie.

"What is it, Connie?" asked Bobby.

"What would have happened if the two rabbits hadn't come out of the clump of reeds by the path, where the large shrub was blacking my way?

If that hadn't happened, then I wouldn't have been able to find this beautiful place," Bobby smiled impishly at young Connie saying,

"The rabbits weren't as random as you think they were, Connie, you see they wouldn't have been there if I hadn't put them there in the first place. As for them rushing out of the reeds. Well, the large stone that I tossed into the middle of the reeds helped a great deal in causing them to make a run for it. You see Connie I was on top of the mound behind the thicket to your left watching your every move. So I would have made sure one way or the other that you would have found the stepping stones."

Connie chuckled to herself at the idea of Bobby hiding two rabbits in the reeds.

By four o'clock that afternoon the two young lovers had eaten their fill of Mrs O'Hara's picnic. So without further ado Bobby began to pack away the debris left over from their picnic lunch before both he and Connie made their way back to the entrance to the forest in search of Mr Powell and Paddy. A few minutes later as both Bobby and Connie walked hand in hand down the long rubble path which led to the entrance of the forest, they could see in the distance both of Bobby's co-conspirators. Both Paddy and Mr Powell were loading their empty picnic basket into the back of Mr Powell's motor car.

"Have you both enjoyed your lunch in the forest today gentlemen?" called Connie mockingly.

Both Mr, Powell and Paddy turned instantly in the direction of Connie's voice.

"As it happens, Connie we did and I am compelled to say that I found the whole experience most enjoyable," replied Mr Powell as he secured the boot of his motor car before turning to face the newly engaged couple.

"Would it be safe to say that your lunch went according to plan Bobby?"

Mr Powell was of course embarking upon a fishing expedition, anxious to hear if Bobby's proposal had been as well received as they all had anticipated that it would be.

"I can safely say that things couldn't have gone any better, Mr Powell," replied Bobby, holding on tightly to Connie's hand.

Both Bobby and Connie came to a halt at the rear of two parked automobiles, were Paddy and Mr Powell were standing. Connie smiled broadly at both men, this was a smile that relieved both men of any guilt in their part in the conspiracy.

"I have to say that I have never before heard of one man who was capable of keeping a secret, never mind two men," joked Connie. "But I am so pleased that you both did."

Mr Powell smiled broadly at his young charge, then he said,

"Both guilty as charged, Connie."

Connie took a few steps forward towards both her godfather and Paddy, then thrusting her hand out in front of her she said,

"Well! Do you like it Mr Powell?" referring to her engagement ring.

Mr Powell was quick to take hold of his goddaughter's hand and inspect the sparkling diamond that Bobby had placed on her finger.

"I couldn't be more pleased for you, Connie," said Mr Powell, "I know your mother wanted this for you, Connie and I am sure she is looking down on you this very instant and smiling with pride."

Mr Powell proceeded to fling his arms around his goddaughter and hug her tightly.

Paddy, who was standing to Bobby's left, smiled wildly as he took hold of his friends hand and shook it firmly saying,

"I consider it an honour to be here with the both of you on this day because for me to witness your engagement to Connie means a lot to me, Bobby. I still remember clearly those long, dark, wet, cold nights as a group of us sat huddled together in our miserable waterlogged trench on the western front. Listening to you talking for hours about Connie, your one love. I can see it now, Bobby, your face would light up and your smile would widen every time you mentioned Connie's name. I really do believe that it was the thought of coming home to Belfast and asking Connie to marry you that kept you going when times were at their worst, Bobby. Night after night as we sat cold and wet drinking that horrible tepid mud coloured brew that passed as tea. I can tell you now, Bobby, your reminiscing not only helped to see you through the bad times, they also helped all of us lonely young men, as we sat and listened to your accounts of your times with Connie, each of us waiting for you to hold her photograph out in front of you, so we could all take a look and admire her beauty. To a man we all thought that we all knew Connie and that helped to keep our spirits high, as we waited uneasily for the dawn. Knowing that at first light we would once again hear the Sergeant's whistle blow loudly, sending us over the top to mount yet another attack. None of us really knew if we would be one of the lucky ones that would return to our water-logged trench at the end of the day. I also remember that there were times, Bobby when we both thought that we would never see Belfast again, never mind be standing in front of a loved one making a proposal of marriage. Thankfully we are here in this wonderful place and you have done it, Bobby and I for one thank God for it. I just wish that I had been a little smarter and had the foresight to bring a few gills of whisky with me because this day needs to be toasted with the golden water of Ireland, that for sure, Bobby."

Paddy turned slowly towards Connie and respectfully offered her his best wishes for which Connie thanked him warmly.

Mr Powell then exchanged a burly handshake with Bobby as he offered him his heartfelt congratulations on his engagement, then giving Bobby a firm slap on his back he added,

"This has been a marvellous day for not only both you and Connie, but also for me because to see the delight on Connie's face this day will stay with me for ever and for that I thank you, Bobby."

Mr Powell was now becoming emotional and had to wipe a tear from his eye.

Bobby stood upright in front of him and in a strong and earnest voice declared.

"You know that I will always put Connie's happiness and her wellbeing before anything in this world, Mr Powell, on that you can depend."

Mr Powell simply bowed his head in acknowledgement. Bobby turned to his new fiancée and kissed her softly on the lips. Then raising his hand slowly, Bobby touched the soft porcelain skin of Connie's beautiful face with his fingers as he said lovingly,

"I have loved you ever since the first day I saw you when you were dressed in white from head to toe. Your long raven hair curled and bounced around your smiling face with every little movement that you made. To my eyes you were the most beautiful thing I had ever seen, perfect in every way and a real prim and proper young lady at only ten years old. There was I a untidy, dirty kneed crabby faced boy of eleven standing beside his mother. I have never forgotten your warming smile as it flashed in my direction as my mother led me into your back garden.

I tell you this Connie as we all four stand her in this beautiful forest on this day. I will love and protect you for the rest of my life, come what may, be it good or be it bad. I will always be there by your side to fight your corner, Connie."

A tearful Connie replied in a soft loving voice,

"I know you will, Bobby and I will love and care for you all the days of my life."

Mr Powell took a step forward and announced boldly,

"Luckily, it would seem that I have a little more foresight than our friend, Paddy here, because in my motorcar, resting safely in the clove-compartment, I have a small hip flask that is filled to the brim with the golden water of Ireland, as Paddy would call the finest whiskey found anywhere in the world." Mr Powell retrieved the hip flask from his motorcar and said,

"Ladies first I think on this occasion."

The hip flask was passed around, each in turn toasting the engagement before taking their swig of the golden water of Ireland.

"Home, I think," said Mr Powell with a wide grin across his face, as he placed the hip-flask on the back seat of his motorcar.

It was early evening when Mr Powell and his passengers returned to Belfast, first stop was to be Connie's house, allowing Mrs O'Hara and Mary to offer their congratulations to both Connie and Bobby on their engagement. Once all engagement congratulations had been tearfully delivered by Mrs O'Hara and Mary, Mr Powell and Bobby prepared to leave for Mr Powell's house, but not before a wedding conference had been arranged between Mr Powell, Connie and Bobby for the following evening at Connie's house for seven thirty. When Mr Powell and Bobby returned to Mr Powell's house that evening, both men relaxed with a rather large glass of Irish whiskey, as they sat comfortably in the fireside armchairs, talking for hours, before retiring for the evening.

The following evening they both arrived at Connie's house just after seven thirty. As the wedding conference got underway, Mr Powell was hit with a bit of a bombshell. As Connie made it clear from the outset that she had decided that there was to be no long drawn out engagement, as was the order of the day. Connie was insistent that she had waited long enough to be with her Bobby, so as far as she was concerned, to hell with customary and practise. Connie was insistent that this was one wedding that was going to take place as soon as it could be arranged. At first Connie's bold statement came as something of a shock to Mr Powell, as he was more of a traditionalist and had expected an engagement of at least one full year. This was not to be, not as far as Connie was concerned, she was most resolute that her wedding to Bobby would take place without delay. After voiding his opposition to Connie's bold proposal, Mr Powell, in the end, convinced himself that he could see the wisdom behind Connie's plan and decided to go along with it.

Some two days after the wedding meeting at Connie's house, Mr Powell made the short journey from his house to St. Mark's church where he talked at length with Reverent Standing, the Vicar. It has to be said, that at first, just like Mr Powell, Reverent Standing was more than a little shocked at the haste in which this wedding was to be arranged. Mr Powell assured the good Reverent that there had been no impropriety taking place and the reason for the haste was due to their long separation because of the war. Reverent Standing appreciated that it was difficult and unusual times that we were all living in and so posted no objections to the wedding going ahead. Promptly, the wedding of Connie and Bobby was fixed for the 25th September 1918.

That evening Mr Powell returned to Connie's house to convey the good news to her and Bobby, that he had arranged a date for the wedding with Reverent Standing. Upon hearing the good news, Connie got to her feet and walked across the sitting room to where her godfather was sitting. Once by his side, Connie took hold of her his hand, then giving him a smile that would have melted the hardest of men's hearts, she said in a low voice,

"I have one more very important thing to ask of you, Mr Powell."

"Anything," replied Mr Powell, "You only have to ask."

"Mr Powell," started Connie, "You have been a lifelong friend of both my mother and my father and I would consider it to be the high honour, if you would please take the place of my late father and walk me down the aisle on my wedding day?"

Mr Powell was speechless, his eyes welling at the thought of walking Connie down the aisle on her wedding day. He got to his feet and gently pulled his goddaughter towards him, hugging her as tightly as he could as tears rolled off his cheeks. Then with some gusto Mr Powell replied,

"My dearest Connie, I would be more than delighted to represent your father and walk you down the aisle on your wedding day. Your father was my closest friend and I made him a promise before he died that I would always look after you and your mother. Regrettably, I failed him in regards to your mother but rest assured I will not fail him when it comes to you, Connie."

Connie kissed him gently on the cheek and said,

"You must not attach any blame to yourself for my mother's death, Mr Powell, there was nothing you could have done to prevent what took place that night. None of that was your fault."

Mr Powell took Connie by the hand and led her across the room to where Bobby was standing. He then placed Connie's hand in Bobby's hand as he declared,

"I have no fears in my heart that you will be nothing but good for this child in the years still to come, Bobby and that means everything to me. This child is the closed I have ever come to having a daughter of my own."

"I will, Mr Powell, rest assured, I will never allow harm of any kind to even come close to her," answered Bobby.

Mr Powell smiled broadly as he made ready to make his next announcement.

"I have one kindness I seek from the both of you and that kindness is that you both agree to allow me the privilege to not only to arrange everything in regards to your wedding, with you approval every step of the way of course, but to permit me to pay for everything. If you both agree to this wish of mine, then I would be most grateful," Connie looked at Bobby and then at her godfather as a smile beamed happily from her face.

"We would both be honoured and most grateful to you Mr Powell," said Connie.

"Then it's agreed," smiled a delighted Mr Powell. "I shall begin making the arrangements first thing in the morning."

The next few weeks proved to be somewhat frenzied in the Kean household, especially for Mrs O'Hara, her niece Mary and not forgetting Paddy. First there was the engagement party to be arranged and catered for and was to take place at the end of July. Fortunately, for Mrs O'Hara, Connie had informed her that she may recruit as much help as she thought necessary to make sure that the engagement party was one to be remembered and it was. Now that the engagement party had been successfully handled by Mrs O'Hara and her staff, the Kean household briefly returned to some kind of normality. This oasis of peace was not to last long, as everyone's attention quickly turned towards the wedding plans. Needless to say, Mrs O'Hara and Mary were kept on their toes for weeks in advance of the big occasions, as a procession of people were visiting the house and all had to be fed and watered.

There was now only one week to go until the wedding day itself and the excitement in the Kean household was mounting by the day. Mr Powell was like a man processed, list after list was being checked and re-checked by the day. The church was ready, the transport was ready, the photographer was ready, the bridesmaids were ready, the young pageboy was ready, the wedding reception, that was to be held at the Grand Central Hotel on Royal Avenue, was ready. Mr Powell was determined that Connie's wedding was going to be the grandest affair ever seen in the City of Belfast.

Mr Powell had made sure that some of the most powerful and influence people in Belfast were going to be in attendance. Although he did make sure that in pride of place and at the top of the guest list were Paddy, Mrs O'Hara and Mary.

Connie's wedding day was also going to uncover a rather well-kept secret, because unbeknownst to anyone, especially Mrs O'Hara, Paddy had been secretly walking out with Mrs O'Hara's Mary. This stealthily formed union was only made known to Mrs O'Hara by a very nervous Paddy on the morning of the wedding, just as all three were preparing to leave for the church. Luckily for both Paddy and young Mary, Mrs O'Hara viewed the newly discovered union in a favourable light, as she had always thought highly of Paddy.

Now that Bobby and Connie were married and living together at Connie's house, Bobby took up a position working full time at the bakery under Mr Powell's tuition. After a few weeks working there, there was one thing that Bobby thought needed changing and so after a short discussion with both Connie and Mr Powell it was decided that Paddy would no longer continued working as Connie's driver and handyman at the household. Bobby had concerns that his close friendship with Paddy might suffer if Paddy continued to see himself as nothing more than a servant to his best friend. So with Mr Powell's full agreement, Paddy took up a position at the bakery as a shift manager, a position that offered Paddy the opportunity for advancement, as well as instantly doubling his wages. This new position and extra money also allowed Paddy to take his relationship with young Mary to the next step and this it did as Paddy and Mary were engaged in late October.

It now seemed to all that the war in Europe was coming to an end, but the situation in Ireland showed no signs of improving. A year earlier in 1917 Eamon de Valera, who had previously been arrested and sentenced to death for his part in the Easter Rising of 1916, but then had his sentence commuted to imprisonment in England on account that he had been born in America and was classed as an American citizen. Upon his release from prison in Sussex he returned to Ireland and was duly elected as the President of Sinn Fein. He immediately began to forcefully resist the rule of London over Ireland, he openly and actively encouraging the people of Ireland to resist British rule at every turn and in anyway the found necessary and so it was that he was rearrested and imprisoned in Lincoln prison. In the spring of 1918 the German high command launched its final offensive in a bid to win the war. The British Government's reaction to this was to attempt to introduce conscription in Ireland, as many men in the southern counties had not volunteered in the same numbers as the men in Ulster had done, but this proposal never got off the ground, because both Sinn Fein and the Roman Catholic Church in Ireland were bitterly opposed to the whole idea of Irishmen fighting for the crown.

As Christmas of 1918 approached, the spirit of the people throughout Ulster was on something of a high, The Great War had come to an end and the young men of Ulster who had been overseas serving in the British army began to return home in great numbers. For the young protestant returning soldiers this was a time of being reunited with their families and a time of great celebrations. Open air street parties were to be seen all over the protestant areas of Ulster, Belfast itself was a beacon of celebration. Sadly the same could not be said for the young returning Catholic boys, as most of them returned home to be seen as traitors to Ireland and shunned, not only by the communities in which they had lived since being a child, but also in many cases they were abandoned by their own families. These young Catholic boys were left homeless and jobless, with nowhere and no one to turn to for help, their plight wasn't helped by the situation which was now raging throughout Ireland. Due to the attitude widely shown by most Catholic Nationalist towards Brittan and the returning solders, many Protestants in every corner of Ulster were now openly voicing the distrust and anger that they felt towards Roman Catholics in Ulster. This distrust and anger was growing by the day, many protestant employers were now reluctant to employ Roman Catholic workers, fearing sabotage and disruption as the Nationalist movement was gathering pace in Ulster.

With the war now at an end, the Catholic Nationalist movement in Ireland quickly sensed that there was now a weakening in the attitudes of some of the British leaders in London towards what was known as the Irish problem. There was now a steadfast determination growing amongst certain members of John Redmond's Irish Nationalist Party to once again push hard for Home Rule. The more extreme Nationalist Party known as Sinn Fein, had now become the leading Irish Political Party and were quickly emerging as a warring force within Irish Politics in the southern counties. The leadership of Sinn Fein now convinced that the whole idea of Home Rule was outdated and a non-starter. Sinn Fein's leaders were now pushing for Self-Rule, they wanted to be completely independent of London. This situation was naturally a concern to the Unionist of Ulster. These concerns widely held by the Unionist in Ulster, resulted in many former members of the U.V.F. who had returned form the war, banding together once again in readiness to defend what they saw as the Nationalist threat to their very existence. In the Post-war General Election in December 1918 Sinn Fein made a breakthrough, sweeping aside the IPP by 73, seats to 6. The Ulster Unionists taking 25 seats in the North. After the Election Sinn Fein decided to boycott Westminster, instead meeting at Dublin's Mansion House using it as 'Dail Eirean', of Irish Parliament. By 1919 the rise of Sinn Fein had worried the Ulster Unionists so much that both north and south had become polarised and Ulster no longer listened to Dublin, then in the January of 1919 Sinn Fein openly declared Ireland as an Independent Republic, much to the annoyance of both the Ulster Unionists and Westminster.

What made matters worse in 1919, when news that Eamon de Valera had escaped from Lincoln prison and had returned to the country of his birth, America, where he remained for 18 months. It was widely reported that he had embarked on a mission of gathering funds for the I.R.A. all over America. It was being reported in many publications, not only in America, but also in some Nationalist newspapers in Ireland that he was believed to have successfully raised more than one Million Pounds for the Nationalist cause in Ireland. As a result the I.R.A. had now an abundance of funds to arm themselves making them a worrying force to be reckoned with in Ireland.

In the March of 1919 amidst all of the upheaval that was going on in Ireland, Connie found herself pregnant with her first child, resulting in her having to giving up her volunteer work at the Somme Nursing Home. Connie's first born was a boy and he was born on the 15th. of August 1919. Connie and Bobby had the child Christened at St. Mark's church on the 29th. of October, naming him, Robert Andrew Gallagher. Robert after his father of course and Andrew after Mr Powell. Connie was becoming increasingly worried about the situation that the young catholic boys, who had returned from the war, were now facing in Belfast. Even though she had just become a new mother, Connie still found time to address this problem in the only way she knew how, straight on.

Connie personally funded the renovation and opening of two of the large empty buildings she owned in Belfast. One of these buildings, when completed, would serve as a centre where young returning Catholic soldiers could go to learn a trade and be helped to find work. The other building, the larger of the two, was furnished and transformed into a lodging house where the homeless catholic boys that found themselves ostracised after returning home from the war could live. This activity did not sit well with everyone in Belfast, the protestant population were outraged that one of their own should want to help the Catholic boys in this way. Some would say that their anger was well founded when you consider everything that was going on in Ireland at this time. On many occasions this outrage that was felt by the Unionists towards Connie's activities would spill over and her buildings would be targeted by Loyalists and at times sever damage would done to both buildings. The inhabitants of these buildings were at times also attacked and beaten severely. As for Nationalists, we all saw the participation of the returning Catholic soldiers in this venture as further evidence that they had sold out to the British. On many occasions it would be the Nationalists that would attack both the buildings and their inhabitants. No matter how many times Connie's buildings were attacked, Connie was steadfast in her belief that she was doing the right thing.

As for Paddy, well he and Mary were now married and living in their own little terraced house in the Short-strand, a strong Catholic area of East Belfast, just a short walk from St. Matthew's Roman Catholic Chapel. Mary was no longer working as a maid at the big house, although her aunt remained as the housekeeper. The situation in Ireland was now worsening by the day, as the Protestant Unionists in Ulster now saw the Nationalist threat of Independence from London as a real worrying to their very existence. Many of the most influential men in Belfast began to get more involved in Ulster politics, as they were determined to protect their culture and way of life, Mr Powell being no exception.

Mr Powell had now become close friends with both Sir. James Craig and Sir. Edward Carson. Sir. James Craig (1st. Viscount Craigavon.) along with Sir. Edward Carson had some years before both been instrumental in the formation of the U.V.F. Sir James Craig had also been an Ulster Unionist M.P. since 1906. Sir Edward Carson was the moving force behind the mass signing of the Ulster Covenant in 1912. He was also an Ulster Unionist M.P. Carson was widely seen in the north as the Father of Protestant ideology throughout Ulster, as well as standing firm and showing uncompromising resistance to The Home Rule Bill in Westminster.

The year of 1920. was now upon us and the I.R.A. were now more active than at any time in Irish history, targeting anything or anyone deemed to have links with Britain. In response to the I.R.A.'s violent activities the British Government sent reinforcements in the shape of the Black and Tans to help the Royal Irish Constabulary in the south of Ireland to help crush what was seen in London as the Irish rebellion. This new force was recruited in England and made up of returning soldiers who were only too willing to sign up as most of them found themselves jobless, but the logistics of providing uniforms for this new force was proving difficult as uniforms were in short supply and so this new law enforcement unit was kitted out with a mix of old uniforms from the army and the police, i.e.: (Black police tops and Khaki army bottoms,) hence their nickname the Black and Tans. This new force were quickly pressed into action fighting an increasingly bloody cycle of reprisal and counter-reprisal with the I.R.A. By the July of 1920, the violence that had mainly been seen in southern parts of Ireland had now erupted in the streets of Belfast. Running battles were being fought on regular occasions between the Nationalists (I.R.A.) and the Loyalist (U.V.F.) then in the August of 1920. things escalated dramatically when the I.R.A. murdered District Inspector Swanzy of the R.I.C. in Lisburn, just a few miles outside Belfast, (The R.I.C. was soon to become the R.U.C.) this act of defiance by the I.R.A. resulted in anger within the Unionist communities and anti-Catholic rioting erupted in many cities throughout Ulster, but the worst was to be seen on the streets of Belfast. Roman Catholic families were burnt out of their homes, beaten and chased out of protestant areas when it transpired that Inspector Swanzy's death was ordered by Michel Collins and his associates in Dublin as reprisal for Swanzy's part in the killing of Thomas MacCurtain, the Lord Mayor of Cork by the R.I.C. at his home earlier that year. MacCurtain was a well-known leader and active participant in the war of Independence against the British in Ireland. At the Coroner's Inquest into MacCurtain killing the jury passed a verdict of wilful murder against Lloyd George and certain Inspectors of the R.I.C. one of the Inspectors named was Oswald Swanzy.

It was at this time that life changed dramatically for Paddy and Mary, although they were relatively safe where they lived, as their house was in the Short Strand area of the city, which was a small Catholic enclave on the edge of the predominant protestant East Belfast. The problem arose when Paddy would leave the safety of his neighbourhood to go to work in the lager protestant area of East Belfast, that's when the danger would threaten his safety. You see Paddy was well known as a Roman Catholic at the bakery and with everything that was happening in Belfast at this time, the workforce slowly began to turn on him. Many workers resented the fact that a Roman Catholic was being employed as their boss. Unrest at the bakery was becoming something of a problem and threats were being made towards Paddy and his wife, Mary. At first both Mr Powell and Bobby tried to ride out this unrest, but things took a turn for the worse in Belfast in mid-August after Swanzy's murder. Things boiled over one Friday afternoon when Paddy was violently attacked in the courtyard of the bakery by four masked men. Paddy was brutally beaten with wooden clubs and left in a heap in the middle of the cobbled courtyard unconscious and bleeding profusely from deep wounds to his head and face. Bobby, hearing the commotion outside of his office window, rushed out into the courtyard to find Paddy laying on the ground surrounded by a group of on looking workers. Paddy was instantly rushed to hospital where he remained for several weeks. Bobby questioned every one of the workers that had assembled in the courtyard, but the answer to Bobby's question was the same from each and every one of them,

"I saw nothing Mr Gallagher."

A meeting was hastily arranged between Mr Powell, Connie and Bobby, Mr Powell making it clear from the outset to both his goddaughter and her husband Bobby, that it would be impossible for Paddy to continue working at the bakery.

This decision had not been taken lightly by Mr Powell, but he made it with Paddy's best interests in mind. His suggestion was this, that at the bakery's expense, they move Paddy to the other side of Belfast, setting him up in his own business. Regrettably, both Bobby and Connie could see the logic in that proposal, leaving them with no choice but to agree to Mr Powell's solution to the problem. Bobby recalled that on many occasions when he and Paddy would sit cold and wet in their trench just talking, that Paddy would say that his dream was to own his own pub when he got back to Belfast when the war was over. Bobby quickly informed Mr Powell and Connie of Paddy's dream, suggesting that they should purchase a public house on Paddy's behalf somewhere in West Belfast, it being a Catholic stronghold where Paddy and Mary would be safe to carry on with their lives. Bobby's idea was that when Paddy was discharged from hospital and had made a full recovery, they would hand over the keys of the bar to him as compensation. Both Mr Powell and Connie agreed whole-heartedly with Bobby's suggestion. Mr Powell quickly announced that he would make all of the necessary arrangements and begin the search for suitable premises. Bobby knew deep down that once Paddy had taken charge of his new pub, then their friendship would come to an abrupt end. You see, this attack on Paddy wasn't an isolated incident in Belfast, crimes of this kind were happening all over Belfast and being committed by both sides of the divide. The sectarian violence in Belfast worsened in the matter of a few short weeks, in August alone 30 people were killed in brutal riots. The only bright spot at this time in the Gallagher household was that Connie was about to give birth for the second time. It was in the early hours of the morning of the 5th. of September that Connie gave birth to twin boys. One was named Terence Gallagher and the other, William Gallagher!

Later that month on the 20th. of September to be exact, Bobby made the short journey to see his friend Paddy at his home in Seaforde Street in the Short Strand area of East Belfast. Bobby had been to visit Paddy several times whilst he was in hospital, but he hadn't seen his friend since he had been discharged from hospital and had returned home. Paddy had now been recovering at home for a day past two weeks and was now just about back to full heath. Bobby knocked firmly three times on Paddy's front door, then waited for an answer. Within a matter of seconds the door was opened by Paddy's wife, Mary.

"Good God, Bobby!" called out alarmingly, so shocked was she to Bobby standing at her front door,

"Jesus, Mary and Joseph, Bobby," continued Mary in the same concerned manner, "What are you doing here?"

"I've come to see how Paddy is recovering, Mary and course to see if you are coping with things." answered Bobby calmly.

"Jesus, Bobby, you will get us all killed, come in, come in before someone see you."

Mary's concern was plain to see, her fear was written all over face her face and it was fully justified, because she knew that if someone was to recognise Bobby, then not only his safety, but that of herself and Paddy too would be in jeopardy, Bobby being a well-known protestant figure and a man of the ruling classes in East Belfast. Mary quickly ushered Bobby into the house, slamming the door firmly shut behind him.

"Paddy, Bobby is here to see you," called Mary as both she and Bobby made their way down the hallway past the parlour towards the sitting room at the rear of the house. Bobby entered the room and warmly shook his old friend by the hand.

"How are you feeling, Paddy?" asked Bobby.

"Feeling a hell of a lot better than I did a few weeks ago, that's for sure thanks, Bobby," replied Paddy.

"I really can't apologise enough for what happened to you, Paddy, it should never have happened," said Bobby.

"Thank you, Bobby, but honestly you really shouldn't have come here, someone might realise who you are and you know what the consequences would be if that were to happen, Bobby," continued Paddy with earnest concern for his friend.

"Listen to me, Paddy, no one in this city is ever going to tell me when, where or even if I can visit any friend of mine, I will decide when I come to see you, Paddy, no one else!" replied Bobby defiantly.

Both friends chatted for over an hour before they got down to business.

"It's really good to see you, Bobby, but I am sure that you haven't just come here today to chew the fat, have you Bobby?"

Bobby smiled as he replied,

"No, I haven't, Paddy, I'm here to sort out the future with you."

"I thought so, Bobby," said Paddy, his tone becoming sombre, "Believe me, Bobby I don't blame you for not wanting me back at the bakery, I really understand the position you are in."

"Listen Paddy," said Bobby, "If it wasn't for your safety I would have you back tomorrow and anyone that didn't like it could leave and find another job, but your safety has to come first, Paddy."

"I understand, Bobby and I thank both you and Connie for all you have done for me since I got back to Belfast, but trust me I do understand what you're saying."

Again Bobby smiled at his friend saying,

"You've got it all wrong, Paddy. Yes, it's true you can't come back to work at the bakery, but we are not going to just leave you and Mary high and dry. Do you really think I could do that to you Paddy?"

"What else is there for you to do, Bobby?" asked Paddy curiously.

"I know that you have always talked about owning a bar one day, Paddy."

"A pipe dream, Bobby, but a nice one while it lasted I have to admit." interrupted Paddy.

"Well it's no longer a pipe dream Paddy" smiled Bobby.

"What do you mean, Bobby?" asked a mystified Paddy.

Bobby took a small bunch of keys from his pocket and tossed them in Paddy's direction.

"What are these keys for, Bobby?" asked Paddy as he caught the bunch of keys in his right hand.

"They are the keys to your future, Paddy." replied Bobby with an impish smile.

"What do you mean, Bobby!?" exclaimed Paddy, having no idea what his friend was talking about.

"The keys you hold in your hands, Paddy will open the doors to Paddy's Bar on the Falls Road. Mr Powell, Connie and myself have talked it over and we decided that this is the least we can do for you and Mary. We have made sure that the bar is fully stocked, cleaned and ready to open, your first beer order has been arranged and it will be delivered on your say so, Paddy. So your bar is ready to open as soon as its new owner wants it to."

Bobby once again smiled at his friend, adding,

"By the way, we changed the bar's name from Duffy's Bar to Paddy's Bar, I hope you approve, Paddy?"

Paddy looked at his wife, Mary with the biggest smile on his face.

"My God, Mary, we own our own bar on the Falls Road!" Paddy shouted loudly in his unhindered excitement.

Marry put her hand to her face in reaction to the shock she felt at hearing the good news. She quickly crossed the room and flung her arms around her husband and hugged him tightly saying,

"It looks very much like we do, Paddy."

Both Mary and Paddy thanked Bobby for his kindness, then they went to get out the whisky in celebration. After a few gills had been downed by both men, Bobby got to his feet and shook his friend firmly by the hand and said,

"The best of luck to the both of you, Paddy. I will miss you both, I really will, but maybe one day I will be able to walk into Paddy's Bar on the Falls Road and order a pint of stout from my old friend."

"If only that could come true, Bobby, it would make me the happiest man in Belfast!" replied Paddy as he once again hugged his friend warmly. Bobby looked his old friend in the eye and said,

"I may never see you again, Paddy but I want you to know that it has been a pleasure and a privilege to have served with you, but it has been more of an honour to have had you as my friend. One day, Paddy, maybe one day we will share that pint of your best stout together in your very own bar, maybe one day."

"I will pray for that day, Bobby," replied Paddy sadly.

And with those sombre wards exchanged between the friends, Bobby left Paddy's house, not knowing if they would ever see each other again!

CHAPTER 20

Bobby returned home with his sprit dampened and his heart saddened by the depressing situation that was raging out of control all across Belfast. This was a conflict that no one wanted, yet everyone seemed to be falling over themselves to get involved in. A conflict so divisive and dangerous that one friend could not speak to another in fear of their lives, unless the friend was of the same religion as them. For several days after Bobby had said his goodbyes to his friend, Paddy, his mood was dreary, his step not as eager as before, his actions not as resolute towards his everyday life. Everything he heard and saw happening all around him, chilled his heart, leaving him fearful for the future. The only ray of light on Bobby's horizon was that the wounds to his leg had now fully healed and although he still walked with a slight limp, he had no further use for the walking cane he had been using.

The year of 1920 saw a rise in brutal rioting throughout Belfast, Lisburn, Bangor and Banbridge. The cause of such fierce and brutal sectarian rioting across many towns and cities was put down to the callous slaughter of Detective Inspector Swanzy in Lisburn by the I.R.A. At its worst there was 22 people killed in one week of fighting. On both sides of this divide many unspeakable atrocities were being committed. Families were burnt out of their homes, people were being attacked in the street, just for being of a different religion. The I.R.A, claiming that Catholic families were receiving little or no protection from the police, began a campaign of falsely luring police officers into carefully set traps then shot down in cold blood.

One morning, in the late winter of 1920 Mr Powell received a visitor, a visitor from the past, this was a caller whom he had never expected to ever see again. The visitor in question was Inspector Nabney. Mr Powell was in his front sitting room reading his morning newspaper when his housekeeper entered the room and announced the arrival of the Inspector. To say that Mr Powell was surprised by the Inspector turning up at his house, would be an understatement.

"To what do I owe this unexpected visit, Inspector Nabney?" asked Mr Powell.

"I'm sorry to say, but I am the bearer of sad news, Mr Powell." replied Inspector Nabney.

"Please do sit down, Inspector," gestured Mr Powell.

The Inspector sat down in a large armchair by the bay window, then taking a deep breath to brace himself he said,

"We were called to the house of William Hastings late last evening, Mr Powell."

"To William's house?" enquired Mr Powell, "And why would the Constabulary have cause to visit William's house late at night, Inspector?" inquired Mr Powell curiously.

"There was a shooting at William's house last evening Mr Powell." answered the Inspector.

"A shooting!" exclaimed Mr Powell.

"Yes, a rather serious shooting I am sorry to say, Mr Powell, a shooting that leaves us with some rather disturbing consequences," said the Inspector.

"Explain please, Inspector," said Mr Powell.

"It would seem that the I.R.A. have not forgotten about the little skirmish we had with them a few years back, Mr Powell. We believe that a new I.R.A. high commander has been sent from Dublin to take control of all I.R.A. activities here in Belfast. This new commander, whose identity we are yet to uncover, is without question responsible for sending two gunman to execute William at his home. It would seem, from several eyewitness accounts of the incident, that William put up a hell of a fight and although he was killed in the attack, he managed to take the two gunman with him."

"Good God, where will it all end?" gasped a shocked Mr Powell.

"One of the gunman is unknown to us, but we believe that he came to Belfast from Dublin along with the new commander. The second gunman is well known to us, Mr Powell. He was known in the Nationalist community simply as Spud Murphy and owned a Public House on the Falls Road. He was a well-known republican activist and his bar is used as a meeting point by the higher ranking I.R.A officers in West Belfast. We have intelligence that shows us that this new I.R.A. commander, is out for revenge, Mr Powell.

We also have intelligence that this same commander is the man who gave the order to have young Connie's mother assassinated, and now that he has done for William, we fear that you, Mr Powell, are also in his sights. I would encourage you to take the upmost care in your daily life from now on. I would also strongly suggest that you purchase a firearm at your earliest convenience, Mr Powell," said the Inspector.

Mr Powell sat forward in his chair, his face in deep thought, then he said to Inspector Nabney,

"I thank you for the information, Inspector and by God I will take steps to keep myself and those close to me as safe as is humanly possible."

"You do that Mr Powell," said Inspector Nabney.

The very next day, Mr Powell arranged a meeting between himself and Bobby in a small Belfast hotel. He thought it best to keep this disturbing news about the I.R.A.'s renewed interest in himself and undoubtedly in Connie as well, as far away from Connie's ears as possible. Mr Powell advised Bobby to carry a firearm at all times until this danger had passed. Bobby agreed and so both men met with Inspector Nabney that afternoon and were both handed papers allowing them to carry firearms.

That year a group of Nationalist sympathisers in The Belfast Corporation sent a letter to the Dail in Dublin. Sean Macentee (Momaghan South) presented the Memorial signed by representative citizens of Belfast, to the Dail in Dublin, it read...

We the under signed members of the Belfast Corporation and others representing the views of Irish Republicans in Belfast beg to call the earnest attention of the Dail to the war of extermination now being waged against us, and we appeal to you to stand by us in this struggle. We assume that you have read the press reports of the program which started on the 21st, of July with the violent expulsion from work of well over 5,000 people, of the murders, wrecking, looting and wholesale eviction of families. The situation for expelled workers grows worse daily, and all signs go to show that the persecution is to be continued with unabated vigour. No one, not being in Belfast can have any adequate idea of what our people are suffering now and must continue to suffer. From the first, the promoters of these outrages have been publicly declaring that they are out to fight Sinn Fein, and drive it from the North-Eastern Pale. Already thousands of young men from every county in Ireland have been forced to fly, and thousands of others are idle here with destitution staring them in the face. The only condition in which they will be permitted to work is that they sign a declaration of loyalty to the British Government. We earnestly appeal to Sinn Fein, through the Dail to take up this straight challenge, and fight Belfast – the spear head of British power in Ireland. The loyalists have repeatedly declared at public meetings and in the town council that this time they are not fighting Popery as such, but Sinn Fein, so that mere sectarianism does not enter in. We suggest that Sinn Fein can strike back with powerful effect by a commercial boycott of Belfast. Drastic action of this kind has already been taken spontaneously in various places, but the movement ought to be made National and throughout. The chef promoters of Orange intolerance here are the heads of the distributing trade throughout Ireland.

We further suggest that the most effective action Sinn Fein can take ...

(To make Belfast realise that it is in Ireland and must be of Ireland)

Is to secure that it's supporters throughout the country immediately withdraw all accounts from Banks having their headquarters in Belfast, and transfer them to Banks with their headquarters in other parts of Ireland. This action is of vital importance. It will deprive Belfast merchants who mostly either support or assent to this war on Irish Nationalism, to the fluid capital on which their business, through the medium of Belfast Banks, is largely run. Other additional measures will doubtless suggest themselves to some of the Gentlemen of the Dial. The above will meet with the fullest approval of nearly 100,000 people in Belfast. It should be strictly enjoined that Protestants in other parts of Ireland are not to be molested in any way on account of the actions of their co-religionists in Belfast. But, of course, those of them who are in business must be given the understanding clearly that if they continue to get their goods from Belfast firms they cannot dispose of them to Sinn Feiners.-

(This document was signed by several members of the Belfast Corporation and dated...5th. August 1920.)

In the Dial itself opinion was split on what they should do, but more were against the idea of action against the merchants and Banks.

Joseph Macgrath (St. James, Dublin) Suggested that the Trades Congress be asked by the ministry to open negotiations with the employers for a settlement.

Michael Collins (Cork South) Spoke of the effect which a boycott of Belfast Banks would have in Belfast. He protested, however, against the attempt which had been made by two deputies from the North of Ireland to inflame the passions of members. Saying... There was no Ulster question.

Others said that if action was taken against the Banks and the merchants in Belfast, then many Republicans would be forced to buy British goods, one of them was...

Liam De Roiste (Cork City) who said, I oppose an economic boycott as it would mean having to purchase English made goods instead of Belfast made articles. Instead he said... Economic penetration was the solution to the Ulster question.

So after further discussion the amendment was put and defeated.

The Acting- President then moved a further amendment-

That the imposition of political or religious tests as a condition of Industrial Employment in Ireland is hereby declared illegal, and that action be taken by the ministry to prevent such tests being imposed in Ireland.

After further discussion, this amendment was accepted by Sean Macentee, and was pasted and carried.

Sadly to say all this activity in Dublin made little difference to the situation in the North, especially in Belfast, as the Loyalists still saw the I.R.A's. activity as a real threat to their very existence. It is believed that at this time probably 10,000 Irish Republicans were driven from their employment in Belfast, leaving thousands of Republican families destitute and with no means of support. Home rule was once again on the agenda, but many saw the Home rule Bill of 1912 outdated and so the new up dated home rule Bill of 1919, which decreed that Ireland would govern itself within the Empire, but with two separate parts, - The South - and the Six Counties of the North, - Which was most, but not all of the old Province of Ulster. - The Bill stated that each of the two parts would have a Parliament, in Dublin and Belfast. Also that Ireland as a whole would still have MP's representing them at Westminster. The Bill also proposed a Council of Ireland which would have representatives in it from both Parliaments. This Bill became an Act in the December of 1920. The North accepted the Act and in 1921. King George V. opened the first Parliament of the six Counties at Stormont in Belfast. In his speech he appealed for calm in Ireland, but his words fall on deaf ears. However, despite the Kings words, the South did not except one part of the Act, the Sinn Fein members that had been elected as MP's in the 'Coupon 'Election of 1919, refused to take up their seats at Westminster.

Sir James Craig, who was now a close associate of Mr Powell, was instrumental in a six County Northern Territory being chosen for Northern Ireland, as opposed to the nine counties favoured by English Ministers and some Unionists. Although at this time Craig had a promising Ministerial career at Westminster, he reluctantly gave it up and accepted the Premiership of the six Counties in 1921. Sinn Fein and the Nationalists were still not happy with the political situation in Ireland and continued with their war of Independence throughout Ireland. With the situation in Belfast being at an all-time low Bobby and Connie decided to take their three boys to their house in the small fishing town of Kilkeel for the simmer, Kilkeel is a peaceful picturesque town, it's central hub being it's small, but busy harbour, which, when they were not at sea, was filled with local fishing boats, the town is situated on the South-East coast of Co. Down at the foot of the Mourne Mountains. It was whilst the Gallagher family were holidaying here that Connie discovered that she was once again pregnant. At the end of the summer the Gallagher family returned to Belfast, and Connie gave birth to yet another son on the 10th. of November 1921, he was christened at St. Marks Church, the child being named... Andrew Gallagher, again after her godfather. Belfast was now in turmoil and the workshop and lodging house that Connie had set up in the city for young jobless and homeless catholic boys who had returned from the war was now coming under repeated attacks from both sides of the divide, but Connie was determined to carry on with her work in this area and so every time it was attacked, Connie simply put it right again and carried on.

The I.R.A. were now stepping up their offensive against anything and anyone linked with the British, then after the I.R.A. attack on the Custom House in Dublin in the May of 1921, that went drastically wrong when they were surrounded and over 120 I.R.A. fighters were arrested. Following this the British Prime Minister Lloyd George calls for an end to the war in Ireland and in mid-July the I.R.A. agreed to a truce. A meeting is hastily arranged in London and Sinn Fein leader Eamon de Valera meets with Lloyd George, but Sir. James Craig point blank refuses to attend such a meeting. An Anglo-Irish Treaty is tentatively discussed, followed in the October of 1921, by the beginning of formal and earnest negotiations on the Treaty, an agreement is eventually agreed and signed. Then in the January of 1922. The Dail Eireann, after a bitter debate in which those in favour of accepting the Treaty were accused of treachery towards the people of Ireland, voted on the issue and the Treaty was accepted by 64 votes to 57, and so the Irish Free State was born, but many Republicans in Dublin were not happy with this situation as they rued the loss of the six Counties to Britain. In the months that followed there was no the end of the violence in the North as the Unionists in Ulster felt betrayed by London and saw the Treaty as strengthening the hand of the Republicans and more worryingly the I.R.A. thus increasing the threat to the safety of the people of Ulster. In the March alone 230 people were killed and over 1,000 wounded in the brutal riots that ravaged Belfast. The majority of the dead and wounded were Roman Catholic Republicans, The I.R.A. in the South quickly send reinforcements to the North to bolster what forces they already had there. The I.R.A. retaliates by targeting and viciously attacking the 'B. Specials' the 'B. Specials' were the part time police force in Ulster and were made up mainly of members of the Orange Order. In the April the R.I.C. (Royal Irish Constabulary.) is renamed, now to be known as the R.U.C. (Royal Ulster Constabulary.)

In the spring of 1921 Mr Powell and Bobby were leaving the Orange Hall on the Albert Bridge Road, after attending the monthly meeting of their Orange Lodge. Both men were walking the short distance from the Orange Hall to Templemore Avenue, where Mr Powell had parked his motorcar. As they turned into Templemore Avenue Bobby noticed a group of four men on the opposite side of the road who appeared to be huddled together in deep conversation. At first Bobby thought nothing of it, but for some reason he decided to keep one eye on them. As Mr Powell reached into his pocket to retrieve the keys to his motorcar, for some odd reason Bobby turned his attention back towards the four man who had been in conversation on the opposite side of the road. Bobby watched as the four men, still fixed in a tight huddle, started to cross the road and in doing so quicken their step as they headed in his and Mr Powell's direction.

Bobby sensed that something wasn't quite right with these four men and as he took a closer look, he realised that these men were wearing black balaclavas and that their only reason for being there was to assassinate Mr Powell and himself. In a flash, Bobby screamed loudly as he pulled his firearm from under his coat, Mr Powell, who was now alerted to the danger, also pulled his firearm from his coat and a gun battle quickly erupted. Within a few minutes all fell quiet and the four I.R.A, gunmen lay motionless on the ground. Bobby was leaning against a shop window clutching his left shoulder tightly, as blood oozed from a gunshot wound he had sustained in the gun fight. Mr Powell was on the ground with his back resting against his motorcar. Blood was gushing at a rapid rate from at least six gunshot wounds that he had suffered in the gunfight. Within seconds several fellow Orange Lodge Brothers were on the scene to lend assistance, two of the Brother were openly carrying revolvers. Both of them moved quickly towards the four I.R.A. gunmen who were lay on the ground, their purpose was to make sure that they were indeed dead and posed no further danger to anyone. What happened next was never given an explanation of any kind, all that is known for sure is that two loud gunshots were heard coming from the area were the I.R.A, gunmen were lay on the ground. By the time medical help arrived on the scene, sadly it was too late for Mr Powell, as hard as Bobby tried to help him and keep him alive, it was a losing fight. Mr Powell's injuries were too severe, as he had received multiple gunshots all over his body. As for Bobby, well he was fortunate he had only received the one gunshot wound to his shoulder.

This terrible news was broken to Connie at her home later that evening by members of the Orange Lodge. After Connie's initial shock at the news of the attack on her husband and her godfather outside the Orange Hall, Connie was grateful to hear that Bobby had survived with just a small wound to his shoulder. But the news of Mr Powell's death was devastating for Connie. Even though Connie was now a grown woman with a husband and children of her own, Mr Powell's death seemed to signal the end of the security she had known from her childhood. You see, when her father died, she understandably felt a great loss, but there was always her mother and Mr Powell looking out for her. In Mr Powell and her mother Connie had two strong parental figures who stood large in her life and that she could always depend on to comfort her when she needed comforting and advise her when she needed advice. After her mother had been murdered by the I.R.A. Connie felt that a part of her died along with her mother. It was Mr Powell that stepped forward and filled the void that she felt in her life, but now he was gone too. Connie felt a sad emptiness deep inside, much like she did when her mother had been murdered by the I.R.A.

For Connie, Mr Powell's passing was the removal of the last link of sanctuary from her upbringing. After the passing of both her father and her mother, Mr Powell was the rug of comfort beneath her feet, a force she had always known and depended upon, but now it too had been pulled from under her. It took Connie a long time to get over her godfather's death, although she mourned his passing for many weeks. Connie thought of him on a daily basis for many years to come, at the same time she would also give thanks every day for her Bobby having survived the incident. Several weeks after Mr Powell's funeral, Connie was contacted by his solicitor, a Mr Pending-Smith, for the reading of Mr Powell's will. Connie was accompanied to this sad occasion by her husband, Bobby. As Mr Powell had never been married and had no children, nor had he any family to speak off, he had bequeathed everything he possessed to his goddaughter, Connie.

Mr Powell's estate was indeed a rather large one, meaning that Connie had inherited his large house at Sydenham, as well as several buildings in Belfast City centre. Also reverting to Connie was Mr Powell's half of the bakery, along with his great wealth, making the Gallagher family one of the richest in Belfast. As for Bobby's recuperation after the attack, it took no longer than six weeks for Bobby to return to full fitness, although in the winters to come, he did suffer with a stiff shoulder.

Because of the worsening situation in Ulster the Government enacts the Special Powers Act, the Act is thought to be controversial in other parts of Ireland, as it permits the setting up of special courts with the power to detain suspects without trail and to pass jail terms and even the death penalty. This act was in response to the callous murder in London of Sir. Henry Wilson, a British General and security advisor to the Northern Ireland Government, by two I.R.A. gunmen. The Free State Government, acts against those within their midst who are opposed to the Anglo-Irish treaty and a civil war breaks out in the newly formed Irish Free State. In Northern Ireland the Government makes Electoral Changes, abolishing Proportional Representation. Also at this time local boundaries are redrawn under the Leech Commission - to the benefit of the Protestants of Ulster. The Border is fixed between the North and the South, officially separating the two parts of Ireland for good and confirming the huge fissure between the two ideologies. The civil war in the Irish Free State rages on and in 1922 the Anti-Treaty Republicans corner and shoot dead Michael Collins, who was one of the Treaty signatories. It wasn't until 1923 that the civil war in the Irish Free State ended.

On a much happier note, also in the year of 1923, Connie was again expecting her fifth child and in the 6th. of October to be exact, Connie gave birth to yet another boy, naming him Samuel Gallagher.

With Connie now having five boys to look after and Mary long gone, Mrs O'Hara's work load was increasing daily and so it was that Connie, along with the support of Mrs O'Hara, began the process of looking for a new housemaid to assist Mrs O'Hara with the daily running of the big house. Also to be recruited was a nanny to help Connie in the day to day activities that go with having five small boys to look after. Within a few weeks, a housemaid was found and her name was Susan Sanders, a local girl of the tender age of twenty one. It was only a matter of days after the housemaid had been employed, that a nanny, with four years' experience of working and looking after children, was also employed. The nanny's name was Martha Morgan, an English girl from Liverpool, aged twenty five. Life at the big house was once again running smoothly and the two new employees had settled in really well and seemed to be enjoying their new positions in the Gallagher household. A warm and relaxing environment had now been created for the boys to be brought up in. As time passed, Connie once again found herself pregnant and a sixth child was born on the 8th November 1924. As you may not be surprised to learn, the child was yet another boy being named Harold Gallagher.

The Christmas of 1924 heralded yet another surprise for the Gallagher family as on the 20th. of December Connie gave birth to yet another son, this time the boy was named Thomas Gallagher.

And so Bobby and Connie were now the proud parents of seven young sons: Bobby, Billy, Terry, Andy, Sammy, Harry and Tommy.

By the year of 1928 the training workshop and lodging house that Connie had opened in Belfast were slowly but surely becoming obsolete. This was due to their success, as the young men that this enterprise had been originally set up help, no longer had any use for them, as all of the young returning solders were now all grown up and had jobs and families of their own. So once again Connie's buildings lay empty and unused. The following years passed quickly for the Gallagher family and their boys were growing bigger with every passing year. It was now the year of our Lord 1932. Trouble was once again brewing all over Ireland, although this time the trouble was not motivated by either politics or religion, but poverty. People on both sides of the divide took to the streets in protest of their suffering in the Great Depression. Then in the October of 1932 the protests on the streets of Belfast erupted into full scale riots, two people are shot dead and fifteen are wounded by the police who opened fire on the rioters. The Government have no option but to increase the amount of outdoor relief available in an effort to quell the riots, but even this was not enough to solve the problem.

As the troubles in the city of Belfast were reaching new and even more brutal heights, the people of the city were now not only fighting over religion, but also over the extreme lack of food. In response to the drastic state in which the people of Belfast found themselves, Connie reopened her empty building in Belfast and self-funded a food relief program giving out free food each and every day. This food relief was open to all, no matter what their political persuasion might be, families with small children being first in line to receive food. Things changed in Belfast in the July of 1935. I.R.A. activity increased in the city, sectarian rioting once again broke out on the streets of Belfast. The violence claiming the lives of twelve people, most of them being protestants, although most of the damage to property due to the rioting, occurred in Catholic areas, Catholic family homes and Catholic owned businesses were set alight and destroyed in big numbers. The I.R.A. saw the disruption in Belfast life as a chance to recruit more and more Catholics into their organisation, knowing that the more members that they had the more chance they would have when the time was right to oust the British from Ireland once and for all,

In the September of 1937, Connie sold the bakery, as neither she nor Bobby had any great interest in running it anymore. Along with the selling of the bakery Connie also sold the buildings she had inherited from Mr Powell in Belfast. As for her godfather's large house at Sydenham, well both Connie and Bobby decided, not only to kept the house, but to move into it with their family and staff, as it was a much superior house in size to the one they presently lived in.

By the year of 1939 the situation, in not only Ulster, but all over Britain was on a sinking downturn, as everyone throughout these home Islands were only too aware that war was just around the corner. But to add to Britain's woes at this time, the I.R.A., sensing that Britain was in turmoil and who are still opposed to Home Rule, preferring a free Ireland with no ties to Britain, embark on a mainland bombing campaign, hitting targets in London, Birmingham and Manchester in January 1939. But their campaign frizzled out after the worst attack of all in Coventry in August, when five people are killed.

In the September of 1939 Germany aided by Russia invade Poland and the chances of war increase massively. Tension all over Britain was growing, although no one said it, everyone knew it, war was on its way. Eire (The Irish Free State) quickly declares itself as a natural state the very next day. On the following day the British Prime Minister, Neville Chamberlain, declares war on Germany. In Belfast the shipyard, Harland & Wolf, along with all heavy industry and agriculture throughout Ulster is immediately turned towards the war effort. The British Government writes to Eamon de Valera (the Irish leader) requesting the use of the 'Treaty Ports' in Ireland as Naval Bases. Eamon de Valera point blank refuses the British Government's request, causing outrage in Ulster. Bobby and Connie's seven sons were now almost grown men. Wee Bobby, the eldest, was now 20 years of age, twins Billy & Terry were 19 years of age, Andy 18 years old, Sammy 16, Harry 15 and Tommy 14 years of age.

Bobby and Connie's oldest boy, Robert, who had become better known to everyone as Wee Bobby, was on the verge of marriage. He had been courting a young lady by the name of Alice Anderson for almost two years. Wee Bobby was captivated with this young lady, he thought of her every minute of the day and as time went by he became devoted to her. Alice was the only daughter of a wealthy whisky distiller in Belfast. She was a very pleasant girl, not only to look at, but also to be in company with. Alice was of the tender age of 19, she was timid in her manner and slight in her build. Bobby would often say, although not in a derogatory way, that Alice reminded him of a little china doll, that if you dropped it, then it would most probably break.

Both the Gallagher family and the Anderson family thought it prudent to delay the wedding for a few months, as the situation in Belfast was frantic to say the least. So it was agreed that the wedding of Wee Bobby to Alice would be delayed for a few months. The wedding eventually taking place at St. Mark's Church on the 10th January 1940. After the wedding, Wee Bobby and Alice came to live in the Gallagher family home. It was only a matter of months later, on the 3rd April to be exact, when the blissful harmony that existed within the Gallagher household was suddenly and somewhat abruptly shattered. As the family gathered in the sitting room after dinner, one of the twins, Billy to be exact, positioned himself in front of the fireplace and tapped firmly on the top of the mantelpiece with a coin in order to gain the attention of his gathered family.

"May I have your attention please? I have something I need to tell everyone!" announced Billy boldly.

Everyone in the room, except for Billy's twin brother, Terry and their younger brother, Andy, looked somewhat surprised by Billy's sudden outburst, as he wasn't accustomed to making public announcements.

"What is Son?" asked his father curiously.

Billy braced himself in order to deliver the news he knew wouldn't go down well with his mother.

"As you all know, we are once again at war with Germany and everywhere I look throughout Belfast, young men are rushing to join the British army in order to defend this country of ours. I listened to Sir. James Craig on the wireless but the other day. He was urging all protestant men of fighting age to join the British army and defend Britain and Ulster against this German tyrant. I have come to the conclusion that I am no different than the other young men of Ulster who have already pledged their allegiance to our king. I also know for fact that my brothers, Terry and Andy, are in full agreement with my outlook on this matter. Therefore, today in Belfast, all three of us signed our names to the papers that now oblige us to go and fight for our King in this war against German oppression. We all three of us, will leave for Liverpool by the end of the month. We pray that you, our father and you, our loving mummy, will understand our reasoning for doing what we have done."

Once Billy had concluded his announcement, he was joined by the fireplace by his two brothers, Terry and Andy, the three boys coming together in a show of unity.

After Billy's untimely and shattering news, the silence around the room was not only deafening, but unsettling for all that witnessed it. Connie sat in her armchair unable to either speak or move for several long seconds, fearing that her sons, once gone overseas, may never return from the hell that they would now surely face. Connie's heart sank as she looked at her three beautiful sons standing by the fireplace, all the old feelings of despair and hopelessness that had plagued her life some years before when Bobby was away fighting, all came flooding back to her without mercy. The difference this time was the heartache would be increased three fold. After a few seconds Connie got to her feet and gave her three sons the sternest look of disapproval they had ever seen.

"What are you boys thinking?" she blasted, "You have done this without first talking to me or your father? I am disappointed with the three of you!"

It was plain for all to see that Connie was not best pleased with the actions of her boys. Bobby crossed the room without saying a word and placed his arm around his wife, pulling her close to him.

"But we had to do this, Mammy," replied Billy, "We just had too, can't you see that Mammy?" he added in a last desperate attempt to convince his mother that what they were doing was the right thing to do.

Bobby held his wife tightly in his arms, knowing only too well how she was feeling, after all she had already been through this before. Bobby looked his wife in the eye and said,

"Don't be angry with them, Connie, be proud of them because they are men now and they have to do what all men must do when their country calls. So, my darling Connie, kiss your brave sons and pray for them every day they are away."

CHAPTER 21

It was on the morning of the 30th. of April 1940, when Connie's three boys left Belfast for Liverpool to begin their army training. Connie gave each of her sons a long loving hug, as she said a tearful goodbye to each of them before they left the family home. This she did because she was unwilling to travel to the docks to see them off, remembering how she felt when she took this very same journey all those years before when she said her goodbyes to Bobby. Bobby did accompany his sons to the docks, hugging each one tightly in turn before they boarded the ship bound for Liverpool. By the August of 1940, all three boys had been deployed to their different regiments, first twin, Billy was with the 1st. Battalion Inniskilling, second twin, Terry was with the 1st. Irish Fusiliers and young Andy was with 2nd. Battalion, the Irish Guards. By now all three boys were in action overseas. In the September of the same year, Wee Bobby's wife Alice brought a welcomed ray of sunshine to the Gallagher family by announcing that she was pregnant. Connie welcomed this news wholeheartedly for two reasons, first this child would be her first grandchild which excited her immensely, and the other reason was that she could now discourage her eldest son, Wee Bobby, from joining his brothers in volunteering his services to the army, as Wee Bobby had been making noises in that direction for some months now. Connie's argument to her son was, how could he now leave his wife and child and go to fight in this second God awful war in her lifetime?

Later in the year of 1940, in the November, Sir James Craig died,
He was succeeded by John Andrews.

As the Easter of 1941 approached, the Gallagher family were gathered around the wireless listening to music, when the program was interrupted by a broadcast from Hamburg, it was of course William Joyce, better known as Lord "Haw-Haw". In his broadcast he announced that this year there would be:

231

"Easter Eggs for Belfast"

Then on 15th April 1941, Easter Tuesday, came a date that would become cemented into the minds of everyone that witnessed it. That night the Luftwaffe Bombers attacked Belfast with devastating results. Belfast lay in ruins and over 1,000 people were killed in the one night and over half of the houses in Belfast were destroyed. Belfast was defenceless against the German Bombers, there was no anti-aircraft guns to speak of, no air raid shelters for people to take cover in, hence the great loss of life. That night in the Gallagher household it was a terrifying experience for everyone, as the German Bombers came time and time again in wave after wave of bombing runs. Even indoors the smell of burning and thick black smoke could be tasted in the back of your throat. Then there was the loud whistling sound from the bombs as they came hurtling down from above. This was followed by ear shattering explosions that mixed with the haunting screams of dying and trapped people all around. There was simply no hiding place, nowhere to turn, no escape from the carnage anywhere. Alice, who was now pregnant and of a delicate disposition at the best of times, suffered more than all the others. The whole night through she was gripped in a state of terror, and showing no possibility of her regaining any kind of normality.

Even after the bombers had done their worst and had returned to Germany, Alice was still in a state of hysteria. It took several hours of comforting from Wee Bobby and his Mother to finally calm Alice down and get her into bed. When the dust had settled and the morning light had arrived, Alice was still feeling the strain of the events of the previous evening. Connie issued instructions that Alice was to remain in bed and rest for the rest of the day. Meanwhile downstairs, in the relative quiet of the morning, after the men of the house had gone to offer their services in the task of looking for survivors, Connie, Alice, Mrs O'Hara and housemaid Susan were the only ones in the house. Connie was relaxing in the front sitting room, enjoying a pot of freshly brewed tea that Mrs O'Hara had made for her? She was sitting by the large window of the room, enjoying her tea, when her tranquillity was abruptly halted by the most horrifying ear bursting screaming that Connie had ever heard. Connie jumped to her feet and moved from her sitting room out into the hallway to investigate the cause of this Banshee like wailing. Mrs O'Hara came running down the stairs towards where Connie was now standing looking flustered, a look of panic fixed upon her face.

"It's Alice, Mrs Gallagher, please come quickly, something's wrong with Alice!" she screamed.

Connie quickly followed Mrs O'Hara up the stairs and into Alice's bedroom. As Connie entered the room she saw Alice laying on top of the bed rolling back and forth and screaming in extreme pain. Connie rushed to Alice's side in an attempt to comfort her, but Connie quickly realised that something was drastically wrong and immediately ordered Mrs O'Hara to phone for Doctor

Woolsey. It was over an hour before Doctor Woolsey arrived, as he was in great demand due to the events of the previous evening. He quickly assessed the situation and realised that Alice and her unborn child were in real trouble. Removing his jacket and rolling up his shirt cuffs, he turned to Connie and in a stern voice he said,

"It seem that the events of last evening have taken a terrible toll on this young lady, she's in shock and her child is now in some distress. I am going need your help, Mrs Gallagher and yours as well Mrs O'Hara, quickly now, there's no time to lose here, both mother and child are in serious danger."

Connie held Alice's hand tightly as she tried to assure her young daughter-in-law that everything was going to be alright.

"I am going to have to deliver the child here myself and the sooner the better, Mrs Gallagher," said Doctor Woolsey.

"What do you need me to do, Doctor?" asked Connie, fearing for the safety of her daughter-in- law and her unborn grandchild.

Doctor Woolsey turned to Mrs O'Hara and ordered,

"We are going to need lots of hot water and clean towels, Mrs O'Hara, and as soon as possible please."

"Right away, Doctor," said Mrs O'Hara as she rushed from the bedroom, returning very shortly after carrying a laundry basket filled with clean towels.

"The hot water, Mrs O'Hara?" asked Doctor Woolsey.

"Susan is fetching it, Doctor Woolsey, she's right behind me," answered Mrs O'Hara. Within seconds Susan arrived with two pails of hot water.

"Put them down there if you please, Susan" said Doctor Woolsey.

Doctor Woolsey then began the procedure of delivering Alice's baby. With no more than the passing of fifteen minutes, the first cries of life came from Alice's new born child. This wonderful sound echoed around Alice's bedroom, bring smiles to all as they strained to get their first glimpse of the child held in the arms of Doctor Woolsey.

"It's a boy, Mrs Gallagher!" declared Doctor Woolsey.

The Doctor handed the child to Mrs O'Hara, asking her to clean him up before handing him over to his mother. Then turning towards Connie, the good doctor joked,

"Looks like there is another one waiting to be born here, Mrs Gallagher."

"Really?" gasped Connie excitedly, as she squeezed Alice's hand gently and smiled at her.

"Yes really, Grandma," joked the doctor.

"Did you hear what Doctor Woolsey just said Alice? You're having twins!" beamed Connie.

Within a few minutes, the life cry of another child was heard resounding loudly around the bedroom.

"It's another boy," announced Doctor Woolsey, as he passed the second child to Mrs O'Hara for a clean-up.

"Good God, Alice, you have given birth to twin boys!" smiled Connie.

Connie, seeing that Alice was becoming stressed and that she was perspiring perversely from her brow, dipped her handkerchief into the bowl of cold water which was on the bedside table and began to dampen Alice's forehead, saying.

"Twin boys, Alice, just think, twin boys."

Both of the new born children had now been cleaned and wrapped in clean warm towels and had been placed on the bed beside their mother. Standing proudly at the bedside, looking down lovingly at the new born twin boys was their grandmother, with a smile of delight that was as wide as the river Lagan itself.

"Are they not the most beautiful babies you have ever seen, Mrs O'Hara?" whispered Connie.

"That they are that, Mrs Gallagher," smiled Mrs O'Hara.

"Are my babies alright, Doctor?" asked Alice nervously.

Doctor Woolsey smiled broadly as he replied,

"Both your boys are just fine, Alice, you have given birth to two fine sons! You should be so proud of yourself," he stated.

Alice lay back in her bed and smiled as she cuddled both of her new born boys close into her body.

"How do you feel, Alice?" inquired Connie.

"Tired," replied Alice, her voice soft and kind of faded.

Connie looked down at Alice and noticed that blood could be seen seeping through the bed sheets.

"Doctor!" said Connie, pointing to the blood stained bed sheets.

Doctor Woolsey lifted up the bed sheets to take a closer look.

"Dear God!" exclaimed Doctor Woolsey, "the girl is bleeding badly, but I don't have the means here to stop it, Mrs Gallagher."

"There must be something we can do, Doctor?" said Connie franticly.

"I'll try my best, Mrs Gallagher, but I don't have the necessary equipment here at my disposal to stop the bleeding, even if I can stop the flow, she is going to need stitches, but like I said I don't have the necessary means to do that." replied Doctor Woolsey.

"Here, Alice, let me take the boys so Doctor Woolsey can examine you properly."

Connie passed one of the twin boys to Mrs O'Hara and the other to Susan. Doctor Woolsey then began his attempt to stop Alice's bleeding. Connie knelt down by the side of Alice's bed and took hold of Alice's hand in an attempt to comfort her.

"Please tell me everything is going to be alright, Connie." pleaded Alice, her voice faint and of a tremble.

Connie looked her young daughter-in-law in the eye, squeezed her hand gently once again and answered with some uncertainty,

"Doctor Woolsey is doing everything he can, Alice, you just have to rest and leave everything to Doctor Woolsey. Whatever you do, you must not stress yourself, just try to relax, Alice."

Alice smiled up at Connie and said,

"Wee Bobby will be so pleased with me giving him twin boys, won't he Connie?"

"He will Alice, he certainly will," replied Connie, as she felt Alice's grip on her hand loosen.

Suddenly Alice's eyes began to slowly close and her grip on Connie's hand was now almost non-existent.

"Alice, Alice," shouted Connie, "please Alice open your eyes, Alice, for God's sake, please open your eyes."

But Connie's frenzied words of encouragement were not to be heard by Alice, whose hand slowly slipped from Connie's and flopped lifeless onto the bed like an Autumn leaf falling from an old favourite tree.

Doctor Woolsey looked at Connie and simply shook his head.

"Please Doctor." pleaded Connie.

"I'm afraid she's gone, Mrs Gallagher, there was nothing that I could do to arrest the bleeding it had all gone too far I'm sorry to say."

Connie got to her feet and kissed her daughter-in-law softly on the forehead. Then moving across the room to where the twin boys were sleeping, first she kissed both boys on the forehead and then in a low compassionate voice she said,

"Both you boys will know your mammy in the years to come, trust me boys, this I vow to you here on this day."

Both Mrs O'Hara and Susan took the new born children out of the room, allowing Doctor Woolsey and Connie to make good Alice's bed and make her look more presentable for when her husband would return. Doctor Woolsey could see that Connie was finding it all too much. He noticed that her body was in a shiver and that her speech was quick and at times repeating the same thing over and over again. Doctor Woolsey turned to Connie and said,

"Go, Mrs Gallagher, go and be with your new grandsons, they need you more than ever now. I can finish off here, Mrs Gallagher, please go be with your new grandsons."

Connie left Alice's bedroom and went down stairs into the front sitting room where Mrs O'Hara and Susan had taken the newly born twin boys. Connie then instructed Susan to go and locate Wee Bobby and the rest of her family and tell them to return home immediately.

"What shall I tell them, Mrs Gallagher?" asked Susan.

"Only tell them that I need them home, Susan." replied Connie.

Within the hour the men had returned home. As they entered the house they were met with the loud crying, as both new born babies were now awake and by the noise they were making they were feeling mighty hungry. This greeting, of course brought a huge smile to their faces as they turned and looked at each other with a sense of excitement. The men rushed into the sitting room from whence the crying of the babies could be heard.

Once inside the sitting room they saw Connie sitting in an armchair with one of the babies on her knee and next to her in another armchair they saw Mrs O'Hara with the other new born child resting on her knee.

"My good God, Wee Bobby, you're the proud Daddy of twins!" roared Bobby excitedly.

"What?" Wee Bobby got no further with his question, as his mother had anticipated it and said,

"Twin boys, Wee Bobby, you are the father of twin boys."

"Twin boys Da," said Wee Bobby excitedly.

Wee Bobby then kissed both his sons one after the other, his face filled with the pride that can only be seen on the faces of a new daddy as he looks at his new born. Wee Bobby's father sensed that that all was not as it should be. He knew by the look on his wife's face that something was amiss. Bobby turned and looked at his wife with inquiring eyes as he asked,

"Is all well with the twin boys, Connie?"

"All is well with the babies, Bobby," replied Connie.

"And how is Alice after the birth, Connie?" asked Bobby.

Connie looked at her husband and then at her son, her eyes clouded as she was losing the battle to fight back her tears.

"Please sit down, both of you," whispered Connie, her voice low and tense.

"What is it, Mammy?" inquired Wee Bobby, as he took his seat.

Connie then ask Mrs O'Hara and Susan to take the babies to another room while she talked with her son.

"What is it Mammy, you're frightening me, tell me what's wrong?"

Connie took a deep breath, looked her son in the eye and said,

"It was a sudden and difficult birth son. Doctor Woolsey did everything he could, but he just couldn't stop the bleeding. I am so sorry, Wee Bobby, Alice died after giving birth to your beautiful sons. But she did see and hold both her sons before she passed. Doctor Woolsey reckons that the bombing of the previous night took too much out of her."

Wee Bobby, unable to hold back his tears, buried his head deep in his hands.

"My God she can't be gone, Ma. What on earth I am I going to do without Alice, Ma? Please tell me that she's not dead, Ma!" Wee Bobby's voice was filled with disbelief, his tears oozed through his fingers and fell to the floor.

"Dear God!" gasped Bobby. "Has Alice's father been informed?"

Connie shook her head indicating that he hadn't.

"Then I must go and see him immediately," said Bobby.

Just then Doctor Woolsey entered the room.

"My deepest sympathy to you, Wee Bobby, I am so sorry for your loss."

"Can I see her, Doctor?" asked Wee Bobby.

"Yes, by all means, she's peaceful now."

Wee Bobby left the room and made the long climb up the stairs to see his wife.

Doctor Woolsey then informed Connie that he had called for an ambulance to take Alice to the Hospital as several formalities and paper work needed to be carried out.

Alice's funeral took place a week later. It was a sad and distressing affair for everyone concerned, but Wee Bobby took Alice's passing particularly hard. As the advance of the next few weeks quickly turned into months, Wee Bobby found it extremely difficult to come to terms with his wife's death and there seemed to be a strained and distant relationship developing between himself and his new twin boys. Wee Bobby also harboured a great loathing for the Germans, a hatred that seemed to eat away at his inside throughout his every waking hour and he would openly curse them at every given opportunity. Without a doubt, Wee Bobby held the Germans totally responsible for the death of his wife, Alice. It was in the June of 194, when both Wee Bobby's babies were christened at St. Mark's church. The children being named George Gallagher and Edward Gallagher.

A week after the twin boys had been christened, the Gallagher family were just finishing their Sunday lunch. Wee Bobby got to his feet and announced that he too had pledged his services to the King by joining the R.A.F. several days before at the recruiting office in Belfast and that he would be leaving for Liverpool within the next week. Connie was devastated by this revelation from her eldest son, because now she would have four sons fighting in this damned war. Connie became withdrawn in the days after her oldest son left to join the R.A.F. Connie now put most of her time and energy into looking after Wee Bobby's twin boys. Day after day she would be with them for hours on end. It would seem that Wee Bobby's twin boys were becoming a great source of comfort to Connie, whilst her own sons were fighting overseas. As the Gallagher family entered into the new year of 1942, Connie was now beginning to receive letters from all of her sons and yes, their letters proved what she had always suspected, that this war was no better than the one that had gone before it. In mid-February of 1942, yet another of Connie's sons announced that he too had joined up to fight for his King and country along with his brothers. Connie's fifth son, Sammy had joined the Royal Navy.

By the summer of 1942, the fighting was fierce all over Europe and Connie feared for her sons' wellbeing. The letters from her boys had stopped coming with the same regularity and all Connie knew for sure was that her sons were fighting in horrendous conditions all over the world. One evening in late summer of 1942, Connie was sitting in her armchair by the garden window, quietly reminiscing of better times spent with her sons around her. Without thinking, Connie's eyes drifted towards her two youngest sons who were playing chess on the other side of the room. Without warning a great fear suddenly consumed Connie's very being, because the inevitable had flashed before her very eyes. Connie knew that one day, in the not too distant future, her two remaining sons would want to join their brothers in fighting for their King and country.

A sinking sadness seemed to fix itself in Connie's deep blue eyes, as the reality of having seven sons fighting overseas in this dreadful, brutal war painfully hit home. Connie raised her hand and wiped a tear from her eye as she feared for the future of her family. By the March of 1944 all of Connie's fears were to come to pass, as both her youngest boys had followed their brothers and joined the army and were both overseas fighting in this God awful war. Harry had joined the Parachute Regiment, and young Tommy was serving with the Allied forces in Burma. As for their father, Bobby… Well after the blitz on Belfast of the Easter of 1941, Bobby had decided, much against Connie's wishes, to offer his services to the A.R.P. in Belfast.

Connie's oldest boy, Wee Bobby, was serving as a rear gunner in a Lancaster Bomber crew, attached to 12 Squadron, Based at Wickenby Lincolnshire, under Bomber Command. Wee Bobby joined the crew after intensive training in 1942.

Oldest twin, Billy, was serving with the 1st. Battalion Inniskillings, their main objective was to attempt to delay the Japanese advance in Burma. The Inniskillings were flown to the North of Rangoon in the March of 1942, to join in an expedition to destroy the oil fields at Yenangyaung.

Second twin, Terry, was serving with the Irish Fusiliers, but in 1942. Terry's Regiment was made part of the new 38th. (Irish) Brigade. Fighting first in Tunisia, after which they were merged with the eighth army who were fighting in the Sicilian campaign.

Younger brother, Andy, was with The Irish Guards, in 1941. The Irish Guards took their place in the newly formed Guards Armoured Division. In 1943. the Battalion embarked for to play their part in the North-Africa campaign.

Brother Sammy, was serving with The Royal Navy, on-board…

HMS PENELOPE. – Light Cruiser.

Brother Harry, was serving with The Parachute Regiment, 1st. Battalion. In 1944. Harry was preparing for one of the biggest air drops ever to be undertaken, this operation was to be known as, - Operation Market Garden. -

Brother Tommy, was serving with The Allied Forces during their capture of Mandalay and Meiktila.

CHAPTER 22

The year of 1943 marked the emergence of a traumatic period in the lives of the Gallagher family. With all of Bobby and Connie's seven sons now away fighting for King and country. The mood within the household was somewhat subdued to say the least. Bobby was well aware that Connie was struggling to come to terms with the fact that her boys had placed themselves in such danger by going and joining in this brutal conflict. Bobby tried his best to lighten the mood within the house and uplift his wife's dragging sprit, but not a day would pass that Connie would not pray for the safe return of her boys. It had been an unusually long time since Bobby and Connie had received any letters from any of their sons and this only served to dampen Connie's spirit even further. It would seem that not knowing, was worse than actually knowing. If it hadn't been for Wee Bobby's twin boys, Connie would surely have drifted deeper into the unknown of sadness. These two little darlings somehow managed to pull Connie back to reality, as she simply adored them and never let them out of her sight for one minute of the day. The morning of the 5th January 1943 began much like any other winters day, The damp Winter wind was fully alive and was whistling chillingly through the branches of the barren apple trees in the family garden. Connie and Bobby were in the dining room finishing off their breakfast. Housemaid Susan was having the day off, leaving Mrs O'Hara alone to look after the family. Mrs O'Hara had been with them now both as the Kean family and the Gallagher family. Mrs O'Hara's service to the family stretched back for many years, although nowadays her duties were light and becoming less by the day, due to her advancing years. Bobby reached across the breakfast table and picked up his morning paper to update himself on the war. Connie was tending to the needs of Wee Bobby's twin boys, George and Edward, when suddenly, from the kitchen, they heard an all mighty crash. Bobby instantly dropped his morning paper and jumped to his feet.

"Goodness me, what on earth was that?" roared Bobby.

"It seemed to come from the kitchen," replied Connie,

Bobby rushed out of the dining room and made his way to the kitchen with haste.

Connie, first securing both George and Edward in their playpen, quickly followed her husband in the direction of the kitchen.

Bobby crashed through the kitchen door to investigate what had happened, but what he saw shocked him. There spread out across the floor was several large cooking pots, along with a full tray of silver cutlery. In the middle of this mayhem, face down on the floor was Mrs O'Hara. Bobby quickly rushed to her aid, but it was too late, Mrs O'Hara had stopped breathing, her body was limp and lifeless.

"Dear Lord, how is she, Bobby?" asked Connie as she entered the kitchen.

Bobby looked up at his wife, this was a look that told Connie that all was not well.

"Is she really gone, Bobby? asked Connie.

"Yes, Connie, she's gone from us."

"Sweet Lord no, please say it's not so, Bobby!" cried Connie,

This loss was as big a loss to Connie as it was when Mr Powell had died. You see for Connie, Mrs O'Hara had been part of her life since she had been a small child. This was yet another link to Connie's childhood that had gone forever.

"You better call Doctor Woolsey, Connie," said Bobby, as he cleared the fallen debris from around Mrs O'Hara's body.

Connie hurriedly left the kitchen and rushed to the sitting room to phone for Doctor Woolsey. Meanwhile, Bobby went to the bedroom and fetched a clean white sheet in order to cover Mrs O'Hara body. When Doctor Woolsey arrived he confirmed that Mrs O'Hara had died from a massive heart attack. Although visually Mrs O'Hara looked to be in good physical condition, she was in fact approaching her seventieth birthday. That fact was one of the reasons why Connie had reduced Mrs O'Hara's work load within the household. Doctor Woolsey then asked Bobby if Mrs O'Hara's body could remain in the house until he had the opportunity to make arrangements for an undertaker to collect it the next day.

"No need to worry on that account, Doctor Woolsey," said Bobby, "Leave everything to us, we will arrange for an undertaker and we will look after all funeral arrangements."

"Is there any family that you know of, Bobby?" asked Doctor Woolsey.

"Yes," replied Bobby, "Mrs O'Hara has a niece called Mary."

"You are in contact with her?" asked Doctor Woolsey.

"No, not in a few years, but I know how to contact her, so informing her of her Aunts death won't be a problem," offered Bobby.

"Right then," said Doctor Woolsey, "I shall leave everything in your capable hands then, Bobby."

The next day Bobby was setting out to go see Paddy and Mary. Connie took hold of Bobby's arm as he was leaving the house and said,

"Do you think that you will be safe going to the Falls Road Bobby?"

Bobby looked at his wife, knowing that she was right to be concerned for his safety.

"I don't have a choice, Connie, I have to inform Mary of her aunt's death. So I will have to take that chance that no one recognises me, Connie. I have to go to the bar and speak with Mary and Paddy personally," replied Bobby.

Later that very afternoon, at around 5-30pm. Bobby arrived at Paddy's Bar on the Falls Road. Bobby parked his motor car a few yards from the entrance to the bar and walked steadily, but with a degree of caution, in the direction of Paddy's Bar. Bobby arrived at the thick wooden door at the front of the bar. He took hold of the large brass door handle and slowly turned it. Instantly, Bobby could tell that the bar was more full than it was empty, if the collection of voices coming from inside was anything to go be. Pushing the large wooden door open, Bobby entered the bar, not really knowing what kind of a reception waited for him inside. Bobby was well aware that once inside he was going to stand out like a priest at an Orange Lodge meeting, but inside he had to go. Bobby took a deep breath and marched smartly up to the bar. Within a seconds of Bobby's appearance, the mood inside the bar instantly changed. All chatter stopped immediately, all heads turned in Bobby's direction and all beer glasses were quickly put out of hand and roughly banged onto the tables in front of the drinkers.

Paddy, who was standing behind the bar with his back turned towards the door stacking bottles of beer onto the shelves, quickly turned to see what had caused the sudden silence.

"Bobby!" howled Paddy, shocked to see his old friend standing in his bar. "What the hell are you doing here?" Paddy's greeting for his old friend was chilled to say the least.

"Sorry to say, Paddy, I am the bearer of bad news," replied Bobby.

"What is it, Bobby?" asked Paddy.

"It's really Mary that I have come to see, Paddy." said Bobby.

Paddy nodded his head, realising that the sad news must be about Mrs O'Hara.

"I'll call her, Bobby," replied Paddy, "But first, let me pour you that pint of porter that we talked about, I owe you that at least, Bobby." He added.

"A pint would be most welcomed right now, Paddy," replied Bobby, taking a seat by the window at the far end of the bar.

All eyes remained fixed firmly on Bobby, all conversations remained suspended and all beer glasses remained firmly on the tables, although the same cannot be said for the hands of many of the drinkers. As Bobby took his first mouth full of porter in Paddy's Bar, Mary came walking towards where

Bobby was sitting and sat on the opposite side of the table. It seemed that Mary's welcome was just as chilly as her husband's had been.

"What is it that you have to tell me, Bobby?" asked Mary somewhat curtly.

Before Bobby had the chance to answer, Paddy had joined them at the table.

"I am sorry to be the one to tell you this sad news, Mary, but your Aunt had a massive heart attack yesterday and passed away."

Mary's eyes filled with tears at hearing the sad news of her much loved Aunt. Paddy put his arm tightly around his wife and kissed her softly on the side of her head.

"Was her death quick, Bobby, she didn't suffer in any way did she, Bobby?"

"Mercifully, she didn't feel a thing, Mary, it was instant," answered Bobby.

"Thank the Lord for small mercies!" said Mary, her voice soft in tone as she dabbed at the tears rolling down her face.

"Both Connie and I thought you might like to make the funeral arrangements, although, Connie would like to pay for everything involved, as Mrs O'Hara was like a second mother to her. Of course that is if you both have no objections to that suggestion," proposed Bobby.

Paddy looked at his wife, then back at Bobby, then he said sharply,

"We know how Connie felt about Mrs O'Hara, but we all live in different worlds now, Bobby!"

"Look, Paddy," said Bobby, "I won't try to kid you, I know things ended badly the last time you were in East Belfast, but I will do everything possible to make sure that no harm comes to you or Mary when you both attend Mrs O'Hara's funeral."

Paddy's response shocked Bobby.

"Listen, Bobby," he snapped, as he frowned angrily in Bobby's direction.

"Things haven't changed, Bobby and they never will. Look around this bar, every one of these men don't like you and what you stand for, Bobby. The only reason that you are not lying face down on my barroom floor with several bullets in your head right now, is out of courtesy to me, Bobby. To a man they all know that you were involved in the killing of four I.R.A. men outside the Orange Hall in East Belfast. I can tell you right now, that nothing would give these men more pleasure than to drag you outside into the street and shoot you down like a dog."

Bobby suddenly realised that this was not the same Paddy that he had fought and served with in the first war. Bobby sat forward in his chair and looked at Paddy, then he said,

"Tell me one thing before I leave, Paddy, do you despise me and what I stand for in the same way as these men that fill your bar room?"

Paddy looked Bobby straight in the eye and simply said,

"Yes, I do, Bobby."

"What is happening to this country of ours when two old friends end up hating each other?" asked Bobby.

Again Paddy looked Bobby in the eye and said,

"One thing, Bobby, this is not your country and it never will be, it's our country, it belongs to us, the true Irishmen of this Island and to the yes men of Westminster and the English Crown. We true Irishmen won't rest until all of the 32 counties become one great country under the flag of Ireland."

Bobby got to his feet, took one last look at his old friend and simply replied.

"Only time will be the judge of that Paddy. Not you or I." Bobby turned around and left Paddy's Bar, never to return and never to see his old friend ever again.

The news of Mrs O'Hara's death quickly spread throughout East Belfast. Mrs O'Hara, along with her niece, Mary, and of course Paddy, when they lived in East Belfast, were well known on the Newtownards Road as Roman Catholics, as they were regularly seen attending Sunday worship at St. Matthews Chapel, needless to say this caused a certain resentment in the Unionist populate. Although the Gallagher family were well respected in this part of Belfast, in certain quarters the fact that they employed Fenians in their household, did not go down that well!

(Fenians being a colloquial term used by Unionist Protestants in the North of Ireland for Roman Catholics living in Ulster. The Fenian movement was founded in 1858 by former young Irish rebels James Stephens in Dublin and John O'Mahony in New York. The Irish Republican Brotherhood in Ireland and the Fenian Brotherhood in the U.S.A. were the predecessor to what we know now as the I.R.A.)

With everything that was going on in Ireland at this time, it meant that parts of Belfast were becoming breeding grounds for sectarian hatred. So as word spread that Mrs O'Hara's body was to be collected and taken to her niece on the Falls Road, which is an I.R.A. stronghold, tension began to grow amongst some local residents in East Belfast. On the day that Mrs O'Hara's body was to be taken from the Gallagher household to her niece's house on the Falls Road, a small crowd, mostly consisting of youths between the ages of 16 to early 20s, had gathered outside Connie's house. Two men aged around twenty two were standing slightly forward of the main crowd. As Mrs O'Hara's body was being transported by the undertakers through the gates at the front of Connie's house and out onto the footpath, this small crowd of young men began to jeer and boo loudly. This distasteful taunting continued as Mrs O'Hara's body was loaded into the waiting hearse.

Connie, who had followed Mrs O'Hara's body through the gates from her house out onto the footpath, was now standing by the side of the funeral car. Connie was absolutely furious at hearing the horrible and vile insults that were being hurled in the direction of Mrs O'Hara's body. Stepping forward to confront this angry crowd that had gathered outside her house, Connie shouted loudly,

"What on earth do you think you are doing? Show respect for the dead."

Suddenly from the middle of the crowd came a barrage of the most sickening and distasteful insults, all of which were aimed at Mrs O'Hara's dead body.

"We don't show any fucking Fenian bitch respect, alive or fucking dead. If you ask me the deader they are, the fucking better."

Bobby came rushing out of the gates into the road outside and gently moved his wife back and out of any danger and then pushed himself to the fore.

"Do you really think that there is any need for that sort of talk here today? If you have no respect for the dead, then show some respect for yourselves for God sake, what kind of people are you?" blasted Bobby angrily.

Then the two young men at the front of the crowd joined in the argument.

"Then stop employing fucking Fenians, Bobby, we don't want them and we don't need them in our part of town."

Bobby took another step forward and confronted the young man who had just voiced his opinion. It is true that Bobby was now in his mid-forties and carried a limp, but he was still a big man and had retained much of the considerable strength from his younger days. Also, Bobby hadn't lost his appetite for the fight when called upon.

"I am telling you and your friends to move away from the front of my house right now!" ordered Bobby.

The two younger men then faced up to Bobby and it was plain that they were itching for the fight.

"Fucking try to move us, you Fenian lover!" snarled one of the young men, stepping forward to confront Bobby.

Like a flash of lightening Bobby punched the abusive young man right in the face, knocking him to the ground. His friend was quick to throw a punch in Bobby's direction, but Bobby was again quick to react and blocked the young man's punch with his arm. Bobby then dished out the same treatment to the second loudmouthed bigot that he had to the first one a few seconds earlier. The end result was the same in both cases, as the second loudmouthed youth ended up on the ground beside his friend. Bobby's speedy action seem to quell the anger of the crowd, at least for now.

Bobby's rage was now about to boil over and in anger he turned to face the rest of the crowd and in a furious outburst he said,

"Don't let anyone here doubt my loyalty or my wife's loyalty to Ulster. I fought for Ulster and its King in the last war and my wife and I have sent all of our seven sons to fight for Ulster and our King in this damn war. So tell me if you can, why are these two loudmouthed young men here outside the gates to my home shouting obscenities at a dead woman's body? Why are they here doing that when they should be in France or Belgium, or in the deserts of North Africa fighting for Ulster and the king, just like my sons are doing? Go on, someone please tell me, why are you both here? I would suggest that they are only brave enough for shouting at the bodies of dead old ladies. Real fighting calls for real men, something that these two are not."

The two young men dragged themselves slowly to their feet, their heads hung with shame. At that moment another man pushed his way to the front of the gathered mob. He was a big man in every way, standing at well over six foot. His age, mid to late fifties. Once at the front of the mob he turned to face them, then pointing to Bobby he said,

"Listen to me, out of all of us that are gathered here this day, this man is more a Loyalist and a friend of Ulster than any of us."

The man turned and looked directly at Bobby as he continued,

"Bobby won't remember me, but I served with this man and his friend Paddy in the last war and I also remember what Connie's mother did for the people of East Belfast when she was alive. Have you all forgotten how Connie's mother was killed and by whom. Yes, Mrs O'Hara was a catholic as was Paddy, but Paddy volunteered to fight for Ulster in the last war, he wasn't made to go, he volunteered to go. Which would appear to be a hell of a lot more than these two loudmouthed fools are prepared to do. So I tell you all, show some respect for the dead and go, go now and leave these good people in peace."

With these words from the stranger, the mob quickly dispersed and Mrs O'Hara's body was able to finally leave east Belfast with some dignity.

As the undertaker's car drove away from the gates outside the Gallagher's house, both Bobby and Connie stood hand in hand watching the car as it disappeared into the distance.

"That's the last we will ever see of Mrs O'Hara, Bobby," said a tearful Connie.

"It's an awful shame that it has to end in this way, Connie, we won't even get the chance to say our final goodbyes at her funeral," he said.

Both Paddy and Mary had decided that no one who was involved in any way with the Loyalist cause, be they friends or not, would be allowed to attend Mrs O'Hara's funeral. Mrs O'Hara was laid to rest at Milltown Cemetery in West Belfast, a strong Republican area, meaning that it would be an impossibility for either Bobby or Connie to ever visit Mrs O'Hara's grave to pay their last respects.

By the middle of January 1943, Andy was with Montgomery's 8th. Army fighting in the North African, in Tunisia Campaign. The Allies had made significant advances in the earlier Battles, forcing Rommel to make a fighting retreat back to the France built southern defences of Tunisia,

- The Mareth Line. - But by now Rommel had teamed up with Hans-Jurgen von Arnim's Fifth panzer army, strengthening his hand considerably. Hitler was determined to hold on to Tunisia at all costs, so Rommel now began to receive even more reinforcements and firepower. Fierce fighting followed for in the next few months, then in the March of 1943. the Allied forces outflanked the Mareth

Defences, after further fierce fighting in the May of 1943. The Axis Forces in North-Africa finally surrendered to the Allies. Young Andy had come through the fighting unscathed, but his war was far from over. After several smaller successful skirmishes in places like Sicily, Montgomery's 8th. Army, as part of the allies forces embarked on the mainland invasion of Italy. Once again young Andy was in the thick of the fighting, landing at Reggio Calabria, located on the toe of the Italian boot, as part of, Operation Baytown, which began on the 3rd. of September 1943. Again the Allies forces were successful and considerable advances were made, as for young Andy, well he had once again survived the fierce fighting and was now a seasoned fighter. -Operation Baytown- was quickly followed by - Operation Slapstick - which began on 9th. September 1943.

At first there was little opposition and fighting was to a minimal.

A few days later on the 11th. of September, it was decided that Allied patrols were to be sent out farther afield, as intelligence on German movement and numbers was badly needed. The deeper these patrols travelled into enemy held ground, the more they came into contact was made with the German 1st. Fallscirmjager Division. Violent skirmishes with the enemy were now taking place on a daily basses. Andy Gallagher had taken part in several of these fierce, brutal encounters, at times finding himself fighting hand to hand with the enemy. Andy was quickly gaining the reputation of being one of the most fearless members of his company.

Just after mid-day on the 20th. of September, with the late summer sun still lingering high in the sky, making everything and everyone feel hot and sticky. Andy Gallagher, along with fifteen of his comrades were sent out on a reconnaissance patrol. At first all was quiet, in fact most of the young men on the patrol were joking that it was like being out on a Sunday stroll after church. As the afternoon progressed and the sun became hotter, the air, what there was of it, remained as still as a sleeping baby. Suddenly every ones attention was fixed on movement that had been detected ahead. Andy, along with the rest of the patrol took cover wherever they could. Between the men on Andy's patrol their expectancy for the fight was beginning to grew, all made ready and waited. Suddenly the commanding officer gave the order to stand down, as the movement that had caused the alert turned out to be Wally and Paul, the two advanced scout. Both men had returned in some haste and were breathing rather heavily.

The scouts inform the officer in charge that he had seen a German attack unit, no more than half a mile away and numbering approximately twenty-five to thirty strong. The scouts informed the officer that the German unit were making their way back to their own lines and that they had wounded men with them, suggesting that they must have been involved in some kind of attack on Allied forces. At this time the German forces were badly stretched and only engaged in swift attacks before falling back to the safety of their own lines. The officer in charge of Andy's patrol came to the conclusion that this German unit had most definitely been involved in a gorilla attack on Allied Forces. The officer gathered his men around and pointed out the objectives of the attack, after a few short minutes Andy's patrol set off to track the German unit and engage them as soon as possible. It must have been some twenty minutes later when Andy's patrol caught up with the German unit. The order to engage the enemy was given by the officer and within seconds all hell broke loose, as a fierce fire-fight quickly ensued. Andy's patrol was gaining the upper hand and were pushing the German unit farther away from the direction of their own lines.

Andy was once again proving himself to be a brave and somewhat fearless solider, he was always there at the head of every advance made by his patrol. This violent skirmish with the German unit lasted well into the late afternoon. Andy's patrol were pushing the German unit in a direction that they did not want to go, back towards the Allied lines. The British officer's intention was to push them as close to the Allied lines as possible and then take as many German prisoners as he possibly could. Andy's patrol made yet another advance upon the German unit and now had them where they wanted them. The German officer, realising what Andy's patrol was trying to do, ordered his men make a stand. A furious fire fight now took place, the Germans being determined not to be taken prisoners. Just as Andy's patrol were about to make their next, and as they thought, their last advance on the German unit, suddenly Andy's patrol came under intense fire form another German unit that were advancing on them from behind. Within minutes Andy's patrol was surrounded, with nowhere to go. Andy's comrades were dropping like flies all around him, within a matter of a few minutes Andy's patrol numbered but four. Their officer lay dead face down on the ground, more of Andy's comrades lay scattered all around, with not a breath between them. Andy looked at his three remaining friends and said.

"You do know that they have no intentions of taking us alive boys don't you?"

The three remaining soldiers, accepting their fate as they simply nodded their heads in agreement.

"Listen boys," said Andy bullishly, "They are to the front of us, they are to the back of us, they are to the right of us and they are to the left of us. I'm charging to the front of us, each of you boys pick your own way to leave this earth."

In a flash young Andy got to his feet and charged the German soldiers that were no more than 30 feet directly in front of him. It seemed that every German gun opened fire on Andy at the same time as he rushed their defences. Andy Gallagher was hit with over twenty bullets all over his body. Andy lay all alone on his back on the scorched Italian earth, his life's blood staining the ground beneath him. Andy smiled as he fixed his eyes on the bright Italian sun which beat down from above burning his young face. Time and time again Andy Gallagher gasped in vain for his last breath ever to be taken in this world, his one and only thought now was of his mother back in Belfast. Her comforting smile that he knew so well when he was but a small boy now filled his dimming eyes, this image of his loving mother he would take with him too which ever world he was now on his way to. Andy Gallagher slowly closed his eyes and ended his time on this earth lying in a pool of his own blood, in the heat and the dirt of the Italian countryside.

With the passing of Mrs O'Hara, housemaid Susan had been promoted to the position of housekeeper. On the afternoon of the 28th September 1943 Susan had just taken a tray of tea into the garden where Connie and Wee Bobby's twin boys were enjoying some later summer sun. As Susan returned to the house she heard several loud knocks coming from the front door. She made her way across the entrance hall to the front door. Upon opening the door Susan was confronted by a Telegram boy, which could only mean one thing.

"Can I help you?" Susan ask nervously.

"Telegram for Mr and Mrs Gallagher." replied the solemn young man.

Susan put out her hand and took the small paper from the Telegram boy.

"Thank you," she said as she closed the door and turned to make her way into the sitting room where Bobby was reading his newspaper.

"Who was at the door?" asked Bobby as Susan entered the room.

She stood in silence for several seconds, not really sure what to say, or even how to say it.

"What is it, Susan, speak up?" said Bobby.

But there was no need for Susan to say anything, because now Bobby could see the telegram in Susan's hand. He quickly he got to his feet and took it from Susan's hand.

"It's ok Susan, you can have the afternoon off it you wish," whispered Bobby softly.

Bobby walked slowly out into the garden. Connie was sitting under her favourite pussy-willow tree drinking her tea while watching the twins at play.

Connie saw Bobby coming across the garden and coming towards her, at first she smiled, hoping that Bobby would join her in the garden for the rest of the afternoon.

Sadly, Connie's wish to spend the afternoon with her husband was instantly shattered the second she saw the telegram in his hand. Connie raised her hand to her mouth and cried loudly,

"No, no, Bobby, please God no, Bobby!" Connie now knew that one of her sons had been killed, the only question was which one?

Bobby sat down beside his wife to open the telegram. He opened it gently and with a soft, stuttering voice he read the content out to his wife. The Telegram read…

- Guardsman Andrew Gallagher Killed in Action 20th. September 1943. -

(Young Andy Gallagher was only Twenty one years old.)

CHAPTER 23

In the days after receiving the shattering news of young Andy's death in Italy, the mood within the Gallagher household was at an all-time low. Wee Bobby's twin boys, George and Edward had now become the only reason to raise a smile in the Gallagher family. To make Connie's fears and worries even worse, was the fact that it had been a long, long time since she had received a letter from any of her boys. Considering that Connie had not long since received the tragic news of the death of one of her sons, it is was no wonder that from time to time she would allow her mind to drift into places where she really wouldn't want it to go. A great fear that all wasn't as she would want it to be, with regards to the safety of her boy, haunted her every waking hour. Bobby would do his best to ease his wife's fears, telling her that no news is good news. Unfortunately, Connie did not find her husband's words a comfort in any way, no matter what he would do or say would make little or no difference to Connie's uncertain concerns for her sons' safety. Connie's fears and worries for her boys began to effect the way she reacted towards the twins. Connie became even more protective towards them and it would seem that she was now reluctant to let them out of her sight even for a single second.

The weeks passed agonisingly slow, with still no word from any of Connie's sons and as the Christmas of 1943 approached, there was little festive spirit to be seen in the Gallagher family. Connie seemed to carry a deep sadness in her heart and in her eyes, because she was fully aware that this year would be the first year that none of sons would be with her on Christmas day. In truth Connie would willingly accept their absences from the Christmas lunch table, if she only knew that each and every one of them were safe and well. Another of Connie's sons, Terry, had also been fighting with Montgomery's 8th. Army in the Tunisia Campaign and had taken part in - Operation Baytown - and - Operation Slapstick – just like his brother Andy had done. Although both brothers were fighting in the same regain, their paths never crossed, in fact Terry was totally unaware that his brother Andy was even in Italy. After the launch of - Operation Slapstick - on the 9th. of September Montgomery's 8th. Army fought it's was along the coast until on the 15th. of September 1943, it linked up with the U.S. 5[th.] Army that had launched its own objective called - Operation Avalanche - which landed at Salerno on the 9th. of September. The 8th. Army went on to capture Boggia and its most valuable Airfields on the 17th. of September. Terry Gallagher was now involved in fierce fighting daily as Montgomery's 8th. Army continued to advance. The battle for the town and port of Termoli began on October 1st. By October 3rd. a landing was made at Termoli, and the enemy was taken completely by surprise. The town and port were captured intact. A desperate battle ensued, but by October 6th, the 8th. Army had consolidated its gains. Within weeks the 8th. Army had begun a slogging advance, progressing from defended ridge to yet another defended ridge, until the troops reached the Trigmo River, an outpost of the Barbare Line. The river was crossed on the night of October 22[nd.] – 23[rd.] and a fierce battle to consolidate this bridgehead began on October 26th. The attack on San Salvo, a town on the top of a commanding height and seen to be of significant importance, began on the 27[th.] of October, but was held up and had to be renewed on the 3[rd.] of November. San Salvo was eventually captured on the 4[th.] of November and in a two pronged drive the 8[th.] Army pursued the enemy to the Sangro River, an outpost of the immensely strong Gustav Line.

The advance to the Sangro was slow and hindered by extensive demolitions blocking the roads, also the unset of a bad winter halted progress to a major extent. On one road alone there were 18 major demolitions in a 15 mile stretch. On another road there were up to 45 major demolitions in a run of 27 miles. But the 8th. Army was about to engage, in what was to turn out to be, the hardest battle of its career. On the Adriatic sector the battle for the

Sangro began on the night of the 21[st.] of November. The battle on the inland sector, where Terry Gallagher was fighting, began on the 27[th.] of November. Fierce fighting continued in both sectors, with many losses on both sides, eventually ending in victory for the 8th. Army on the 2[nd.] of December. By the 20th. of December a firm bridgehead across the Moro River had been secured. But this success came at a great cost, sad to say, but the 8th. Army's loses were heavy after months of constant fighting.

On the morning of the 19[th.] of December, Terry Gallagher was part of a large advanced party that were sent out with orders to push forward and secure the land beyond the newly secured bridgehead over the Moro River. The farther they advanced into unknown territory, the stronger the resistance that they faced from large numbers of German units. At one point the fighting was so fierce that the advanced party were forced to separate and find cover wherever they could. Terry Gallagher now found himself in a group of twenty men. Sergeant Fielding, who was in the same group as Terry, took charge and ordered that all men must stick close together as the search for better cover. Needless to say this order raised a few eyebrows between the men, as the usual order would be to spread out, making a much larger target. Sergeant Fielding began to move off to the north, again eyebrows were raised, because most of the men knew that they should be heading west, because that's where they left the bulk of their comrades when they were forced to split.

Terry, along with a few of the other soldiers in the group, raised this with Sergeant Fielding, but their questioning was met with the strongest rebuke from Sergeant fielding.

Terry's group headed north in their search for the rest of their comrades. The group had been tracking for over an hour, when again Terry raised the question of the direction in which they were heading. Again sergeant Fielding's rebuke was strong and this time also threatening. Terry's group suddenly emerged from a dense thicket that they had been moving through for over half an hour. They were now confronted by a small stream about forty foot wide. Sergeant Fielding told the men to stay close together as they crossed this small stream. Again eyebrows were raised, as the men knew that the better idea would be to follow the stream going west, not crossing it and certainly not in a bloody huddle. Terry's group began to cross the small stream. Led by Sergeant fielding. The stream was not a deep one, by the time they had reached the middle of the stream, the water was waist high, making advancement slow. Terry, who was by the side of Sergeant Fielding in the crossing, suddenly stopped, because there on the opposite embankment, partly hidden behind thick undergrowth he could see a warren of well dug in German machine-gun posts. Terry nudged Sergeant Fielding, who could now see them for himself. What the sergeant did next was probably the most stupid and nonsensical action any officer had ever done, Sergeant Fielding raised his weapon and opened fire on the German machine-gun posts.

A devastating bursts of automatic gun-fire rained down on Terry and his comrades, giving them no chance what so ever, due to the fact that they were all so close together. Terry and his comrades had nowhere to go, they were totally defenceless against the German machine-guns. Within but a few short minutes it was all over and all that was left were the dead bodies of twenty brave young men floating helplessly in a stream reddened by their own blood. Here were a group of men who had been led to their deaths by arrogance and ignorance, a brave band who were cruelly cut down and lost for ever to this world for ever.

Terry Gallagher lost his life on the 19th December 1943.

(By the end of 1943 Montgomery had been recalled to U.K. in order to take charge of the D-Day landings at Normandy.)

Meanwhile back in Belfast, with the Christmas of 1943 approaching fast, mixed feelings existed within the Gallagher household. It was difficult for Bobby and Connie to be filled with the season's usual good spirit, as they had recently lost their son Andy in the war and with their remaining sons' still away fighting, thoughts of keeping the Christmas celebrations to a minimum had been mooted. But the Gallagher's were church going people and held Christmas in high regard and felt that they had a duty to celebrate the birth of Christ. Also they had Wee Bobby's twin boys to think about, as this was the first Christmas that they were old enough to realise just what it was all about. Connie decided that Christmas must be celebrated as normal. So the Gallagher's had dressed the house in the manner befitting the occasion, gifts for the twins had been purchased, wrapped and put to one side awaiting the big night. The closer they came to Christmas Day, the more excitement and good feeling the Gallagher family began to experience. Presents were not only bought for the twins, but also for all seven sons, including lost son, Andy. Connie had decided that the Christmas tree, with her seven sons' presents underneath it, would remain standing until all of her sons had returned home. There was now only one day to go, as it was now the afternoon of Christmas Eve and the Gallagher household, including housekeeper, Susan, were gathered together in the sitting room enjoying a glass of Christmas punch. Susan had been with the Gallagher family for many years now and although she was a pretty girl, for some reason she had never married. Both Connie and Bobby treated her as a friend, not just as an employee. As everyone was relaxing and enjoying the conversation and the Christmas punch, they all heard the doorbell ring.

"Who on earth can that be on a Christmas Eve?" muttered Connie.

Susan placed her glass of punch on the table and got to her feet to go and answer the door.

"No Susan," said Bobby, "You stay and enjoy your punch, I'll see to the door."

"Thank you, Sir." replied Susan, taking her seat by the fireside once again.

Bobby left the sitting room heading for the front door but almost a whole minute later Bobby still hadn't returned.

"Who is it Bobby?" called Connie.

Bobby didn't respond to Connie's call, which along with his absence, caused Connie some concern.

Again Connie called out to her husband. Bobby appeared in the doorway of the sitting room, in his hand was a small sheet of paper. Bobby's expression was now one of gloom. Seeing the paper in her husband's hand, Connie realised instantly that this could be nothing but bad news. She jumped forward in her chair, her eyes swelling with her gathering tears, there were no need for words, because Connie knew that the outcome was not going to be good.

"Please God, oh please God no, not on Christmas Eve!" sobbed Connie, as she got to her feet and crossed the room to be by Booby's side.

Bobby placed his arm around his distraught wife, in a futile attempt to comfort her.

"Read it to me please. Bobby, I need to know which one of my sons is named on the telegram," Connie's voice was soft and filled with the fear and torment of a mother knowing that she was about to be told of yet another of her children was lost to her for ever.

Bobby raised his hand and began to read out the words:

- Fusilier Terrence Gallagher Killed In Action 19th. December 1943. -
(Terry Gallagher was only Twenty Three years old.)

From the moment that Bobby read out the telegram, Christmas had ended for both himself and his wife Connie. The next morning, being Christmas Day, Bobby and Connie were awakened early by Wee Bobby's twin boys, because for them, this was Christmas morning and they wanted to see what Father Christmas had brought them. Connie looked at her husband and then at her two grandsons and said to Bobby,

"No matter how hard this day will be for us to get through, we must get through it for their sakes, Bobby."

Bobby smiled at his wife and then kissed her softly, then he simply nodded his head in agreement. As Christmas Day progressed, both Bobby and Connie tried their upmost to put their sadness and great sense of loss to one side in order to allow the twins to have a troubled free Christmas day. Not once throughout the day did Connie or Bobby not hold dear their thoughts for each and every one of their sons. Up to this point in their lives, getting through this Christmas Day was the hardest thing they had ever done, but do it they did.

Sammy Gallagher was serving as a navy gunner on-board H.M.S. Penelope, nick-name (The Pepper-pot.) she was given this nickname because of the amount of times she had been hit and holed by bomb fragments. It was ironic that Sammy should be serving on this particular ship, as it was built in his home town of Belfast at The Harland & Wolf Shipyard. Beginning on the 22nd. Of January 1944. Sammy's ship was deep in action carrying out bombardments in support of military operations at Anzio beachhead. The Penelope, along with USS. Brooklyn an American Navy light cruiser, were engaged in the constant blasting of the beachhead at Anzio, in readiness for Allied landings. As for the crew, well they found the repetitive bombardment of unseen targets monotonous to say the least and were happy when their time was up. Later the Penelope returned to the harbour at Naples, when the crew were given shore-leave, the Penelope remained at anchor at the port of Naples until the 18th. of February 1944, when she set sail once again for Anzio.

Unfortunately the old Pepper-pot sailed into the path of a German U-Boat, the Penelope and her crew were unaware that they were being stocked by the Germen U-boat. Without warning the U-boat launched its attack. The U-boat's first torpedoed hit the Penelope in her engine room. This direct hit was followed some sixteen minutes later when the U-Boat's torpedo made yet another direct hit, this time hitting the Penelope in her boiler room. This hit instantaneously set off several other explosions within the ship. Fire quickly followed, raging uncontrollably throughout the ship, the explosions and the resulting fire killed a number of sailors instantly. The Penelope's sinking was now inevitable and indeed the ship started to go under almost immediately. Many sailors jumped into the sea in an attempt to save their lives as the ship went down, but unfortunately as the Penelope went under, the drag took many a sailor down with her. Other sailors didn't even make it off the ship, as they were trapped by fire and mangled iron and they too went down with their ship.

In total 415 men, including the Captain went down with the ship, miraculously 206 men survived the attack, regrettably Sammy Gallagher was not amongst the survivors, Sammy had gone down with his ship, one of many souls to be lost at sea that sad day. The most remarkable thing about the sinking of the (Pepper-pot) was that the Penelope was making 26 knots when first hit. As far as can be ascertained, this was a unique case in the history of U-Boat attacks in world war two. No other ship travailing at such a speed was ever successfully attacked by a U-Boat. On the afternoon of March 12th 1944 the slim figure of a lone Telegram boy made his way to the front door of the Gallagher household for the second time. He knocked timidly three times on the door and stood back waiting for a response. Housekeeper Susan opened the door to the young man and took the telegram from his hand without saying a word. She took it directly into the sitting room where both Bobby and Connie were resting. Bobby had seen the Telegram boy arrive through the sitting room window, so he knew what to expect once Susan had returned to the sitting room. Bobby got to his feet and walked towards the door, stopping Susan from entering the room. No words were spoken between Susan and Bobby, he simple took the telegram from Susan's hand and thanked her.

"My God Bobby not another one so soon?" gasped Connie, seeing that it was yet another telegram that her husband was holding in his hand. Bobby stood by the open fire as he opened it up and, with a reluctant voice, read out the contents of the telegram to his wife.

- Naval Gunner, Samuel Gallagher, lost at sea, believed killed
18th. February 1944-
(Sammy Gallagher was only Twenty years old.)

Upon hearing the tragic news of the death of yet another one of her sons, Connie fell back into her armchair and broke down in tears. The days that followed brought no comfort to Connie what so ever, there was to be no relief from the sadness and despair that now consumed her every waking hour.

The war in Europe was intensifying by the day and Harry Gallagher, who was serving with the 1st. Battalion Parachute Regiment, had completed his training and was preparing for the first action of his young life. For his first taste of action Harry was to take part in what was to be known as… - Operation Market-Garden. -

There was great excitement amongst the young men of the regiment as, like Harry this was their first action after their long training. The regiment was now based at Grimsthorpe in Lincolnshire and preparations for D-Day were well under way. It was on the 16th. of September, just before midnight when Operation Market Garden was launched, this was to be the biggest Airborne battle in history. 200 Lancasters and twenty-three Mosquitos from RAF Bomber Command pounded four German fighter airfields in northern Holland.

Harry Gallagher's oldest brother, Wee Bobby, a rear-gunner on one of the Lancasters that was talking part in the same raids. The raids, when completed, were followed up by 822 B-17 Flying Fortresses from the 8th Air Force the next day, their mission was to bomb the 117 identified anti-aircraft positions along the route that the transports would take, as well as airfields at Eindhoven, Deelen and Ede. These were backed up by another fifty-four Lancasters and five Mosquitos, while another eighty-five Lancaster's and fifteen Mosquitos would attack Walcheren Island. Losses were light (two B-17s, two Lancasters and three Mosquitos) Sadly Wee Bobby's aircraft was one of the Lancasters that was brought down due to intensive anti-aircraft fire. Reports say that the Lancaster that Wee Bobby was serving in was brought down over Eindhoven. Wee Bobby's aircraft was said to have been hit several times giving the crew no time at all to bail out. Disastrously, none of the crew of Wee Bobby's Lancaster survived the attack, tragically all on-board were killed when the air-craft burst into flames upon contact with the ground. At this point in the operation things were mostly going well for Bomber Command.

The first gliders of the British 1st Airborne Division touched down just after midday (1st Air-landing Brigade) they were closely followed by the divisional artillery and troops. Fortunately, glider losses were light, the only major losses was the failure of two gliders to arrive, each carrying a 17pdr anti-tank gun. The 101st jumped north of Eindhoven. The 501st Parachute Infantry Regiment landed correctly on its drop zone south of Veghel, apart from the 1st Battalion, which dropped by mistake at Heeswijk, 3 miles on the wrong side of the Willems Canal and the River Aa. The 502nd Parachute Infantry and 506th Parachute Infantry landed with the divisional headquarters just north of the Sonsche Forest. The 82nd Airborne dropped with the minimal loss of two Dakotas. The 504th Parachute Infantry dropped at Grave (with a company of the 2nd Battalion dropped west of the bridge) while the 505th Parachute Infantry and 508th Parachute Infantry dropped on the Groesbeek Heights with the 376th Parachute Artillery Battalion (the first ever parachute deployment of artillery into battle).

The British 1st Airborne Corps headquarters landed near to Groesbeek village at around 13.30 while the 1st Parachute Brigade dropped at 13.53 west of Arnhem to complete the British landings. Some 20,000 troops, 511 vehicles, 330 artillery pieces and 590 tons of stores had arrived safely. As the transports departed, Brereton flew back to IX Troop Carrier Command Headquarters at Eastcote to oversee the second wave. Once that had taken off, the Market deployment would be fixed and his role would be over. There would be no-one in England to coordinate the land battle with the air plan and no contingency plans had been made.

Harry Gallagher had now landed with the rest of his regiment at Renkum Heath, west of Arnhem. As Harry's Battalion advanced in an attempt to capture the high ground North of Arnhem, they were engaged in fierce fighting and their commanding officer was wounded and taken prisoner. As the fighting continued in the area of Den Brink, the 1st. Battalion endured severe casualties, as they tried to complete their objective, which was to rendezvous with the 2nd. Battalion, who had unfortunately been cut off at the bridge at Arnhem. Harry's Battalion was forced to withdraw to the Division perimeter that became besieged at Oosterbeek. Reduced to only 100 officers and men they defended with Lonsdale Force, until forced to withdraw across the Rhine to Driel and then to Nijmegen with the survivors of the 1st Division. Harry's Battalion had been evolved in some of the fiercest fighting seen at Arnhem and as the survivors were counted in when they reached Nijmegen, sadly Harry was not one of them. Harry Gallagher had been killed earlier that day shortly after his Commanding Officer had been taken prisoner.

Harry was with a group of young soldiers, numbering twenty-five in total, they had found themselves separated from the others after their Commanding officer had been captured by German forces. For most of the morning Harry and his comrades were involved some fierce fighting against a force much bigger in numbers and armed with much heavier weaponry. Attack after attack was fought off bravely by Harry and his comrades. As the day progressed, Harry, along with the rest of his group, found themselves being forced back into the ruins of a small village, being totally outnumbered by the enemy, Harry and his comrades found themselves trapped and surrounded by up to one hundred heavily armed German troops.

Their situation looked grim to Harry and his comrades, although they had put up one hell of a fight for most of the day, the young soldiers quickly realized that their ammunition was rapidly running out. With no realistic way out of their situation, six of the young soldiers at the fore of the group, put down their guns, lifted their arms high in the air and holding aloft their white handkerchiefs, they abandoned their cover and walked out into the open ground and offered themselves up as prisoners of war. As these young men walked forward, their white handkerchiefs plain to see, the German troops opened fire killing all six of them in a matter of seconds.

Harry and the others immediately returned fire in an attempt to save themselves, but their response to the German unwarranted aggression was to be in vain. Later that day the inevitable happened, Harry and his comrades ran out of ammunition, the British guns fell silent. The German troops advanced on Harry and his comrades in the safe knowledge that they had no more ammunition to fight back. Sadly the German troops declined to show any mercy what so ever to the unarmed British soldiers, as each and every one of them were brutally murdered. It was on the afternoon of 29th September 1944 that Connie was in the garden with twins George and Edward and they were enjoying the last of the summer sun. Bobby had gone into town to meet with some friends, leaving Connie alone with Susan and the twins. Susan, the housekeeper, suddenly appeared on the edge of the garden, she was just standing there motionless looking at Connie. The moment that Connie's eyes fell upon Susan her heart sank, because she could tell from Susan's expression, that yet another telegram had been delivered. Connie got to her feet really slowly and walked towards a tearful Susan. Connie raised her hand slowly and touched Susan gently on the side of her face, clearing away several tears that trickled down her cheek. Connie realized that Susan was finding the arrival of these telegrams just as stressful and depressing as Connie and Bobby themselves. Connie took, not one, but two telegrams from Susan's grasp.

"Would you please take the children into the house, Susan?" asked Connie, her voice low and devoid of spirt.

"Yes of course ma'am," replied Susan.

Connie walked to the end of the garden and sat on the swing that Bobby had built for their sons many years ago. Connie's heart was beating fast as tears filled her eyes. She held the two telegrams tightly in her hand, reluctant to open them, fearing their content. Connie sat there on that old swing for over half an hour, both telegrams were held tightly in her hands, but remained unopened. The late afternoon sun was now beginning to fade as it drifted slowly behind the hills that surrounded Connie's house. Connie watched as small teardrops fell upon the envelopes in her hand. Then with on deep breath, Connie opened the first of them. In a soft, tender whisper Connie read the out the content of the first Telegram…

- Airman Robert Gallagher Killed In Action 17th. September. 1944. -
(Wee Bobby was the oldest of Connie's seven sons and the father to twin boys George and Edward, Wee Bobby was aged Twenty Four.)

Slowly Connie folded the telegram and placed it gently into the pocket of her dress. Then, with her handkerchief in hand, she cleared several tears from her swollen eyes and opened the second telegram. Connie began reading it in the same fashion as she did the first time one had ever been handed to her.

- Para-trooper Harold Gallagher, Killed In Action on the 17th.
September 1944. -
(Harry was only Twenty years old.)

Connie and Bobby now had only two son left alive and both of them were overseas fighting. The last Connie had heard from them was when she received a letter from each, in the November of 1944. Both Billy and Tommy were in Burma fighting the Japanese, although not together and completely unaware of the others presences in the same regain.

But since Connie had received their letters, things had moved on considerably and the Allied forces had advanced successfully into central Burma, the Allied command thought it vital that they captured the port of Rangoon before the monsoon arrived, in order to avoid a logistics nightmare. In the spring of 1945, the other factor in the race for Rangoon was the years of preparation by the liaison organization, Force 136, which resulted in a national uprising within Burma and the defection of the entire Burma National Army to the side of the Allies. In addition to the Allied advance, the Japanese now faced open rebellion behind their own lines. And so an attack was mounted by the Allies down the Irrawaddy River valley against stiff resistance from the Japanese, casualties were high and a large number of Allied soldiers were taken prisoner and transported to Rangoon Jail - POW Camp. - The main attack came down the "Railway Valley", this attack was quickly followed by the Sitting River attack. They began by striking at a Japanese delaying position at Pyawbwe. The Allied advance was initially halted by a strong Japanese defensive position. Only to be undone by a clever flanking manoeuvre by Allied forces, involving tanks and mechanized infantry, struck at the Japanese from the rear and shattered their defences. From this point onward, the advance by the Allies moving down the main road to Rangoon, faced little organized Japanese resistance.

As yet neither Billy nor Tommy's paths had crossed, although both were in the thick of the fighting, Billy since 1942 and young Tommy since the March of 1944. By now in the early spring of 1945. Billy was with the leading Allied troops when they met the Japanese rear-guard just north of Pegu, 40 miles north of Rangoon. At this time the Japanese army was in some disarray, the situation looked grim for the Japanese, forcing General Heitaro Kimura, who was the highest ranked officer of the Imperial Japanese Army in Rangoon, to hurriedly form the various service troops, naval personnel and even Japanese civilians in

Rangoon into the 105 Independent Mixed Brigade. This scratch formation was able to hinder the British advance until the 30th. of April. This action by the Mixed Brigade not only held up the Allied advance, but helped to covere the evacuation of the Rangoon area. It was during a skirmish with this Japanese Mixed Brigade on the 26th. of April, that Billy was taken prisoner by the Japanese and moved to the Rangoon Jail - POW Camp - The sight that met Billy when he arrived shocked him to the bone. Billy looked on in horror as once strong young men now huddled together like neglected kittens, beaten and broken, their bodies withering from lack of eatable food.

Everywhere Billy looked, all he saw was walking skeletons with the look of terror in their eyes. Young men laying on the ground unable to pull themselves to their feet, they were so weak, their bodies covered with open untreated sores. The treatment handed out by the Japanese guards to anyone that got in their way, or was simply too slow to move out of their way, was brutal in the extreme. Prisoners would be whipped across their legs and lower body with long bamboo canes for no reason at all. Billy, along with the other new arrivals, were taken into a small wooden hut at the far end of the camp, there they were stripped off his uniform and dressed in what could only be described as old disused sacking. This sacking was rough on the skin of these men that their bodies were covered with an angry red rash, which in many cases had torn open and was bleeding due to irritation.

The Japanese made the prisoners work hard every day and Billy was no exception. Roll call at 7 o'clock, each morning, after which the prisoners were split into different groups, some were put to work unloading armament crates and storing them away. Other groups of prisoners were taken to a nearby quarry where they were worked like dogs under the hot sun. Others would be set to work on the railroad, both old and new. There was no let-up in the daily work routine, the only break throughout the day came at mid-day. That's when the prisoners would each be given small drops of water. As for food for the prisoners, well that consisted of stale, almost rancid, scraps of food that had been salvaged from what the Japanese soldiers had left from days before. This food would be placed in a wooden trough first thing in the morning and left in the open under the blazing sun until mid-day. The men were then forced onto their knees in front of this wooden trough and made to eat like pigs. The work day lasted until six in the evening, the men would then be taken back to the prison for final roll call and dinner, before being locked up for the night. One sad fact is that not all of the prisoner that set out for work in the mornings, made it back home that night.

The work was backbreaking, and unending, prisoners were made to work even though their hands were blistered and cracked. The evening's dinner back at camp was no better that the pig-swill the men were forced to eat at mid-day. The amount of food given to each prisoner each day was only just above starvation level, but yet the prisoners were expected to carry out arduous tasks day after day. Most days, but not all, there were eight pumpkins and four marrows to be shared amongst the 200 men in the camp. Due to the lack of Vitamin B in their food, the health of the men had reached catastrophic levels and was progressively getting worst.

The living conditions of the prisoners were simply atrocious, small wooden huts big enough for ten men, were housing up to twenty-five men at one time. Hygiene within the camp was non-existent, no proper washing facilities, no proper toileting facilities, just three holes that had been dug in the earth at one end of the camp. Throughout captivity no Red Cross food parcels or medical supplies were allowed to be passed on to the prisoners, all parcels were quickly confiscated by the Japanese soldiers. It was Billy's second day in the camp and whilst morning roll call was in progress, Billy suddenly heard something that caught his attention and made his ears prick up. The Japanese Officer, who was in charge of the morning roll call, had just called out the name Tomas Gallagher. Billy then heard a weak trembling voice from further down the line answer -here Sir- in response. Billy knew immediately that this voice, although weak, belonged to his younger brother Tommy. Billy tried to look down the lines towards where he had heard his brother's voice, after a few seconds Billy saw his brother. Tommy was no more than twenty feet from where Billy was standing, Tommy looked weak and thin, his face was covered with deep untreated cuts and multiple bruises. Unable to control his excitement at seeing his younger brother, Billy called out loudly,

"Tommy, it's me Billy."

This was an action that didn't go down well with the Japanese Officer who was calling out the morning roll. Tommy, upon hearing his older brother's call, moved out from the ranks to see where his brother was. Tommy saw Billy standing but a matter of feet away from him.

"Is that really you Billy?" Called Tommy.

The Japanese Officer went into a rage and barked something loudly in Japanese. In an instant the guards manhandled both Billy and young Tommy out of the ranks of prisoners and into the clearing in front of the Japanese Officer. The Japanese guards that were dragging young Tommy into the clearing, were doing so with unnecessary brutal force. Billy, being the older brother and who had always looked out for young Tommy, took exception to the treatment being handed out to his younger brother, as it was plain to see that young Tommy was far too weak to put up any kind of resistance. Billy wrestled hard with the two Japanese guards that were hauling him into the open ground where the Japanese Officer was standing. Eventually breaking free from their grasp and running to help his younger Tommy. Billy barged into both of the Japanese guards, knocking them to the ground as he grabbed his younger brother in both arms hugging him tightly as he shouting loudly.

"Leave my brother alone you fucking bastard."

Billy could see that his brother Tommy was in a really bad physical state, due to the treatment and beatings that he had endured at the hands of the Japanese.

"How long have you been here Tommy?" Asked Billy.

"I don't know how long Billy, I know I was brought here at the beginning of December, but I have no idea how long ago that was Billy." Answered Tommy.

The Japanese Officer yelled something in Japanese and both brothers were instantly surrounded by up to ten heavily armed Japanese guards. The Officer in charge was now in even more of a rage and again he screamed something in Japanese to the guards. Billy was brutally handled by the guards as he was dragged clear of his brother Tommy and hauled in front of the Japanese Officer. At this point another Japanese Officer arrived on the scene, this Officer was of a higher rank that the first Officer, in fact he was the camp's Commandant and he could also speak English. At first he seemed to be tearing a strip of the first Officer for his poor handling of the situation. When he had finished with the first Officer he turned angrily towards Billy, his face no more than a few inches away from Billy's face as he screamed loudly.

"Tell me," he said, "Do you think that it is alright for you to put your hands on a soldier of the Imperial Japanese Army, you English dog."

"I'm not an Englishman, I'm a fucking Ulsterman and we always look after our own."

Billy's obvious lack of respect for the camp Commandant only seemed to aggravate him more. In a flash the Commandant had wacked Billy across his face with a short bamboo can that he always carried in his hand, instantly Billy's cheek opened up and blood began to gush from the open wound.

Young Tommy made a move to help his brother, but he was brutally beaten to the ground by two Japanese guards. At this point the camp Commandant had flown into a frenzied rage, because of the insolence and disrespect shown towards, not only himself, but towards the uniform of the Japanese Imperial Army by the two brothers. Again he barked out further orders in Japanese. Four of the camp guards quickly caught hold of Billy and dragged him forward towards a wooden block situated in the centre of the camp compound. Billy's hands were then tied behind his back and a gag was brutally forced into his mouth, lodging at the back of his gullet. Billy was then forced by two down onto his knees by a hard kick behind his right knee from one of the guards. With a guard at either side of him, each taking hold of an arm with one hand, whilst the other gripped him roughly by the back of his neck, Billy was forced over the wooden block. The camp Commandant turned to the first Officer, his face blood red with furry and howled something in Japanese. The shamed first Officer stepped forward and positioned himself to the side of Billy, who was being held in position over the wooden black by two Japanese guards. The shamed Japanese Officer took his Samurai sword from its sheath and slowly he raised it high above his head and waited. Tommy's frantic cries for mercy for him brother were met with a vicious beating by several Japanese guards.

The camp Commandant looked at Billy and said.

"You Ulsterman, today you have insulted me the Camp Commandant, also you have insulted the uniform of the Japanese Imperial Army, which is also an insult to our Great Emperor. You have also insulted and shamed this Officer of the Japanese Imperial Army. For him to regain his pride and his honour, he must dispose of the one that caused his dishonour."

The Commandant then nodded in the direction of the shamed Japanese Officer. At First he waited nervously and took no action. The Camp Commandant then bellowed a second and even stronger order for the shamed Officer to do his duty. Suddenly, with a merciless strike the shamed Officer lashed downward with his Samurai sword in an attempt to decapitate Billy. Unfortunately his first strike was unsuccessful, as all he had achieved in doing was to make a deep cut into the side of Billy's neck. Again Tommy's cries for mercy for his brother only met with yet another callous beating. Nervously the shamed Japanese Officer raised his sward high above his head once again, his eyes now flitting uneasily back and forth from the camp Commandant to Billy. Billy's muffled, yet chilling screams of agonising pain, echoed loudly in the ears of every one of his watching comrades. Sadly the Japanese Officer's second attempt at decapitation, was even less of a success than his first attempt.

As a result of the botched second attempt to decapitate Billy, the shamed Japanese Officer, had only succeeded in making yet another and even deeper cut into the side of Billy's neck. Billy's stifled cries of pain sent shivers through each and every one of the watching prisoners. Billy's blood now covered the ground beneath him, finally, on his third strike, the Japanese Officer had succeeded in severing Billy head from his body. Once and for all ending Billy's blood curdling shrieks of hurt and ending the agony he was undoubtedly suffering. This callous act of inhumanity was carried out in full view of Billy's younger brother Tommy, who, throughout the whole terrible ordeal, had himself been on the wrong end of several viscous beatings at the hands of two prison guards.

Billy's body lay shaking on the ground, blood still squirting from his neck where his head once was. Young Tommy screamed loudly as he broke free from two guards and rushed franticly towards his brother. Sadly Tommy never reached his brother, but he was quickly restrained by three camp guards.

"You love your brother, do you." snarled the Commandant.

"Yes I do you bastard." yelled young Tommy angrily.

"Then you shall spend time with him, would you like to do that." laughed the Commandant.

The three Japanese guards, who had a firm hold of Tommy, physically dragged him in the direction of his dead brother, while a fourth guard skewered Billy's blood soaked head on the end of his samurai sword and then thrust it into Tommy's hands, forcing him to hold his brother's severed head. The camp Commandant then ordered that Tommy, along with his dead brother's head, was to be locked up in the small darkened wooden shelter, which had been christened, THE HOLE, by the P.O.W's, Normally this harsh punishment of, serving solitary confinement in the hole, was reserved for prisoners that had either, attacked, insulted or disrespected a Japanese soldier, or even worse, had tried to escape. Three Japanese guards dragged Tommy across the compound to the hole, once there the corrugated iron roof was lifted off and Tommy, along with his brother's severed head, were dumped unceremoniously into the hole and then the roof was replaced and bolted down.

The only daylight that could enter into the hell hole, was through three small holes that had been drilled into the roof. The space inside was minimal, it was only big enough for a man to sit up in, totally impassable for a man to stand up, or to even stretch out his legs. Any prisoner in the hole would be forced to sit with his legs tucked under his chin. Here, in these cramped conditions young Tommy remained cradling his brother's severed head tightly in his hands. At mid-day each day, Tommy was given a small bowl of putrid rice to eat and a quarter cup of water to drink. The heat inside the hole was tortious, reaching over 100% at the height of the day. This torment continued until the 5th. of May 1945, when the camp was liberated by advancing Allied forces.

When the British Officer who led the Allies into the camp was told of Tommy's incarceration in the hole, he instantly ordered that the roof be ripped off and Tommy released immediately. When Tommy was liberated from this pit of suffering, the British Officer and the watching British soldiers were all physically sick. From the day the British Officer had released Tommy from the his hell hole, he never once uttered a word, he would just perfectly still and gaze aimlessly into space. As for Billy's head, or what was left of it, the British Officer gave orders that Bill's body was to be dug up and reburied along with his head somewhere outside the confines of the camp. Within a day Tommy was transported to a military hospital, sadly the whole terrifying affair had affected Tommy's young mind to a considerable degree. Sadly Tommy was now a very disturbed young man, who was going to need, months, if not years of intense treatment before all of this could be put behind him. A week later Tommy was put on-board a Royal Navy Ship heading for England. Tommy found sleeping extremely hard, as nightmares of what he had witnessed, as well as what he had gone through in the camp, continued to haunt his darkened hours. Tommy felt that there was to be no escape from the hell that he now found himself trapped in. So much so that even being in the confinement of his ships cabin was too distressing for young Tommy Gallagher to cope with.

It was on the evening of May the 18th. at 2. A.M on a warm still tropical night, young Tommy Gallagher went for a walk on the top deck of the ship. Tommy stood looking out into the dark emptiness that surrounded him. The night air all around was still and quiet, so, so quiet, the shimmering light from the full moon that danced across the gentle heaving waves was the only factor to interrupt the blackness of the vast empty ocean. A sailor recalled speaking to young Tommy Gallagher as he gazing out into darkness of the night, the sailor also commented that he received no replay for Tommy. The sailor remarked that Tommy seemed to be in some kind of trance, he was there, yet not there. When asked, the sailor reports that the time of the encounter to be three minutes past three in the morning. That was the last recorded time that anyone had seen young Tommy Gallagher. The Army records show that on the morning of the 18th. of May 1945, the time estimated to be ten minutes past three in the morning, Tommy Gallagher is believed to have ended his life by jumping over the side of the ship into the sea, his soul is to be forever lost to the sea.

Meanwhile back in Belfast, as the chill of the winter of 1945, was becoming but a faded memory and the spring of that year was about to begin its blossom, the good people of the city were filled with an overwhelming excitement. Everywhere, in every little shop, in every bar-room, in every place of work that Belfast had to offer, the message was the same, this terrible war was about to end. It was on the 8th. of May when an official announcement, by the Prime Minister Winston Churchill, was broadcast on the wireless. Prime Minister Winston Churchill declared openly that Germany had surrendered and that the war in Europe had ended. This news was welcomed by everyone and it sparked wild celebrations all over Belfast, as the people's expectation of loved ones returning home escalated, fathers, brothers, husbands, uncles, sweethearts, all would be home soon.

The news was also greeted with great enthusiasm by Bobby and Connie, although they had lost five sons to this war, they awaited with great anticipation for the return of their two remaining sons, Billy and Tommy. Although Bobby and Connie were well aware that the war in the Pacific was still ongoing, but like everyone else they were convinced that victory over the Japanese was just around the corner. It was 30th May and Bobby and Connie were resting in the garden enjoying the warm spring sunshine with twins George and Edward. Connie suddenly looked towards the house only to see through the haze of the spring sunshine housekeeper Susan standing at the edge of the garden. Connie raised her hand to block the sun from her eyes, only to see that a British Army Officer was walking beside Susan and coming their way. Connie grabbed hold of Bobby's arm and pulled hard upon it.

"For the sake of God stop them, Bobby, please stop them!" cried Connie loudly.

Bobby, who at this point had not seen Susan and the Army Officer, turned quickly towards the house to see what had upset wife so badly. That's when Bobby noticed Susan and the Officer approaching. Connie, who was sitting on the ground, slumped back against the Pussy-Willow tree and buried her face in her hands. Bobby got to his feet and began to walk towards Susan and the Army Officer, wanting to intercept them before they reached his wife.

"Excuse me, Sir," said Susan as Bobby now stood before them on the edge of the garden.

"This is Captain Harwood and he would like to speak with you, Sir."

Susan was somewhat subdued.

Unlike Connie, Bobby really didn't think that the Captain was there to deliver any bad news, after all, the war was all but over and never before had the Army sent an Officer to inform them of the deaths of their other sons. Bobby shook hands with the Captain and said,

"Can we take this into the house please, Captain?"

"But of course," replied Captain Harwood.

"Please take a seat, Captain," said Bobby as he and Captain Harwood entered the front sitting room.

Captain Harwood sat down and removed his hat.

"What is it that we can do for you, Captain Harwood?" asked Bobby.

It was at this point that Captain Harwood's expression changed and instantly Bobby feared the worst. Captain Harwood then expressed his deep sympathies and proceeded to inform Bobby of the dreadful events surrounding the deaths of both Billy and Tommy at the hands of the Japanese.

"My God!" Groaned Bobby, "Not Billy and Tommy as well, how the hell do I tell Connie that her two remaining sons have also been killed, hasn't she suffered enough in this damned war?"

Captain Harwood sat forward in his chair and said softly.

"Would you like me to stay and explain everything to her, Mr Gallagher?"

Bobby raised his head and looked at Captain Harwood and said,

"I think that would be a good thing to do Captain Harwood. But for God sake please don't make it too graphic, I can do that when the time is right."

Bobby and Captain Harwood left the sitting room and headed for the garden where Connie was sitting under the Pussy-Willow tree with her two grandsons. Bobby and Captain Harwood walked across the garden and sat down beside her. Susan, who had followed Bobby and the Captain into the garden, gathered up the twins and took them into the house. Captain Harwood then informed Connie, without too much detail, of the fate of her two sons, Billy and Tommy. At first Connie showed no emotion whatsoever, she simply sat with her back against the old tree and glared directly at Captain Harwood.

"Are you all right, Connie?" asked Bobby, seeing that his wife didn't look so well.

Suddenly Connie thrust both of her hands to her face and screamed out loudly.

"Please God tell me why you have taken all of my sons, why all of them, tell me why?"

As the words left Connie's lips, she instantly passed out, falling sideways in a crumpled heap. Bobby picked Connie up in his arms and he, along with the Captain, returned to the house. Bobby lay his wife down on one of the large sofas in the front sitting room. He then called for Susan to bring some water and a clean cloth. If was a few minutes before Connie regained her senses, Bobby continued to dab her face with the cold water until she was sitting up and back in control of her movements.

Bobby put his arms around his distraught wife and hugged her tightly in an attempt to comfort her, although he knew in his heart that there was to be no comforting for Connie for a long, long time to come.

Captain Harwood, being a little curious after hearing Connie's outburst, suddenly said.

"May I ask how many sons have you both lost in this war, Mr Gallagher?"

Bobby's answer was short, but yet it shocked Captain Harwood to the core.

"Seven, all seven of them."

"Good heavens, have you really lost seven sons to this war Mr Gallagher?" gasped Captain Harwood.

"Yes, we have Captain," answered Bobby.

Captain Harwood left the Gallagher house that day stunned by what he had just been told by Bobby Gallagher.

- Fusilier William Gallagher Killed in Action 27th. April. 1945. -
(Young Billy Gallagher was only twenty-four years old.)

~~~~~

- Fusilier Tomas Gallagher Lost at Sea 18th. May. 1945. -
(Young Tommy was only nineteen years old.)

For months after Captain Harwood's visit, Connie became something of a recluse. Preferring to spend hour upon hour alone in her bedroom, staring lovingly at hordes of photographs from times gone by of her sons that she would spread out on her bed.

CHAPTER 24

All through the war years relations between Eire, (the Republic of Ireland.) and London were for the most cordial, but they did become somewhat strained from time to time. On one occasion in 1941, cross boarder cooperation was at its best when after the Blitz on Belfast, De Valera did come to the aid of the people of Belfast by sending, within hours of the Blitz, 13, fire tenders from Dublin, Drogheda, Dundalk and Dun Laoghaire to assist in the fighting of the inferno that ravaged Belfast. Again to de Valera's credit throughout the war years when dog fights had taken place and aircraft would be forced to crash land on Irish soil, British pilots would be immediately escorted to the Ulster boarder and released, were as German pilots would be instantly interned. But then on other occasions de Valera had a tendency to shoot himself in the foot, for instance, he seriously angered both London and in particular the Ulster Unionists, when in late 1941, the Irish Taoiseach, Eamon de Valera, annoyingly remarked…

'I wish there was some way of knowing who will win the war.

As it would make my decision making much easier.' -

This comment was followed up later when Eamon de Valera verbally attacked Ulster Unionists by condemning the North of Ireland for allowing a string of U.S, Bases to be established on, what he referred to as, Irish Soil.

Then on the 2nd. May 1945, just at the close of World War Two the political leader of the Irish Free State and embodiment of the Irish Republican movement, de Valera, failed to even be discreet in his support for Nazism. Eamon de Valera, the survivor of the 1916 Easter rising (who had a track record for helping the German war efforts) saw fit to sign a petition of condolence at the German legation in Dublin to express his grief on the death of Adolf Hitler. Furthermore, he then went to personally commiserate with the Nazi representative in Eire, Dr Eduard Hempel on the death of their beloved Fuhrer. Later on in the same month of May, a Dublin mob vandalised both the British High Commission and the US Embassy in Dublin. When news of the Allied victory broke, both countries, bitterly complained and were outraged at Southern Ireland's attitude and actions.

This outrageous event took place a full three months after the liberation of the Auschwitz-Birkenau concentration camp. When the revelation of the full horror of the Nazi genocide was exposed to the outside world. It was also only two weeks after British troops had liberated Bergen-Belsen. As it happened the British liberators were accompanied by an Irish doctor, so there could be no possibility that de Valera and the Dail (The Irish Government.) were unaware of the Nazi treatment of the Jews. Yet the leader of supposedly neutral Ireland still wished to pay his respects to one of the most evil men in the history of the world. It was a display of support that no other national leader on earth ever made. At the time it was defended as a diplomatic gesture by the Dail, but this was a gesture that not even General Franco was insensitive enough, or to be honest, stupid enough to make. It is clear that De Valera was sympathetic to the Nazi slaughter of the Jews, and he was still willing to be open about it when it was clear that there would be no comeback for Nazi Germany and no united Ireland. It is also interesting to note that de Valera's visit to Dr Eduard Hempel was publicly applauded in the Irish Nationalist press by the Irish republican supporting literary genius, George Bernard Shaw.

Many European Leaders openly criticised de Valera and his Government for remaining neutral through the war years and not making a stand against the nuisance of Fascism. At the end of the war de Valera further angered Britain and Ulster, when he permitted Dr Eduard Hempel to remain in Ireland, de Valera, then first resisted requests from Britain and the U.S.A. for the return to Germany of all German agents that had been interned in Ireland, then later, at Hempel's request, de Valera and the Irish Government opposed the outcome of the Nuremberg trails. Documents produced by the Department of External Affairs in Dublin refused to accept the concept of a war criminal and compared the Nuremberg trials to that of the British use of the judicial system in Ireland against Nationalists. As at the end of the First World War, returning Irish volunteers came home to indifference and in many cases, even hostility. At the end of the war United States personnel were permitted to wear their uniforms in Ireland, but not those who had served in the British forces. In addition, the Irish Government callously cancelled the Remembrance Day march. So once again tension between north and south was brewing. Many Ulster Unionist now feared that with de Valera as the leader of the Republic of Ireland, then the safety of Ulster, and its people, would be in jeopardy.

As the summer of 1945. began to fade into autumn, more and more of Ulster's young men began to return home from the war, but things weren't as idyllic as everyone thought that they were going to be. After the Blitz of 1941. Belfast was left with a huge housing problem and many soldiers returned home to find they had nowhere to live and those that did, found the standard of housing wasn't what it should be. Also many fathers had been lost in the war and so did not return home to their families. This sad fact, along with the realisation that countless mothers had also been killed in the Blitz of 1941, resulted in countless numbers of children in the city being left orphans.

On the evening of 10th November, Bobby was relaxing in his armchair reading his evening paper, The Belfast Telegraph, had printed the headline in big, bold letters on the front page…

- The Hundreds of Children Whom No One Wants. -

Connie, who was sitting quietly by the fireside with her two grandsons by her feet, happened to glance across the room at her husband. That's when the headline in Bobby's newspaper caught her attention.

"What is that article about, Bobby?" Connie asked curiously.

"Which one, Connie?" enquired Bobby, knowing quite well which article Connie was referring too? You see, he had purposely folded and held up the paper in this way, knowing that Connie would see it. Bobby's hopes were that when Connie saw the headline it would take her interest and hopefully encourage her to get involved in the whole tragic situation.

First Bobby straightened his newspaper, then he folded it to reveal the article that Connie was referring to. Bobby then began to explain to his wife that the article was telling the dismal story of the city's children left orphaned by the Blitz and the war.

"Let me read it please, Bobby," she said, her curiosity now aroused. She wanted to know more about this terrible situation that she hadn't realised existed.

"Dear heavens above!" said Connie after she had read the article in full.

"Shocking, isn't it, Connie?" said Bobby.

"Why is no one doing more to solve this dreadful problem?" Connie's undoubted love of children and her annoyance that the city of Belfast could allow this scandalous situation to continue was plain to see.

First thing the next morning Connie set about addressing this immoral and appalling situation. First she tracked down the orphanages that were attempting to care for these poor children. Connie was shocked and revolted when she saw the conditions that these children were forced to live in. There were up to eight children sleeping in a room that was hardly big enough to sleep three children. The beds provided for these children were nothing more than potato sacks filled with straw. The clothes on their backs were old, tatty and unwashed. The food put on the table for them was tasteless, unnourishing and almost always cold. Connie raged into a fury as she ranted angrily to the superintendents of the orphanage.

"These poor children deserve better than this. It's no fault of theirs that their mothers were lost in the Blitz, it's no fault of theirs that their fathers lost their lives fighting for this country, sacrificing themselves to ensure that the likes of you are able to go on living safely and not in fear of the Jackboot. And you treat them like this!!"

Connie left the orphanage that day disgusted at the treatment these poor children had to endure because there was no one to speak up for them. Sadly, the story was the same in the next five City Council run orphanages that she visited.

Connie decided that she would personally provide the funds that these institutions so badly needed to instantly improve the living conditions for the children. Regrettably, after almost six months of providing funds to over six orphanages throughout the City, Connie discovered that very little had changed for the lives of the children inside these places. As far as Connie could tell, the only people whose life standards had increased dramatically, were the Council officials and the Superintendents in charge of the orphanages. Angry and outraged at this so obvious deception, Connie decided to withdraw her funding instantly and instead put the funding towards the renovation of three of the large buildings that she owned on the coast, transforming them into her own private orphanages. Two of these establishments were situated in the seaside town Holywood, overlooking a long stretch of sandy beach. The third building was located in the middle of a beautiful woodland, but a short walk from the town of Bangor's sea front.

The work on all three of Connie's buildings was completed in a matter of a few months, transforming them into appropriate clean accommodation for children. The children's educational needs were also catered for, as Connie had an agreement in place with several schools in the area of all three orphanages. Although it must be said that this agreement was only reached after Connie had made a sizeable donation to all schools. Sports of different kinds were also catered for at all three orphanages. Although the orphanages were to be for both boys and girls, the sleeping arrangements were to be in dormitory fashion, ten beds to each dormitory. The boy's dormitories were to be situated at one end of the building and the girl's dormitories at the other end of the building. Leaving a respectful distance between them.

There was one thing in the structure of these orphanages that Connie was most insistent upon, this idea Connie refused to be moved on and it almost ended the whole scheme before it got off the ground. Connie began to lobby the business community in Belfast to help with this project. Although help was forth coming at first, Connie had to use a lot of her own money to kick-start the venture. But Belfast, being Belfast, Connie soon hit a problem. You see Connie's idea was to end years of tradition by ending religious divides and having children of all religions living together. Now the two main religions in the Ulster were of course Protestant and Roman Catholic, but also there were a large number of Jewish children who had been orphaned in the City. Connie was reluctant to segregate the religions, instead she wanted them to live together, hoping that a degree of tolerance for each other's religion might thrive between the children and if proved a success, then one day might be adopted by the Government at Stormont. Connie also had the idea that if her non-denominational orphanages were to be a big success, then the next step could be non-denominational schools.

All three of Connie's orphanages opened their doors in the summer of 1946 although sadly, it didn't take long for the first objectors to Connie's new idea to raise their ugly heads. The Roman Catholic Church was the first to openly object to Connie's new non-denominational orphanages, branding them as total lunacy. The Roman Catholic Church made their position clear, they were bitterly opposed to this idea and wanted it to be stopped forthwith. Next to openly attack Connie's new orphanages, were the Jewish Synagogues in the City of Belfast. Protestant Church leaders weren't that far behind in their condemnation of Connie's idea for religious co-inhabitancy.

Come what may in Connie's direction, the lady was determined to see her idea come to fruition. This of course meant that the three religious leaders in the city withdrew their support for Connie's newly formed orphanages by the seaside. Not only did they withdraw their support logistically, they also refused to help finically, leaving Connie having to finance the project, mainly in the beginning, with her own money. Fortunately, within a few months of opening the doors to her orphanages, Connie was able to convince some in the business Sector of the benefits of this idea and they began to support Connie's orphanages finically. Connie's orphanages were now full to capacity, with over one hundred children of different religious denominations being catered for. Connie insisted that the orphanages were to be staffed only with people that agreed with the ethos of the orphanages and they too were to be of various religions. No religious education was ever to be taught within the walls of the orphanages, that was left to the schools and churches the children attended. There was to be no more physical punishment handed out to the children within the orphanages.

Discipline was to be to the fore of course, but it was to be administered in a civil and respectful way. All the children were to receive three healthy meals a day and were to be kept clean and tidy at all times. In the July of 1948 the interdiction of the N.H.S. in Northern Ireland was to prove to be a huge help to the finances of the orphanages. The burden of health costs was now lifted off their shoulders of the orphanages. In all, Connie's idea was proving to be a huge success, as the children that lived in Connie's orphanages were happy, well-adjusted and were receiving an education to match that of other children throughout Ulster.

It has to be noted that at first Connie had to fight tooth and nail to get her orphanages opened. Connie had truly made a huge success of her project, but this great achievement wasn't gained easily, far from it. From the very beginning Connie came up against stiff opposition from organised religion in the city. The Catholic Church tried to block Connie at every turn, sending inspectors to the orphanages several times in an attempt to have them closed down, but all they found were well run, clean and friendly institutions, filled with happy well-nourished children. Connie also received death threats from the I.R.A. who backed the Catholic Church in their condemnation of Connie's orphanages, referring to the idea of mixed religions living together as nothing but a front, claiming that Connie was only trying to poison the minds of good Catholic boys and girls.

The Jewish leaders in the city, along with the chief Rabbi, also attacked Connie at every chance that came their way. The chief Rabbi, writing in the Belfast Telegraph called Connie a modern day Delilah, saying that she was trying to cloud the word of the Lord God Jehovah, by tainting the young minds of the sons and daughters of Israel with the teachings of the false prophet that spawned this new Christianity. The Protestant Church leaders in Belfast also strongly opposed Connie's new brand of orphanage living and they too did everything they could to close down the three orphanages that Connie had opened. The Orange Order in Belfast, although confirming that they believe in civil and religious liberty for all, cynically decried Connie's multi religious orphanages, calling them perverse in the extreme. Towards the end of 1946, Bobby was called to a meeting of the senior Brothers of his Orange Lodge at Knock. At this meeting Bobby was informed that if he could not convince his wife of the errors of her misguided approach to running her orphanages, then, in their option, it would be best all round if he were to resign from the Orange Order. Bobby smiled broadly at the Assembled Brethren, then answered in four simple words...

"Consider it done gentlemen."

With those words, Bobby removed his Orange Order Regalia (orange sash and white gloves) and laid them on the table in front of the Master of the lodge. Bobby then turned around sharply, bid a farewell to the watching Brethren and left the lodge-room, never to return.

In spite all the animosity and threats that came Connie's way, she never once, not for a second, faltered in her belief that what she was doing was right for the children and for the future of Ulster. Connie's fight with the organised religions in the City of Belfast, lasted for several years and because of this under current, funding for the orphanages became harder and harder to secure. Come what may, Connie was determined that her orphanages would never close and this meant that Connie had to increasingly use more and more of her own money to keep them afloat.

As if things weren't hard enough, in the October of 1949, the darker side of Belfast raised its ugly head. Without warning, a raging fire swept through the Gallagher family home in the middle of the night, killing poor housekeeper, Susan. The rest of the family had gone to the coast for the weekend, leaving Susan at home to look after the house. The blaze ripped through the house so quickly that Susan had no chance to escape the flames. The fire totally destroyed the Gallagher family home, leaving nothing standing. No one ever claimed responsibility for this despicable act and no one was ever prosecuted for the death of Susan, even though it was proved beyond all doubt that the fire had been started deliberately. Connie, Bobby and their two grandsons moved to a smaller four bed roomed detached house on Martinez Avenue in the affluent Bloomfield area on the outskirts of East Belfast. The Gallagher family were not in a bad state financially, but with the orphanages eating up a lot of their money, they were now not as affluent as they once were. In the June of 1950 Connie received some good news when the Stormont Government eventually recognised her achievements in the care of the orphaned war children and came to her aid with much needed yearly founding.

By 1952, the war years seemed to be but a distant memory to the people of Ulster, sadly though, once again sectarian rumblings were beginning to surface in the City.

This new Irish Republic, that had become official back in 1949, was growing by the day, causing Ulster unionist to be worried for their future. The Dail in Dublin had now began to flex their muscle and were once again making constant noises about an all-Ireland. This issue was to haunt Ulster for years to come, even though the British Government had given new constitutional guarantees to the Northern Ireland Parliament in Stormont. Still, fear and mistrust loomed large in the minds of Ulster Protestants.

By 1956. Wee Bobby's twin boys, George and Edward, had now reached the age of fifteen years old, both boys were attending Sullivan Upper Grammar School, a private school which was situated in the seaside town of Holywood, near to where Connie's orphanages were situated. Both boys were excelling at their studies, reaching considerable academic standards and it was widely believed that they were both destined to become great scholars. Both boys were also keen sportsmen, representing their school in football, rugby, cricket and swimming. Sadly though in this year, the I.R.A. had upped their campaign of violence against the North, blowing up important electrical installations and attacking several R.U.C. stations, as they pushed their claims for an all-Ireland. Unfortunately for the I.R.A., work at this time in Ulster was plentiful, Both Protestants and Catholics alike could see the benefits of being part of Britain and as a result the I.R.A. campaign was met with apathy by Nationalists in the north and the I.R.A.'s campaign to recruit new members, died out with a whimper in 1962.

At this time Connie's grandson George was studying Law at Queens University, whilst Edward was studying Medicine at the very same University. Also in the year of 1962, most of the war orphans that had been living in Connie's three orphanages had now grown up and left. It would seem that Connie had beaten the organised religions and bigots in the City that had so vigorously opposed her idea of non-denominational institutions. Connie's orphanages remained open until they were no longer needed by those who were living in them and, by the end of 1962, with so few children remaining in Connie's well run orphanages, they were taken over by the state. Within a few months of the state taking charge, reorganisation of all three orphanages had begun. This meant that all of the Catholic children being sent back to Catholic Church run orphanages, the Protestant and Jewish children, also being returned to orphanages run by their own religious Churches. Connie's dream had been ended without a thought, the buildings were shut down less than six days after the last child had been relocated. This development came as a blow to Connie, as she had hoped, due to the success of her orphanages, that the state might have adopted her blue-print, especially in province's schools, for multi religious education. Sadly that was never to happen.

By the spring 1966 Connie was approaching her sixty-seventh year, Bobby his sixty-eighth. Grandson Edward was now working at the Royal Victoria Hospital in Belfast, after securing a Surgical Residency position, Edward had bought his own house on the Malone Rd, an Affluent area of Belfast. Twin brother George had married a Scottish girl by the name of Alison, whom he met at University and they were married at St. Mark's Church in the spring of 1964. George, along with his new bride and their baby son Ross, who was of the tender age of fourteen months, were living with Connie and Bobby at their house on Martinez Ave. George was in chambers with the crown public prosecution service in Belfast. Things in the City of Belfast were relatively peaceful and people were getting on with their lives, although still keeping a safe distance from each other. In this year of 1966, there was one thing that was never far from everyone's thoughts, because in the summer of 1966 the football world cup was to take place in England. Could England really win the Football World Cup?

This big event in England allowed all football fans in Ulster a wonderful opportunity to make the short journey across the Irish Sea to England and see this great sporting spectacle for real. Imagine it, some of the best footballers in the world playing in your own back yard, well almost. Edward and George had decided to make the short trip across the Irish Sea and take in several games in the tournament. Two weeks before the tournament was due to kick off, both George and Edward announced to their grandfather over Sunday lunch, that they were going to the World Cup.

"Really!" exclaimed Bobby, feeling excited for his grandsons.

"Yes…really, Granddad," replied Edward.

"You lucky boys, can you believe that you are going to see the world's best footballers for real. Most of us will only be able to read about it in the paper," mused Bobby.

"But that's not the best news, Granddad," added George.

"What could be better than going to the World Cup, George?" asked Bobby.

"Well," interrupted Edward, "We have both taken a few weeks off work and we have tickets for five games, but the thing is Granddad, we have three tickets for each of the games, so we were wondering, if you would like to come with us, Granddad?"

"Are you serious?" gasped Bobby.

"We are, very serious." laughed both boys.

"Then too right I would like to come with you!" answered Bobby excitedly.

"Then it's settled, we're all going to the Football World Cup in England."

Connie smiled at her two grandsons saying...

"You two boys look after your Granddad."

"We will, Granny," answered George.

It was on the morning 9th July 1966 that Bobby and his two grandsons left Belfast by aeroplane for England, arriving in London that very afternoon. Their first taste of this great football event was on the 11th of July when they went to Wembley Stadium to watch England take on Uruguay in the opening game of the tournament. In the end this game was a game to forget as it ended nil- nil. The next day the boys took their Grandad to see the sights of the City of London, followed by a lavish dinner at the newly opened, but already fashionable Eatery, the Admiralty Restaurant.

Two days later, Bobby and his grandsons got their second taste of the football World Cup when they returned to Wembley Stadium on 13th July to watch the game between France and Mexico, again the game was something of a disappointment, it would have to be said, as it ended one –one. The game between England and Mexico followed on the 16th. of July, a better game and a better result was achieved this time as England won the game two – nil.

England's game against Argentina on the 23rd. of July was the next game they attended, England wining 1-0. The boys now had a few days before, the next game they had tickets for and so Bobby and his grandsons decided to take in as much of the London sights as they could. On the morning of the 24th July, both George and Edward were sitting at the breakfast table waiting for their granddad. George was the first to notice, as his granddad entered the hotel's restaurant, that he seemed to be walking rather slowly and cumbersome as he crossed the restaurant coming towards them. George nudged his brother, Edward to take a look. They both noticed that their granddad seemed sluggish in his movements, his eyes were red and he looked so tired. Both brothers watched carefully as their granddad repeatedly stopped to take deep breaths. Edward became concerned by his appearance and decided to take him to St. Bartholomew's hospital, where he was immediately admitted.

After tests were carried out, the boys were told that their grandfather had suffered a slight heart attack and that the doctors would like Bobby to stay in hospital for a few days, just for observation. On Bobby's second day in hospital he told the boys that he really needed to go back home to Belfast, as he needed to see Connie. George and Edward agreed to return home to Belfast once he had been released from hospital. The brothers picked him up from the hospital on the morning of the 27th July. Bobby and his grandsons returned to Belfast that very afternoon. Once on the aeroplane, Bobby positioned himself on the inside of the row of three seats, next to the window. George sat next to him and next to Edward on the aisle seat.

"How are you feeling, Granddad?" asked George as the flight was about to take off.

Bobby smiled at his grandsons and said,

"Relax boys…I'm fine…just a little tired."

"A nap might just be the best thing for you, Granddad," said Edward.

"You might be right, Eddy." replied Bobby.

All three settled themselves for the flight back to Belfast. George and Edward opened their newspapers, whilst Bobby sat back and closed his eyes, as he was more than ready for a cat-nap. Within minutes Bobby was fast asleep.

"Do you think Granddad will be okay, Eddy?" asked George.

"I think so, Geordie, but when we get home I will take him to see a colleague of mine at the hospital, just to be on the safe side," answered Edward.

The flight home was nearing its end, crew were now busying themselves preparing the passengers for landing.

"Shall we wake Granddad up?" said George.

"Wait until we touch down Geordie, that will be time enough," replied Edward.

So it was that Bobby was left sleeping, as the wheels of the airplane could be felt bumping down onto the tarmac, George turned to his granddad and gave him a gentle nudge. But there was no response from their sleeping grandfather. Again George shook his grandfather, this time a little harder, but the response was the same. Again he tried to wake his granddad, saying,

"Come on, old man, it's time to wake up, the airplane has landed and we're back home in Belfast."

But Bobby never moved, not so much as a flinch was detected from his body. George quickly alerted his brother, Edward to the fact that he couldn't awaken their granddad.

Edward quickly changed places with his brother, George and began to examine his granddad. Sadly, it was of no use, as hard as Edward tried, there just wasn't a pulse to be found. Bobby had closed his eyes to sleep, thinking of his beloved wife, Connie, but he just simply never woke up again. Bobby had passed peacefully away in his sleep, thinking of Connie.

"Oh good Jesus, Geordie, he's gone!" mumbled Edward.

"What!" screeched George?

"It's Granddad, Geordie, he's dead, he's bloody well dead," muttered Edward softly.

Both boys each took hold of one of their grandfather's hands and held it tight until everyone had left the aircraft. George and Edward remained with him, holding tightly to his hands until an ambulance arrived to take Bobby off the aeroplane.

Bobby's body was taken to the Royal Victoria Hospital in Belfast, coincidently the same hospital where Edward worked. Both George and Edward accompanied him to the hospital, not once leaving his side. Bobby's death hit both George and Edward really hard, because both boys adored their granddad. It wasn't long before Bobby's body was taken for examination by a team of Doctors to determine the cause of death.

Edward and George left the hospital in solemn mood that day and made their way to their grandma's house, knowing that the news that they had to break to her was not going to be an easy task. George and Edward were walking up the garden path towards the front door of the house, when the front door was opened by George's wife Alison, who was leaving to go shopping.

"What are you both doing here?" she asked, somewhat surprised to see them standing there on the garden path, as they were not expected home for another two days.

"And where's your granddad?" she said with a chuckle, "Don't tell me that you have left him at the bar, because if you have you know that your granny will kill the both of you," added Alison with yet a bigger smile.

Sadly, the second that she had said the words, she realised that something was terribly wrong.

"Dear God, what is it George, what has happened to your granddad?" asked Alison.

"We all best go inside." suggested George.

Alison suddenly gasped with fear as she realised that something bad must have happened to her father-in-law.

Alison turned and went back into the house, followed closely by George and Edward. Alison led the brothers into the sitting room, where Connie was playing with her great grandson, Ross.

"Have you forgotten something Alison?" enquired Connie, surprised to see Alison entered the room.

"The boys are here, Connie," said Alison with a whimper.

Connie, who was on the floor playing with her great grandson, Ross, looked up to see both of her grandsons standing in the doorway of her sitting room. Connie's eyes dropped, almost to a complete close, but she never said another word.

"Please sit down Granny, we have something to tell you," said Edward.

"No need, Edward, I already know," said Connie softly, her heart aching just like it did for her lost sons.

"But how?" asked Edward.

"I just do," was all that Connie said.

"Do you need anything grannie?" asked George.

"Please tell me he didn't suffer," said Connie.

Edward braced himself, then kneeling by his grandmother's side he took hold of her frail Tiny hand and held it softly in his. Then he explained the full and heart-breaking story of her Bobby's sad departure.

"Are you okay, Granny?" asked Edward, once he had told her the full story.

"No," said Connie softly, "My Bobby is with my beautiful boys now and I know they will keep him safe for me until we are once again reunited."

Connie sat back in her chair as her eyes moved slowly towards the small table beside her armchair, slowly she reached out and picked up Bobby's photograph which sat in pride of place in the middle of this small polished table. Still not a word passed Connie's lips as she lovingly kissed the tips of her fingers before tenderly pressing them against Bobby's face on the photograph. Connie then pressed Bobby's photograph tight to her chest, as a single perfectly formed tear oozed from her right eye and nestled precariously in the corner of her eye. The bright sunshine that beamed intrudingly through the bay window, suddenly caught the tear in Connie's eye, making it sparkle and shine like a newly cut diamond. Connie sat Silent and still in her armchair holding Bobby's photograph tight to her breast for over an hour. Then with Alison's assistance, both George and Edward convinced Connie to go upstairs and rest on her bed. Connie nodded in agreement and with a little help from her grandson's, Connie got to her feet and left the sitting room and went to her bedroom.

Once in her bedroom, Connie lay back on her bed, still clutching Bobby's photograph tight to her breast.

"Is there anything you need Granny?" asked Edward.

Connie smiled at both of her grandsons and replied in a soft gentle voice, "Nothing thank you, Edward."

"Okay, Granny we will leave you now to rest, but if you need or want anything, please just call," said Edward.

Alison, George and Edward left Connie's bedroom and returned to the sitting room.

Connie now lay alone on her bed thinking of Bobby and her seven sons. Slowly Connie closed her eyes, still holding Bobby's photograph tightly in her small hand, then in a soft whisper she said,

"I only ask one thing of you my Lord, please take me before you take my grandsons. I couldn't stand it if I had to see them go too. I have buried enough of my loved ones and I hold no fears for leaving this world. I know in my heart that one day Bobby and my boys will come for me, and I tell you now my Lord. When that day arrives, I will be ready, whenever they call me."

Connie's eyes remained closed as she drifted off into a deep sleep.

Bobby's funeral service was held at St. Mark's Church at Knock, attended by a small group of family and friends. On the afternoon of 30th July 1966. Bobby's body was laid to rest at Roselawn Cemetery at Crossnacreevy, just outside Belfast.

- Robert Gallagher Senior Was Sixty-Eight Years Old.-

CHAPTER 25

After Bobby's death and subsequent funeral in 1966, Connie was never quite the same lady ever again. Yes, it is true that Connie had suffered terrible losses in the past, losing each of her seven sons to the war and without a doubt those devastating events in her life took a great toll on her. But this was different, Connie's zest for life had now gone, events happening around her, no matter how good or even how tragic or how devastating they turned out to be, Connie's indifference to them was there for all to see. No matter how hard George and Edward would try to engage their grandma in open conversations about the talkative events of the day, not only Belfast but all over the country, Connie refused to show any interest in such conversations whatsoever. No longer did this grand lady jump to defend the rights and wellbeing of the underdog, as she had done all of her life. It was as if something inside her had surrendered to life's woes, Connie's determination to do the right thing by helping her fellow man had faded. It would seem that she had given up the fight to help those who needed help the most. The flame that had, for so many years, burnt so brightly within her, had been extinguished. Connie became something of a recluse, rarely leaving her house on Martinez Avenue. Connie's entire existence now revolved around her great-grandson Ross, whom she cherished dearly.

The next two years passed in relative quiet and without any real major incidents in the city of Belfast, or indeed in the Gallagher household. This said, there remained a worry in the minds of the people of Belfast. Although everything seemed normal, unrest was brewing just under the surface amongst the Catholic Nationalist community. Rumblings of discontent could be heard almost on a daily basis in the Nationalist press and also on the radio. As for Connie's immediate family, well her grandson, Edward was now a surgeon at the Royal Victoria hospital in Belfast and her other grandson, George was a Q.C. with the C.P.S. in Belfast. George, Alison and young Ross were still living with Connie on Martinez Avenue, as George was reluctant to move out of the family home after his grandfather's death, not wishing to leave his grandmother living alone.

The year of 1966 saw the troubles begin to escalate in Belfast when on May the 21st, following several P.I.R.A. attacks, the Protestant Paramilitary force the U.V.F. issued this Statement.

(From this day onward we declare war against the IRA and all its splinter groups. Known IRA men will be executed mercilessly and without hesitation. Less extreme measures will be taken against anyone sheltering or helping them in any way, but if they persist in giving them aid, then more extreme methods will be adopted. We solemnly warn the authorities to make no more speeches of appeasement. We are heavily armed Protestants dedicated to this cause.)

Following this worrying statement by the U.V.F. on the 11th. of June 1966, the U.V.F. shot and killed a Catholic store owner in west Belfast. On the 26th. of June 1966, another U.V.F, gun attack in west Belfast killed a Catholic barman and seriously injured three others.

The year of 1968, saw changes across the Atlantic, America was griped in the seemingly unstoppable advance of the Civil Rights Movement, which had first surfaced years before in 1955. The movement was led by black religious leaders such as the Rev's. Martin Luther King, Ralph Abernathy and others. Their idea was to call for social change in America by the use of Non-violent Resistance, the movement was originally started in response to, what the black population saw as discrimination in, Jobs, housing, public transport, schools, universities and many other everyday ways of life. Before long their ranks were swollen as countless white students across America joined the Black protesters in their marches. The movement were now organising marches all over the country and news teams from all over the world were flocking to capture it all on film, the plight of the black population was now to the fore.

This phenomenon that was taking place in the U.S.A. wasn't to be lost on the Catholic Nationalists of Northern Ireland, who had grievances of their own, as they felt that ordinary Catholic's were being discriminated against by the Stormont Government and Unionists in general, in regards to decent housing in catholic areas, also Catholic's complained that they found it hard to obtain jobs, sighting that most employers in the Province were Unionists and only employed other Unionists, those Catholics who were in work, bitterly complained that they were always overlooked when it came to promotion in certain occupation, especially in those institutions run by the Government, the Civil Service being named as one of the biggest culprits. They called for an end of inequality throughout Ulster.

In the October of 1968. The Irish Civil Rights Movement took to the streets of Londonderry, or as the Nationalists preferred to call it…

(Free Derry, because in Ireland it would seem that even a place name could be objected to and considered controversial.)

The authorities at the time believed that the route the march was about to take would prove to be too provocative to Protestant residents in that area and instruct the police to halt the advance of the march. The Royal Ulster Constabulary do exactly that with the use of baton attacks and water cannon on the marchers. This action by the R.U.C. was seen world-wide on television, casting them in a dubious light, this was something the organisers of the march not only hoped, but knew would happen. But following the terrible event in Londonderry, unfortunately, it now seemed inevitable that Ireland would now undoubtedly topple over the brink and tumble head long into its second prolonged spell of sectarian violence. Because Unionists throughout the Province took exception to these marches, seeing them as no more than Republican marches. This idea that the Unionists held was seen to be vindicated, when during these marches the Republic of Irish's tricolour would be openly paraded on the streets of Ulster by the marchers.

The Stormont Government, under Terence O'Neill, needed to act quickly in an attempt to quell the situation before it got totally out of hand. So in the November of 1968, reforms were rushed through the Ulster Parliament to meet some of the campaigner's demands, but this too had an adverse effect, as it angered ordinary Unionists throughout Ulster. As for the Nationalists campaigners themselves, well their response to the reforms was to say, it's all too little too late, so the reforms failed to stem the rising tide of sectarian violent confrontation. Fighting between Catholic Nationalists and Protestant Loyalists broke out on the streets all over Ulster. On the 30th. of March 1969, a U.V.F. bomb exploded at an electricity station in Castlereagh resulting in widespread black-outs. A further five bombs were to be exploded at electricity stations as well as at water pipelines throughout the April of 1969. It was hoped that these attacks would be blamed on the I.R.A. thus forcing moderate Unionists to increase their opposition to even further reforms being brought into force by Terrence O'Neill's Stormont Government.

Then in the January of 1969, another Civil Rights March is organised in Londonderry, Loyalists in the city strongly object, but the march goes ahead. Unfortunately, the march is ambushed and attacked by over 200 angry Protestant Loyalists at Burntollet Bridge south Londonderry. Once word of the ambush got out, Nationalists in the Bogside area of Londonderry began rioting and furious violent street battles between Nationalists and Loyalists continued long into the night. One of the turning points in the Nationalists view of the R.U.C. was to take place that very night, when Officers of the R.U.C. went into the Bogside and fought long violent battles with the residents, Nationalist were convinced that the R.U.C. were only there to back up the Loyalists rioters, relations between Nationalists and the Royal Ulster Constabulary were never to be the same again.

(The Bogside area of Londonderry was to become famous all over the world in the years to come, but sadly for all the wrong reasons.)

Following these terrible scenes of sectarian violence at Burntollet Bridge, (Londonderry) and later in the Bogside, some of the more extreme members of the I.R.A rebelled against its leadership saying that,

> (The I.R.A. - as it stands - are not doing enough,
> to protect Roman Catholics throughout Ulster.)

As a result, a Hugh number of them decided to break away from the established Paramilitary Force, (The I.R.A.) and form a new force, to be known as (The Provisional I.R.A.) this splinter group would vigorously advocate the renewed use of terrorism throughout Ulster. Their activities in turn further enraged the Protestant Loyalists of Ulster, prompting the reformation of Protestant or ('Loyalist') Paramilitary groups, such as the long since disbanded U.V.F. in order to protect Protestant areas that would be at risk from this new threat from,

(The Provisional's.)

The extreme acts of violence, by both sides, caused the British Government to send troops to the province, at the request of the Nationalists it has to be said, to maintain order.

At first the soldiers were welcomed by the Catholic Nationalists and tea and sandwiches were handed out to the soldiers when on patrol on the streets of Nationalists areas. Sadly this situation was not to last for long. Maintaining order on the streets of Ulster was to prove to be an almost impossible task for the army, as riots and terrorism flared up spasmodically in the two main cities, Belfast and Londonderry. In these early days of the sectarian violence that was taking place on the streets of Londonderry and Belfast, East Belfast, the side of the city where Connie and her family had always lived, hadn't seen as much violence on its streets as other parts of the city, but that was to change on the Saturday evening of the 27th. of June 1970.

(Later to become known as the Battle of St. Matthews.)

The exact turn of events of how this all started is unclear, it depends who you ask. There are two versions of what happened that night, the Nationalists version and the Loyalist version.

First the Nationalist side of the story...

On the evening of Saturday 27th. June 1970, a mob of loyalists gathered and began making their way from the Newtownards Road towards the "Short Strand" A mainly Catholic and republican area of East Belfast, the "Short Strand" was almost totally surrounded by Protestant and loyalist areas. Many of the loyalists were returning from an Orange Order parade that had been held in another part of the city, during which sectarian violence had erupted. Local Catholics say that they believed that they were about to be burnt out of their homes and claimed that the British Army and R.U.C. stood by and watched as the Loyalists entered their area. It was claimed that among the mob of Protestants were an unknown number of loyalist gunmen. In response to this attack by Loyalists a group of P.I.R.A. armed volunteers took up sniping positions in the grounds of St. Matthew's Catholic Church as well as some of the surrounding streets.

A shootout began between the P.I.R.A. and the Loyalists gun-men, this gun-battle lasted at least five hours. Ending only when the Loyalists retreated.

This story of the P.I.R.A.'s desperate defence of Catholics in the area quickly spread and the nationalist community from that day on saw the P.I.R.A. as their defenders. Following the events of this night the Catholics of the Short Strand say they lived in fear of their lives from the Loyalists that surrounded their small Nationalist community.

As for the Loyalist view of that night, well that is a totally different story...

It has been said by many who say they witnessed the event on the morning of the 27th. of June 1970, that a string of buses pulled up outside St. Matthews Catholic Chapel and mothers and children by the hundreds were loaded onto them in the pretence that it was a Sunday-school trip to the seaside. Most convenient don't you think.

On the Evening of Saturday 27th. of June 1970, as a group of Loyalists were returning home to East Belfast from an Orange Order Parade that had been held on the other side of the city, on their return they had to pass by the Short Strand area and then Seaford Street, both being a Catholic strong hold, then they had to make their way past St. Matthews Catholic church, this was a rout they had no option in taking, as it was the only way back to East Belfast from the city. It is said that as they passed Seaford Street a group of Nationalists gathered and angry words were exchanged between Protestants and Catholics, missiles were also thrown between the two. When the group of Orange Men and their followers reached St. Matthews Roman Catholic Chapel on the Newtownards

Road, in the heart of the Protestant East Belfast, they were suddenly fired upon from the grounds of St. Matthews Catholic Church by P.I.R.A. gun-men, who had taken up sniper positions within the grounds of the Church, killing two Protestants in the crowd. As the Loyalists scattered taking cover anywhere they could a group of armed Loyalists Para-Militaries, U.V.F. Men, arrived on the scene and returned fire. This gun-battle was to last for over five hours. All in all two Protestants and one Catholic were killed that night and several more wounded.

Following the events of this night the Protestants of East Belfast regarded the Catholic Enclave of the Short Strand as a danger to their very lives.

(From that day on the situation in Ulster worsened over the next two years.)

The Civil Rights Movement continued to gain momentum, as did the sectarian violence. Further marches were organised in Londonderry and Belfast, but the defining moment came in Londonderry on the 30th. of January 1972.

(Later to become known as Bloody Sunday,)

When confronted by a Nationalist Civil Rights March that had been banned by the Government, British Para troops, in an attempt to halt the match, open fire on the marchers, killing thirteen people and wounding many others, again all seen worldwide on television. After this the British Government decides that Stormont, the Northern Ireland Parliament, which had run the province for just over half a century, had now lost control of the situation. The Ulster Parliament was then suspended indefinitely. Direct rule from London was imposed on Ulster, under the guidance of a secretary of state for Northern Ireland, who, to the bewilderment of the people of Ulster, would be based at Westminster. But sectarian violence is now endemic throughout Northern Ireland from that point on. The year of 1972, was to prove to be a terrible year in Northern Ireland history, as there were 467, deaths, 321 of them civilians, all due to the troubles.

Connie was now in her seventy-third year, but she remained alert of mind, fit in body and in general good health, her great-grandson Ross was growing by the day and was now seven years old. Connie's grandson Edward was now a consultant surgeon at the royal Victoria Hospital in Belfast, but he remained unmarried, preferring to continue living alone in his large house on the Malone road. Connie's other grandson George was now beginning to be involved in the situation in Belfast, due to his role as a Q.C. for the Belfast C.P.S. George had recently, and successfully, prosecuted two men charged with rioting in Belfast, they were believed to be members of the Provisional I.R.A. although this was never proven. At this time George was advised by the Security Forces to start carrying a gun for his own protection, as the P.I.R.A. would now see him as a legitimate target. George's wife Alison was now expecting their second baby, due to be born in the May of 1973, this was something the Gallagher family was absolutely thrilled about. As the situation in Ulster worsened, Connie slowly began to show an interest in the terrible events that were ravaging the Cities of Belfast and Londonderry. Connie's new found interest in the events of the day, were of course prompted by both her Grand-sons.

Connie could never be accused of being a bigot, yes she was a Protestant and a lifelong church goer, Connie was also someone that throughout her life was loyal to the crown, but she believed totally in religious tolerance. Connie deplored the actions of all paramilitaries throughout Ulster, saying that the violence that they inflicted upon the people of Ulster only served to make victims on both sides of the divide. Connie's annoyance at what was now going on in Ulster reached a height in 1972, when after the Provisional I.R.A. had agreed to a ceasefire which was to last from 26th. of June until the 9th. of July, a British Government delectation, led by William Whitelaw, felt the need to hold secrete talks with a group of Provisional I.R.A. leaders. This group of Paramilitary Leaders included, Gerry Adams and Martin McGuinness. The I.R.A. leaders point blank refused to consider any peace settlement that did not include a commitment to British withdrawal from Northern Ireland, a retreat of all British Army personal back to barracks and the release of all republican prisoners. The British delegation of course refused and the talks ended abruptly. When word of this meeting broke the Loyalist communities throughout Ulster were outraged. By 1974, tit for tat killings were rife all over Ulster. On January the 5th. 1976, an I.R.A. unit in Armagh shot dead ten Protestant building workers at Kingsmills, in reprisal for Ulster Volunteer Force (UVF) killings of six Roman Catholics the previous day. The P. I.R.A. did not officially claim responsibility for the killings, but justified them in a statement on January 17th. 1976, saying...

("The Irish Republican Army has never initiated sectarian killings... (But) if loyalist Elements responsible for over 300 sectarian assassinations in the past four years stop such killing now, then the question of retaliation from whatever source does not arise")

(Earlier in similar incidents, the I.R.A. deliberately killed 91 Protestant Civilians in 1974.)

(Another statement made by the Provisional I.R.A. was that their war was not against the Ulster Unionist population. But was against the British Forces that had occupied Ireland.)

This was yet another statement from the P.I.R.A. that only served to anger the Unionists, as the Provisionals continued to blow up, shoot, maim and kill Protestants in Ulster.

The I.R.A. continued with their campaign of planting bombs all over Ulster, as well as launching murderous attacks on both civilians and the security forces, unspeakable tit for tat reprisals would follow by the Loyalist U.V.F. as a result, killing was tragically becoming a part of Ulster life. Early one Friday evening in July 1976, a British Army foot patrol, consisting of eight soldiers, was monitoring the Divis Flats area at the bottom of the Falls Road, as this area was a well-known P.I.R.A. stronghold and the scene of numerous rioting in the past. Deep in the heart of the back streets of the Divis area a Provisional I.R.A. unit, consisting of six operatives, lay in wait for the army patrol, the P.I.R.A. gun-men were hidden in several small terraced houses on the back streets of the Lower Falls. The gun-men had positioned themselves by opened windows in the front upstairs bedrooms of the houses. This position gave them a commanding view of the street below. The Army patrol rounded a row of terraced houses and proceeded to cross an expanse of wasteland. This was when the army patrol were at their most vulnerable, as they were now in open ground with little or no cover to speak of. It was when the army patrol had reached the middle of this wasteland, that the P.I.R.A. unit opened fire on them. The army officer ordered his men to find cover and return fire, but by this time, two British soldiers had been seriously wounding.

A short but fierce gun battle fallowed, lasting eight to ten minutes. This short gun battle wasn't unusual, as it was a tactic often used by the P.I.R.A. They found it easy to lay in wait and then ambush an army patrol, then after a short fire fight, make a quick withdrawal. Unfortunately for the P.I.R.A. unit, the British army officer hadn't read the script, as he ordered his men to give chase, killing one of the gun-men and wounding two others, as they tried to make good their escape. It wasn't long before army reinforcements arrived on the scene, but the P.I.R.A. gun-men had made their escape through the maze of back streets and back entries that littered the whole area. The fact that the local residents had opened the front and back doors of their houses, allowing the P.I.R.A. unit to move quickly from one street to another. The two wounded gun-men escaped with the rest of the unit, but the dead gun-man was left lying where he fell in the middle of the road. The Army were unable to pursue the P.I.R.A. unit, as countless numbers of youths blocked the streets and bombarded the army patrol with missiles of all kinds, this too was a typical P.I.R.A. tactic.

Later that evening Edward had been working late at the Hospital, it was just after eight-thirty and Edward, along with three nurses were standing chatting in the A. & E. department. Suddenly a loud disturbance could be heard coming from the far end of the corridor. Edward turned to see mayhem erupting before his eyes, nurses were screaming and running in all directions, Edward then saw two armed masked men advancing up the corridor at speed. Their behaviour was erratic and seemed disorganised, one of the gunmen was shouting loudly for everybody to get out of their way. When they reached the nurses station where Edward was standing chatting with the nurses, the gunmen stopped.

"Are you a fucking doctor?" one of them yelled at Edward.

"I am a surgeon." replied Edward nervously.

One of the gunmen then pointed his revolver at Edward and screamed loudly...

"We have two wounded colleagues and we need a fucking doctor quickly, so gather whatever it is you need, because you are coming with us Doc."

Fear was quickly setting in with the young nurses and they were in danger of forcing one of the gunmen to do something that would have disastrous results, because the gunmen themselves were not showing the most stable of behaviour. Edward told the nurses to be calm and not to panic, telling them that everything was going to be all right. Edward then instructed the nurses to gather everything that he would need to tend to a gunshot victim. Within a few minutes the nurses had filled a doctor's bag, with bandages, medicines, antibiotics and various other equipment that Edward would need.

"Is that it?" yelled the gunmen, as the nurses handed over a bag to Edward.

"I think we have everything we need now," said Edward, noticing that the gunmen were getting really nervous.

"Listen to me," said Edward, "please don't do anything stupid, I'm coming with you, so there is no need for anyone to get hurt here."

One gunman, the one that was doing all of the shouting, suddenly grabbed Edward by the arm and began to pull him down the corridor, then he stopped and turned to one of the other gunmen and said,

"Bring one of them fucking nurses as well, we might need her."

"No we won't need a nurse, leave her here," shouted Edward.

"I give the fucking orders here, not you, Doc, ok? snarled the gunman.

Edward, along with a young nurse, whose name was Jill, were roughly dragged from the hospital and bungled into a waiting car, which drove off at speed.

The hospital instantly informed the R.U.C. of the armed abduction of Edward and the young nurse, sparking several army patrols, along with a fleet of armoured Police Land Rovers filled with armed R.U.C. officers, being dispatched to the Lower Falls, (Divis flats) area of Belfast in search of the seized doctor and nurse. It was just after nine o'clock in the evening when Edward and Nurse Jill were ushered into a small terraced house on the lower Falls. The house looked as though it was uninhabited, as the windows were blocked out with whitewash, the inside was sparsely furnished, consisting of only two well-worn old armchairs. There were no carpets on the floor and the interior was undecorated, dusty and unkempt. Edward realised immediately that this house was, what was known as, a safe house, used by the P.I.R.A. Both Edward and the young nurse were rushed up the stairs and into the front bedroom, the rooms two windows were also whitewashed, with a small peep hole in the centre of each. A further two gunmen watched the street below from the two windows in the small room, a third stood by the door watching the stairs and entrance to the house.

The small bedroom, housing the two wounded men, consisted only of a double bed covered only with a blood-stained sheet. The two wounded men were stretched out on top of the bed, both bleeding from the wounds they had sustained earlier in the gun battle with the army. The thing that worried Edward the most as he entered the room, was that the gunmen had now removed their masks revealing their identities.

"Fucking hurry it, Doc, you need to save them both, and fucking quickly, understand me Doc? screamed the first gunman loudly.

Edward and the young Nurse began to attend to the gunshot wounds the two men on the bed had received. The first job was to clean the wounds. Luckily both men had only been shot the once, the first man wasn't too seriously injured, he had been shot in the shoulder, easy enough to tend to. The second man was more of a problem, as he had been shot in the gut. It transpired that the more seriously injured man was in fact the brother of the gunman with the big mouth. Edward and the nurse worked tirelessly until the early hour of the morning, removing the bullets from both men and stitching their wounds, before administering strong antibiotics and injecting pain killers.

As the dawn broke two further men entered the house, these two men turned out to be P.I.R.A. West Belfast Brigade Commanders and they weren't best pleased to see Edward and the nurse attending to the wounded men. The two Commanders ordered two of the gunmen out of the room onto the landing, where a bitter argument took place between them. Edward overheard one of the Commanders, a big man, well over six foot tall and strongly built, he was furiously arguing with the big-mouth. It seems that the Commander was fuming that they had brought Edward and the nurse to the safe house. In his opinion the wounded men should have been left outside the hospital, not brought back to the house. The Commander seemed more concerned that both Edward and the nurse now knew, not only the existence of the safe house, but also the identity of at least six P.I.R.A. activists. Things then turned very worrying.

As Edward overheard the Commander ordering the wounded man's brother, the big-mouth, that it was up to him to bring this fuck-up that he had stupidly created, to a satisfactory conclusion. Needless to say this last statement by the Commander left Edward in no doubt what was going to happen to the young nurse and himself. Edward could see that the young nurse was becoming anxious about the situation that they found themselves in. Edward tried to calm her, by telling her that she had no need to worry as they would soon be released.

As the time approached seven thirty in the morning, both Commanders left the safe house. The not so badly injured gunman, was now sitting up in the bed and feeling stronger. Edward noticed that he was in deep conversation with the other P.I.R.A. men. As for the other, more seriously, wounded gunman, well he was now conscious and talking to his brother. Although this second gunman was talking, he was still very weak and in considerable pain, leading Edward to insisted that he remained lying flat on his back. Edward checked once more on both wounded men, then satisfied that he had done all that he could for them, he moved forward to the centre of the room and said,

"There's nothing more we can do for them now, it's just a matter of time, but I suggest that you get a doctor to check on them in a weeks' time and get someone to change their dressings daily."

"Okay then, Doc," mumbled the first gunman sheepishly.

"Then it's time for you both to go," he added, trying his best to avoid eye contact with either Edward or the young nurse.

"Look," said Edward, "Just let us go, we did everything you asked us to do and both your friends will be okay, just let us go, please."

The gunman didn't answer, he just pushed Edward towards the door.

As Edward, the nurse and three of the gunmen walked through the door of the small terraced house into the bright fresh morning air, Edward sensed that all was not well for the future of Jill and himself. None of the gunmen spoke a word, instead they bundled both Jill and Edward into a car that was waiting outside the small terraced house and they were driven off at speed.

After a short drive lasting no more than 5 to 6 minutes the car pulled to an abrupt halt. Edward and Nurse Jill were dragged from the car and marched down the road towards the main thoroughfare in front of the Divis Flats. As the group rounded a corner, they were confronted by an army foot patrol at the far end of a short street, no more than thirty yards away. The army foot patrol instantly took cover, some diving behind several parked cars, others positioning themselves behind the gable end of a row of terraced houses. The P.I.R.A. gunmen, who were once again masked, shielded themselves behind Edward and Nurse Jill, as they moved back behind the houses that they had just rounded. The army captain instantly realised that this was the missing doctor and Nurse.

"Let the doctor and the nurse go!" ordered the army Captain.

"What happens to us if we do?" screamed the gunman who previously been making the most Noise.

"All we want is the safe return of the doctor and the nurse,"
answered the army Captain.

"Yeah, fucking right, Brit, and when we let them go, you are simply just going to let us walk away?"

"You have my word on that, all we want is the safe return of the doctor and the nurse," repeated the army Captain.

"Wait one minute then," the gunman.

A conversation took place between the P.I.R.A. men, because they knew that the army officer would have already radioed their position and would have asked for back up.

"Are you and the nurse okay, Doctor?" shouted the army Captain.

"We're both fine," replied Edward nervously.

Again the army Captain shouted out his request.

"Just let the doctor and the nurse start walking towards us and we can end this here and now, no need for anyone to get hurt here today."

"Okay Doc, take the nurse with you and start walking towards the army officer, nice and slow, okay Doc?" ordered one of the gunmen.

"You're really going to let us go?" asked Jill nervously.

"No choice girl, not now the fucking Brits are here!'" snarled the gunman.

"You're doing the right thing, no need to make things worse," said Edward.

With a hefty push from P.I.R.A. man, Edward and Nurse Jill were on their way to freedom. Edward took hold of Jill's hand in an attempt to calm her. Both Edward and Jill began walking slowly towards the army patrol.

"That's good, Doctor, just keep coming, nice and steady, "instructed the army Captain.

Edward and Nurse Jill continued walking gingerly along the road towards the army patrol. Edward was still holding nurse Jill's hand tightly, as she was now shaking furiously with fear,

"Nice and easy, Jill," said Edward,"we are almost there, just a few more steps Jill.

Jill began to relax and she smiled at Edward and said,

"We are really going to make it, aren't we, Mr Gallagher?"

The army patrol was now no more than ten foot away.

Edward smiled back at Nurse Jill and said,

"We…

But before he could finish what he was about to say, suddenly two loud shots rang out from behind Edward and Jill. In an instant both Edward and Nurse Jill fell to the ground with blood gushing from the backs of their heads. The P.I.R.A. gunmen had fired both lethal shots. The P.I.R.A. men had used this confusion in order to make good their escape, knowing that the Brits would be more concerned with attending to the Doc. and the nurse than following them.

Immediately on hearing the shots and seeing Edward and the nurse fall to the ground, the army patrol opened fire on the P.I.R.A. gunmen, but it was all in vain, as they had fled the scene within seconds after they had fired the shots that killed Edward and Jill. The army patrol advanced, but the P.I.R.A. gun-men were long gone like thieves in the night into the maze of back streets of the lower Falls, that were filled with willing helpers. As if by magic the streets around the Divis Flats area, even at this early time of the morning, were suddenly bursting with angry youths, all shouting abuse and throwing missiles at the army patrol, preventing the Captain and his men from pursuing the P.I.R.A. gunmen. The army patrol was subjected to this, verbal, as well as physical, attack for over fifteen minutes before back up arrived in the form of four R.U.C. (Royal Ulster Constabulary.) Black Maria's, filled with heavily armed police officers. The arrival upon the scene of the R.U.C. sparked something of a scramble by the rioting youths, resulting in this vicious mob vanishing just as quickly as they had assembled.

Once the area had been brought under the control of the R.U.C. and they had deemed that it was now sake to recover the bodies of Edward and Jill, two ambulance crews, accompanied by the army Captain and three R.U.C. officers, advanced slowly towards the slumped motionless bodies Edward and Jill. But as they were approaching the bodies, a strange thing happened, several elderly ladies appeared in the street and walked to where Edward and Jill's bodies were lying and covered them with blankets.

"Thank you very much for your kindness. I know that what you have just done, can't have been an easy thing for you to do," said the army Captain,

One of the elderly ladies turned to the army officer and said,

"What has happened here this day is a shame, we have no fight with doctors and nurses, but they just seem to have gotten in the way of our fight against you Brits."

With those words now said the group of elderly ladies disappeared back into their small terraced houses.

Later that afternoon at around one thirty, Alison was in the kitchen making a pot of tea for herself and Connie, who was in the garden playing with her two great grandchildren, Ross, who was now eleven years old, and his little sister Molly, now aged three years. As Alison was leaving the kitchen carrying the tray of tea, she heard three firm raps on the front door. Placing the tray of tea on a small hallway table, she rushed to see who it was knocking on the door. Alison opened the door to see two tall well-built men in smart suits standing there.

"Can I help you, gentlemen?" enquired Alison.

"Does George Gallagher live here madam?" asked one of the men.

"Well yes, George is my husband, do you have business with him?" asked Alison.

"Allow us to introduce ourselves madam," said one of the men.

"My name is Captain Johnson and this is Sergeant Woods, we are with the Anti-Terrorist Squad. We would like to speak with your husband George Gallagher if we could please?" said Captain Johnson.

Alison was now somewhat shocked when she had discovered who the two unexpected visitors were.

"Is there something wrong?" she asked worriedly, "You see my husband is involved in some high security cases involving the P.I.R.A. Please don't tell me that they are targeting my George."

"No ma'am, it's not your husband that has brought us here. It's his brother, Edward,." said Captain Johnson.

"Oh. Right, then you best come in." said Alison, fearing the worst. "Is Edward all right, please say that nothing has happened to him?" asked Alison, as she moved to one side allowing the two Anti-Terrorist officers into the house.

Alison showed the officers into the front sitting room.

"Please sit down," she said, would you like some tea, I have just made a fresh pot?"

The two officers thanked Alison and said that a cup of tea would be most welcome.

Alison told the officers that she was expecting her husband home any minute, as he had just gone to the newsagents.

"In that case we will wait for him," said Captain Johnson.

Alison left the sitting room to fetch the tea and that's when George returned home.

Alison met her husband in the hallway as she was returning with the tea. She explained to her husband that two Anti-terrorist officers were in the sitting room and that they wanted to talk to him about Edward. George's expression changed, because he knew that something had gone horribly wrong. George opened the sitting room door, allowing his wife to enter with the tray of tea and he followed directly behind her into the sitting room.

"Good afternoon, gentlemen, my wife tells me you are here about my brother, Edward, has something happened to him?" asked George nervously.

Once again Captain Johnson introduced himself and Sergeant Woods to George.

George smiled, saying.

"Your names have crossed my desk on several occasions gentlemen,

"Please tell me if my brother is all right?" asked George nervously.

"I'm afraid to say that there's was an incident involving your brother in the early hours of the morning, Mr Gallagher," said Captain Johnson.

"Tell me please, what has happened to my brother, Captain Johnson."

"I think it best that you take a seat, Sir," suggested Captain Johnson.

George sat down in an armchair by the window. Alison gave everyone a cup of tea before leaving the sitting room and taking Connie's tea to her in the garden.

Once Alison had left the sitting room, Captain Johnson then proceeded to inform George of his Brother Edward's abduction from the hospital, along with a young nurse called Jill and the subsequent murder of both of them by the Provisional I.R.A on the lower Falls earlier that morning. This dreadful news was a devastating blow to George, as he and Edward were very, very close. George sat in his armchair for several long seconds without saying a word and then he said,

"My God, where will this all end?"

That's the question we all ask ourselves every day, Mr Gallagher," said Captain Johnson.

"How am I going to tell Granny, this horrible news could kill her!" said George worriedly.

"Is there anything we can do for you and your family, Mr Gallagher?" asked Captain Johnson.

George looked at both Captain Johnson and Sergeant Woods and said softly,

"No, nothing, thank you. I just need a minute before I have to tell Grandma this horrendous news, he said.

Now that Captain Johnson had delivered and explained in full, the horrific details of what had happened to Edward and Jill, the two officers left the Gallagher's house, leaving George alone in the sitting room. George sat in silence for several long agonising minutes, pondering just how he was going to tell his grandma the deeply disturbing and unpleasant news of Edward's death.

CHAPTER 26

George got to his feet and walked slowly into the garden, his grandmother was relaxing in a colourful wooden deck chair, under the shade of several large trees which stood tall at the far end of the garden. Alison, who was sitting next to Connie, could tell by her husband's face, as he approached, that all was not well. Instantly Alison jumped to her feet, gathered her children around her and headed back towards the house, leaving husband, George alone to talk with his grandmother.

"What is it, George?" asked Connie sheepishly, sensing that something was very wrong. "I am aware that we have just had visitors, George and by the look on your face it's not good news, would I be right, George?"

"I'm so sorry that I have to tell you this, Grandma, but I'm afraid it isn't good news at all, in fact it's the worst news possible, Grandma, "replied George.

"Sit here beside me, George," said Connie. "Now, please just tell me what has happened. I'm too old to play games, George."

George sat down beside his grandmother and took hold of her hand and with a heavy heart he told her of the terrible abduction and murder of her grandson, Edward by the Provisional I.R.A. Connie sat back in her deck chair, her eyes firmly closed and her hand tightened in George's hand.

"Are you okay, Granny, do you want anything?" asked George.

"Nothing George, just leave me here in the garden by myself, I want to be alone, please George, if you don't mind, son?"

George gently kissed the back of his grandma's hand, before leaving her alone sitting quietly in the garden. Connie shut her eyes and whispered softly,

"I know that you must have a reason for what has happened to me over the years. But Lord, all I asked of you was to allow me to go before either of my grandsons. Were you not listening that day, my Lord? Now I have but one grandson and two great-grandchildren left, if anyone has to go Lord, let it be me."

Connie simply sat alone in the garden with her eyes firmly closed for almost three hours. Due to the manner in which Edward had been killed, the authorities did not release Edward's body to his family for five days, Edward's funeral took place one week to the day he was murdered by the P.I.R.A. Edward's funeral service took place at St. Mark's church. his body being laid to rest at Roselawn Cemetery, close to where his grandfather Bobby was buried.

Whether it was by design or just a coincidence, no one really knows for sure, but on the evening of Edward's funeral, a news bullion on the television announced that a man's dead body had been dumped outside the R.U.C. station on the Newtownards road. This body was draped with the Tricolour, (The flag of the Republic of Ireland.) The dead man's face was clad with a black ski-mask, a trade-mark item worn by the P.I.R.A. Resting on his chest, on top of a sheet of paper, was a revolver, minus the bullets. The message written on the sheet of paper read as this.

(We the P.I.R.A. take no pleasure in the deaths of Edward Gallagher, Surgeon, nor Jill Jacks, Nurse. Our deepest sympathies go to the families of both Edward Gallagher and Jill Jacks.)

Following forensic examination on the revolver that had been found on the dead man's person, it was proved that the revolver was the same gun that fired the bullets that killed both Edward and Jill. The dead man was identified as Sean O'Malley, resident of the lower Falls Road. A father of three boys, all under the age of ten years. He was a well-known member of the P.I.R.A. and was thought to have been involved in several murders and shootings that had been carried out in the City.

In the days and weeks that followed Edward's funeral, the situation in Ulster worsened and it seemed to a mournful Connie, that human life in her beloved Ulster was now becoming worthless. When the people of Ulster would open their morning newspapers to read of yet another atrocity had been committed, in either the name of freedom from the oppression of the British by the P.I.R.A. Or it would have been carried out in the defence of their country by the U. V. F. (Ulster Volunteer Force.) No matter which of these two para-military forces carried out these atrocities, the result would be the same, loss of even more lives. This news in the morning newspapers, would not cause as much as a blinked by the readers, it would seem that these outrages had been relegated to nothing more than a short comment during a morning coffee break.

Then something happened that shocked everyone in Ulster. An event that tugged at the heart strings of even the hardest of blackened hearts.

On the Finaghy Road that bright summer's afternoon was a young mother and her four small children. Her name, Anne Maguire, she was pushing a pram containing her young baby son Andrew, aged six-weeks, alongside the pram riding her bicycle, was Anne's daughter Joanne, aged eight, on the other side of the pram was her other son, toddler John, aged two. A few yards further along was Anne's older son, Mark, aged seven. A young family out for a stroll enjoying the afternoon sunshine. When suddenly, and without warning, the car containing the dead I.R.A. man and his comrade swerved wildly out of control and crashed into the family group and then into the railings of St. John the Baptist school. Joanne, aged eight and baby Andrew aged six-weeks were killed instantly. Son John aged two, was pronounced dead in hospital the following day. Anne herself was severely injured, suffering leg and pelvic injuries, she also suffered brain bruising, and was unconscious for days.

When the wreckage, of the car, baby Andrew's pram and little Joanne's bicycle were removed from the crash scene, local residences quickly set up a shrine by the mangled railings of the school, leaving flowers as a mark of respect. To blame either the British army for shooting the speeding driver or to blame the escaping republicans, who were travelling recklessly through a built up area in an attempt to escape the chasing soldiers, for the tragedy, seemed irreverent, as the core reaction of the community was one of pure anguish and sadness at the needless deaths of the young family. Over the next few days, chapels in the area were packed to the doors with people saying prayers, groups of people even stopped and prayed spontaneously at the death site itself, countless local women then took it upon themselves to go from door to door asking residents to sign a petition calling for an end to the violence that was ripping Ulster apart. All over Northern Ireland plans were made for protests against the continuing violence, by paramilitaries on both sides.

After a visit to her house by one of the petitioning neighbours, a woman called Betty Williams rang a local newspaper. The Irish News, she talked to veteran reporter Tom Samways. She gave him her number asking that it be published in the paper, so that anyone who felt as she did should contact her. Meanwhile, Anne Maguire's sister, Mairead Corrigan, having just returned that very evening from her holiday, accompanied her stricken brother-in-law Jackie Maguire, Anne's husband, to the hospital, for the formal identification of his dead children, this was to be one of the sadist sights ever to be seen in Northern Ireland. Afterwards this unwelcomed task had been completed, Mairead Corrigan went down to the television studio and asked to go on the Ulster Television in order to make an appeal for an end to the violence on the streets of Northern Ireland. This appeal moved people around the world, Connie being one of them,

(The appeal was also shown on BBC)

Later Mariread Corrigan contacted Mrs Williams to thank her for her reaction to the news of the death of the children. On Friday the 13th, of

August the Maguire children's funeral took place. Later Ciaran McKeown, who was the N. Ireland correspondent for the Dublin Based Irish Press group, met with Betty Williams and Mairead Corrigan for the first time. Out of this meeting was born the movement to be called the 'Peace People' this movement would later play a part in helping move the Northern Irish people towards a peace process, and eventually the Good Friday Agreement...

The three co-founders of the movement, (Peace People.) Betty Williams, Mairead Corrigan and Journalist, Ciaran McKeown worked endlessly to harness the energy and desire of many people in Northern Ireland for peace...

Ciaran was the one who named the movement, "Peace People", she also wrote the Declaration, and set out its rally programme. The People of Northern Ireland showed their great desire for peace and when thousands marched throughout Northern Ireland as well as in the South of Ireland. Within the first 6 months of its life there was a 70.

Percent drop in the rate of violence and things would never return to the terrible rate of death and destruction experienced in 1976 when it looked like the community was spiralling out of control and tumbling into an all-out civil war.

(Sadly with her mind shattered, and her waking hours haunted by the images of the three children that she would never to see again, this broken woman, Anne Maguire finally took her own life in 1980, after failing to start a new life in New Zealand.)

Connie, after seeing Anne Maguire's sister Mairead's appeal on television the evening of the tragedy, then reading the full horrible story of the tragic deaths of the three children in the newspaper, became involved in the movement called the "Peace People." as she could completely identify with Anne's sister, Mairead, having just suffered the loss of her grandson, Edward to the troubles. Connie now devoted most of her time to the movement as well as supporting it financially. Although the movement was making inroads in its stance against the violence on the streets of Northern Ireland, trouble was still rife through Ulster as the P.I.R.A. continued in their campaign of sectarian violence. The efforts of the "Peace People" movement was recognised in late 1976, when the movement won the Nobel Peace Prize. The "Peace People" had organized large demonstrations calling for an end to paramilitary violence. Sadly though their campaign lost momentum, when after they appealed to the nationalist community to provide the authorities with information on the I.R.A. the (Peace People) were now perceived by the Nationalist communities as being more critical of the Nationalist paramilitaries than of the security forces that, in their eyes, were occupying Ireland.

But make no mistake, the legacy of this Peace Movement went a long way to eventually bringing about place in Ulster.

In the late summer of 1976 Connie's grandson, George, in his role as a Q.C. with the C.P.S., had been a very busy man over the past few years, as he had successfully prosecuted fifteen P.I.R.A. gun-men, sending them to prison for many years. At this point in time George was in the middle of a high profile case, prosecuting two men accused of being P.I.R.A. Brigade Commanders in West Belfast. The Crown Prosecution Service were convinced that these two men had authorized countless civilian murders, as well as causing explosions and organizing attacks on the security services through Ulster. It was now a bright Sunday morning in late September and George was at home relaxing with his family. The breakfast table was in the midst of being cleared and George was talking to his two young children whilst they waited for Connie to ready herself for the family's weekly trip to church. Even all these years later Sunday mornings in the Gallagher household hadn't changed one little bit since Connie had been a little girl. The routine remained the same, everyone up early for breakfast, then on to morning worship at St. Marks's church. This Sunday morning was to be no different.

Connie entered the sitting room and sat down in her favourite armchair. The last of the summer sunshine was bright in the sky, its warming rays bursting through the large window next to Connie's armchair. George, his wife Alison, their son, Ross, now aged eleven and their young daughter, Molly, now aged three, were all ready to leave for church. Connie remained sitting by the window gazing out into the gardens outside.

"Are you almost ready to go, Granny?" asked George.

Connie was now Eighty-Six years old, but still very fit and in good health as a rule.

Normally Connie would be the first one in the household to be ready to leave for church on Sunday morning. It would seem that today was to be different as on this occasion Connie was feeling rather tired and a little unwell with a stomach upset. She had missed breakfast, which in itself was unusual, as she was a great believer that everyone should start the day with a good breakfast. Today though, Connie made do with just a cup of hot sweet tea for breakfast. As the rest of the family were almost ready to leave for church, Connie began to make her way down the stairs. Still dressed in her dressing-gown, Connie wanted to inform the family that she didn't feel well enough to go to church on this occasion, but had come to see them off.

"Are you not feeling very well, Grandma?" asked George.

"I'm just feeling a little tired, George, nothing to be concerned about," said Connie.

"You all go on to church without me today, I'll be fine here until you all return home," she added.

"Are you sure, Grandma?" asked George.

"Yes George I'm fine, now go!" insisted Connie.

George was a little concerned about the health of his grandma, but he also knew that to push the point with her would be a rather pointless thing to do. George ushered his family out onto the driveway where his car was waiting. Suddenly young Molly stopped and turned back towards her great grandma and said,

"Will you watch us go from the window Nanna as we leave for church? I want to wave goodbye to you from the car."

Connie smiled at little Molly and replied,

"Of course I will my little darling."

Connie moved gingerly to the window and pulled back the curtain, allowing her to see George's car in the driveway.

George opened the back door to his car allowing Ross then Molly to clamber inside. His wife, Alison was already sitting in the passenger seat. With every one now settled in the car, George climbed into the driver's seat ready for the off. George gave Connie a short wave, but young Molly, who was on her knees on the back seat of the car, was waving furiously with both hands to her great Grandma. Connie smiled at young Molly as she waved back, George turned once more towards the house to wave goodbye to his Grandmother as he put the key into the ignition.

Connie smiled lovingly out of the window at the young family grouped together in the car ready for church. Young Molly was still waving furiously through the back window of the car at her great grandma. She was also shouting something, but Connie couldn't quite make out what she was saying. Then without any warning what so ever, a deafening, stomach-wrenching blast erupted on the driveway. The blast turned George's car into a raging inferno, an unserviceable fireball that was so fierce that it shattered the windows at the front of the house. The small trees and scrubs that decorated the front garden, now lay flattened in a smouldering heap. George's car had been transformed into knotted mass of burning metal. The blast was so strong that it knocked Connie of her feet as splinters from the shattered windows made several cuts to Connie's face and arms. Connie now lay unconscious on the sitting room floor. Within seconds of the explosion a crowd had gathered in the road outside Connie's house.

Two men from the neighbourhood rushed past the mangled wreckage of George's car which was blacking the driveway and burst into Connie's house looking for any survivors. Within a few short minutes both men emerged from Connie's house, one of the men holding the frail unconscious and bleeding figure of Connie in his arms. Connie was rushed to the safety of Dr Philpot's house but a few doors away. There her wounds were attended to by Dr Philpot, luckily Connie only sustained several small cuts and bruises. Connie remained at Dr Philpot's house until an ambulance arrived to take her to the hospital.

The scene outside Connie's house was quickly becoming chaotic, and tempers were close to boiling over once the word was out that George, his wife, Alison and the two children, Ross and Molly were in the car when it was blown up. Within ten minutes of the explosion, the army, the R.U.C. the fire brigade and several ambulances had arrived on the scene. Once the burning remains of George's car had been extinguished, the task of removing the wreckage from the driveway could take place, in order for forensic examination. Sadly there was little left of George and his family that could be identified!

Connie had been taken to hospital where she remained for a full week before returning home. A traumatic funeral service for George's family was held at St. Mark's Church a week later. What was left of the young family was laid to rest at Roselawn Cemetery, close to the graves of George's brother, Edward and their grandfather, Bobby. In the weeks that followed, Connie felt that she could no longer carry on living in the house on Martinez Ave and so the house was sold and Connie moved to a smaller, yet stylish, three bed-roomed detached house on Cyprus Avenue, yet another very fashionable and wealthy area of East Belfast. A week after the funeral of George Gallagher and his young family and whilst the hurt and heartache of the terrible ordeal was still fresh in both Connie's mind and heart. Something happened that almost caused Connie to have a breakdown. A thoughtless, heartless statement was released to both the television and the newspapers by the high command of the Provisional I. R. A. in Dublin. This statement read…

(The Provisional I.R.A. were responsible for the car bomb which was detonated on Martinez Ave. on Sunday the 20th. of September. This was carried out because of Mr George Gallagher's involvement with the British Crown and his subsequent work on behalf of the British Crown against the P.I.R.A. We, The High Command of the P.I.R.A. considered Mr George Gallagher to be a legitimate target. We do regret the deaths of his family, but we do take the view that people who attach themselves to agents of the British Crown and benefit from such attachments, undoubtedly make themselves legitimate targets.)

This statement from the P.I.R.A. only succeeded in adding even more torment to Connie's life, as she struggled to come to terms with this despicable act of inhumane horror. Connie's every waking hour was now haunted by the image of young Molly waving to her from the back of her daddy's car.

Several months of deep mourning had now passed and Connie, although never fully getting over this latest horror that had been inflicted upon her family, began to look for ways to stop this terrible violence that now gripped Ulster.

Using her wealth, she set up several schemes and initiatives throughout the city in an attempt to help those who were suffering as a result of the violence in Ulster, be they Loyalists or Nationalists. Connie realized that there must be so many more families in the City of Belfast that have suffered and lost loved ones to the violence that now gripped Ulster. The decade ended in tragedy in terms of the loss of human lives, when there was a double attack by the P.I.R.A. against the British. First to be attacked, on the 27th. of August 1979, was Lord Mountbatten of Burma, a member of the British Royal Family. Lord Mountbatten was the great grandson of Queen Victoria, the attack took place whilst he was on holiday with his family in Mullaghmore, Co. Sligo, in the Republic of Ireland, a place he had visited on many occasions. The P.I.R.A. had planted a bomb on board Lord Mountbatten's boat. Three other people who were on board the boat were also killed along with Lord Mountbatten in the explosion. Including a local teenage boatman who was in the employ of Lord Mountbatten. The second attack came on the very same afternoon, when eighteen soldiers, mostly members of the Parachute Regiment, were killed by two remote-controlled bombs at Warrenpoint, in County Down.

In response to the continued Provisional I.R.A. campaign of violence both in Ulster and also on the English main land, in the mid to the late 1980's loyalist paramilitaries, including the Ulster Volunteer Force, the Ulster Defence Association and the Ulster Resistance, began to import arms and explosives from South Africa. The weapons obtained were divided between the U.D.A. the U.V.F. and Ulster Resistance, this led to an escalation in the assassination of Roman Catholics throughout Ulster. These killings were said to be in response to the 1985. Anglo Irish Agreement which gave the government of the Irish Republic, a "Consultative Role" in the internal government of Northern Ireland. In opposition to this agreement, an estimated 200, thousands Ulster Unionists gathered outside the Belfast City Hall to cheer the Reverend Ian Paisley's famous 'No Surrender' speech against the Anglo Irish agreement signed by British Prime Minister Margaret Thatcher and the Irish Taoiseach, Garret FitzGerald.

After the tragic car bombing of Connie's grandson and his family outside her house in 1976, Connie had entered into a self-motivated and totally self-financing campaign of trying to help families that had been affected by the violence carried out by the Paramilitaries on both sides. Connie had set up several drop-in centres in the city, staffing them with highly trained and willing professional people, such as solicitors, councillors and financial experts, all providing help in areas that were sorely needed. Advice in how to escape the persecution of the paramilitaries that gripped certain areas of the city, was freely available. Help in moving house, sometimes setting up the exchanging of houses between Catholics living in, or near Loyalists areas with Protestants living in, or near Republican areas, also economical help could be offered, these centres were opened to all no matter what their religious or political persuasion happened to be. It has to be said that these centres proved to be a huge success over the years, helping countless numbers of Belfast citizens.

As the decade of the 1980's was drawing to an end and the situation in the City of Belfast was becoming even more depressing by the day. Connie, now in her late eighties, remained alert of mind, strong and fit of body, light of foot and more then capable of looking after herself in every aspect of her everyday life. Health wise, Connie had really only the one problem and that was her hearing as, sadly to say, it had been deteriorating for some time. In normal conversation, Connie now found it difficult to follow everything that was being said, unless it was being said in a high volume. Most of the people that Connie had around her, realized her problem and always spoke that little bit louder when in conversation with her.

Despite Connie's advancing years, in the late 1980's Connie decided to embark upon a mission to try and help the youth of the city because in Connie's opinion they had been neglected by the authorities and left alone and vulnerable to influences of the paramilitaries for far too long. Connie's idea was that if she could keep the youth off the streets and away from the clutches of the likes of the I.R.A. and the Provisional I.R.A. in Nationalist areas and the U.V.F and the U.D.A. in Loyalist areas, then these kids just might have a chance of a better way of life. Connie's idea was to try to keep the youths of the City, both boys and girls, occupied with useful activities, such as football, rugby, boxing, swimming, athletics, netball and hockey. In the case of kids from Nationalist areas, Irish sports were also to be included, sports such as Gaelic football and hurling.

Connie also wanted the youth of the City to have the chance to experience and explore all the pleasures of music, be it classical, traditional folk or rock and pop.

Alongside music, there was also the arts to be considered, there was the theatre, dance, in all of its forms and of course there was painting and the old Masters to be discovered. There was so much that most of the Children of the City had missed out on because of, what had become known as the "Troubles." Connie realized that for young people to move around the City would be madness, a strange face seen in the wrong place could mean a severe beating, or even death. Connie's first task was to employ several experienced youth leaders from across the Religious divide, their mission was to convince youth club leaders throughout the City to join in and embrace her project.

Connie was well aware that this was not going to be easy, but she believed deeply that in the end, her idea would bear fruit.

By the March of 1990, Connie's vision for fully filled and functioning youth and sports clubs had come to fruition. Many of the clubs now played the different sports against each other, creating the competitive, yet friendly aspect that the boys and girls seemed to like. As time went by, Connie wanted clubs in

Nationalist areas, to play against clubs from Loyalist areas and so these matches were introduced, without any animosity taking place it has to be said. This more than anything pleased Connie no end, Connie always had the belief that given the chance, kids from across the great divide, could live and play together. Most of the girls preferred to take part in the music, dance and Theatre activities, a few boys also signed up for these activities, but not in any great Numbers it has to be said.

On several occasions girls from different clubs would merge together to put on performances in music and dance, as well as dramatic plays. These events helped with the financial running of the clubs, as a small fee would be charged on entry. As time went by funding for these youth clubs became a little easier to obtain, as local businesses began to get involved more and more, because they could see the benefits of these clubs working together. Business sponsorship aside, there were still occasions when Connie had to help the finances along a little, but she considered every one of her donations well worth it. The pleasure Connie got from seeing the smiles on the faces of the youths of Belfast, when one of their dramas, or one of their music concerts had proved to be a success. Knowing that these young people were succeeding, when the adults of the City had failed.

As the 1980's drifted into the 1990's, once again feelings were running high in the City of Belfast, both in the Loyalist and Nationalist communities. There just seemed to be no end to their hatred for one another, causing the situation to disastrously spiralling out of control. As Ulster entered into the new decade of the 1990s, both the loyalist and republican paramilitaries in the City of Belfast began to increase their violence towards each other, more attacks and more killings followed. A new kind of target was now emerging, these targets were named by both the P.I.R.A. and the U.V.F. as,

(Enemy Civilians, or, to you and me, innocent bystanders.)

A cycle of killing continued over the next few years, one slaughter followed another, in fact this excessive round of sectarian violence continued right up to the P.I.R.A. called a ceasefire in the August of 1994. This act of sanity was followed by the Combined Loyalist Military Command declaring a cessation of military action only six weeks later. Before this glimmer of hope for the future had raised its head above the parapets in 1994. many atrocities had taken place, the most horrific single attack to be perpetrated in these black days in Ulster, came in the October of 1993, when the P.I.R.A. planted a bomb in a fish shop on the Protestant Shankill Road area of Belfast. This bomb was planted in an attempt to kill the U.D.A. leadership. But this Shankill Road bombing by the P.I.R.A. only succeeded in killing nine innocent Protestant shoppers, as well as one of the bombers.

In the September of 1994 Connie was approaching her ninety fifth birthday, sadly her situation was about to changed drastically, turning her life upside down, in a way she could never have envisaged. As Connie sat in her sitting room early one Tuesday morning opening her mail. Connie's attention was drawn to one particular latter. On the top right hand side of the envelope was the crest of her bank. Connie had received a letter from her bank manager. The letter was a request asking Connie if she could make the time to come and see him at ten thirty on the following Friday afternoon. On the following Friday afternoon Connie set off for her meeting with her bank manager. This meeting brought the most devastating news imaginable to Connie. It would seem that due to all of Connie's good works and projects that she had undertaken over the years, was now finally taking its toll on Connie's finances. The bank manager informed Connie that as from that day she was now bankrupt. Sadly this devastating news was not the end of Connie's troubles. The bank manager also informed Connie that the bank had covered a large bill that they had received for work carried out on two youth clubs that Connie had set up. This bill was for one hundred thousand pounds, a sum which needed to be repaid as soon as possible. It would seem that Connie's youth project proved to be the last straw, as it had eventually bankrupted her. Connie was left with no choice but to sell her detached house on Cyprus Ave. in order to repay the bank and buy a much smaller house in which to end her days.

So it was in the October of 1994 that Connie moved to a small two-up-two-down terraced house on Wolf Street on the Newtownards Rd. Wolf Street was situated on the edge of the Loyalist working class area of East Belfast and adjacent to the notorious Nationalist Seaford St. and Short Strand area. Connie remained hopeful for the future of Ulster and all who lived in it. Not once did Connie feel bitter in the slightest about the situation in which she now found herself. In fact when asked by the bank manager if she now regretted flittering away her fortune on the many youth projects that she had started in recent years, Connie gave the bank manager a long disapproving stare, then she told him in a manner that sat him back in his seat. One, I did not flitter away my fortune as you so foolishly said, I used it to help those that need help, and two, if my youth projects saved only one young person from the evil clutches of the God-forsaken Paramilitaries, then every penny I spent was worth it. So my answer to you is, regrets, No, not in the slightest and given the chance I would do it all again. Connie got to her feet and marched proudly from the bank manager's office.

In time Connie settled into her new surroundings and life took on a much slower pace as Connie didn't have the same responsibility of the many projects she once had to fill her day. Something that Connie was going to have to get used to is the fact that she now had neighbours on both sides of her new, but small terraced house. This was a new and strange experience for Connie, as never before had she lived so close to other people. This was something that proved to be a blessing, because Connie's health had begun to decline and she found getting around under her own steam much more difficult than it used to be. Connie found the working class people of East Belfast that now surrounded her to be the most friendly and caring and considerate people she had ever met. Not a day went by that one or another of her neighbours failed to call in to see if she was okay, or if she needed anything from the shops. Connie now lived her life in total anonymity, because not one of her neighbours ever realized who she really was.

CHAPTER 27

By the summer of 1995, Connie had past her ninety sixth birthday and her body was weakening as the years passed. Connie now had real difficulty remaining steady on her feet, but her mind was still as bright and alert as it always had been. One summer afternoon Connie was relaxing in a white plastic garden chair outside the front door of her house on Wolf Street. She was enjoying the afternoon sunshine when a middle-aged man approached her.

"Good morning, madam," he said, "Are you Mrs Connie Gallagher?"

Connie looked up at the strange man, then replied,

"Yes I am, but do I know you?"

The strange man smiled at Connie and answered,

"No, you don't know me Mrs Gallagher, but please let me introduce myself to you. My name is Colin Woodard and I am a reporter for the Belfast Telegraph."

Connie extended her hand and shook Mr Woodard's hand.

"Pleased to meet you Mr Woodard, is there something I can do for you?"

Colin Woodard smiled broadly and replied.

"There is that, Mrs Gallagher. I would like your permission to tell the world your life story. I have heard several small parts of it in my work as a reporter and I would like to hear the full and true story from your own lips. If what I hear about your life is only half true, then if has to be put into print, Mrs Gallagher."

"Please call me Connie, and if you think my life story is that interesting, then by all means I will tell it to you," smiled Connie.

Colin Woodard then produced a small hand recorder from his coat pocket and said,

"Shall we begin?"

Connie smiled and said,

I think this conversation would be better continued inside, don't you, Mr Woodard?"

Colin Woodard helped Connie up from her plastic garden chair and they both entered Connie's humble little home.

"Whenever you are ready, Connie," said Colin.

"What would you like to know first, Colin?" asked Connie.

"Well, like I said, I have heard bits and pieces of your story, so maybe we could begin at the very beginning, maybe with your very first memories, Connie? I did hear that you had two sons, are they still alive, Connie?" asked Colin.

Connie smiled at Colin Woodard and said,

"You have been misinformed, Mr Woodard."

"I am sorry, Connie, I really do have to learn to stop trying to put words into people's mouths."

Again Connie simply smiled at Colin Woodard and said,

"I had seven of the most wonderful and beautiful sons any mother could ever wish to have, Colin. Each one of them was a pleasure, all be it a pleasure that was to be short lived, Colin."

"You had seven sons, Connie?" said Colin, "but what do you mean when you say the pleasure was short lived, Connie?"

"We will come to my boys in time, Mr Woodard," she said.

Connie began her story by telling Colin about her mother and father.

"First there was my father, Mr Terrence Kean, a handsome man, everyone said so. But to me he was the most wonderful, kindest father a girl could ever wish for. I remember that in the summer months, that on some Sundays after church, my father would take me to what I thought to be the most beautiful and magical place I have ever known.

That place was Tollymore Forest, a place I came to love for more than one reason. My father was a very successful businessman, but he was an employer that cared deeply for the welfare of his workforce. I remember him telling me on more than one occasion, that they are people, people with families to support, they are not just workers. Every evening when he would return home my eyes would light up at the sight of him coming through the door. No matter how hard a day my father had, there was always a smile and a hug for me the instant he got home. My father, along with my mother, gave me the most wonderful, happy and secure childhood imaginable. When my father died of a heart attack shortly after my thirteenth birthday, I was devastated. It felt that a part of me had died along with him, and only for my mother I am not sure that I would have come to terms with the huge loss that I felt.

My mother, Edwina was a tall slender woman with long silk like hair. She was elegant in her movement and possessed a face so pleasurable to look at, that many a man was stopped in his tracks the moment his eyes would fall upon her. My mother was kind of heart to everyone around her, just as my father was. Only once did I ever hear her speak ill of anyone, but as you will discover, trust me, they both deserved the lash of her tongue. After my father died, my mother devoted her every free minute of her time to my wellbeing, something that made a deep impression on me. It was also something that I hope I had achieved with my own boys. My mother loved my father dearly and after his death she recoiled somewhat within herself, never once did she look at another man. Trust me when I tell you, Colin, she was never short of suitors, but my godfather was able to keep them at bay, at my mother's request.

Then there was Bobby, my beloved Bobby. When I was only ten years old, a woman came to visit my mother. This woman was slim of build, although a little raggedly dressed and by her side was a grubby faced boy with dirt on his knees and on his hands, but from the first instant I set eyes on him, I was gripped by his smile. As I looked in his direction I could see his eyes drop as he began to slowly slink behind the cover of his mother's long flowing dress. Once behind his mother, this ragamuffin of a boy only peeped out to look at me the once and that was only for a few seconds. As it turned out, this lady was at our home to teach me to play the piano. Twice a week, every Tuesday and Thursday afternoons after school she would turn up at our house with this grubby boy by her side. Once my lesson had ended, my mother would sit with her and have tea and a chat, leaving myself and this grubby boy to pass away the time together in the garden. I have to say, that after his second visit, he would now always turn up looking much cleaner that he did in the beginning.

Over the weeks and months, I got to know this shy pleasant looking eleven year old boy really well. I remember he had the biggest and most engaging smile I had ever seen. Twice a week we would play together in the garden. His name was Bobby and as time went by we both became inseparable. I would wait impatiently by the window on the afternoons that he and his mother were due, as I couldn't wait to see him again. By the time I was fourteen I needed no more piano lessons, as I had become something of an accomplished pianist. Luckily for both Bobby and myself, my mother then decided that she too wanted to learn how to play the piano. By the time I was fifteen my mother had ended her piano lessons, but Bobby and I were now close friends and he would still come to my house every day after school to see me. After one hell of a lot of water had passed under one hell of a lot of bridges, Bobby and I were married in the September of 1918.

When my father died, his business partner and best friend, Mr Powell, who was also my godfather, became a huge influence in my life. He looked out for both my mother and myself. Mr Powell had been my father's best man at his wedding to my mother. In the days after my mother was murdered by the I.R.A. and Bobby was away fighting in the first war, I felt very much alone, but Mr Powell made sure that I was never left alone for long. Calling to see me every evening on his way home from the bakery he and my father started years before. Mr Powell also thought highly of Bobby and was instrumental in Bobby asking me to marry him, as you will discover later in my story. Mr Powell never married himself, but he always looked upon me as his own daughter and became like a father to me in the years after both my father and my mother had passed away. I believe that now in these most modern of times that Mr Powell would have been referred to as gay. Although, to the best of my knowledge, he never once entered into any kind of relationships with a man. Mr Powell preferred to live a life of celibacy, sharing his house only with his life-long housekeeper as his preferred company.

But I have to say that I loved my godfather very much and I was devastated when he too met with an untimely end.

On 15th August 1919, our first son was born and we named him Robert after his father. Although he was always known as Wee Bobby, he was a big healthy baby boy when born, with a full head of thick black hair. From an early age we knew he was going to be a single minded young man. When he would set his mind to something, he wouldn't stop until he had completed it. As he began to grow and his personality began to form, we discovered that truth was all important to Wee Bobby. Wee Bobby would be the best friend you could ever wish for, but you only had to cross him the once. Once you crossed the line and disappointed him, you were gone with no way back, no second chances were ever given. Wee Bobby didn't ever forgive dishonesty or deception from his friends and once he had lost your trust, you were finished as far as he was concerned.

On 5th September 1920 I gave birth to identical twin boys, William and Terrence, better known as Billy and Terry. They were the most beautiful baby boys you could ever see, both boys had their father's cheeky smile. From being one year old everyone who saw them would remark upon their devilish smile. As they got older it was obvious to everyone that both boys were full of fun, never wasting a second of their time feeling miserable. People that didn't know them that well, would be taken for a ride at times each boy would pretend to be the other. Leaving whoever was the butt of their joke feeling confused to say the least. But both boys were as honest as the day was long, they would always reveal the prank to their victim in the end. They were two of the kindest, gentlest boys I have ever known. So, so close to each other.

Just over a year later, on 10th November 1921 I gave birth to another baby boy we named Andrew, called Andy by his brothers as they grew up. From being a toddler to growing into a young man, Andy never ever lost his temper. Not even when his older brothers would tease him. I never once saw him get angry about anything, he just accepted whatever came his way and dealt with it in his own way. As the years advanced and he became a teenager, this trait remained part of his makeup, making him a very pleasant boy to be around. Young Andy was at his happiest when he was in my company. As a small child he would always tell me, that when he grew up he was going to marry me, because he loved me so much.

My next child to be born was on the 6th 0f October 1923 and was named Samuel, Sammy to his brothers, Now Sammy could be a miserable child at times, finding fault with almost everything he came across. I must add that he was also a loving child, who loved to be in the company of his brothers, it was just that he never found anything outside of the family good enough. My husband, Bobby use to laugh and say that young Sammy would even find fault with Father Christmas, if he was to ever meet him. The one thing that young Sammy really enjoyed was to go sailing. He loved to be on the water and he found the idea of the wind on his face and the sea beneath him exhilarating. We bought him a small boat that he sailed every chance he got. He would stand in front of myself and his father and say,

I am going to sail around the world one day, you watch if I don't!

Then there was Henry, he was born on 8th November 1924. Harry was a very noisy baby, always wanting out of his pram? Even as a small baby, Harry loved the freedom of being on the floor. From being just over six months old, once young Harry was awake we had to get him out of his pram or cot, whichever he happened to be in at the time. Harry loved the idea of being free, if not, then the noise he would make could raise the dead. Harry always needed to be able to feel his limbs free of restraint and uncovered. As long as these rules were followed, then Harry was a very happy child who was always smiling. As he got older he loved the outdoors and playing sports of all kinds. Harry played both football and rugby for his school. Playing football on Saturday mornings and then rugby on the Saturday afternoon.

My next son to be born was on the 20th December 1925 and his name was Thomas. Again his brothers would shorten his name, so he was always known as Tommy. Tommy would follow his older brothers around all of the time as a child, much to the annoyance of his brothers it has to be said. But by the time he reached the age of ten he had become something of a loner. Harry would sit in his room with his little story books, reading them time after time. As he got older he would take my books, two at a time, to his room and read them from cover to cover. Tommy was never a child for the open air, instead preferring to remain indoors reading his books. All of my boys reached a very high standard of education at school, but Tommy was head and shoulders above all of them. His one ambition in life was to become a school teacher but sadly he never got the chance to fulfil his dream.

I also had the great privilege of raising the identical twin boys. They were the sons of my first born Wee Bobby. The twins were named George and Edward and both boys were scholars from an early age. But unlike young Tommy, both boys were excellent sportsman, representing their school in many different events. But when it came to their future, both boys always knew just what they wanted to do with their lives. From being as young as fourteen, George knew he wanted to be a lawyer and Edward, a surgeon. Both boys were very close to me and both would willingly look after me as I began to get a little older. It was a real pleasure for me to see both of them reach their goals in life. George, his wife Alison and two children lived with me until their tragic deaths in 1976.

Edward lived alone in a large rambling house on the Malone Rd. Sadly, Edward's life also ended in 1976, a few months before the death of his brother George.

I loved all of my sons equally, the happiest time of my life was when I had all my sons around me. When they were with me in my house, it became a home and they brought a joy to my life that I have never experienced since the day I lost them to the war.

Connie suddenly sat forward in her chair and said in a soft gentle voice,

"Shall we have a cup of tea, Colin?"

"Yes, if you wish, Connie?" replied Colin. "Would you like me to make it for you Connie?" added Colin.

"Please, it you would," replied Connie.

Colin returned with the tea and he and Connie continued with their chat for over another hour. Colin could see that Connie was getting tired so he said,

"I shall leave you now, Connie, but may I return tomorrow and talk with you some more?"

"Yes of course you can, Colin, I will look forward to it," answered Connie.

Colin returned many times to Connie's house over the next few months, eager to listen to the rest of her life story. Colin's visit to Connie's house on 18th March 1996 proved to be his very last visit. Connie waited in vain for Colin to return, but he never did, much to her sadness. Connie had come to enjoy Colin's visits and she had become very fond of him, but his non-return left Connie confused. Eventually the mystery of why Colin stopped calling to interview Connie was solved one day in 1999, when two young men arrived at Connie's front door. Their names were Bill Clark and Thomas Westwood. Both boys explained to Connie that Colin had died suddenly and that was the reason that he never returned to visit her again.

Bill Clarke and Thomas Westwood then explained to Connie that they were going to finish Colin's story about her life story. But only if she wanted them to do so. Connie told both the young reporters that she would be delighted for them to complete her life story that Colin had started. Both Thomas and Bill took it in turns to visit Connie and on this occasion it was Thomas Westwood that had come to interview her. In the late afternoon, as Connie and Thomas were deep in conversation, Thomas received a phone call on his mobile phone. This was a call of great importance. It was Thomas's friend, Bill Clarke that had called him to inform him of this breaking news on the radio. Thomas put down his mobile phone and turned to Connie and said,

"You are never going to believe what I have just been told, Connie."

"What is Thomas?" asked Connie curiously.

Thomas sat forward in his chair and said,

"The I.R.A. have just released this statement, Connie."

This statement released by the I.R.A. was regarding, what a lot of people in Ulster consider to be one of the worst and shameful atrocities to be committed in all the years of the Troubles.

Thomas quickly turned Connie's old radio on and they both listened as the I.R.A.'s statement was being read out.

The I.R.A. this day have openly admitted that between the years of 1972 and 1985, that they had kidnaped, murdered and buried sixteen people in a secret location somewhere in the Republic of Ireland. Their crimes, treachery against the Nationalist people of Ireland. These victims were both male and female, fathers, husbands, sons, daughters, wives, and mothers. They were to become known as…

> THE DISAPPEARED
> With the news of the I.R.A.'s statement now released to the
> public, Thomas left Connie's house to return to the newsroom
> at the Belfast Telegraph.

The most shocking episode of all the sixteen kidnaps and subsequent murders of these unfortunate people, was surely the kidnap and murder of Jean McConville. Jean was a Protestant woman from the Loyalist East Belfast area of the City. Jean married a Roman Catholic man and she converted to the Catholic religion. Jean was forced to move from East Belfast by intimidation from the Loyalist community and she went to live with her husband in the Divis Flats, a staunch Republican and I.R.A. stronghold. Jean was the mother of ten children. Sadly, in 1972 her husband Arthur died from Cancer, leaving her to bring up their ten children alone. In the months leading up to her kidnapping, she was forced to withstand a barrage of abuse from her neighbours, who didn't trust her. It was reported on several occasions that she had been attacked in the street by women in the neighbourhood. It was reported that on the 29th November a British Army patrol found her wondering the streets bleeding, bruised and confused.

The army patrol brought her home and put her into her house where her ten children were waiting for her to return home. One of her children claimed that their mother was kidnaped from their home on the following evening, although this date of the kidnapping is in dispute. On the night of her kidnapping, four young women took Jean McConville from her home at gun point, in front of her ten distraught children. Jean was driven to a secret location, a woman named Dolours Price later admitted that she was one of the women involved in the abduction. Jean was taken to this secret location, interrogated, it is believed that she was first tortured, as years later the post-mortem revealed that she had broken bones and mutilated hands. Jean was then shot once in the back of her head, apparently while on her knees. Jean's body was recovered from this secret location many years later.

Searches have been carried out by the Independent Commission for the Location of Victims Remains, which was established in 1999 by a treaty between the British and Irish Governments to obtain information in the strictest confidence, which might lead to the discovery of the location where these missing bodies are buried. Seven of these bodies have to date been confirmed as found, but sadly the others have not as yet.

In the October of 1996, the P.I.R.A. moved their campaign of terror from main lane England back to the streets of Ulster. It didn't take long for the loyalist paramilitaries to respond to the P.I.R.A.'s terror campaign. Once again Ulster was in the grip of the terrorists. In the May of 1997. Tony Blair won the Westminster election, his first act as Prime Minister was to attempt to kick-start the stalled peace process in Northern Ireland. He announces in the June 0f 1996, that talks on the future of the province will begin in September, regardless of whether or not there is a cessation of violence. Adding that Sinn Fein will be welcome to join in the talks six weeks after the P.I.R.A. had declared a new and unequivocal ceasefire.

Fortunately this introduction of a deadline, after which Sinn Fein will be absent from at least part of the talks, proves effective. Then on July 19th, the P.I.R.A. announces a ceasefire to begin on the following day. Resulting in Sinn Fein's participation when the talks begin at Stormont in the September. The Unionist side object and briefly walk out in protest, fortunately sanity prevails and the Unionists return to the talks within a few days. There was to be several setbacks in the peace process over the following months, but Tony Blair's original programme had placed a time limit on the talks, insisting that a package must be agreed by the May of 1998, to be used as the basis for a referendum. - The deadline is met. - In Belfast, on the 10th. of April 1998. (Good Friday), both governments and all the relevant political parties formally agree to the holding of a referendum – along the lines close to those jointly proposed by Blair and Ahern, (the republic's Prime Minister.) The referendum takes place in the May of 1098, and the Good Friday agreement is accepted.

In the July of 1998, the Northern Ireland Assembly meets for the first time at Stormont. Ulster Unionist Leader, David Trimble, is elected First Minister.

But he is unable to form a Cabinet or begin the proper business of Government for over a year. The reason being the long-standing problem of the decommissioning of arms by the P.I.R.A. Unionists insisting that Sinn Fein can in no way be part of the Government until decommissioning had begun. But the P.I.R.A. insist that they will not consider decommissioning until Sinn Fein are part of the Government. Prime Minister Tony Blair is outraged and in desperation attempts to enforce another deadline. Saying...

Unless there is an agreement by the end of June 1999, there will be no Stormont Parliament.

Long nights of intense bargaining follow right up to the end of June, (the deadline) and past June into the first two days of July, ending with yet another ultimatum from the British and Irish Prime Ministers. They jointly propose that Sinn Fein should be allowed to take part in the proposed executive on the promise that the P.I.R.A. begin arms decommissioning, that must begin within a short period and be complete by May 2000. A strict monitoring system for all decommissioning is set in place. Stormont will be suspended if the P.I.R.A. fail to meet the stipulated deadlines. If all parties accept these new terms, and agree to meet together in Stormont on the 15[th.] of July, to select the members of the executive, once this is completed, then devolved powers will be transferred from Westminster to Northern Ireland on the 18[th.] of July.

Intense discussion continues over the next two weeks, particularly between David Trimble, on behalf of the Ulster Unionists, and Tony Blair. Trimble expresses his concerns that no clear evidence has been provided that the P.I.R.A. really do intend to hand in their arms, and that no strict timetable for this to happen has yet to be agreed. Without stronger guarantees on this front Trimble refuses to recommend to his party the proposed arrangements for immediate power-sharing. This is a tense time for everyone in Northern Ireland. On the 15th, of July Northern Ireland's elected politicians assemble at Stormont. The business of the day is the nomination by all party of their representatives on the power-sharing executive. But the main problem was that the Ulster Unionist seats remain empty. The assembly progresses solemnly through something of a hollow procedure. The SDLP along with Sinn Fein are the only parties to nominate ministers, so the ten-member executive becomes exclusively a Nationalist one. Ministerial portfolios are allocated. Then the speaker announces that the new executive is invalid because it does not meet the power-sharing requirement.

For now the peace process is back in limbo, but with a profound public sense of disappointment. The Good Friday Agreement and the referenda remain good as the basis for future progress, but devolution has been snatched once again out of the hands of the people of Northern Ireland. But after the intervention of U.S. negotiator George Mitchell common ground is found between Sinn Fein and the Ulster Unionist leaders, Gerry Adams and David Trimble. Their joint efforts end in a breakthrough when both men issue an agreed and conciliatory statements on the 16th, of November 1999. But there are still hurdles to overcome as the Ulster Unionists had always maintained that they would not cooperate with Sinn Fein until the P.I.R.A. had at least began to hand in its weapons. The next obstacle was for David Trimble to persuade the Ulster Unionist Council that the party should share Government with Sinn Fein on the mere promise of this happening. Then on the 27[th.] of November Trimble wins the agreement he needs, with the proviso that the party will pull out of Government if the P. I. R. A. fails to hand in any of its arms by the February of that year.

Then on a historic day in Ulster's history, on the 2nd. of December 1999, both sides convene at Stormont and a ten-man-strong cabinet is selected with David Trimble, the leader of the largest party, being installed as the First Minister. But the next crisis looms all too soon. By the February the P.I.R.A. has shown no sign of decommissioning any weapons. Well aware of the harm to the peace process if the Ulster Unionists withdraw from Government, the British Government pre-empts the issue early in the month by re-imposing direct rule from Westminster - while emphasizing that the Stormont executive is being temporarily suspended rather than being dismantled.

After quiet diplomacy there is sudden progress made again when in May, the P.I.R.A. release their most unequivocal statement to date, offering to put all of their arms... - completely and verifiably beyond use. –

Their proposed method of doing this is the opening of their arms stores to full and regular inspection by independent observers. The question is whether David Trimble can sell this as significant progress to an increasingly sceptical Ulster Unionist Council. In late May he narrowly succeeds in convincing them (by 459 to 403 votes, a closer margin than six months earlier), winning the party's agreement to share power again with Sinn Fein on this new basis. Power is once again transferred from Westminster to Stormont. The Ulster executive at Stormont resumes its devolved work once again in the early June in the year 2000. It would seem that Connie witnessed peace at last in her beloved Ulster. Her days of living through a war seemed to be over, although she had nothing left to lose, nothing that any war could now take from her.

CHAPTER 28

On the afternoon of 20th October 1999, Bill Clarke returned to the offices of the Belfast Telegraph, after returning from, what he believed was going to be his last ever visit to interview Mrs Connie Gallagher at her modest home on Wolf Street in East Belfast. Bill Clarke's reason for thinking that he wouldn't be returning to Connie's house, was that he had now completed Connie's full life story. Bill Clarke strode briskly through the large glass door leading to the open planned pressroom office, where he knew he would find his friend and colleague Thomas Westwood. Just before Bill Clarke reached the desk that he and Thomas shared, something stopped him in his tracks and suddenly all that his mind could focus upon was the image of this wonderful ageing lady sitting alone in her small terraced house in East Belfast. For the first time since he had started recording this elderly ladies story, he realised that she was not just good copy, because in truth, Connie was without a shadow of a doubt a majestic figure of a mature lady. A lady whose life had been lived through the most bitter of times, through the most joyful of times, through the most violent of times, through the most compassionate of times. Here was a lady who deserved more attention and one hell of a respect from every single person who walks upon the streets of this Ulster, be they Loyalists or be they Nationalists. Bill Clarke was now determined that Connie's name and her deeds were never going to be forgotten by, not only the people of Northern Ireland, but by the people of the world.

Bill reached his desk and sat down on his seat. His friend, Thomas was typing furiously on his keyboard, bringing what information they had gathered up to date for their story on Connie's life. Bill just sat there staring into space as if in deep thought, not even speaking a word to his friend, Thomas. The thing about Connie that remained embedded in his thoughts the most, was not the tragic events that had happened to her throughout her long life, of which there had been many. Nor was it the countless selfless deeds that had been attributed to this wonderful lady through her life, for Bill it was just as Colin Woodard had noted in his manuscript upon meeting Connie for the first time. It was that small perfectly formed tear that seemed to be permanently fixed in the corner of her right eye. A tear that never seemed to move, a tear that was destined never to roll down a cheek and fall to the ground like tears are designed to do. Something that, even more puzzling to Bill, was that this small perfectly formed tear had never wiped away. On every occasion that he had visited Connie, never once did she make any kind of attempt to clear it from her eye. It was as if this small tear was patiently waiting for one last great event to happen in Connie's life, thus rendering it unnecessary.

After a few minutes of silence between the two friends, Thomas suddenly said,

"Ah Bill, you're back."

Bill didn't answer his friend at first, he just sat blank faced, as if in another world.

"Bill!" shouted Thomas, trying to grab his friend's attention.

Bill turned towards his friend and said,

"Yes, sorry, Thomas, I was just thinking about something."

"Is it don, Bill." asked Thomas, referring to Connie's story.

"It's done, Thomas." answered Bill.

"Good, now we can whip it into shape, Bill," said Thomas.

Bill still seemed to be miles away, lost somewhere, because he surely wasn't in the pressroom with his friend Thomas.

"Is it finished, Thomas, is it really finished, or should there be more to come?" said Bill, sounding a little downcast.

Thomas looked up from the screen of his computer and peeped with some dismay at his friend, Bill. After all, the story was all but completed and Thomas would have anticipated a little more enthusiasm from his friends.

"What is it, Bill?" asked a bemused Thomas.

Bill shook his head, with a puzzled look fixed firmly on his face.

"Do you know something, Thomas, I'm really not sure. It's just that I have this nagging thought at the back of my head and it's telling me that we should be doing more than just putting her story in the fucking newspaper, she deserves much more than just this," groaned Bill, as he pointed to the stack of papers containing Connie's life story that were in a neat little pile on the desk.

"Really, Thomas can this be it? Surely we just can't leave it like this, can we Thomas, really, can we?"

Thomas sat back in his chair and scratched his head thoughtfully, then he said,

"No, you're right Bill, we can't just put her story in the newspaper and then forget all about her. There has to be more for us to do. We have both read her astonishing story, we have both also had the privilege of meeting and talking with that wonderful lady. Truth be told, Bill, the lady is bloody infectious, once met never forgotten, wouldn't you say, Bill?"

Thomas now had the biggest smile beaming across his face.

"You agree with me then, Thomas, we can't simply leave the lady, not now that we have grown so close to her?" said Bill.

"No, we can't and we won't," agreed Thomas.

"The lady is like our favourite great Aunt, someone we can't wait to visit and see time and time again," smiled Bill.

"We must do something that will be so spectacular, something that Belfast will talk about for years to come. Something that will place Connie back amongst the cream of Belfast society. We need to organise some kind of social gathering, something so grand that the cream of Irish society will be fighting each other to attend. A glittering summit of the great and good that this wonderful Province of ours has to offer. What do you think, Bill, can we do it?"

Bill's face lit up with delight at hearing Thomas's idea.

"Christ yes, Thomas, oh yes, what a bloody excellent idea!" grinned Bill wildly before he to continued. "Look, Thomas, its Connie's 101st birthday on the 22nd March 2000. Why don't we do it for her on the night of her birthday?"

"Shit yes, Bill, that's the one for me!" roared Thomas loudly, his excitement growing by the minute.

Thomas then jumped to his feet, straightened the papers on his desk and said bravely,

"Right, Bill, we need to talk to Mr Packingham right away. We need to convince him that we need the newspaper to back us all the way on the one."

"Yes we do, Thomas, you're right and there's no time like the present, so let's do it now," said Bill.

Filled with excitement, both young men took a deep breath and began their determined march to Mr Packingham's office. Mr Packingham was the Editor in chief of the newspaper, the big boss. Unbeknownst to Bill and Thomas, the rest of the pressroom had been listening to their conversation and had also been following their progress on Connie's story over the weeks that they had been working on it. As both young men crossed the pressroom floor, making for the glass doors at the far end, a chorus of support spontaneously erupted and echoed around the pressroom. Shocked at what had just happened, both Bill and Thomas stopped and turned to see every one of the reporters in the pressroom on their feet and cheering support for the two boys. With the biggest smiles on their faces both Bill and Thomas acknowledged the support shown to them by their fellow reporters. But the biggest cheer was coming from old Peter, who was standing by the coffee machine. As both Bill and Thomas walked slowly passed old Peter he said,

"Go boys, go do this for Connie and for Colin."

Minutes later, Thomas and Bill arrived in the outer office of Mr Packingham's domain. Gloria, Mr Packingham's personal secretary was relaxing in her rather large leather chair behind one of the biggest desks to be found in any office in the whole of the newspaper. Now Gloria hadn't been Mr Packingham's secretary for very long, and to be perfectly frank, Gloria fell more into the category of eye-candy, than that of efficiency. It was well known on the pressroom floor that from the first day she moved into the big boss's office, she instantly came down with a really bad case of dilutions of grandeur. The two boys slowly approached Gloria's desk, but Gloria's eyes never flinched from the magazine that she was reading. After standing there for a few long silent seconds, Tomas stepped forward and tapped gently on Gloria's desk.

Still Gloria's eye's never flinched from her magazine.

"We need to see Mr Packingham. It's really important we talk to him," said Bill.

"Sorry, you can't, he's not to be disturbed," mumbled Gloria in a dismissive manner.

"But we really need to talk to him right now, today," repeated Thomas.

Gloria, who rudely still hadn't taken her eyes off her magazine, raised one eye in the direction of the two boys, licked her finger and flicked over the page of her magazine, then in a unconcerned voice she repeated curtly,

"I have told you once, he's busy, not to be disturbed, now go away please. I have things to do."

Bill was not amused in the slightest by Gloria's flippant and offensive attitude towards himself and his friend, Thomas. Bill took one step forward, then leaning bullishly on Gloria's desk, he pushed his face so close to hers that their noses were almost touching. Then in a loud voice he said forcefully,

"Gloria, put down your magazine right now, because you need to listen to me when I tell you, we must talk to Mr Packingham right now, and I mean right now, do you understand what I am telling you Gloria?."

Gloria fell back in her chair, totally shocked by Bill's somewhat aggressive and unexpected approach.

"But he..."

Bill was quick to interrupt Gloria as he said,

"No buts, Gloria, just tell Mr Packingham that we are here to see him, okay, Gloria?" Gloria tentatively picked up the telephone as she looked at Bill, then she muttered nervously,

"I'll see if he's free for you."

"Thank you, Gloria, that would be most helpful," replied Bill sarcastically.

"I'm sorry to trouble you, Mr Packingham, but Bill Clarke and Thomas Westwood are here and they insist on seeing you right away. I did tell them that you were really busy and not to be disturbed, but they are most insistent, Mr Packingham," said Gloria.

There was a short pause before Gloria spoke again.

"Yes very well, Mr Packingham, I'll show them in right away."

Gloria put the receiver down and sheepishly told Bill and Thomas to go right in as Mr Packingham was expecting them.

"Well thank you, Gloria, you have been most helpful today," smirked Bill, as both he and Thomas made for the door to Mr Packingham's office.

The reason Mr Packingham was expecting the two boys was simple, old Pete, who held a certain amount of sway with the big boss, had called him telling him that they were on their way to see him, explaining that the two had really discovered something really special.

Bill and Thomas entered Mr Packingham's office, shutting the door firmly behind them. Both the young reporters took a seat at Mr Packingham's large oak desk, which was only marginally bigger than Gloria's. Once seated and convinced they had Mr Packingham's full attention, they began to outline Connie's life story in some detail. The boys also explained the idea that they had discussed earlier of how to celebrate Connie's 101st birthday. Mr Packingham listened intensely to what the two young men had to say, taking in and studying every little world that they had to say. He then wanted to discuss at length the finer points of their idea on Connie's 101st birthday celebrations. It was almost three hours later before Bill and Thomas's meeting ended and needless to say that both boys left Mr Packingham's office with the biggest smiles imaginable.

Not only was Mr Packingham willing to back the two young men fully in their endeavours over Connie's life story, but he had expounded greatly upon their ideas. Mr Packingham told Bill and Thomas that he wanted their story finished by the end of November, as he decided that it would be better to publish Connie's story as a book instead of just printing a shortened version of it in the newspaper, as was first planned. Mr Packingham instructed the boys that he wanted the book to be released by mid-January.

Mr Packingham also revealed that as a prelude to the book being released, from the beginning of December to the beginning of the new millennium, the newspaper would be serialising Connie's story in their evening edition. Mr Packingham's thinking was that the best thing they could do was to let everyone hear some of this ladies amazing story before releasing the book. Mr Packingham also told the boys that the bulk of the proceeds would go to Military Charities of Connie's choice, plus Connie would receive remuneration from the newspaper that would see her live out her life in a great more comfort than she was at present.

Even more exciting was Mr Packingham's response to their idea for Connie's up-coming birthday celebrations. He informed the boys that he would speak with the Lord Mayor of Belfast, also the first and second Ministers of the N. Ireland Assembly, plus all the major political leaders of the Province, insisting that Connie's birthday celebrations were to be turned into a full blown civic reception to be held at the Belfast City Hall. Mr Packingham's idea was to set the cost of the tickets at such a high price that only the cream of N. Ireland society would be able to attend. Making this event the most glamorous ever to be held in the Province, he then guaranteed the young reporters that all proceeds from the Gala would also go to Connie's charities. Mr Packingham also assured the boys that he would help them in any way they wanted him to in the organisation of this wonderful occasion. He was most insistent that the guest list for this function would be something that would be talked about for a long time to come in N. Ireland.

It was around 7.30 in the evening when Bill and Thomas returned to the pressroom. As they walked through the glass doors, to their surprise the office was jam-packed with reporters. This was a surprise because by 5.30 on any other evening, all of these reporters would have abandoned their desks and headed for the nearest bar. The deeper into the press-room the two boys travelled, the more they noticed just how quite the pressroom was. What were they all still doing here, thought Thomas to himself? That's when old Peter could constrain himself any longer and suddenly he shouted out at the top of his voice,

"Come on lads, put us all out of our misery. Tell us how did it go with the boss?"

Both Bill and Thomas looked at each other and smiled broadly, then Thomas called out loudly in triumph,

"It's a goer people, it's a bloody goer!"

This news was greeted with great roars of celebration all around the pressroom. Then, as if by magic, bottles of Irish whiskey were produced from almost every desk in the pressroom. Suddenly, the front of the ill-fated coffee machine was opened up and its contents of plastic cups were quickly removed and handed out to everyone there. Not one person left the pressroom that night until all of the golden water of life had been drank.

Over the next few weeks both the young reporters had to put in long arduous hours at the newspaper, but this they did willingly and with a feverish endeavour that hadn't been seen in the pressroom for some years. It had now become something of a frantic race to get Connie's life story finished in time, because a lot of their time was now being taken up working vehemently on organising Connie's birthday bash. Mr Packingham, in his willingness to help Bill and Thomas, was setting up meeting after meeting with the most powerful movers and shakers of Belfast life. The result of this was that Bill and Thomas's time on each project was now being spread rather thinly. On the afternoon of 21st November 1999, the pressroom was brought to a standstill, when suddenly a euphoric cheer roared out from Thomas and Bill's shared desk, a cheer so loud that it reverberated around the pressroom for several seconds. Bill and Thomas walked to the front of their desk and held two compact-discs aloft above their heads. Both boys were now resembling a pair of Cheshire cats that had just licked the cream of the Queen's birthday cake. The reason for all of this joyful hullabaloo, well, it would seem that our dynamic duo had completed Connie's life story. Bill then shouted out aloud, with some vociferousness and relief,

"That's it people, we've done it, it's finished, Connie's life story is finished!"

Again a rapturous cheer echoed around the pressroom, everyone delighted that the two young reporters, Bill and Thomas, had finally done it.

Bill called for the pressroom runner. On his arrival, Bill handed him the two discs containing Connie's full life story. Bill told the pressroom runner to take the discs to the editing office right away. Their next step was to inform Mr Packingham that they had at last concluded Connie's life Story and that it was now in the hands of the editing office. That evening our two young essayist decided to give themselves the night off and retired to the bar with the rest of the pressroom, where they intended to celebrate in some style.

From that day forward, on Mr Packingham's direct instructions, both Bill and Thomas were to spend all of their working hours working exclusively on Connie's birthday celebrations. The time now seemed to pass really quickly and suddenly it was 1st December 1999, and the time had come for the first instalment of Connie's story to be published in the newspaper. Eight instalments in all of Connie's story were being published in the newspaper, suddenly the whole of Belfast was talking about it.

Everywhere you went in the city, in bars, in supermarkets, on buses, in the work place, everywhere, just everywhere, the topic on everyone's lips, was Connie's story. Even people that didn't know each other, people that had never even seen one another before, would willingly engage in discussion about Connie's life. It seemed that the people of Belfast had taken this remarkable elderly lady to their hearts. It would appear that Connie's story had gripped the imagination of people on both sides of the political divide in Belfast. Protestant and Roman Catholic alike came together and talked openly about Connie's story. It wasn't long before the whole of N. Ireland was clambering to get their hands on the Belfast Telegraph. Everyone, from farmer to doctor, from banker to bus driver, everyone wanted to read about Connie.

Later in the month, towards the middle of December, word was leaked that the book of Connie's story was to be released just after the millennium celebrations. Well, talk about excitement erupting in the Province. Within days of the news breaking, every book shop in N. Ireland, announced that they had reached a level of advanced booking for Connie's book, that they had never seen the likes of before. Connie's story had now truly become the biggest thing to hit N. Ireland in years. So big in fact that Ulster television got involved, reporting on Connie's story every night on their early evening bulletin. By the end of December, the synopsis of Connie's story that had been published nightly in the Belfast Telegraph had come to an end.

This only raised the feverish appetite that the population of Ulster had shown in Connie's life story. Everywhere you looked people were now waiting with bated breath for the book to be released. Then on 4th January 2000, the book detailing Connie's life was released to the public.

Just when you think that the situation surrounding Connie's story couldn't get any crazier, incredibly the television news agencies on the mainland had now gotten wind of Connie's story and were falling over themselves to get involved. Film crews by the dozen were suddenly littering the street of Belfast, all in search of any scrap of information they could find on Connie. Connie's story had now gripped N. Ireland tighter than anything had ever done before. Mr Packingham had anticipated that this frenzy might well take place and he had the foresight to move Connie from her house on Wolf Street to a secret location in Belfast. There she was being looked after around the clock by two private nurses who were well known to Mr Packingham.

It would appear that all of this feverish publicity surrounding Connie's story was having an outstanding effect on the preparations for Connie's birthday bash. Before all hell had been let loose, it looked like the guest list was going to be around the one hundred mark. Now, since the outbreak of mass hysteria, the list of celebrities wanting to attend Connie's birthday celebrations, had exploded beyond all expectation. The way things were going, almost everyone famous who was born in the Province wanted to be at Connie's birthday celebrations. Countless celebrities from the world of sport, Football, Rugby, Boxing, Olympians. Celebrities from the world of entertainment, Rock Stars, Film Stars, Television Personalities, Movers and Shakers from the world of Business, Politicians from all political parties across the Province, they all wanted to be in on the act. Every one of them wanting to be there at Connie's birthday celebrations.

Applications for a place at the party were escalating by the day, so much so that Mr Packingham decided to double the price of the tickets. Surprisingly, this made no difference whatsoever to the amount of celebrities wanting to attend. As the event was now looming large, Bill and Thomas were working harder and harder, making sure that every eventuality was covered.

It was now the morning of 22nd March 2000 and the day of Connie's birthday celebrations had eventually arrived. The plan Bill and Thomas had devised to manage the events of the day was this, Thomas was to host the occasion and he was also to be in attendance at the City hall to welcome the guests as they arrived. Bill was to remain with Connie for all of the day and in the evening he was to accompany the guest of honour to the gala. Needless to say, the day was something of a worrying time for the boys, both of them constantly checking their to-do list at every possible opportunity throughout the day. Thomas, who was in attendance at the City Hall, looked at his watch for the 100th time that day, but on this occasion his watch told him that it was time for the first guests to begin arriving. Normally it would have been a total nightmare to have hundreds of celebrities being moved through the streets of Belfast City at the same time. Knowing that the people of Belfast were sure to turn out in their tens of thousands, not just to cast an eye over the famous guests that would be attending, but to show their support for Connie. The Chief Constable was well aware that the roads around the City Hall were sure to be swamped with well-wishers, making movement on this scale an impossibility. But on this occasion, thanks to the forward thinking of the Chief Constable, he had everything under control. The police, who were there in their hundreds, had created a human corridor of excess carved through the crowds of onlookers on Royal Avenue, which led up to the City Hall. Under his orders no one was allowed to enter the grounds of the City Hall, accept for a few selected Television crews, invited newspaper reporters and of course invited guests. The Chief Constable had also taken charge of delivering all the guests to the gala event, staggering their arrival over almost two hours.

Bill, who was with Connie, the two nurses that Mr Packingham had employed, as well as the two lady stylists, also employed by Mr Packingham, at their secret hideaway. Again Bill glanced at his watch, it was now six o'clock and Connie was dressed in her dressing gown and she was resting in an armchair. Connie's hair and makeup had already been fashioned to the highest standard by the two stylists. All that remained to be done before leaving for the gala, was for Connie to put on her dress and then she was ready to go. Bill knew that there was time enough for that last activity. With the nurses tending to Connie's needs, health ways and the two stylists looking after Connie's appearance, Bill was able to relax, as everything his end was moving along nicely. Bill decided to leave Connie resting in her armchair for as long as possible. Moving into another room, Bill gave Thomas a call on his mobile phone.

"Hello Thomas," said Bill, "How's everything going your end?"

"Bill," he shouted, "You wouldn't believe it here, it's just incredible, everywhere you look there is a famous face, Rock Stars, Footballers, Film Stars, even the Commanding officer of the British army in N. Ireland is here. I tell you Bill, it's just bloody mindboggling, just wait until you get here and see it for yourself."

"Really, Thomas, is it looking really special there?" asked Bill.

"Mate, just wait until you get here, it's bloody fantastic!" said an excited Thomas.

"Tell me," asked Bill, "Who can you see right now, Thomas?"

"Well there are still lots of people to arrive yet Bill, the Secretary of State for N. Ireland will be here later as a guest of the Lord Mayor. Some of the ministers from the N. Ireland Assembly are here already and more on their way. Wait Bill, let me look around for you.

To my left sitting at a table are the Film Stars, Sam Neil and Liam Neeson, next to them I can see stars from the world of sport, George Best is here, so is Dennis Taylor, also Martin O'Neill, Eddie Irvine is here too. From the world of television there's, James Nesbitt and Eamonn Holmes and Gordon Burns. Then at the back of the room there's the Rock Stars, I see Van Morrison and Feargal Sharkey chatting with world renowned flutist James Galway O.B.E., now where in the world would you be able to see that Bill?" Thomas took a deep breath before continuing loudly. "There are also lots of people here I really don't know, but never the less famous, Bill. There's numerous playwrights. Authors, Poets, Scientists. You have no idea what it's like here, you have to see it for yourself, Bill, there's just so many, it's just so bloody fantastic!"

"Christ, Thomas, it all sounds incredible, I can't wait to get there, said Bill.

"How long before you and Connie get here, Bill?" asked Thomas.

"We will be there around eight, Thomas," answered Bill.

"Okay, I'll see you both then," said Thomas.

Bill ended his call to his friend, Thomas, then again he looked at his watch, it was now six thirty. Bill returned to the room where Connie was resting, both nurses were sat but a few feet from Connie's armchair, the two stylists were just waiting for the word to put the final touched to Connie's appearance before leaving for the Gala.

Bill approached Connie quietly, her eyes were shut firm. Bill tapped Connie gently on the arm as he whispered softly,

"It's time for you to finish getting dressed, Connie. Go with Angela and Helen to the bedroom, they will help you in getting dressed, Connie."

Both Angela and Helen escorted Connie to her bedroom where they prepared her for the evening ahead. Bill waited patiently in the sitting room for Connie's return. Although everything was going well, Bill began reflecting on all of the hard work both he and Thomas had put into this one very special evening. All that was left now to do was to bloody well enjoy it. After a relatively short time, Angela and Helen returned to the sitting room where Bill was now chatting with the nurses, again he glanced at his watch, it was now Seven o'clock. Bill was standing in the middle of the sitting room when Connie entered the room. Bill took one look at Connie and said with an enormous approving smile,

"You look just fantastic, Connie!"

Connie smiled and replied in a soft refined voice,

"Why thank you kind Sir. It's nice of you to say so."

"We have a few minutes if you want to sit, Connie?" said Bill.

Connie gave a slight nod of her head as she sat down in the same armchair she had been resting in a few moments earlier.

Bill thanked Angela and Helen for all their hard work in getting Connie looking so stylish, so majestic in appearance for her big evening. Ten minutes or so had passed and Bill decided to tell Connie that it was time to leave for the Gala. Connie looked really relaxed as she rested in the armchair, her head slightly tilted to one side and her eyes shut tight. Bill really didn't want to disturb her, but he knew that he had to. Bill smiled as he tentatively approached this elegant lady. Not wishing to startle Connie as he woke her from her nap, Bill took a gentle hold of her hand and stroked it softly with his right hand, then he whispered softly,

"Connie, can you hear me, Connie, it's time to go, if you are ready to go now?"

Connie opened her eyes slowly, Bill noticed how bright they had become, he even detected a slight twinkle as Connie looked up at him. After a few seconds Connie suddenly smiled broadly in Bill's direction, then in a soft silky voice she murmured tenderly,

"Bobby you're here, you're really here, and you look so handsome in your army uniform."

Bill smiled at Connie, realising that she mustn't be fully awakened as yet. Bill replied sympathetically,

"No, Connie, it's me Bill and it's time to go, are you ready to go now, Connie?"

Connie's face suddenly came alive, the twinkle that Bill had observed in Connie's eyes a few seconds ago, had now been transformed into a sparkle that glittered brightly. The smile now on Connie's face was the sort of smile that would be normally reserved purely for the one true love in someone's life. Connie's actual features had also suddenly changed, they seemed enhanced, making her look younger in a strange sort of way. Bill really didn't understand what he was seeing before his very eyes. Connie raised her head and said in a low and tender voice,

"Have you come for me, Bobby, do you want me to go with you now. Because if you do, I think I'm ready to go."

Bill took Connie's hand in both of his and whispered softly,

"No, Connie, it's me Bill, it's not Bobby and it really is time for us to go."

Bill suddenly realised that Connie wasn't really looking at him, she was more looking past him, as she continued.

"I knew you would come for me one day, Bobby. I've waited such a long, long time for you, and now your here, my love."

One of the nurses tugged at Bill's arm and whispered for him to leave her be, as there was nothing they could do for her now. Best just to move out of her eye line, because if looks like her time is now. Connie's eyes were focused straight in front of her and suddenly she sat forward in her armchair, her voice was now even softer, yet clear and precise as she whispered warmly,

"Oh Bobby, you have brought my babies with you to see me, each one of them dressed in their uniforms too. Oh Bobby don't they look so handsome, just like their daddy did on that day when you first went off to war. I can still picture you on that day, Bobby, looking so smart in your new uniform, I was the proudest girl there that day on the Newtownards Road as I watched you march bravely with the other boys. I was so proud of you that day, Bobby, so proud that I just didn't want to let you out of my sight. I followed you all the way until you boarded the ship that took you away from me on that cold, cold morning."

Connie slowly shuffled to the edge of her armchair and continued.

"Let me look at my boys, let me fill my eyes with the sight of their beautiful faces. Wee Bobby bring your brother forward, bring them closer to me and let me touch every one of you. Good God just look at my sons, every one of them so handsome in their army uniforms. Come close boys, because it has been such a long time since I have seen you all standing together in front of me. I'm so proud of each and every one of you. My good, good boys, Wee Bobby, Terry, Billy, Sammy, Harry, Tommy and Andy. You are a mother's joy to behold it is true."

Again a surprised look came across Connie's face as she raised both of her hands to her lips, kissing her fingers before reaching out, as if to touch something or someone, then she said,

"My God, Wee Bobby, you have brought your twin boys to see me. Are they not the most beautiful babies you have ever seen?"

Connie then took a linen handkerchief from the petite diamond evening bag that was resting on her lap, folding it neatly several times, before raising it towards her face. Connie then gently dabbed the tear that rested in the corner of her right eye with the soft linen. In that one poignant movement, the tear that appeared to have been resting in Connie's eye for most of her life, was gone, it was no more. Connie kissed the linen handkerchief tenderly then she folded it one more time and held it tightly in her hand, as she reached out with her hands and uttered the heart breaking words,

"Yes I am ready to go now, Bobby, if you are ready to take me."

Connie sat back in her armchair and gently rested her head upon one of the side wings of her armchair. Gradually Connie's eyes began to close, that delightful smile that had filled her face for the last few sad moments, still remained firmly fixed in position. Bill watched in complete sadness as in that one fleeting second, in that one flash in time, in that one blink of an eye, just as Connie's eyes were about to close shut, Bill truly believes that he saw Connie change from the elegant elderly lady that he knew so well, into that of an eighteen year old beautiful young girl. A vision so stunning with long raven hair and the deepest bluest eyes he had ever seen. But this sudden flash in time startled Bill, making him flinch and recoil in shock. Once he had regained his senses, he quickly looked again, but now all that he saw was Connie, as he had always known her, an elegant, lovely lady. But now she was gone.

For the first time Bill now realised the full extent of the sadness that had haunted Connie's life. The realisation that Connie was no ordinary lady suddenly hit him, because without a doubt Connie really was the epitome of the real Irish Colleen. Bill remembered that he had heard somewhere, that it had been said that Connie was so beautiful as a child, that people, who had set eyes on her, declared that she must surely have been touched by the angles at birth. If indeed that had been said about Connie, then Bill agreed whole-heartedly with those sentiments.

It was now Seven Forty Five and Thomas was becoming a little nervous as he waited for Bill and Connie to arrive at the City Hall, knowing that this great event was about to begin for real. Coming from the back of the room, Thomas could see Mr Packingham approaching him. Thomas was hoping that nothing had gone wrong, as he didn't want to be on the receiving end of Mr Packingham's wrath. As it happens, Thomas couldn't have been more wrong, as Mr Packingham took hold of Thomas's hand and began to shake it warmly saying,

"Wonderful job you and Bill have done here, Thomas, just Bloody wonderful."

"Thank you Mr Packingham," answered Thomas.

At that very moment Thomas's mobile phone began to ring.

"Excuse me Sir, I have to take this call, it could be important," said Thomas.

"Yes of course, Thomas, take the call," said MrPackingham, "I'll speak to both you and Bill later, okay, Thomas?"

"Yes, yes, later Mr Packingham," muttered Thomas, fumbling with his phone. Mr Packingham then turned and walked away, leaving Thomas in peace to answer his phone call.

"Hello Bill, where are you, you both should be here by now," said Thomas anxiously.

Within a split second, Thomas's expression quickly changed, it was as if his whole world had collapsed around him, his excited enthusiasm ended, his anticipation abandoned, his hope crushed.

"I see, Bill," was all Thomas said.

Standing alone at the end of the Banqueting Hall of the Belfast City Hall, Thomas look around the room at the host of celebrities all waiting for Connie's arrival. Slowly Thomas closed his phone and put it back into his pocket. Thomas raised his hand and lazily cleared a tear from his eye and took a deep breath. Thomas then walked briskly past the waiting multitude of celebrities to the stage at the far end of the Banqueting Hall. Thomas now found himself standing alone in the middle of the stage with the microphone in his hot sweaty hand. He took one more deep, deep breath and said,

"Ladies and..."

Before Thomas could say any more, he was interrupted by loud spontaneous applause which rebounded loudly around the room. But a minute later the room fell silent again, all ears waiting to hear what Thomas had to say. Thomas made every effort to compose himself, then once again he raised the microphone to his mouth with his right hand. Thomas's voice dulled and somewhat shaky, as he began to speak.

"Good evening My Lords, Ladies, Gentlemen and Honoured Guests. First I would like to thank you all for attending this historical event this evening. This event here at the Belfast City Hall this evening was arranged to Honour a wonderful Lady. A Lady who lived through every minute of the 20th. Century. A lady who took everything that this passing Century had to throw at her, and as we all know, it tossed more than enough heart-break in her direction. But this lady, this wonderful lady came through it all with her dignity, her poise and her pride remaining for all to see. This was a lady that, despite her own difficulties and her own sorrows, always found time to help and care for the unfortunates of this great Province throughout her life. This was a lady that devoted her life to helping others less fortunate than herself. A lady who worked tirelessly to serve the interests of those who needed help, this she did without bigotry or prejudice of any kind. Most of you, if not all of you will have read Connie's powerful and moving life story, so there's not much more that needs to be said by me on the subject of Connie's truly compassionate and selfless life. So I will keep what I have to say next as short as possible."

Thomas stepped back from the microphone for a second, then he cleared his throat and wiped several falling tears from his eye, only for them to be quickly replaced by others. Thomas looked all around the room, no longer did he feel bewitched or overwhelmed by the people within it. No longer was he star struck by the sights before him, because deep in his heart he knew that he had befriended the most important, the most influential and the most remarkable person this Province, this Ulster, this Island had ever known. Thomas again picked up the microphone and a glass of red wine from the nearest table to him and said sadly,

"What I have to convey to you all now, I would rather not have to do so, I can assure you all of that. Just ten minutes ago I received a phone call from my friend and colleague, Bill Clarke. Sadly, Bill informed me that this world has just been deprived of the existence of one of its most gracious, most outstanding, most loving and most compassionate citizens, to have ever walked upon this earth."

Bill raised up his glass of red wine and said dejectedly,

"My Lords, Ladies, Gentlemen and Honoured Guests, please charge your glasses as we toast a marvellous human being for the last time. Connie Keane was lovingly bestowed upon a world not yet ready to receive such a wonderful human being on 22nd March in the year of our Lord 1899. Connie Gallagher was a Wife, a Mother of seven Sons and a Granny to two grandsons. Connie was sadly taken from us on this day, 22nd March in the year of our Lord 2000. People of N. Ireland, people of the world, please charge your glasses one more time, as we pay one last deserving tribute to a truly astonishing lady."

As one, the room got to its feet in complete silence, the only sound to be heard was the gentle clinking of glass on glass which echoed unnervingly around the forum.

This eerie, yet respectful silence lasted but a minute and was only broken by the Spontaneous outbreak of the deafening chanting of one name...

"CONNIE, CONNIE, CONNIE, CONNIE."

THE END

Printed in Great Britain
by Amazon

73010224R00203